In her second romantic caper, Starr Ambrose raises the stakes *and* the heat as a woman on the trail of her missing sister teams up with the wrong—or is it right?—kind of man.

Callista smiled at Drew. "I'll see you there," she purred. "Come alone."

Lauren lowered her drink and watched Callista strut away. "Wow. You're good with sluts. You must get a lot of practice."

She looked so genuinely impressed Drew nearly laughed. "Not that much."

"How are you with good girls?"

His amusement died in a rush of heat, and he took a closer look at her. He didn't know if it was the alcohol or the dancing that had raised the pink glow in her face, but he found himself suddenly imagining what it would be like to press his mouth to her flushed skin and lick the champagne off her wet lips. The flirtatious look she was giving him wasn't making her easier to resist.

"Stop looking at me like that," he whispered harshly.

"Like what?" The pink tip of her tongue ran over her upper lip and wide eyes blinked innocently at him.

"Like you're n— married to my father!"

"I'm not."

More praise for Starr Ambrose's debut novel,
Lie to Me

"Likeable characters and an intriguing premise."

—*Publishers Weekly*

"Ambrose adds a welcome, bright new voice to the genre. Her lighthearted repartee imparts a special charm to this novel."

—*Winter Haven* (FL) *News Chief*

"This book really grabs you and doesn't let go. I was hooked from the first page."

—BookBinge.com

"In her debut novel, a light romantic suspense Starr has been born."

—Reviews for CompuServe.com

This title is also available as an eBook.

OUR
Little
SECRET

STARR AMBROSE

Pocket Books
New York   London   Toronto   Sydney

Pocket Books
A Division of Simon & Schuster, Inc.
1230 Avenue of the Americas
New York, NY 10020

This book is a work of fiction. Names, characters, places, and incidents either are products of the author's imagination or are used fictitiously. Any resemblance to actual events or locales or persons, living or dead, is entirely coincidental.

First Pocket Books paperback edition December 2009

POCKET and colophon are registered trademarks of Simon & Schuster, Inc.

For information about special discounts for bulk purchases, please contact Simon & Schuster Special Sales at 1-866-506-1949 or business@simonandschuster.com

The Simon & Schuster Speakers Bureau can bring authors to your live event. For more information or to book an event contact the Simon & Schuster Speakers Bureau at 1-866-248-3049 or visit our website at www.simonspeakers.com

Cover photo © Pando Hall/Getty Images

Manufactured in the United States of America

10 9 8 7 6 5 4 3 2 1

ISBN 978-1-4391-0223-7
ISBN 978-1-4391-2686-8 (ebook)

For Mom and Dad

Acknowledgments

Special thanks to Kevan Lyon, who saw the rough version of this story and knew what it could become.

Thanks to Abby Zidle and Danielle Poiesz at Pocket Books for their brilliant editorial insights.

For expert advice, thanks to Lori Toth and Julie Vokwinkle. Any mistakes are my own.

Thanks always to Jim, Stevie, and Ariana for too many reasons to name, and to Key, who insisted I could type while holding a cat.

Chapter One

Lauren Sutherland stood on the slush-covered Georgetown sidewalk and reminded herself that wrecking her sister's marriage was the responsible thing to do.

Sisters looked out for each other—especially when one sister insisted on being an irresponsible idiot. Meg would thank her for it later.

Probably.

Lauren cast a speculatve glance at the house. The red brick edifice to old money was exactly the home she would expect for the third most influential man in Washington, D.C. Meg always had been attracted to power, so that was no surprise. That was why she'd taken a job with Senator Harlan Creighton III in the first place. The lecherous creep. But marrying the elusive and infamous—not to mention much older— bachelor was a surprise even to Lauren's jaded expectations. She already chewed through three fingernails on the plane ride.

Lauren clenched her hand into a fist, hiding the

evidence of her nervous habit. Being a good example took its toll.

A gust of wind snuck under her coat and up her skirt, reminding Lauren that she didn't need to stand outside in the chill March air. Might as well go inside where she could warm up, get into some comfortable clothes, and confront Meg. Her sister would put up a fight, but Lauren knew the best solution was a quick annulment. Meg would see that—eventually.

Briefcase in one hand and suitcase in the other, Lauren dragged herself up the walk to the front door, weaving a path around spots of melted snow that were trying to refreeze. She would have worn hiking boots and jeans instead of her prim black business suit, but Jeff objected. Her fiancé said she had to make a good impression on the senator, and besides, the suit went with the expensive-looking red wool coat Meg had sent her. Lauren didn't know why she should care what the senator thought when he wasn't going to be a family member for longer than it took to get Meg to an attorney. And the expensive coat was obviously some sort of bribe to buy Lauren's approval. Well, Meg wasn't going to get it. What she *was* going to get was a lecture on inappropriate behavior and old men who use power and money to buy everything they want, including women.

With her indignation nicely pumped up, Lauren set down both pieces of luggage and rang the doorbell, prepared to burst her sister's bubble.

She didn't hear footsteps behind the heavy door, but seconds later a deadbolt clicked and the door opened. Prepared for Meg's ecstatic grin, Lauren blinked in confusion. She stood face-to-face with a frowning dark-haired man in worn jeans and a crew-neck sweater.

He couldn't be the hired help, not in those clothes. And he was far too young to be the senator, though his demeanor said he belonged here. Lauren's first thought was that she had the wrong house. But she couldn't; the limo driver dropped her here, and he certainly knew where Senator Creighton lived.

Which led to her second thought: Holy cow, why hadn't Meg mentioned this guy? He wasn't the type who escaped notice, especially by someone as fond of good-looking men as her sister. Lauren was certainly noticing. She noticed the flashing blue eyes full of sharp intelligence, the strong jaw implying decisive action, and the athletic build . . . well, a woman could spend a long time appreciating a man with a body like that. Even an engaged woman.

As she stared, the man's expression changed, his attractive mouth curving into an ironic smile.

"Well, well, well," he drawled in a voice as richly masculine as the rest of him. "Look who's back."

Before she could respond, his hand darted out, grabbed her sleeve, and he yanked her inside.

"Hey!" Startled, Lauren swatted at the hand that had already released her, and backed away until she felt the wall. She'd been right about the decisive action. He had a commanding presence, too. But she hadn't expected a physical assault, and she eyed the man warily.

Steely blue eyes assessed her in return. He crossed his arms and planted his feet firmly in front of the door.

"What did you forget?" he asked. "The number for the offshore account?"

Lauren tried to find an appropriate response, but between his confrontational attitude and his distracting, um, distraction, all that came out was, "Huh?"

His appraisal was more frank than hers had been, and downright disconcerting as his gaze traveled her body from head to toe. She squirmed and tried to ignore the little shiver that crept across her shoulders.

"I see why he fell for you," he finally said. It might have been flattering if he hadn't sounded so disgusted.

"You do?" Her brain was regaining traction.

"Don't get your hopes up. I'm not here to congratulate you on your marriage."

"My marriage?" She suddenly understood the problem. "You think I'm Meg!" She didn't question why this drop-dead gorgeous hunk would be angry with Meg. Her sister went through men like candy, and he wouldn't be the first guy she'd dropped like a day-old sucker.

One dark eyebrow lifted, a good look for him. "Is this part of the game? Who do you expect me to think you are?"

"I'm Meg's sister, Lauren."

He smiled, appearing genuinely amused—an even better look. "The mistaken identity routine—I thought you'd be smarter than that. Sorry, it won't work. Gerald described you. Red coat, Pendleton scarf, medium-length dirty blonde hair." He looked her up and down pointedly, causing a curious flutter in her stomach. "That's you. I'll admit the diamond ring's a bit small, but that's your problem."

The last comment jolted her out of her fantasies. His description of her might be right, but his attitude was all wrong. It had always been irritating to be mistaken for her sister, even though they were identical twins. But insulting the sensibly priced ring Jeff had picked out was crossing the line.

"Look, I don't know who you are, but I told you, I'm not Meg. I'm Lauren. And whoever Gerald is, he's wrong."

The man actually laughed, and Lauren noted with irritation that he looked good doing it. "Gerald's never wrong."

If he hadn't sounded so arrogant about it, she'd have been more sympathetic. Maybe he thought she was easily intimidated. She stepped toward him, right up to the creamy-beige sweater, stuck her face close to his and said in slow, distinct words, "I'm not Meg. Gerald's wrong."

She was close enough to smell him, a clean, open-air smell, like pine trees and sunshine. She could even feel the heat from his body. Or maybe it was hers. Someone was overheating.

He held her gaze for several seconds, then yelled, "Gerald!" loud enough to make her flinch.

Footsteps pounded down a staircase and vibrated through the gleaming floorboards until a young man appeared at the other end of the spacious foyer. He pushed wire-rimmed glasses back up his nose and put a hand over his tailored vest as he fought to catch his breath. "What?"

The man lifted a hand as if he were presenting Lauren for an introduction. "Well? Is this her?"

"Megan!" the young man cried happily.

Lauren felt her frown deepen and she spoke to Gerald in carefully enunciated words. "I am not Meg."

"Give it up, lady," her accuser began, but Gerald interrupted.

"Wait, wait, Andrew," he said, staring at Lauren intently while flapping a hand at his handsome but pushy friend. Stepping closer, Gerald peered at her face, then made a slow circle around her. Lauren stood still, shifting her eyes cautiously to follow him. He was small, but he had an air of authority and she knew his judgment was going to carry weight.

He finally spoke, using one arm to support his elbow as he tapped a thoughtful finger against his chin. "She does look like Megan, but the hair is too long."

"Too long?" Lauren blurted in disbelief. "If anything, mine is shorter. Do you even know Meg? Her hair is halfway down her back!"

"She cut it two days ago," Gerald informed her with a superior air, as if she should have known.

Lauren hesitated. She hadn't actually seen her sister in several months. "She did?"

He nodded, an arrogant sort of affirmation that said he knew many things about Meg that she obviously didn't. "Megan now has a very stylish feathered cut that just brushes the top of the collar, with a few wispy bangs." His fingers sketched invisible locks on his own forehead in demonstration. "Plain, but striking, if you have the right sort of face. Which, of course, our Meg does. She—"

The man he'd called Andrew wasn't listening to the rest of the fashion commentary. "It could be a wig," he suggested. Before Lauren could duck, he reached out and tugged a lock of her hair.

"Hey, back off!" She instinctively kicked him in the shin.

"Ow!" Bending his knee, he grabbed his throbbing leg. "Jesus, lady, I wasn't attacking you."

"You grabbed me," she said, then tacked on, "twice," in case he thought she had overlooked the way he'd pulled her in the door. In fact, the way he'd reached out and pulled her toward him had been quite memorable.

While they glared suspiciously at each other, Gerald mused, "No, that's definitely not Megan. She had her hair layered for fullness. She would never let anyone style it that way, all straight and flat and . . ." He stopped as Lauren shot an annoyed glance his way. "So you must be Meg's sister, Lauren," he concluded.

"Ha! Finally!" Lauren flung her hand toward Gerald in an exasperated gesture as she turned to the man who, gorgeous or not, had the audacity to imply that she was a liar. "See?"

"Okay, okay." He tested the ability of his right leg to hold his weight. It looked sturdy enough to Lauren, so he'd better not be expecting an apology. "You're not Meg. I was wrong. Not that it wasn't a logical mistake," he added in an undertone.

She crossed her arms and sniffed her dissatisfaction.

"Probably cracked my shin bone," he muttered, taking a few limping steps to enhance his performance.

She watched, unmoved. His leg looked perfectly fine to her. "Who are you, anyway?"

"Drew Creighton," he said absently, concentrating on his wounded leg. The big baby. With a slight sneer, he added, "Nice to meet you, Aunt Lauren."

Time shuddered to a halt. Lauren felt her mouth open stupidly. "What?"

She had his attention again, and his slow grin was

wicked with satisfaction. "I'm Senator Creighton's son. Which makes me your sister's new stepson. And, it seems, your nephew. Aren't blended families fun?"

What had Meg done to her? Engaged women might be allowed to have semi-sexual feelings about other men, but aunts definitely weren't supposed to have those feelings about their nephews. Lauren was in big trouble here. Besides, Drew was too old to be her nephew. He had to be about thirty-five or -six, which would make him no more than five years older than she was. Her sister hadn't mentioned any grown children from the senator's first marriage. She cleared her throat and asked hesitantly, "Do you have any sisters or brothers?"

He seemed to enjoy that one even more. "Yes, your newly acquired niece, Miranda, is forty years old. Congratulations."

He probably thought Miranda's age was the reason for her stunned expression. In actuality, she was still grappling with the idea that the man who had stirred her lust at first sight was her nephew, albeit her not-so-nice nephew.

A related thought occurred to her. Her sister had always preferred the studly types. If Drew's father still looked this virile in person, she might be forced to rethink Meg's impulsive marriage: The attraction could be based on more than money.

While Lauren recovered, Gerald retrieved her luggage from the porch and coaxed her out of her coat. She looked at him over her shoulder as he hung it in the front closet, cautiously assessing the smaller man. He didn't look anything like Drew, but you never knew. "Are we related, too?"

Drew snorted back laughter, but Gerald answered her seriously. "Not at all. I'm the senator's personal secretary. A man of Senator Creighton's means has many business interests outside the Senate. Meg is his assistant for all that political stuff." He dismissed the United States Senate with a wave of his hand. "Come in and sit down, Miss Sutherland. Perhaps you can help us determine the whereabouts of your sister."

Lauren fought against a familiar, sinking feeling. Her irresponsible sister had stood her up—why should she be surprised? This was exactly what she hated about Meg, and exactly why she was with a dependable, sensible man like Jeff. Meg could stand to adopt a few of his values.

"Call me Lauren," she murmured, trailing Gerald into the living room. She could feel Drew's presence behind her. All the hairs on the back of her neck stood on end, as if carrying a magnetic charge pulling them in Drew's direction. She tried to ignore him as she addressed Gerald. "What did you mean about determining her whereabouts? Where is Meg?"

"Pay no attention to Gerald, he worries too much," Drew said as he settled onto a yellow sofa. The silk brocade upholstery was patterned with pale green flowers, and the contrast with his plain sweater and jeans only made him look more masculine. Lauren didn't realize she was staring until she caught his lazy smile. She quickly looked away.

Gerald clasped his hands, apparently too nervous to sit. "Meg stopped by the house two days ago on her way to the bank. No one's heard from her since." Concern was evident in his voice. Gerald obviously considered Meg a friend, and he was worried about her. Lauren wondered if she should be worried, too.

Drew gave a soft snort. "They haven't heard from her with good reason. Either my father is keeping his new bride occupied, which I'll admit is possible, or she's already ditched him in favor of his assets, and she's long gone." When Lauren frowned at him he pointed toward the matching sofa across from his. "Have a seat. I can't wait to hear what excuses you come up with for Meg's behavior."

She eased onto the edge of the sofa, knees together, purse tucked under her arm, the antithesis of Drew's relaxed sprawl. Angling her body away from him and toward Gerald, she tried to allay his fears. "I don't know why you haven't heard from Meg. I have. She called around noon the day before yesterday to say she'd reserved a plane ticket for me, and begged me to come. She knew I had to use my vacation time for the trip, so I'm sure she wouldn't just"—she waved a hand and quoted him—"disappear. She knows I can't stay here long. You'll see, she'll be back soon. She must be with Senator Creighton." She slid a dark look at Drew as she quoted him again. "Who is keeping her occupied."

"Maybe," Gerald mused. Lauren didn't like how grudgingly he said it. "We called his Senate office, but he wasn't available. Committee meetings or something. We're waiting for him to call back."

"Stingy with vacation time, are you? Even to celebrate your sister's marriage."

She glared at Drew, annoyed that he'd sorted out the one fact that made her sound prissy and rigid. "Not that it's any of your business, but my fiancé and I have resort reservations that I made months in advance."

God, she *did* sound rigid. *And* prissy.

"Oh, I know what her reason was."

"You do?" She and Gerald said it together.

"It's obvious." He scanned Lauren from her turtle-neck sweater to her sensible low-heeled shoes. "Do you and your sister always dress alike, some cute little twin thing?"

"We're not six years old," Lauren snapped.

"So why did you dress exactly like her today?"

Had she? Lauren recalled his description of Meg's coat and scarf, the reason for the mistaken identity at the front door. She hesitated, then admitted, "I didn't know Meg owned the same coat and scarf. She Fed-Exed these to me. They were a gift, and she said if she knew exactly what I was wearing it would be easier to spot me at the airport." It did sound weird, now that she said it out loud. They just didn't know that weird behavior was the norm for her sister. As far as weird went, sending Lauren a new coat and scarf for her trip to Washington didn't stand out.

"But she didn't pick you up at the airport," Drew objected.

"She sent a limo instead because she'd been delayed."

"Uh-huh. And why didn't she just ask you what you'd be wearing? Wouldn't that be easier than play-ing identical dress-up games?"

Damn, his logic was even better than Jeff's, who had impeccable reasoning skills. It didn't seem to be puzzling Drew, though. "If you're so smart, you tell me why she did it."

Drew made himself comfortable first, arms crossed and long legs stretched beneath the coffee table. It was the sort of careless confidence she might have found

sexy in someone less obnoxious. "I don't think Meg
sent you an identical coat and scarf. I think she sent
you her own."

Lauren recognized the truth as soon as he said it.
She recalled noticing the faint scent of Meg's perfume
on both items. But she wasn't about to admit anything
to this stranger. "So what?"

"So, she set you up. You were a decoy."

"What? That's ridiculous." Even as she denied it,
Lauren was aware that was exactly how it sounded.

He didn't respond, just picked a piece of fuzz off
his sweater while she thought about it. He was right,
damn it. Meg had arranged for Lauren to arrive at the
house looking exactly like her sister, while she was
somewhere else.

"She even cut her hair recently," Drew reminded
her. "She might have gone too short, but it made her
look enough like you to fool Gerald at first, and no
one is better than Gerald at noticing those sorts of
details."

"That's right," Gerald agreed without a trace of
false humility.

Double damn. What was going on here? Lauren
lifted a hand to her mouth and nearly started on a
fourth nail before catching herself. She really needed to
break the habit, but dealing with the screw-ups in her
sister's life made it difficult. Grabbing a lock of hair
instead, she twirled it around her finger as she glanced
at Gerald. He looked worried—no help there. Drew
watched her impassively. "She must have had a good
reason," Lauren insisted finally.

At least, she'd *better* have.

"Of course she did," Drew told her. She was

beginning to hate his certainty about the whole confusing situation. "She wanted whoever was watching to think she hadn't left town. Anyone who saw you would think you were Meg."

It made sense, and she nearly put a knot in her tortured strand of hair at the implication. "Who would be watching Meg?"

"The press. My father's marriage would be big news."

She'd forgotten about that. It would explain Meg's ruse. If the press got wind of the biggest playboy in politics getting married, to his much-younger secretary at that, it would be all over the news.

But it wasn't. She tipped her head toward the front window and the empty lawn outside. "If the reporters were supposed to be watching for Meg—for me—why aren't they here?"

He shrugged. "Maybe you were Meg's ace in the hole and she didn't need you. She got away without the press getting a whiff of it. But if she hadn't, you would have been here to divert their attention." Drew suddenly dropped his placid pose and leaned forward, his gaze intense. "Your sister used you, Lauren. Convinced you to take off work and messed up your perfectly organized vacation schedule, just so she could avoid the press for a few days. How do you feel about that?"

Pissed as hell, but not about to let him know it. Her infuriating nephew had already identified her weak spot, her obsessively regulated life, and it irritated her more than she wanted to admit. "Why do you hate Meg? You don't even know her."

Drew's expression hardened. "I don't have to know

her; I've met her type before. This town is full of them."

"Really? What type is that? Bright, efficient, and hard working? Yes, those are pretty suspicious qualities."

His lip quirked into a cynical smile that she tried not to think of as sensuous. "Oh, I don't doubt she's bright—they usually are. She's also young, pretty, and ambitious enough to land a top job in a Senate office. Then a few short months later she marries her boss, a wealthy senator thirty-three years her senior." Drew affected an innocent look. "Gosh, you don't think that looks suspicious, do you?"

At least now she knew why Meg had passed on any romantic involvement with Drew Creighton. The man was a butthead of the first degree.

Lauren had nearly forgotten Gerald was there until he stirred at Drew's words. "Now, Andrew, I told you Meg's not like that."

"You don't know Meg well enough to say what she's like, Gerald." He spoke sharply, without taking his eyes off Lauren.

She fumed. "And you don't know her at all. You want to know why this marriage is such a bad idea? The way I see it, an older man—much older—used his position and wealth to seduce a gullible young woman into his bed." She only stretched the truth a little. Knowing Meg, Lauren had no doubt it was a mutual seduction. "Then he talked her into a marriage that would give him some classy arm candy to show off at banquets and parties, and even better, on the campaign trail—voters love candidates with pretty wives, don't they?—while still keeping her available in his bedroom. Maybe Meg believed he'd give up his other women for her, but I'm not that naive. She's just another conquest."

She expected him to be furious at the picture she'd painted of his father, but she didn't care. They both knew it was true.

Drew nodded. "Dad does have a reputation as a ladies' man," he agreed, undisturbed.

Lauren bristled. "Is that the politically correct term? I do listen to the news, you know. The man's a tom-cat!"

Drew nodded again. "Yup. I wonder what sort of sexual tricks it took to maneuver him into giving up two decades of happy bachelorhood. Your sister must be pretty skilled in that area."

She narrowed her eyes at him and willed her nephew to burs̶.̶ ̶─̶─̶─̶─̶─̶─̶─̶.̶

Drew stared back, serenely unaffected.

That made one of them.

Confusion fogged her mind. As irritating as Drew was, talking about possible sexual antics had side-tracked her brain. The sharp blue gaze that fastened on hers should have been cold and intimidating, but an unexpected heat began building inside her. Something had to be wrong with her.

Maybe it was a lack of sex. Meg's phone call had upset her, and she hadn't kept her usual Thursday evening date with Jeff, which meant canceling one of their biweekly sex nights. Two sessions a week of making love in Jeff's bed had always been enough for her, but she could be wrong. Maybe she needed more. Or maybe she'd thrown her hormones out of whack worrying about Meg. That would explain why she kept having all these conflicting thoughts about Drew.

She had to admit, though, if the man weren't such a jerk, he'd be every one of her fantasies come true. Family loyalty rated high with her, not to mention being quick-witted and handsome as sin. Just like Jeff, she assured herself. Except Jeff's body was a little softer, and she couldn't imagine calling him handsome as sin. Handsome, yes, but in a safer, more . . . bland way. She couldn't figure out what it was about Drew that gave his looks a dangerous edge. Maybe it was the intensity in his gaze, or maybe the way his smile had a mischievous slant, making her wonder about things she had no business wondering about.

She caught Drew watching her with frank curiosity and realized she'd sucked her lower lip between her teeth while staring thoughtfully at his mouth. Embarrassment flooded her cheeks.

"This is not helping," she said.

Gerald stepped closer and placed his hands on his hips. "Arguing over motives isn't getting us anywhere. We still don't know where Meg is."

"Yes, we do." Drew turned his attention toward Gerald. "She's on her honeymoon." The heat inside Lauren waned as soon as he said it.

She looked at Gerald, too. Anything to avoid meeting Drew's eyes. "No, she isn't. Meg wouldn't have told me to drop everything and come here just so she could sneak out of town."

"I agree," Gerald said.

His approval gave her enough courage to risk a glance at Drew. He raised his eyes in silent appeal to the heavens, apparently at their misguided loyalty to Meg. "Okay then, where is she and why can't we reach her?"

Frustration surged through Lauren, pulling her to her feet. "How should I know? But I'm not leaving until I see her. My sister thought it was vitally important that I come here today. And I'm glad I did because I plan to convince her to disassociate herself from the Creighton family as soon as possible."

It was much easier to meet Drew's eyes when she glared.

He smiled. "Well, Aunt Lauren, at least we agree on one thing—my father's marriage to your sister is a mistake."

She gritted her teeth. "Don't call me that."

"But I'm beginning to like the sound of it."

Gerald threw his hands up. "Oh, for crying out loud! Will you two behave?"

The reprimand, coming from such a slight young man, carried a surprising amount of authority. Lauren gave him a sheepish smile. "You're right."

"The voice of reason." Drew stood, an act which, however unintentional, dramatically reduced Gerald's presence in the room. "It looks like we have no choice but to wait for the happy couple to show up. So what do you say we make ourselves comfortable? I'm willing to play nice if you are . . . Lauren."

Since he dropped the Aunt, she forced her lips into a brief, upward curve. "Works for me."

He smiled back with seemingly genuine pleasure. Probably at the prospect of having several more hours to insult her sister.

"We've forgotten our manners, Gerald. Lauren is

our guest." Drew turned back to her. "Can I get you anything?"

It was about time someone asked. "Yes. Food."

He grinned, a look entirely too erotic for comfort. "Right this way."

Lauren spent the next hour eating her way through soup, a sandwich, and a large slice of pie. She tried to clean up, but Gerald shooed her out of the room along with Drew, who seemed no more familiar with Senator Creighton's kitchen than she was. Growing up with money, he was probably used to having cooks make his food.

Meg still hadn't shown up, or even called. Neither had Senator Creighton.

Lauren stood at the senator's leaded glass living room window, brooding over the darkening Georgetown street. She felt Drew enter the room.

"I just tried his office again. They haven't heard from either of them, but apparently it's not unusual for my dad to be out of touch for a day or two. He has an active, uh, social life."

Lauren nodded without turning and crossed her arms. At least he was keeping her updated without dropping further insinuations about her sister's loose life and shady motives.

"Why don't you try your sister's cell phone?"

"I did. I'm still getting her voice mail."

He was silent for a moment. "Would you like to watch TV?"

"No, thank you."

Another short silence. "How about—"

Lauren spun around. "Stop being so nice to me. It's

like someone's died and you're afraid to say the wrong thing."

Drew ducked his head and scratched at a lock of dark hair on his forehead, but she thought he hid a smile behind his arm. "Sorry. Would you like me to say something insulting about your sister?"

"That would certainly sound more like you," she grumbled.

He bit his cheek, and this time she was certain it was amusement he held back. It made her feel a little better to know he was laughing at her. No one laughed at tragedies.

"You were starting to look as worried as Gerald," Drew said. "Is it unusual for Meg to change her plans without telling you?"

Lauren shot a hard look at him, wondering if he'd known the answer before he asked. "No, unfortunately, it isn't."

"Not the responsible type, eh? Just takes off on a whim and never considers that someone might worry?"

She shifted uncomfortably. "Don't push it, Creighton."

He didn't try to hide his enjoyment. "It bugs you, doesn't it, having to be the responsible one? The one who has to clean up her messes?"

How did he do that? It was like she had the words written across her forehead: *Good sister and martyr.*

Lauren straightened her spine. "There's nothing wrong with being responsible. It shows consideration and maturity."

Drew laughed. "Spoken like a true adult."

His superior act was getting on her nerves. "I'm

thirty-one years old, Drew. I *am* an adult. And so is Meg. She has a wonderful career just like an adult, and she pays her taxes and her bills like an adult. It's just that sometimes . . ." Her voice ran down along with her temper. "Sometimes she doesn't act like one."

Admitting Meg's faults to Drew made Lauren angry and depressed all over again. She turned back to the window. Why couldn't Meg just pull in the driveway so Lauren could yell at her, talk her into a divorce, then go back home?

"I'm willing to bet Meg is acting like an adult right now." Drew's suggestion cut through her dark thoughts. "I'll bet she and my dad are holed up in some cozy hotel room, drinking champagne like adults and screwing their—" He stopped with a mild look when she whirled around. "What? A little *too* adult for you?"

A succinct two-word response had barely formed on her lips when he stopped her with an outstretched hand. "Wait, don't say it. I wouldn't want to be the one to spoil that proper image. Maybe we should just change the subject, forget about the honeymoon couple for awhile."

"Maybe we shouldn't talk at all." She stalked past him, but he caught her by the arm, pulling her around to face him. She should have looked at him with all-out fury, but a pleasant shiver accompanied his touch, and heat flared through her when he pulled her close. She had no idea her body craved physical contact so much. It wiped the intended fury out of her mind, and she looked at him blankly.

"Hang on, Lauren." With his free hand Drew rubbed at his forehead until the lines of frustration eased. "Look, I'm sorry. It's Meg I'm angry with, not you. I actually admire your sense of loyalty."

"Really?" she said, dripping sarcasm. "I couldn't tell."

He chuckled softly and it reverberated inside her like a hundred butterflies taking wing. "Feisty. I like that about you, too. And I really do understand. If someone accused my sister of"—he cleared his throat—"bad things, I'd be just as protective as you are. And just as worried."

His expression suddenly became sincere. Damn, he really meant it. "Thanks."

"The problem is, you're all wound up, worrying about your sister while she's obviously not sparing a thought for you. Why don't you cut yourself a break? Let Meg live her own life, make her own mistakes."

He'd hit the bull's-eye with that one, and it shook her nearly as much as the touch of his hand on her arm. She had to fight to keep her voice steady. "I don't want to talk about it."

"Fine, we won't."

"Let go of me."

His gaze flicked to his hand, then back to her. He didn't release her.

Oh God, that shook her more than anything; he felt something, too. She couldn't look away from his eyes. Something wavered in their blue depths, something that transferred itself to her body, settling in her stomach. It was fluttery, but nice. Something she'd never felt with Jeff.

Lauren sucked in a breath. "Jeff!"

Drew's lip twitched. "It's Drew."

"No!" She pulled her arm from his unresisting hand

and held up her ring finger. "My fiancé, Jeff." She wiggled the finger at Drew, who gave it a puzzled glance.

"Yes, a diamond ring. I see it." He squinted.
"Barely."

"I forgot to call him. I said I would as soon as I got
here, and he'll be wondering what happened to me."

"Ah. Another person you look out for? You could
tell him the truth, that you were distracted by . . .
events."

Earthshaking events. She pretended not to understand even as the heat rose in her cheeks. "He won't
understand," she said, twisting the ring nervously on
her finger, already formulating an explanation.

"No, I guess he wouldn't. Because you would never
be that irresponsible."

Stung by the rebuke, Lauren raised her eyes to his
face and found it much too close to her own. Taking
a quick step back, she pressed her mouth into a stern
line. "Don't make fun of me."

"I wouldn't do that, Lauren."

Not Aunt Lauren. Lauren. Distracted by how
different that one softly-spoken word could sound,
she didn't realize he'd lifted his hand until she felt it
against her cheek. She froze, eyes wide, as he stroked a
light path down the side of her face.

"I could never make fun of you. In fact, I find
I'm taking you quite seriously." Two fingers lingered
beneath her chin for one long moment during which
the world might have tipped off its axis for all she
knew. Something about him affected her equilibrium
and made her head swim.

Another something that never happened with Jeff.

The thought stirred her. She took another step

backward, causing Drew's hand to fall away. She swallowed. "I have to go now."

"Okay."

"To call Jeff, I mean."

"Yes, I know."

"I'm going upstairs. For privacy."

"Okay." He raised an eyebrow and waved. "'Bye."

"'Bye." She stumbled, turned, and darted toward the stairs.

Lauren spent the rest of the evening in the guest bedroom, too humiliated to face Drew. And too scared.

Talking to Jeff didn't help. She couldn't answer his questions and didn't care to hear his demands.

"When will your sister stop these crazy games and grow up? Her wild impulses interfere with my life as well as yours. They already ruined tonight's dinner with my parents. Aren't you tired of putting up with this kind of nonsense?"

"Yes, I guess so."

"You *guess so?*" Jeff's annoyance came through loud and clear.

"It's just that I'm not sure it's nonsense. Meg asked me to come, nearly begged me. She should be here. But she's not, she's missing, and she doesn't even answer her cell phone. No one knows where she is. I can't help thinking something might be wrong."

"What's wrong is that you've let Meg's problems affect our lives again."

Lauren's brows puckered with irritation. "I don't see how Meg's disappearance affects your life, Jeff." Unless he was missing their Thursday night sex date, too. The possibility took her by surprise. She liked to think that wanting her more would make him irritable, but she wasn't sure, since he'd always been uncomfortable talking about sex.

"Lauren, are you listening? I want you here. Do I have to spell it out for you?"

Bingo! She chuckled, relieved that she'd figured it out. Relieved, too, that the secret doubts she'd had about their relationship might be so easily solved. "No, you don't. I understand. You think we need more quality time together, and I couldn't agree more. In fact, I'm in the mood for some quality time with you right now."

"Good." He sounded happier already. "Then you'll come home right away?"

He was more eager to expand their sex life than she'd thought. "As soon as I can." Trying for an appropriately playful mood, she asked, "Do you have something planned already?"

"I will, just as soon as we get off the phone."

Trust Jeff to plan everything, even sex. He'd never do anything kinky, but she had to admit to some curiosity. "Give me a hint. Is it something we've never done before?"

"Sure, if that's what you're in the mood for. I can probably find someplace we haven't been."

"That shouldn't be hard." Jeff wasn't good at thinking outside the box, and the box was his bedroom.

"Well, I suppose if we drive to another town . . ."

She actually frowned at the phone before putting it back to her ear. "Another town? What are you talking about?"

"I'm talking about rescheduling our dinner with my parents. What are *you* talking about?"

"Sex! I'm talking about our sex life, Jeff."

Silence filled several seconds. Then several more. "Excuse me?"

She sighed, feeling defeated before she began, but unwilling to back down. "Our quality time together—get it? I think you should take me to bed more often."

She waited through another long pause. "I thought you were happy with our sex life."

She couldn't help noting that he hadn't jumped at the chance for more sex. "I just thought I would enjoy having more. That I might be even happier with more. Is that too much to ask?"

"Um, no. It's fine. What night of the week were you thinking of?"

That wasn't the level of enthusiasm she'd been hoping for. She was fairly certain if Drew's girlfriend demanded more sex, he wouldn't ask her what night of the week. He'd probably do it right then and there.

Don't think about that.

"It doesn't matter when, Jeff. For God's sake, just pick a night."

"Fine. Um, fine. How about we discuss it during our vacation?"

"Fine." She didn't mind putting it off. The idea was already beginning to lose its charm.

"You will be back in time to salvage our trip, won't you, Lauren? You only have two weeks off work, and we've already lost one day we can't make up. Maybe two."

It was a valid complaint, but somehow it sounded petty when Jeff said it. "I don't want to talk about it tonight, Jeff."

"What will you do tomorrow if Meg doesn't call?"

"I don't know. Why don't we wait and see what happens?"

"You need to change your plane reservations as soon as possible, Lauren, or it'll cost you a fortune."

Lauren usually found Jeff's frugal common sense admirable, but it didn't seem to be the most important consideration right now. "I know, I just don't want to think about it now."

"I need to know your itinerary so I can schedule our dinner with Mom and Dad."

Lauren squeezed her eyes shut. "I have a splitting headache, Jeff. I'll call you tomorrow." She hung up before he could reply. A minute later she realized the headache hadn't been a lie and searched her purse for aspirin before crawling into bed.

Incredibly, she slept a full nine hours. With the early spring sunrise still a gray line in the eastern sky, she made as little noise as she could, washing and dressing.

It didn't matter. When she padded silently downstairs in stocking feet, lights blazed in several rooms. She heard the low rumble of Drew's voice from the kitchen, followed by Gerald's softer tone.

She found them standing at the granite-topped island. Lauren took in Drew's disheveled hair and Gerald's tie-less shirt, with open collar and rolled sleeves.

"Have you two been up all night?"

They exchanged looks, as if her question required consultation. Drew came up with the answer. "Yes."

She didn't need a premonition to guess that something was wrong. A quick stab of fear sent a shiver through her as she walked to Drew's side, refusing to think about why standing next to him might offer reassurance.

"What is it? Have you heard from Meg?" An icy feeling gripped her stomach. "Is she okay?" At least a dozen more questions flew through her mind in the second before Drew shook his head.

"No, we haven't heard from her."

Maybe no news is good news, she told herself. "Senator Creighton?" she asked.

Across from her, Gerald shook his head.

"Then what?" She looked from Drew's weary face, unshaven and shadowed with stubble, back to Gerald's pinched expression. "What were you doing all night?"

"Searching the house," Drew told her. "We hoped there might be a letter, or a notation on the computer, something that would hint at where they'd gone."

They wouldn't look this concerned if the search hadn't been successful. "You found something," she guessed.

"Not right away. Not until Gerald thought to check the safe. Meg told him she was going to the bank when she left here, and she'd been in Dad's office, so we thought—"

"*You* thought," Gerald corrected.

Lauren suddenly realized where this was going. The icy dread inside her mixed with hot anger as she turned toward Drew. "You son of a bitch. You thought she might have stolen something from the safe?"

He didn't flinch. "It was a logical possibility."

A rush of fury pulled Lauren's hands into tight fists at her sides. With her remaining fingernails biting into her palms, she growled at him, "No, it's not logical,

not if you know Meg. My sister would *never* steal."
She whipped her head toward Gerald. "You claim to
know her. Did you really think Meg would do something like that?"

Pain creased Gerald's forehead. "No, I didn't."

A tiny wave of relief washed over her. At least
someone believed in Meg.

Gerald's sad gaze shifted toward Drew. "I still
don't."

Responding to the defeat in his voice, Lauren's
stomach clenched with dread. "Still?" She turned back
to Drew, nearly shrinking from the hesitation in his
eyes.

"Lauren . . ." Drew began.

She shook her head to emphasize the denial because
she knew her voice would sound weak. "No. She
wouldn't."

Drew's voice was as hard as steel. "I'm sorry. But
she did."

Chapter Two

She didn't believe him. He wasn't sorry. And Meg certainly hadn't stolen anything from Harlan Creighton's safe.

"Andrew," Gerald scolded. "You don't know that for sure."

"You said yourself, the key was there two days ago. Now it's gone."

Lauren frowned. "What key? I thought you were talking about money."

"All the money's there," Gerald told her, with a meaningful glance at Drew. "Three thousand dollars. She didn't take it."

"No, she aimed higher," Drew said. "A fortune in jewelry, left to Miranda and me by our mother. It's in a safety deposit box, and one of the keys to that box is missing. It was in the safe."

"And you think Meg took it?" Her voice fairly squeaked with outrage. "Do you have any idea how incredibly stupid that is?"

Drew closed his eyes. "No, but I'm sure you'll tell me."

"Damn right." She poked his chest for good measure, ramming her finger into a solid wall of muscle. "My sister is the most honest person I know. She might be a little irresponsible at times, and she might go to a lot of parties, and spend too much money on clothes instead of saving it, and go out with the wrong kind of men—"

Lauren noticed Drew's interested look and changed direction. "The point is, Meg would never do anything to harm anyone else. She wouldn't lie, she wouldn't cheat, and she certainly wouldn't *steal*."

"That's a moving testimonial," Drew said. "But it's not proof. I've met plenty of women in this town who are nice on the surface, but that doesn't stop them from being manipulative gold diggers beneath it."

Lauren flushed with anger. "My sister isn't a gold digger."

"I guess time will tell, won't it? Either the newlyweds show up together with an explanation for the missing key, or my dad shows up alone, while his new wife scampers off with the spoils of her brief but profitable marriage."

She refrained from hitting him, but just barely. "And your dad's office still hasn't heard from him?"

"It happens. You're talking about the Playboy of the Potomac."

Gerald sighed. "In other words, we wait."

Great. Another day of listening to Drew's cynical views on women in general, and Meg in particular. Or, worse yet, risking the disturbing effect of his quiet blue gaze piercing hers. Causing the very sort of wild feelings Meg sought from life, and look where that had gotten her—married to a notorious, skirt-chasing playboy twice her age, raising eyebrows and suspicions, and leaving it to sensible Lauren to straighten out the mess.

No, thank you. Lauren would choose her perfectly ordered life over that sort of chaos any day. In fact, she'd be glad to go home right now and leave Drew to break up the misguided marriage if it weren't for the fact that Meg's disappearance had Lauren worried.

She'd stay just long enough to ensure that Meg was safe. Jeff wouldn't like it, but he'd understand that it was the responsible thing to do. In fact, he'd just lectured her on the virtue of taking responsibility.

Thank goodness she was engaged to a reasonable man.

And in the meantime, she didn't have to listen to Drew's cynical opinions.

"I'll be upstairs," she told Gerald. "I brought some work with me from the office. Let me know as soon as you hear from Meg or Senator Creighton."

She'd almost reached the doorway when Drew called, "Enjoy your phone sex with Jeff."

There was no way she'd give him the shocked reaction he was looking for. "Thanks, I will."

"Who's Jeff?" Gerald asked behind her.

She strained to catch Drew's careless reply. "No one special."

She waited until nine o'clock, when Jeff would be at his desk, finishing his second cup of coffee. He dealt with problems better after a good dose of caffeine.

"What do you mean, you aren't coming back today?"

Lauren could almost hear his scowl through the phone. "I thought we agreed that you would change your plane reservations."

"Actually, you suggested it; we didn't agree. I want to be sure Meg is okay before I leave."

A long moment of silence followed. Lauren knew Jeff was taking a deep, meditative breath to calm himself. "Okay. We can still salvage our trip. Instead of just sitting around waiting to hear from Meg, you can rent a car and drive to my aunt and uncle's house in Virginia. They've wanted to meet you for over a year now, ever since we got engaged. It'll be a nice, relaxing drive, and you can forget about Meg for a while."

She didn't *want* to forget about Meg, she just wanted to know her sister was safe.

"I can't do that, Jeff. I wanted to stick around here in case she calls."

"For Pete's sake, can't anyone there take a message?"

After dealing with Drew, Lauren didn't feel up to an argument with Jeff. She refrained from commenting as he laid out the reasons why a two hour drive to the Virginia countryside to see John and Betty Duchaine would be a good way to spend her time. As he finished, Jeff added, "I'll be free tonight between dinner and my racquet ball game. Give me a call at eight fifteen, okay? I want to hear how your visit went."

"Hmmm," Lauren said, still wondering how to tell him she'd rather sit in Georgetown and worry about Meg than drive to Virginia to see people she didn't know. Still, the evening phone call to him could ease part of her problems. "How much time will you have between dinner and racquetball?"

"Twenty-two minutes. Why?"

It might help if she had some experience at this, but you had to start somewhere. "Do you think that's enough time for phone sex?"

"What? What's gotten into you, Lauren?"

She wondered about that herself. "I don't know. Do you want to help me find out, or not?"

"I don't even know how to do that."

"You just describe what you're doing." The idea of hearing Jeff whisper suggestive things in her ear intrigued her.

"Lauren." She could already hear disapproval in his tone. "Don't you think that's a little low class?"

"No. Lots of people do it, and it has nothing to do with class."

"*We've* never done it."

"There's a lot of things we've never done. That doesn't mean we can't try them." She tried to be patient, reminding herself that she was pushing against the very thing that had drawn her to Jeff, his predictable, conservative nature. He was her anchor, the person who kept her grounded whenever Meg's lifestyle threatened to throw her calm life into chaos. Years of rescuing Meg from disastrous relationships had made Jeff appealing. She just hoped he could stretch those sensibilities a little.

"I'll, um, think about it," he said.

"Okay." It looked like she'd have to settle for that for now.

"In the meantime, meeting Uncle John and Aunt Betty will be the perfect antidote to spending a couple days in Meg's world."

Back to that again. "Meg's world isn't so bad, and

I'm concerned about her. Anything could have happened—"

He cut her off. "Meg is a big girl, Lauren. She'll come home eventually, no doubt with some sordid explanation of why she disappeared for a day."

"Three days, actually."

He hadn't heard her. "Trust me, you're better off spending your time with my aunt and uncle. Just don't tell them about Meg. After all, we're hoping she gets this marriage annulled, right? So there's no need to mention it. I'm looking forward to hearing what you think of Uncle John's antique car collection. You can tell me all about it when you call tonight."

"At eight fifteen."

"Right. Great, I'll talk to you then. 'Bye." The phone went dead before she could respond.

Disgusted, she tossed it aside. No one seemed to be concerned about Meg but her—and Gerald. And he was downstairs with Drew.

She'd already decided it was best to avoid Drew. When they weren't arguing, she found herself noticing the devilish appeal of his smile, or the snug fit of his jeans. But by early afternoon, when she'd read the airline's in-flight magazine cover-to-cover and her stomach was growling, she went downstairs.

She found Drew and Gerald right where she'd left them.

Gerald stood at the kitchen island, surrounded by enough food to stock a small deli. He looked up with a smile. "Hey, Lauren. Did you get caught up in your work? We were about to send out a search party, weren't we, Andrew?"

Drew twisted the top off a beer and drank before answering. "No."

Gerald gave an exaggerated sigh. "It's an expression, stupid. And it was rhetorical."

"But inaccurate." Drew popped a pretzel in his mouth and smiled sweetly at her. "She wasn't lost. I'm willing to bet Lauren Sutherland has never been anywhere but where she was supposed to be, and never caused anyone a moment's concern. Am I right?"

She didn't know what she'd done to get under his skin, but he was definitely displeased with her. She lifted her chin, determined not to let him get to her. "That's right, Creighton. Dependable and predictable, that's me. You know what else? I'm always on time, too. What horrible qualities."

She helped herself to lunch, standing next to Gerald as they passed condiments back and forth. Drew was in constant motion, pacing restlessly from sink, to refrigerator, to table, to window. When he grabbed a piece of cheese from the counter in front of them, Gerald lowered his sandwich and addressed him in a firm tone. "Andrew. Stand still. I can't eat when you're running circles around me. I'm getting winded just watching you."

"Sorry." Drew stuck his hands in his pockets and stood still. Half a minute later he grabbed a handful of chips, chomping through them with the efficiency of a wood chipper sucking in branches. Then olives. Then deviled eggs. Then he cracked his knuckles.

Gerald's sandwich hit the plate. Throwing a sharp glare at Drew, he picked up his food, grabbed a beer bottle, and stalked across the kitchen to sit at the table. Lauren stayed at the island. She might not feel as hyper as Drew, but she was too unsettled to sit down.

"I know, I know," Drew grumbled. "I'm not good at waiting. I prefer action." He picked up a plum, looked at it, then put it down. "And I'm starting to get worried."

Lauren lowered a forkful of potato salad. "You, too?"

"Of course me, too." His gaze speared her. "Why wouldn't I be worried? My dad calls to say he got married, I scramble to get here, and no one knows where he is. For over three days now! He's a United States senator, for God's sake. *Someone* must know where he is. You don't just lose track of those people."

"Oh." She'd nearly forgotten that his father couldn't be located either. "I understand. I feel the same way about Meg."

Drew smiled, a cold gleam in his eyes. "I wouldn't worry too much about her. You'll probably get a postcard any day now from some tropical island, one that doesn't have an extradition treaty with the United States. I just hope she tells you in what remote location she ditched my dad, so we can rescue him."

Her resentment flared. "Did it ever occur to you that something might have happened to Meg, too?"

Drew studied her, looking much more calm now that he had her riled up. "You mean other than fleeing the country? No, I can't say that it has."

The arrogant bastard. Lauren pushed her plate away and faced him. "You're wrong. All you have to do is check that stupid safety deposit box and you'll see that all your precious jewelry is still there." Even if it were gone, Meg had every right to take it as Harlan

Creighton's wife. Yet she didn't think pointing that out would make Meg look any better.

He lifted an eyebrow. "What a brilliant idea."

Gerald spoke up from across the room. "I told you, only the senator or Mrs. Creighton can open the safety deposit box."

Drew nodded. "And they aren't here. And the bank closes in"—he checked his watch—"three hours. Tomorrow's Saturday, so it won't be open. I guess we'll have to wait until Monday before we'll know for sure how much Meg ran off with. If they don't show up by then, we can probably persuade the police to open the box."

No way. Whether they ended up calling the police, or not, Lauren wasn't going to have Drew Creighton accusing her sister of theft all weekend, especially if it might delay a search for Meg. "Take me to the bank. I'll pretend I'm Meg and you can open that damn box, which will prove she didn't take anything. I can forge her signature, and we look so alike that no one will question me."

Drew slapped his hand on the granite countertop, suddenly energized. "Excellent. I'll get your coat. Get the spare key, Gerald, and some sort of ID for Lauren that says she's Meg. If they ask, she can pretend she left her driver's license at home." He strode toward the doorway as he talked, then paused to look back at Gerald, who frowned at him from the table. "Let's go," Drew said. "The bank closes soon."

Gerald looked as surprised by Drew's enthusiastic acceptance as she was. And suspicious. "Just hold on. I don't like this. It's not legal."

"It's close enough to legal," Drew rationalized.

"We're family. And we're just going to look, we're not going to take anything."

Lauren could tell Gerald had stubbornly processed "close enough to legal" to mean illegal. "If it's okay for family members to open it, then why don't you have a key to the box?" he argued, and shook his head. "Uh-uh, I won't do it."

Drew watched him, considering. "Gerald, you're in charge of Dad's finances, so I know you've been there before. You'll be there to watch, to make sure we don't touch anything else." When Gerald still didn't budge, he said, "What if something's happened to my dad? Look, I know you like Meg. But what if Meg really did take the jewelry and skip the country? Do you really want to wait until Monday to panic and call the cops when they could be looking for them both by tonight?" He let Gerald waver a moment before delivering the final punch. "What would my dad want you to do?"

Gerald nodded slowly. "You may be right."

Drew gave him a sharp look. "You aren't afraid of what we'll find, are you?"

Gerald narrowed his eyes, taking the dare. "No." Standing, he adjusted his vest with a determined look and began putting food away. "Just give me a minute. And Lauren has to change into a skirt. Meg is very stylish, and she'd never visit the senator's bank looking like *that*." He gestured at Lauren's jeans and sweater, then noticed her expression. "No offense, sweetie. Meg is aware that Senator Creighton has an image to uphold and it applies to everyone close to him, too. You don't see the First Lady going around town in jeans, do you? Same thing."

Not exactly the same, but she sighed and shrugged

it off. He was probably right about the image. "I'll change."

Drew turned a smile on Lauren, gesturing toward the door. "After you."

He was entirely too eager. She gave him a measured look. "Why do I feel like you wanted me to suggest this very thing?"

"Are you waffling?"

She glared. "I never waffle." She strode from the room, eager to prove Drew wrong and get on with a proper search for Meg. And to pretend it didn't worry her that he knew exactly which button to push.

Any doubts they had about Lauren passing as Meg were quelled as soon as they walked into the bank. Passing through the double doors, a man hurried in the opposite direction, bumping Lauren's shoulder as they passed. He glanced back with a muttered apology, then stopped and stared.

"Mrs. Creighton!" The words were an astonished gasp.

"Hello," Lauren began, already playing her part, but the man was backing away, mumbling more apologies. He bumped into the outer door, then turned and dashed out to the parking lot.

"What the hell was that?" Drew asked. He took her by the elbow. "Are you all right?"

"I'm fine." She glanced outside where the man was jogging toward his car at a fast clip. "I guess he knows Meg."

"Looks more like he owes her money, the way he ran off." Drew kept a protective grip on her arm until they reached the counter.

"Mrs. Creighton! How nice to see you again," the bank clerk oozed. While Lauren carefully forged her sister's signature, the clerk slipped curious glances at Drew and Gerald. The signature didn't receive even a cursory inspection. So much for security.

Lauren tried not to fidget while Meg's and the bank's matching keys were inserted in the tiny door. The box that slid out was long and wide, large enough to hold several fortunes in jewelry. She grudgingly conceded that Drew might have reason to be worried. He was wrong about Meg, of course, but he had no way of knowing that. In a couple more minutes, she was sure he would.

They followed the clerk to a tiny room, barely big enough for all of them to fit comfortably inside. No one spoke while she laid the box on the wide ledge that passed as a table, then squeezed around them, closing the door with a muffled click.

The three of them exchanged looks. Drew motioned at Lauren. "Go ahead."

She took a step back. "Not me, it's not mine." Now that they were closed in this private room, she was reluctant to look inside. She told herself it was because the box wasn't hers, not because she was worried about what she'd find.

Apparently it had also occurred to Drew that his father's safe deposit box might be private for a good reason. He hesitated.

"Oh, for heaven's sake," Gerald muttered, and stepped between them, taking the solitary chair. "It's a good thing you have me here to take charge, since you two obviously fold under the slightest pressure." Lauren and Drew ignored the insult and stepped closer as he flipped back the lid. Lauren felt her heart kick into overdrive as she leaned forward for a better look.

Silk- and velvet-covered jewelry cases fit like puzzle pieces inside the larger box. Lauren released a breath she didn't know she'd been holding.

"Open them," Drew instructed.

She threw him a resentful glance, even though she knew they had to be sure.

They watched as Gerald lifted each case out and opened it. Jeweled necklaces and large gemstone dinner rings glittered in the strong overhead lights as each lid sprang open, then was snapped shut again. With each sparkling item, Lauren felt her heart rate slow, until the anxious pounding returned to normal. Eight boxes covered the table when Gerald reached a light blue document-size envelope at the bottom of the box. He picked it up.

"What's that?" Drew asked.

"I don't know. I was with the senator last week when he stopped to get a necklace out for Miranda to wear at a charity ball. This wasn't here." He looked at them, eyebrows raised. "Should I open it?"

"Hell, yes," Drew said.

Lauren nodded, an unexpected dread turning her hands icy. If Meg didn't take anything out of the box, then she must have left this in it. What would she need to keep in a safe deposit box? It was probably completely harmless, her marriage license or an updated will, and of no concern to anyone but Harlan and Meg Creighton. But the fact that Meg seemed to have vanished after leaving it here sent ominous prickles down Lauren's spine.

Gerald undid the clasp and peeked inside, then slid

something out. Before Lauren could tell what it was, he shoved it back inside and looked up in alarm.

"What? What is it?" she asked.

Gerald swallowed. "Pictures."

Drew scowled. "What kind of pictures?"

His shoulders shuddered. "The wrong kind. Naked people. Two naked people."

Drew and Lauren exchanged a quick look. "Who?" Drew demanded.

"I don't know. I don't want to know." He handed the envelope to Drew. "You look."

Drew's face was determined as he reached inside the envelope. Lauren thought it would be unseemly to rush to his side and peer over his shoulder, even though she was dying of curiosity. Gerald's comment left the possibilities wide open, and none of them fit her image of Meg.

He slid the pictures out slowly. She eased onto her tiptoes but could only make out a black and white blur. But she could see his reaction.

The pictures weren't all the way out before he shot them back in again. His face was drawn and serious as he held the envelope out to her. "I don't need to see any more."

Lauren stared at the envelope, suddenly wary of what neither Drew nor Gerald had wanted to see. She'd never seen a man flinch at viewing nude pictures before. "What is it?" she asked.

"It's exactly what you think it is. A man, a woman, and a mattress. The kind of pictures most people don't want to star in." Drew scowled. "But you'd better be the one to look because I think the woman might be

Meg, and I doubt either she or my dad would want me to see that."

Definitely not. "But the man . . ."

"Is not my father," Drew finished grimly.

What he was suggesting wasn't possible. She grabbed the envelope from his hand. "Give me that."

She reached inside, half expecting to feel something cold and slimy. All she encountered was the slippery surface of a photograph. Several photographs. Pulling them out, she dropped the envelope on the table before raising the pictures to her eyes, unconsciously bracing herself for whatever had caused Gerald and Drew to recoil so quickly.

She expected something grainy and sleazy, but the photos were surprisingly well-focused, glossy, eight-by-ten black-and-white shots. Sleazy still applied.

The bed had no headboard, and the bare walls were only a few shades darker than the white linens. Nothing that would help them identify a place or time. Lighting was barely adequate and from the side, as if a single lamp across the room provided the only illumination. It shone softly on the man's white legs and backside—unquestionably the lean, muscled body of a young man—and turned his long blond hair into a pale glow around his head. A well-built Scandinavian hunk. His body shadowed the naked woman beneath him, although not enough to hide the prurient details for anyone who cared to look, from the tight buds of nipples to the darkness between her thighs, ready to accept his—Lauren's gaze darted toward the woman's head on the pillow. The man's head hovered above hers, high enough to allow light to fall directly on her face.

Lauren stared at an image of herself. Except it wasn't her. It was Meg.

Sudden embarrassment washed over her. Drew had seen enough to guess this naked woman was Lauren's sister. Her nearly identical sister. He might as well have been looking at Lauren's splayed, aroused body, and he knew it.

She steadied her hands with an effort. No matter how much she wanted to shove the pictures back in the envelope, she had to look at them again. They had to know why Meg had hidden them. If there was information to be gained from these pictures, she was the one who had to look. And she had to do it without imagining what Drew thought about them, or what he thought about her.

Lauren closed her eyes and swallowed hard. Shuffling the first photo to the bottom, she took a cautious peek at the second one in the thin stack. The same man and woman, this time their positions reversed. The woman knelt upright on the bed, long, silky hair cascading back from her tipped head, while the man beneath her clasped her buttocks. Her knees were spread on either side of his head, while he—Lauren felt herself blush and flipped quickly through the others. Teeth clenched, she looked at four more pictures in various poses, some showing the perfectly featured and strangely characterless face of the handsome young man, and all showing the mussed hair, naked body, and ecstatic face of Lauren's sister.

She shoved them back in the envelope. Her hands had gone cold and her heart pounded. Her mind scrambled to deny what her eyes had just seen. There had to be another explanation. Secret photos from a wild college fling, or a mad, aberrant impulse to pose for one of those slimy sex magazines. Lauren grasped at explanations, but knew they weren't true. The pictures weren't of Meg ten years ago, they were Meg now.

Lauren felt ill. She handed the envelope back to Gerald, avoiding his and Drew's gaze. Thankfully, they said nothing. But it was an uncomfortable silence, filled with questions no one wanted to ask.

The little room was starting to feel claustrophobic. Lauren nibbled a fingernail and willed Gerald to go faster as he fitted the jewelry boxes back inside the metal safe deposit box, recreating the snug pattern. She needed to get out of there, to find fresh air and open sky. She needed to think.

Her mind was preoccupied all the way to the parking lot. Drew took her elbow as she stepped over a slushy curb, noticeably less antagonistic now that the jewelry had been found in its proper place. In fact, his hand on her arm felt gentle, almost affectionate. Or maybe he was simply worried that she'd trip over the curb in her inattentive state.

"Those pictures really upset you, didn't they?" he said. It was a simple question, but she thought she heard a trace of sympathy.

She didn't want Drew's sympathy. "They made me think." Disregarding the cold wind that blew inside her open coat, she voiced the hope that had been going through her mind. "Pictures like that can be faked, can't they?"

She watched them. Gerald's morose expression turned thoughtful, but Drew gave a weary sigh like he'd expected her to say it.

"Did anything about them look fake?" he asked.

"No, of course not. At least, I don't think so, because I didn't look closely. But I know that couldn't be Meg. It couldn't be. She's never done anything like that before."

"That you know of," Drew finished.

True. And she didn't want to think about that. "Did you notice the quality of those pictures?"

"It wasn't exactly art, Lauren."

"But it wasn't amateur photography, either. They didn't have that grainy look of candid shots from some hidden location. I'll bet that camera was right in the room with them. They must have known they were being photographed. And no matter what it looked like, I can't believe the woman was my sister."

"Hmm." It was grudging, but at least he considered it. "Cameras can be hidden in walls, you know. You just make sure you have a good angle beforehand. And that no one can accidentally block the view. If the guy was in on it, the poses would naturally be good."

"Good?" She didn't care for that description.

"Revealing."

Lauren imagined the Nordic hunk manipulating his partner into the best position for revealing pictures to use as blackmail. Disgusting. But the deliberate nature of the act made her think about what she'd seen.

She turned to face Drew as he stopped at their car. Impatiently brushing aside windblown strands of hair, she ignored the door he held open for her. "You called those pictures poses. I think you might be right."

His eyes were slitted against more than the wind. "How so?" he asked, probably already suspicious of her explanation.

"Did you notice how her face was well-lit even though her body was shadowed? Every picture was like that," she said. "I could see her face clearly, even though her body was obscured. Maybe it was Photoshopped, where one person's head is put on another person's body. Maybe they couldn't show the body clearly because it might not look enough like Meg's. You know, because of birthmarks, an appendectomy scar, a belly button that's an innie instead of an outie, something like that."

She'd made him think. "All the pictures were like that? The woman's body was shadowed?"

"Yes." She nodded vigorously, more convinced as she thought about it. "Everything was shadowed except faces. I could see the shape of her body, but no details on the skin."

"You could see the shape?" A humorless smile tugged at his lips and the icy blue eyes watched her intently. "So what did you think? Was that Meg's shape? The contours, the form, the size . . ."

When his glance strayed to her chest where the wind whipped against her and flattened her sweater to her breasts, she understood. He wondered if the naked body he'd seen was similar to hers. Before she could snap out a nasty retort, he held up a hand to stop her. "It's a legitimate question, Lauren. Only you would know if that body could belong to your sister."

She bit back her impulsive response to tell him to go to hell, and thought about it for several seconds. Reluctantly, she had to admit, "I can't be sure. It could be."

"Really." He seemed to give it serious consideration, but eventually an eyebrow quirked and he looked her up and down.

"Get your mind out of the gutter, Drew. We're talking about my sister."

"*You* are." He smiled lazily. "I'm not."

She met his smile with a glare and hoped the sharp wind blew away the heat she felt sweeping through her body. He was obviously his father's son, and she couldn't stand the fact that some brainless, primitive part of her responded. From his smug look, he knew it, too. She dropped onto the front seat and slammed the door.

Without another glance at her, Drew got behind the wheel. Gerald had been quiet during her theorizing about faked photographs, but as they pulled out of the parking lot, he leaned forward from the backseat. "I don't know who was in those pictures, but I have one thing to say. If somehow I got hold of photos like that of myself, I wouldn't be stashing them in a safe deposit box like they were a priceless keepsake. I'd destroy them." Flipping his cashmere scarf over his shoulder, he plopped back against the seat.

Lauren and Drew looked at each other. She should have thought of it. "He's right," she said. "Meg would have ripped them and burned the pieces."

Drew nodded. "Most convincing thing I've heard so far."

"So you agree it can't be Meg in those pictures?"

"No. I agree it's one possibility. There's also the possibility that she didn't put them there." He frowned as he drove. "But that doesn't explain why she kept them. Or where she is." His mouth pulled into a grim line. "Where either of them are."

Chapter Three

Lauren worried her lower lip, sparing a nail. "I think we should call the police."

Drew shook his head without taking his eyes off the road. "We need to be sure she's missing before we do that. Wait until we talk to my dad. His staff seems to think he's in town and will check in soon. Since she obviously didn't run off with the family inheritance," he tipped his head and smiled ruefully, an acknowledgement that he'd been wrong, "he might know where she is. After all, she is his wife." He added under his breath, "Incredible as it seems."

Lauren nodded, reluctant to wait, but wanting to believe there was a simple explanation for her sister's disappearance. "How long will that take? You said you haven't been able to reach him."

"Not long." His gaze lifted to the rearview mirror and met Gerald's eyes. "I know the Senate just ended a session, but Dad's office staff will still be there, won't they?"

"You mean now, late afternoon? Sure, most of them."

"Then we'll go there. I'm not getting anywhere with them over the phone. Maybe I can be a little more persuasive in person."

Lauren had no doubt about that.

They fought rush-hour traffic toward the Hart Senate Office Building. Lauren had never seen the Capitol complex before, and trudging through blustery winds and freezing slush was not making a good first impression. At least the Hart Building was warm and dry.

Senator Creighton's fourth-floor offices were open, and Lauren was confronted by a breathless young woman as soon as she walked in.

"Meg! Thank goodness! Why didn't you answer your messages? We have to knock one of these groups off the Senator's itinerary for next week, and I don't know whether to dump the church ladies' auxiliary or that conservation action group from Austin. The church ladies aren't important, but the minister is, and—"

Lauren started to correct her, then saw an opportunity she hadn't expected. She cut the woman off, raising a hand in front of the papers she was shoving under Lauren's nose. "Not now. I need to, um, check something first. Could you just leave these on my desk? I'll get back to you."

The woman hesitated and looked at the papers as if she hadn't intended to part with them. "Yeah, I guess I can. But I need to know today. Yesterday, really." She stressed the urgency of deciding between the church ladies and the conservation people as she led the way toward one of two empty desks. Relieved to know which one was Meg's without having to ask, Lauren sat down and began rifling through files on the desktop.

The woman hadn't left. "Hey. You're not Meg."

"I'm her sister," she said without looking up. "And I need to find Meg immediately. Family emergency."

"So why don't you just call her?" The woman sounded truly confused.

Lauren looked up. "You just told me she hasn't answered her messages. Have you heard from Meg today?"

"Um, no, but—"

"Neither has anyone else. I need to find her." Spotting an agenda book, she flipped to the current week and began reading the cryptic notes Meg had made.

Across the room, Drew had collared the first staffer he saw, identified himself, and demanded the woman find his father, *now*. Impressed with his urgency, the woman began dialing, but questioned him as she did. "Actually I've already called a few places today. We've been looking for him, too. What happened?"

"I don't know. But he's dropped out of sight, and we have reason to believe he might be in danger."

That bit of exaggeration helped. Lauren could hear the concern in her voice as the woman began pestering half of D.C. with phone calls.

Lauren gave up on the date book and began examining three loose leaf notebooks on the desktop. The woman who first accosted her had disappeared, but another woman watched her with a frown. "She can't do that," she announced to no one in particular. "That's Meg's desk, and a lot of that stuff is confidential."

Lauren didn't bother answering as she continued flipping through meeting notes, but Gerald stepped between her and the young woman. She was a good three inches taller than him in her heels, but lacked the confidence of Senator Creighton's personal secretary. Hands on his hips, Gerald faced her down. "Did you hear what young Mr. Creighton just said? Are you aware of the seriousness of this situation? We have a missing United States senator here. And his wife. You can either let Meg's sister look for clues to their whereabouts, or we can notify the authorities and you can have a squad of policemen and forensics experts ripping this place apart, including your desk and all the other ones in here. Your choice."

Lauren nearly snickered at the part about the forensics experts. But it intimidated the woman enough to have her looking at other office staff for support. Lauren glanced up to see what would happen. Two other staffers shrugged helplessly, and the one making calls at Drew's command paused long enough to snap, "That's Senator Creighton's personal secretary. Listen to him." With a sullen look, the woman returned to her desk but kept her eyes on Lauren.

"Wise choice," Gerald said, nodding sagely. "The senator will appreciate you handling this discreetly."

"I thought you said the senator was missing," the woman challenged.

"He is. But when we find him, he'll appreciate how you handled this. Believe me, I'm his personal secretary, and I know how he would want—"

"Gerald," Lauren interrupted.

He turned. "What? Did you find something?"

"No, but I need you to hold these files so I can check this stuff underneath them." More like, she needed to keep him from pissing off the secretary who was already on edge about them going through Meg's desk.

"Oh. Sure thing."

She searched for another ten minutes while Gerald held a stack of files and looked important, but her efforts yielded nothing. Lauren put her elbows on the desk and rubbed her forehead. She was becoming more worried about her sister's disappearance with every passing hour. At least she wasn't the only one. Drew wasn't having any luck either, and she could tell his concern was rising, too.

"Did you try Senator Steinberg's office?" he asked the secretary as he paced.

"Yes, sir."

"How about the environmental lobbyist from that clean water action group?"

"Already tried him," she said, then motioned for silence as she spoke into the phone that had been glued to her ear for the past fifteen minutes.

Drew turned to Gerald. "Help me out. What else has he been working on lately?"

Gerald had been absorbed in thought for several minutes. "All I can think of is that trade thing the White House has been pushing—"

"That ended last week," the secretary interjected, then returned her attention to the phone. "Are you sure? No one? Okay, thanks, Eddie." She hung up and looked at Drew with finality. "I'm sorry, sir. I can't find him anywhere. In fact, I can't even find anyone who saw him after ten o'clock yesterday morning." She seemed more puzzled than worried. "He usually tells us where he's going, but with the Senate in recess, it's not like he's missing any meetings. And sometimes he likes to take off for a few days with a, uh, friend."

Lauren could guess what kind of trips those were.

Rising from Meg's chair, she told Drew, "I think we can assume they're together, wherever they are."

Drew's eyebrows pulled together into one tight line. "Looks like it." Although reaching that conclusion didn't seem to make him any happier. He shook his head and banged a fist against a file cabinet. "Damn it. What the hell's going on?"

He brooded about it as they returned to the lobby and were greeted by freezing rain and sleet. Lauren looked from the icy sidewalks to her black leather pumps with dismay.

"No sense in all of us freezing," Drew said. "You two stay here. I'll get the car."

At least he had *some* redeeming qualities.

Fifteen minutes later Lauren spotted his car pulling into the long line of cars waiting to pick up passengers. "Come on," she told Gerald, plucking at his coat. "Let's save time and meet him down there. It's going to take him forever if we have to wait for all these cars."

Lauren clung to Gerald's arm as they started down the icy sidewalk.

They passed an idling black Lincoln, its driver slouched against the passenger door, head tucked against the freezing rain and trench coat flapping in the wind. Gerald gave the man an appraising stare and leaned close to Lauren.

"That's money, honey," he said in a confidential murmur. "Chauffeurs must be well paid these days. That's a Burberry trench, and not the low end, either. Nice." Lauren smiled, half expecting a wolf-whistle from Gerald.

She stole a few curious glances at whatever arrogant

VIP in the backseat made his driver stand outside in this weather. She wouldn't recognize ninety percent of the senators or cabinet members, but who knew, it might be the secretary of state, or even the vice president. She mentally matched the few political faces she knew against the dark hair and hawkish nose of the passenger as they drew closer.

Lauren paid no attention to the driver leaning against the front of the car and had almost passed him when he leapt toward her, grabbing her arm with one sharp yank.

She yelped in surprise. Gerald yelped, too, and staggered as her arm slipped from his.

The man who grabbed Lauren braced himself, legs apart and both arms grasping her waist. He'd expected her slip and caught her nicely. "Get in the car," he ordered. He let go with one hand to open the front passenger door.

"Stop!" Gerald yelled, then uttered a short scream as the passenger threw open the rear door and barreled into him. They both landed on the slick pavement, the larger hawk-nosed man on top of Gerald.

"Gerald!" Lauren fought her confusion. For some reason the two men had attacked them—one of them, anyway. Gerald was obviously being attacked; the other was intent on abducting Lauren. It didn't matter that they were in a public place. All that mattered was getting away.

Lauren wriggled against the man's arm and was surprised to pop free of his grasp. His grip hadn't been very tight. Perhaps he'd expected fear to make her to do as she was told. The force of her efforts jerked her forward, feet skittering on ice. Unfortunately, the slippery black pumps were made for looks, not traction, and Lauren landed with a jarring thud.

Several feet away, Gerald wiggled frantically under his captor. "Get off me, you overweight ox! This is an Oscar de la Renta suit!" When his squirming had no effect, Lauren saw him reach out and grab a handful of hair.

"Ow! Damn it, he bit me! Hurry up with the woman!" Hawknose yelled, grappling with Gerald as he pried at the fingers clutching his hair.

Lauren scrambled to her feet. Several people stopped to stare at the spectacle, and she felt one of them assist her from behind. She turned to thank him as her feet regained purchase and stared into the face of the trench-coated driver. It was the first time she'd looked at his face, and she gasped with recognition. It was the man who'd bumped into her at the bank.

"You!" she said.

"Get in the car, Mrs. Creighton!"

"What? No!" She pulled her arm from his grasp as they both slipped and dropped like stones.

Fear mixed with confusion, but one thought was inescapable: Her assailant had mistaken her for Meg. A horrible possibility skittered through her mind. This was what Meg had run from, and if Drew was right, it was what she'd known would happen to Lauren in her place. Lauren didn't want to believe it, couldn't believe it, but had no time to reason it out while some strange man tried his best to kidnap her.

With four people down, bystanders seemed reluctant to risk ending up on their backsides. No one made a move to help, but Lauren noticed a couple of people had pulled out cell phones. She hoped they were calling the police. She placed her bare hands on the cold pavement and rose cautiously. Trenchcoat would have the same disadvantage and wasn't likely to be any quicker getting to his feet. She turned, noticing the man was on hands and knees, attempting to stand, when something crashed over the hood of the car behind him and landed on his back like a panther pouncing on prey. He flattened with an audible "*Oof.*"

Lauren stared at Drew, spread-eagle across Trenchcoat's back, forcing him to the pavement, and took back all the bad thoughts she'd had about him. No matter what doubts he'd voiced about her sister, he'd just turned her kidnapper into a Burberry pancake. She tried to imagine Jeff leaping to her defense, but couldn't. Pulling out his cell phone and calling 911, yes. Hurdling parked cars and smashing bad guys to the ground, no.

Drew looked up from atop Lauren's assailant, hair mussed and concern puckering his brow. "Are you all right?"

She did a mental inventory of body parts, all of which seemed to be in working order. Discounting her bruised tailbone, she nodded.

Trenchcoat raised his head. "You fuckin' asshole, I'm gonna—"

His words ended with a loud smack as Drew's fist connected with his mouth. The man's head hit the pavement. Lauren saw his eyes roll upward. If he wasn't knocked out, he was at least badly stunned. She was liking Drew more every second.

"Hey!" Hawknose looked in horror at his crumpled partner and let go of Gerald. "Get away from him!"

Planting a knee on Gerald's back to keep him in place, he reached into his coat and came out with a gun. With a two-handed grip, he took dead aim at Drew's chest. "Don't move, asshole!"

Lauren froze. Barely aware of the stinging pellets of sleet hitting her face, she stared at the gun. It looked even more terrifying than the ones she saw on TV. As unreal as this whole situation was, that black cylinder pointed at Drew was too real, too horrifying to comprehend.

"Lauren!" Drew's yell penetrated her dazed mind. His gaze was on the gun, but his words were aimed at her. "Get out of here, now!"

Was he kidding? Run, and make herself a target? Or run, leaving Drew and Gerald to be shot? She couldn't do either. Gerald was still pinned under Hawknose's knee, cursing up a storm. And Drew . . . Drew had saved her from a kidnapper. She couldn't just cut and run.

Undecided, but knowing she should at least get to her feet, Lauren backed against the Lincoln. Grabbing the outside mirror for support, she watched the gun as she pulled herself up and eased around the front of the car, putting it between herself and the drama playing out on the sidewalk.

As she suspected, the gun stayed on Drew. She'd bet on the fact that they wanted her alive and wouldn't shoot her. But they might have no compunction about shooting someone else. She couldn't let that happen.

Drew's attention was on the gun, too. He held perfectly still as he knelt over Trenchcoat's body.

"On the ground, asshole! Hands behind your head!"

She heard Hawknose bark orders at Drew as she crept around the car. She couldn't see him, which meant he probably couldn't see her, either. With his partner out cold, at least for the moment, and Gerald pinned beneath his knees, Hawknose focused on Drew as the threat to eliminate. He'd either forgotten about Lauren or didn't consider her a threat. If she played it right, that would be his mistake.

Drew saw her as she rounded the back of the car, coming out behind Hawknose with Gerald struggling and cursing beneath him. Drew's mouth dropped open as his expression changed from caution to fear. She knew he wanted to warn her off yet didn't dare give her position away. Tension vibrated from every muscle as he froze in place, watching her stealthy advance on Hawknose.

"Now! On the ground!" Hawknose screamed at Drew, sighting along the gun as he braced his other hand on the back of Gerald's neck.

Bystanders scattered at the sight of a gun. She couldn't blame them, but it meant there was no one to help Drew but her.

She saw only one option. Her purse was too small to be an effective weapon, and bashing Hawknose over the head with her shoe wouldn't even give him a headache. But she could land a kick that would make him see double for hours. The trick would be staying on her feet.

The back door handle of the Lincoln provided the best support. Grasping it with her left hand, she raised her knee, turned her foot sideways, and kicked as hard as she could. Her leather pump impacted with Hawknose just behind his ear with a satisfying smack.

Hawknose pitched forward. His out-flung hands hit the pavement and the gun slid across the frozen surface.

It happened fast, but Drew wasted no time deciding on a course of action. "Go!" He was already on his feet, and lunged toward the car, grabbing Lauren's hand. "This way," he said, tugging her into the drive. "There's no ice."

She hesitated just long enough to see Gerald scurry across the ice on hands and knees to the trunk of the car, where he pulled himself to his feet.

Drew wasn't waiting for Gerald. He practically shoved her past the Lincoln to an area where traffic and vehicle exhaust had kept the ice melted. Pulling her down the row of waiting cars, they ran for Drew's rented Taurus with Gerald on their heels.

Lauren spared a glance backward. The man had retrieved his gun and tucked it back inside his coat before turning to his prone partner. By the time Drew shoved her into the passenger seat, the black Lincoln had roared to life. Tires spinning, it slid into traffic and fishtailed, disappearing up Second Street with Hawknose at the wheel.

"They aren't coming after us," she said with relief.

"Too many witnesses." Drew swerved the Taurus around the waiting cars, eliciting angry honks, and took a cross street away from the Hart Building. His gaze left the street for several seconds to sweep over her with concern. "Are you okay?"

"I'm fine." It wasn't exactly true. Her whole body shook from the inside out.

"You sure? No cuts or bruises? Sprained ankle?"

She shook her head.

"Torn fingernail?"

She managed a small smile. "Not many here to tear. I'm fine, Drew, really. You can watch the road, I'm not going to pass out or anything."

She concentrated on taking deep, calming breaths as Drew sped along the wet streets, casting occasional glances at her. He followed a weaving course through the city that looked to Lauren like a tour through her high school civics textbook.

"Are you afraid they'll try to find us?" she asked.

"I'd say that's a given." He looked at her. "They think you're Meg. And it's no secret where Senator Creighton lives."

She flopped back in her seat, stunned at the implication. "You're right. So you think they'll come after me at the house?" she asked.

"I don't know. But if those two goons are looking for Meg, she's in some big trouble. She must have been dodging more than the press when she used you as a decoy." Drew shot a glance at her as he drove. "By the way, nice sister you've got there. Setting you up to meet those guys without a warning."

"Meg wouldn't . . ." Lauren's protest trailed off. What was the point? She would. She had. Lauren's mind rebelled at the idea of her own sister purposely putting her in danger, but clearly Meg had been trying to mislead someone when she'd arranged Lauren's arrival. Lauren simply couldn't believe that her sister had known how dangerous things would get. She fell into a brooding silence, watching the ice-slicked city go by while she pondered Meg's actions.

Drew shifted his attention to the backseat. "Any major injuries back there?"

"Yes, damn it," Gerald responded, still brushing grit off his coat. "Besides all the potentially fatal internal injuries I might have, that overgrown grizzly bear ripped a button off my vest and tore the pocket on my London Fog topcoat. He'll get the bill, too, once they catch him."

Drew smiled at the rearview mirror. "I hope you get to collect."

"Oh, I will," Gerald's voice rang with certainty. "I got a good look at the behemoth before he landed on me. That man's going down."

Detective Rasmussen of the metropolitan police department sat at the Creighton kitchen table, pen poised over his notebook, eager to take down the facts. But his face grew more confused as he listened to Gerald's description.

". . . and his hair was dark, a burnt sienna, barely long enough for me to get a grip on. His eyes were a deep umber, with evil little glints sparkling in their depths." Gerald wiggled his fingers in front of his eyes in demonstration.

The detective stared.

Drew sighed and tapped the notebook. "Brown hair, brown eyes. Just write it."

"And he wore this godawful sepia overcoat, probably from Sears." Gerald shuddered. "I mean, can you imagine?"

Rasmussen looked at Drew.

"Brown coat."

"Oh, and he had one of those college-type rings on his right hand, a big hunk of gold with an oversized fuchsia stone." He wrinkled his nose. "Terribly garish.

Probably from some lower-rung community college."

"Red stone," Drew supplied, rubbing his forehead as if he felt a headache coming on.

Rasmussen wrote it down, muttering, "Man's a goddamned walking box of Crayolas. Spell that red one for me."

Gerald patiently spelled out "fuchsia," then added, "He has a bite mark on that hand, too. Put that down as an identifying feature."

Rasmussen stopped writing and looked at Gerald. "You bit him?"

"Right on the fleshy part between the thumb and index finger. No blood, but lots of bruising. I ground my teeth." He flashed a perfect set in a satisfied grin.

Detective Rasmussen lifted an eyebrow and nodded slowly. "Good man." He wrote it down. "Anything else?"

The three of them looked at each other, then shook their heads. Lauren was impressed with the descriptions Gerald had provided of both men, right down to the lapels on the Burberry overcoat. She'd been so stunned she couldn't even be sure her attacker had hair at all, much less what color it was.

"They weren't very distinctive," Drew told him. "And it all happened so fast, we didn't have enough time to get a good look."

"He did." The detective indicated Gerald with grudging approval. "Very observant." Gerald took the compliment as his due. "If that's all, then, I'll notify the Secret Service and someone will be in touch with you tomorrow."

"The Secret Service? Isn't this a matter for the D.C. police?" Lauren asked.

"We'll let them decide that, but I think they'll be interested. You have a connection to Senator Creighton, and he seems to be pretty important, as senators go."

"No kidding. He's president pro tem of the Senate." Gerald's tone implied he'd have to be a complete moron not to know that. "That means he's third in the presidential line of succession."

"And if no one has been able to reach him for two or three days, I think those boys will want to look into this," added the detective.

Lauren noticed he wasn't too disturbed by the idea of handing over the case to another agency, and wondered if that meant there wasn't much chance of finding the culprits.

As if sensing her thoughts, Rasmussen said, "Don't worry, we got a couple nine-one-one calls about the incident. One of those people might be able to provide more information. Although, I doubt we'll get a better description of the men." He cocked his head thoughtfully. "I doubt we've *ever* gotten a better description of a perp. Thanks again. Someone will be in touch."

Drew stood to follow as the officer left. Passing Gerald, he leaned down to mumble, "Burnt sienna? Umber?"

"I was being precise."

Despite Drew's grumbling, Gerald seemed pleased with himself. He winked at Lauren. Lowering his voice so the departing Drew couldn't hear, he said, "He's always worried I'll piss someone off and he'll have to defend me. He's the protective type."

"Do you need protection?" As slight as Gerald was, Lauren had the feeling he was resourceful enough to take care of himself.

"No, but he's cute when he gets all gruff and grumpy." He slid a glance at Lauren. "Don't you think?"

She almost answered that Drew was far too masculine and sexy to be called cute, but stopped in time. Waving a finger in Gerald's face, she said, "Uh-uh, you aren't playing those games with me. I have no opinions about Drew Creighton."

"Whatever you say, honey." He patted her hand and winked. "Denial is cute, too."

"Shut up." Lauren gave him an irritated swat but wondered just how transparent her face was when she looked at Drew. Half the time she was annoyed with the man, and when she wasn't, she tried hard not to notice how his upper lip had a sexy little curve, or how incredibly well his jeans fit. She thought she'd hid it well. But as the detective said, Gerald was very observant. She'd have to remember that. She'd also have to do a better job of remembering Jeff.

She hurried after Drew. He was standing in the open doorway, speaking to Detective Rasmussen.

"Listen, can we keep this stuff about my father out of the press?" Drew said. "If they turn up in a motel in Fairfax, having a belated honeymoon, it might be kind of embarrassing."

"Sure, no problem. Good night, Mr. Creighton."

She ground her teeth. As soon as Drew shut the door, she asked, "A belated honeymoon? Are you serious?"

"Of course not. But I don't want anything in the media until we know what's going on." After a second's reflection, he added, "Probably not then, either. You never know what might damage re-election chances."

She marched after him into the living room. "You've got to be kidding. Your father and my sister have disappeared under suspicious circumstances, and you're worried about damaging his chances at re-election?"

"Believe me, Dad would want me to consider it." He stopped as he saw the large suitcase and briefcase on the floor. "What's this?"

"It's mine. I packed it when I went to wash up."

He turned toward her, frowning. "Going somewhere?"

She'd known he'd object. From what she'd seen, Drew was used to taking charge of situations, a natural leader like his father. He probably wasn't used to defiance.

"I think I should stay at Meg's old apartment. They just got married this week, so I'm sure it's still leased to her. I can look through her things for a clue to what's going on, like you did here."

"I don't think so." He grabbed the suitcase and started toward the stairs. "Don't you think those two men might look for her at the apartment?"

"But you said they knew she lived *here*."

"Yes, but here you won't be alone, and there's a good security system."

Lauren watched as he went upstairs without waiting for an answer. In the kitchen doorway, Gerald lounged against the doorframe. "Protective," he mouthed silently, and winked.

She gave him a stern look as she grabbed her briefcase and followed Drew. Way to be defiant, she grumbled to herself. But he'd found her weak spot—security. She wasn't eager to meet the armed kidnappers again.

He tossed the large suitcase on the bed like it weighed no more than her briefcase.

"If you need anything, I'm right across the hall."

"What?" She dropped the briefcase. She'd assumed he'd only stayed last night to help Gerald search the house. "You're staying here, too?"

One eyebrow lifted in mild surprise. "Yes. I said you wouldn't be alone if you stayed here."

"I thought you meant Gerald."

"Gerald only works here. He has his own house."

"Don't you?" She didn't mean to sound rude, but he had to be in his midthirties. Drew didn't seem like the type who would still live at home with Dad.

"Yes, in Colorado." He looked her over, head cocked, his mouth pulled sideways with wry amusement. "Are you afraid to stay here alone with me, Aunt Lauren?"

Not until he'd looked at her like that. Tiny prickles raced over her shoulders, and her insides squirmed. Mortified, she reminded herself that she had a fiancé who fulfilled all her squirming desires quite, um, adequately. Imagining Drew in that role was unacceptable.

"Why would I be afraid of my own nephew?" she asked, glad he'd tacked on that reminder of their family relationship.

He smiled with a lazy confidence she found unsettling. "I didn't mean to suggest you would. I thought you might be afraid of your own—" He paused while he raked her with another gaze. "—impulses."

Heat rose to her face. First Gerald and now Drew. She might as well have "Lauren is hot for Drew" written on a T-shirt. "You'd better hope so, because my impulse is to kick you again."

He smiled. "Feeling threatened, huh?" Before she could come up with a huffy retort, he added, "Come downstairs when you've unpacked. I'll see if I can find us something to eat."

She stood frozen in place until he was gone, desperately fighting the desire to massacre another nail. Ah, hell with it. She stuck her finger in her mouth and viciously bit at number four. Between her missing sister and her hot nephew, she didn't give the remaining six long odds for survival.

Drew lined up all the condiments he could find on the kitchen island next to the meat and cheese. He was slathering mayo on a slice of rye when Lauren walked in.

From the corner of his eye he could see she'd changed into jeans. He could no longer see those appealing legs, but the jeans hugged her even-more-appealing hips and butt. Even though he had no intention of sampling the merchandise, he enjoyed looking.

Drew would never make a serious move on the sister of one of his dad's bimbos. He knew their type well. Typically, the senator's female "friends" were short on morals and long on ambition, neither of which appealed to him. He'd give up women entirely before he'd mess with the sexually aggressive game-playing nymphets he'd met in Washington. Even if Meg Sutherland hadn't made off with his mother's jewelry—yet—he was sure she had some nefarious motive for marrying a man thirty-three years her senior. At the least, she was probably obsessed with power and prestige, hoping to move up to an even more politically influential lover. If Lauren was anything like her sister, her unknown fiancé had his condolences.

But there was the little matter of the chemistry between them. Drew had enough experience with women to know that physical attraction went beyond the superficial tits and ass consideration. After the initial "wow, what a babe" reaction, there was something more. An unexplained tingle when they touched, or a pleasant flash of heat in his groin when a particular woman smiled into his eyes. He'd felt it before, but not like this. With Lauren, the tingle had almost been a visible jolt of electricity arcing between them, and the flash was a hot rush of sexual desire that aroused thoughts of crushing her to his chest and kissing her breathless. He knew she felt it too. She hid it well, but he saw her green eyes widen and her breath catch when he touched her. The sexual tension was intriguing as hell. It was too bad he couldn't do anything about it.

The object of his fantasies was standing on the opposite side of the kitchen island, watching his preparations. He took a second look at her. Not green eyes—gray. Strange. He could have sworn they were green.

"Help yourself," he told her, applying mustard to a second slice of bread. "I'm not much of a cook, but I found enough to make sandwiches. I was hoping for something hot, but Gerald is Dad's secretary, not his cook, as he informed me just before he left. So this is it."

"Gerald's gone?"

The timid question made him glance up, and it happened again. As soon as his gaze met those luminous eyes he could feel the electricity spark between them. This time it came with a predatory impulse that told him how simple it would be to turn those little shocks into a bolt of lightning that could set them both on fire. Tempting, but not wise.

He kept his voice nonchalant. "It's late, Lauren. He'll be back in the morning. Have something to eat."

"I'm too worried to eat."

"Suit yourself." He wasn't about to feel guilty for having an appetite.

She frowned as he piled more meat on his sandwich. "Isn't there anything else we can do?"

He flicked a quick glance at her, his mouth twitching with amusement at the thought of what else they could do. But she was talking about her sister, so he answered seriously. "You can help me look through my dad's office for some clue to what he's been involved in lately," he told her. "*After* I eat."

She pursed her lips but didn't say anything. He waited for another fingernail to get nibbled off, but she began twisting a lock of hair instead. He smiled and took a leisurely bite of his sandwich.

The kitchen phone rang midway through chewing his first bite. After three rings Lauren said, "Aren't you going to get that?"

He shook his head. "I don't live here. It's not for me. Let the machine get it."

She didn't seem happy with his answer. Probably the responsible, compulsive type who felt she had to respond to every request and jump at every summons. She fidgeted while the machine played its recorded message. Drew waited for the caller to hang up or leave some boring "call me when you can" request.

What he heard next stopped his mouth in mid-bite.

"Drew? Are you there? Pick up if you are."

Drew lowered his sandwich. *His father.*

A female voice cut in as if someone had grabbed the phone from him, adding, "Lauren, are you there?"

For one frozen second they both stared across the kitchen, then they both scrambled for the receiver. Drew reached it first, but tilted it toward Lauren so she could listen too.

"Dad? What's going on? Where are you?"

Lauren's excited voice cut across his. "Meg! Are you okay?"

"Lauren!" the woman's voice answered joyously, before Senator Creighton chimed in. "I'm fine. We're both fine. Sorry if you were worried."

"Dad, I called the police! No one knew where you'd gone, and Gerald hasn't seen Meg since Tuesday."

Lauren's hand closed over his as she forced the phone closer to her mouth. "Meg, someone thinks I'm you, and they tried to kidnap me! What's going on?"

An odd moment of silence hung in the air, and as Lauren's concerned gaze locked with Drew's, the moment nearly took his breath away.

"I'm sorry, Lauren, really. I didn't think it would get dangerous for you. I just needed to get away from them. When they realize you're not me, they'll leave you alone."

Maybe Lauren had heard numerous apologies for idiotic adventures in the past, because she didn't seem to be moved by Meg's words. "Who are 'they'?" she demanded.

Drew wanted to know the answer to that one, too,

but instead his father's voice interrupted. "We can't tell you, but we think we're out of danger for now."

"Danger? What sort of danger?" Lauren's voice was edged with panic.

"Never mind," Senator Creighton answered. "If we tell you, then you'll be in danger, too. Just stay out of it."

"Please, Lauren," Meg implored. "Let us handle it. We know what we're doing."

Lauren didn't seem reassured. Drew was pretty sure his dad could take care of himself, but he didn't want to see Lauren worry over her sister's safety for however long it took them to "handle" things. Besides, she was running out of fingernails.

He tilted the phone back toward his mouth. "You'll have to do better than that. We don't even know what or who to avoid."

"Everyone," his dad's voice replied firmly. "Just stay where you are, and we'll explain when we get back."

"When will that be?"

It didn't seem like a difficult question, but it received a lot of thought at the other end of the line. Finally, his dad's voice said, "I don't know. It could be a while. Just wait. We'll call again when we can, okay? Take care."

He sounded hurried. "Dad, hold on a second—"

"Sorry, son, gotta run. We're on a tight schedule."

"Watch *Capitol Talk*!" Meg added quickly.

A second later the phone clicked off. Drew laid the phone back in the cradle and turned to Lauren.

"What the hell was that?" he growled. "We still don't know what's going on."

She shook her head and twisted a lock of hair. "What's *Capitol Talk*?"

"It's a local show that's half news, half rumor and gossip." He headed back to the island for his sandwich. He'd think better with food in his stomach.

"When is it on?"

"I don't know. I don't live here, remember? I just visit occasionally."

"Morning, afternoon, or evening, do you know that much?" Her voice was edgy with anxiety.

"Beats me. Check the TV listing."

"I'm not going to waste time tracking it down." She grabbed the phone, marched over to him and slapped it into his hand. "Ask Gerald." When he raised his eyebrows, she told him impatiently, "He seems to know everything else. I'm sure he'll know that." She pointed at the phone. "Hurry up. I don't want to miss whatever the hell she's talking about."

He smiled and began pressing numbers. "Results oriented, aren't you? What do you do for a living?"

"Financial management." Her finger tapped rapidly on the countertop while he held the phone to his ear. He laid his free hand on top of her fingers, stilling them.

"Hi, Steven? It's Drew Creighton. Is Gerald there?" Drew said into the phone. He waited about ten seconds, aware the whole time of the way her hand had frozen beneath his. But she didn't pull away. "Gerald? We've heard from Dad and Meg." He cut off the expected barrage of questions with, "I'll tell you about it later. They said we're supposed to watch *Capitol Talk*. When is it on?"

He could hear the surprise in Gerald's voice when

he answered, "Right now. I'm watching it. Channel six."

"Thanks." Drew hung up the phone. "It's on *now*," he told Lauren, finally feeling some of her anxiety. "Come on." Pulling on the hand he'd been holding, he tugged her toward his father's office, the closest room with a TV. Her warm fingers squeezed his as they rushed along, then pulled away when they entered the dark room and he turned on the TV. They stared at the silver blur of a sports car as it slid across wet pavement to the bass-heavy sound of rock music.

Lauren sighed with frustration at the commercial and stuck a fingernail between her teeth.

"Bad habit. Relax," he told her quietly. He pulled her hand away and held it gently in his. She didn't resist, just bit her lip and stared at the screen. He entwined their fingers, enjoying the softness of her hand while telling himself it was only to keep her from decimating her remaining nails.

After another minute of commercials and two minutes of the first lady speaking at a charity luncheon, Drew stiffened and felt Lauren's fingers tighten around his. Behind the female anchor, an insert photo of Senator Creighton beamed out at them.

"And in our hearts and flowers segment today," the woman said, "Capitol Hill was taken by surprise when Texas Senator and notorious ladies' man Harlan Creighton unexpectedly announced his marriage to his secretary, Megan Sutherland." She emphasized the word "secretary," as if listeners might have missed the significance of Meg's lowly position. "Dana Zamecki caught up with the happy couple at the airport shortly before they boarded a plane for the Virgin Islands."

The screen flashed to a reservation desk where Meg clung to Senator Creighton's arm, both smiling self-consciously into the camera as a pretty, blonde reporter stuck a microphone in their faces.

"Senator, you've been difficult to find since the announcement of your marriage," she said.

Drew recognized the practiced chuckle his father was able to emit at will. "Well, that was the plan, Dana. And we almost snuck out of town without getting caught." He tipped his head in amused acknowledgment. "Now, don't you put this on the air until we're outta here," he said, letting a down-home Southern drawl creep into his voice. It always played well in the public opinion polls. "Newlyweds deserve a little privacy on their honeymoon." Drew nearly choked as his father looked fondly at Meg. She gazed adoringly into his eyes before they turned and headed for the VIP security line.

The picture flashed back to the anchorwoman. "We don't know Senator and Mrs. Creighton's final destination, but his office assures us it will be a short trip, due to the upcoming hearing on the senator's offshore drilling bill."

"Huh," Drew snuffed. "His office. Nice of them to contact us with the news. I wonder when that was?"

The picture changed to the next story, and Drew automatically hit the mute button. He stared at the silent TV while his mind tried to grasp what he'd seen. Lauren hadn't moved, apparently as stunned as he was.

The ringing desk phone jolted him out of his trance. Reluctantly, he released Lauren's hand and picked it up, knowing who it would be. "We saw it," he said in greeting.

"That was weird!" Gerald pronounced.

"In what way?" Drew had his own opinion, but no one had spent more time with Harlan Creighton over the past ten years than his personal secretary.

"They don't act like that. At least, not in front of me. The senator *never* gets that goofy expression on his face. And Megan was *hanging* on him, and practically *dripping* syrup all over him. You don't know her, Andrew, but let me tell you, Megan is *way* cooler than that. That was Megan being played by Marilyn Monroe. Badly."

Drew smiled. "Thanks, Gerald." He hung up and looked at Lauren's shocked expression. "Well?"

She shook her head. "What happened to all that stuff about being in danger? And Meg never acted so silly about a man in her life. Sexy and confident, but not silly. Something's up." She frowned. "What about your dad?"

"That seems to be the consensus. I thought I'd seen him in every possible mood, but I've never seen *that* Harlan Creighton before."

Lauren twirled a string of hair around her finger, another habit he'd noticed her resort to whenever she thought about her sister. "But how would he act if he fell in love? Maybe he's just head-over-heels in love."

Drew ran a hand through his hair. His parents must have been in love at one time, but not in his memory, and he had no idea how his father would act if he fell in love again. In lust, yes. That happened frequently. But in love? "I don't know, maybe that's exactly how they'd act if they fell in love. Maybe they'd be as surprised by it as we are." He found it hard to believe, but he didn't have a better answer at the moment.

Lauren screwed up her face in an effort to imagine that scenario. "Maybe," she said, doubt obvious in her voice. She glanced sideways from under lowered lashes. "Would falling in love make you act silly?"

He smiled. "Bad word choice—men don't act *silly*. Although I couldn't say for sure. I've never loved anyone enough to want to spend the rest of my life with her. It sounds confining." His gaze drifted down to her left hand. How had he held that hand and noticed its warmth and softness, without ever feeling her ring? "But you must have," he said, nodding at her hand. "Fallen in love that much, I mean. You know, with old what's-his-name. How does it make you feel?" He hoped his relaxed stance reflected courteous interest rather than the strange tension that gripped him. Despite knowing how dangerous this line of thinking was, his question had nothing to do with his father and her sister.

"Oh." She held her left hand in her right and looked at the ring, as if she'd forgotten it was there. She caressed it thoughtfully. "I felt happy, I guess. I mean, I feel happy." She corrected her tenses, but must have realized how tentative that sounded. She smiled at him. "Satisfied and happy. Contented," she added more firmly, apparently still searching for the right term. She shrugged helplessly. "Our relationship hit a point where we knew it needed to go somewhere. So we took the next step. It just felt right."

Past tense again, but he didn't point it out. He watched her closely. "That sounds . . . nice." It sounded like a huge mistake, but he couldn't say that when she looked so vulnerable. He forced a smile in return. "So, no acting silly, eh?"

She straightened. "Well, that's me. Practical through and through. I guess I'm not much of a romantic." She tried to sound light-hearted, but seemed nervous beneath the surface. Her hands went in her pockets, and the ring disappeared from sight.

Now, that was flat-out wrong. She was either covering up her emotions, or she really didn't know she had them. Lauren was getting more intriguing by the minute.

"Speaking of romance and stuff, I really should call Jeff. My fiancé," she explained unnecessarily.

"I remember."

"I was supposed to call at eight-fifteen, and it's nearly eight thirty. He'll be wondering what happened to me."

God, what an uptight prick. "Sure, go ahead. You can use the phone in here. I'll go finish my sandwich." He clicked the desk lamp on and turned off the soundless flickering of the TV. "Maybe you'll feel more like eating after you've talked to Jeff."

They exchanged overly sincere smiles as he left, closing the wood paneled double doors behind him.

Maybe talking to the anonymous Jeff would calm her nerves. Although he didn't know how that was possible. He thought a relationship that bland and *satisfying* would give him a stomach ache. He hoped it gave Jeff one.

Chapter Four

"Where have you been? I've been worried sick! You were supposed to call fifteen minutes ago. Were you delayed in traffic coming back from Virginia? I've heard the D.C. traffic can be murder."

Lauren scrunched her eyes shut and put a hand to her forehead. She knew he'd be like this, and she was getting tired of dealing with his picky rules just because she hadn't called at eight fifteen on the dot.

Blurting it out was probably best. "I'm fine, Jeff. And I wasn't delayed in traffic, because I didn't go to Virginia."

"You didn't?" It was the cool, controlling tone usually reserved for Meg, and never before directed at her. Of course, she'd never gone against his wishes before. He'd just have to learn to deal with it.

"I didn't call you because there have been a few problems here." She took a deep breath and began explaining about the trip to the bank and the Hart building. Before she could get to the TV coverage, Jeff's anxiety turned into full-blown panic.

"A gun! He had a gun?" She could picture him jumping to his feet, his perfectly chiseled face going pale. "You could have been killed! What's going on there?"

She had to admit, it was gratifying to hear his concern. "I'm not sure, Jeff. But Meg and Senator Creighton apparently left for the Virgin Islands today, so I'll have to wait a few days for her to get back before I know the whole story."

His voice held a low note of warning. "Lauren, if Meg is mixed up in something bad, you should come home right now. Let the authorities deal with it."

"The authorities *are* dealing with it," she said, a bit defensively. She didn't know if that made her any safer, but she wasn't going to leave without knowing what was going on. It bothered her that Jeff thought she should. But Lauren reminded herself that he loved her and wanted to protect her—a noble objective. Drew Creighton wasn't the only man with protective instincts.

"Lauren, are you listening? I asked if you were able to reach my aunt and uncle."

"What? Oh, that. I haven't had time yet, Jeff. But I promise to get in touch with them. I'd like to meet them, but things are just too unsettled right now. Maybe after Meg gets back."

"Of course." His voice was a little more strained than his words. "I didn't mean to rush you. I know how responsible you feel for getting your sister through these messy relationships she keeps falling into. But, honey, she's married now. We talked about this. It's not your problem."

Lauren sighed. Jeff had never understood Meg, or

the bond between Lauren and her sister. But in his defense, he barely knew Meg, so why should he understand her? And it's not like he had experience with any impulsive or overly dramatic members in his own family. She doubted that anyone had ever called a Duchaine a colorful character. She let his comment go by without protest. "Maybe I can call your Aunt Betty and Uncle John tomorrow, after Drew and I check out Meg's apartment. We're hoping to find some clue about those awful photos or about the two men who are after her."

"Drew?"

"I thought I told you, he's the senator's son, the one who's been helping me look for Meg."

"You didn't tell me his name." He seemed to take a polite interest. "So this guy is probably quite a bit younger than you. College age?"

She laughed. "Drew? No, he's about your age. Senator Creighton's sixty-four, you know."

"Oh." From that one sound, she knew what was coming next. "I imagine he's as much of a bed-hopping playboy as his father is."

"I wouldn't know." Although she had to admit she'd wondered.

"Lauren, do you think it's wise to be seen around town with that man?" Disapproval oozed from his tone. "Hanging around with a man like that is the kind of thing that can destroy a woman's reputation."

"I don't have a reputation to destroy in Washington, Jeff. No one knows me here. They probably don't even know Drew very well, either. And besides, he seems to be a very nice man." And deeply unsettling in a way she didn't feel comfortable describing to Jeff, or even examining too closely.

"I still don't feel good about you spending so much time with him. It might put even more strange ideas in your head."

Even more? These phone conversations were becoming very enlightening. "What strange ideas do I have, Jeff?"

"I'd call phone sex a little strange."

"Oh." She smiled to herself. "I'll admit it's different for us. But we can't say it's strange if we haven't tried it."

"God, I knew it. You really expect me to do it, don't you?"

"Well, there's nothing wrong with trying something once . . ." She faltered, finally catching the resignation in his voice. "Are you willing to do it?"

She heard a long sigh, the kind Jeff made with his mouth pressed into a tight line with his nostrils flaring. The kind that warned he was being pushed to the edge.

"I still don't approve, but you seemed to have this harebrained idea that it would help our relationship, so I looked into it."

She had no idea how one looked into phone sex, but the fact that he had was too incredible to pass up. If she didn't ask, she'd always wonder. "So what did you learn? Go ahead, I'm very curious about this. Who knows, it might revitalized our sex life." God knew it could use something.

She heard mumbled swearing and throat clearing, and what sounded like pages turning.

"Jeff?"

"Wait, wait, I'm trying to figure out how to start."

"Um, probably by taking off clothes."

"Yeah. I guess I would describe that, like I'm taking

off my shirt now. Then my pants. Hell, I don't know how to do it."

No, he didn't. And she was trying as hard as she could not to laugh, which was probably not a good sign for their relationship.

She heard more paper shuffling sounds. "All right, I, um, take off all my clothes, then . . . Jesus, I can't say that!" Furious rustling filled the phone, like paper being crumpled. "This is obscene, Lauren. Embarrassing. Does it really do something for you?"

She rolled her eyes. Hardly. "Well, I guess I'll never know."

"Because frankly, this sounds like something your sister would do."

Whoa. She started to protest, but he'd found his momentum and spoke over her.

"You got this idea from Meg, didn't you? She was never afraid to be outrageous and a little distasteful."

She knew she'd pushed him into this so she tried to control her anger, even though he'd just crossed the line. "Jeff, I hardly think that's fair."

"Lauren, stop trying to cover for her and face the facts. Your sister's morals leave a lot to be desired. I know more than you think I do, and it worries me when you act like her."

She did a few of Jeff's nostril-flaring breaths to calm herself. "What do you mean? What do you know that could possibly worry you?"

He sighed heavily. "I didn't want to tell you, but I suppose you should know since so many other people must by now. Do you remember when Meg visited you last summer and I arranged for her to double date with us and my friend Charlie?"

"Yes, we went to the lake. It was fun, and Charlie seemed to have a good time."

"Oh, he had a good time, alright. I heard about it later. Remember how we were all sunning ourselves on the raft, and taking turns diving off it?"

"Sure." The wooden platform anchored in deep water was a favorite place to spend a few hours, laughing and swimming.

"And remember how we went back to shore first, so we could take a walk in the woods? Well, guess what happened while we were gone?"

"Uh, I don't know."

"Meg and Charlie had sex! Right there in the lake. How does that make you feel?"

Jealous probably wasn't the right answer.

"Because I can tell you I found it pretty embarrassing that Charlie thought I was engaged to a woman who was probably just like her twin sister, who was so free and easy with her body that she probably had a string of one-night stands with God knows how many men before I came along."

The little red coal of anger that had begun glowing inside her was being fanned by a hot breeze. "Are you saying this is all about you, Jeff? About how my sister's sex life makes you look?"

"No, I'm saying it's about how Meg's sex life makes *you* look. I know you aren't like your sister, but other people don't know that. Stuff like that gets around, Lauren. It won't make me look bad—hell, some guys would probably envy me—but I don't want people looking at you and thinking you're just like your sister."

He sounded sincerely concerned. She made an effort

to douse her smoldering anger. "I don't know what to say, Jeff."

"Just say you'll forget about trying to spice up our sex life for now, and concentrate on getting back home. Then we can talk about your concerns and see what we can do."

"That's fair." Also vague. But he claimed to have her best interests at heart, which was hard to argue against.

She hung up, realizing their relationship was going to require a lot of work. But since he was willing to try, she could put in a little extra effort herself.

Her gaze fell on a notepad on the senator's desk. She ripped off a square sheet of paper and wrote "Call Betty and John Duchaine" and stuck it in her pocket. Satisfied, she left to find Drew.

He was putting his plate in the dishwasher. With a wave he indicated the food on the kitchen island. "How do you feel about eating now? Have you found your appetite?"

She'd nearly lost it forever, but she wasn't going to let him know that. "I believe I have." She began constructing a sandwich every bit as big as the one Drew had finished off, humming to herself as she did.

Drew leaned against the counter and watched. "Did you give what's-his-name the whole story?"

"Jeff," she reminded him clearly. "Yes, I told him about the pictures, the two guys, and the Virgin Islands."

"So loverboy's all right with you being chased around Washington by armed kidnappers?"

"Of course he isn't," she said with a haughty air, irritated by his flippant tone. "He's a sensible person, and he loves me. He would prefer that I come home right now."

Drew was silent a moment. "He expects you to leave while your sister is gone and people with guns are looking for her?"

She frowned at him. "He wants me to be safe. That's what you do when you love someone." But Drew wouldn't know because he'd never loved anyone that much. She felt a small pang of sympathy for him, and tried to help him understand Jeff's point of view. "Assuming you had a fiancée, what would you do if she called you from another city and said her sister had disappeared and armed men were trying to kidnap her?" She watched him think it over, certain he'd come to the same conclusion Jeff had. "You'd tell her to come home," she answered for him.

"No, I wouldn't." His voice was quiet and full of certainty.

She laid down her knife. "You wouldn't?"

"No." She thought he was teasing, but his blue eyes met hers with a steely, direct gaze. "We're talking about your *sister*," he said, pausing to let it sink in. "If it were me, I'd be on the next plane, offering to help."

She stared back, wordless, until the corner of his mouth curved into an ironic smile. "But, hey, what do I know? I've never been engaged." He straightened. "I'll be in my dad's office going through papers. If you want to help when you're done eating, you know where to find me."

She watched him walk away, wanting to say something in Jeff's defense, but unable to come up with the words. He'd made it sound like Jeff didn't care about her. Even though she'd begun to see how self-centered

Jeff was, accusing him of not caring was going too far. He just believed in going through the proper channels and letting the police and Secret Service handle it. Drew didn't understand Jeff's need to protect her.

On the other hand, she was getting pretty damn tired of making excuses to justify Jeff's behavior.

Lauren slapped a second slice of bread on her sandwich and stuck it in her mouth, viciously ripping off a bite. Better that than another fingernail.

Drew tried to focus on the pile of documents he'd pulled from his father's safe, but he couldn't.

His instincts could be wrong. He'd watched two men try to abduct Lauren, and he'd never suggested she leave town and let the police handle it. Maybe he should have. What made him think he could keep her safe? He didn't even know what those men wanted. But letting her go might not keep her safe, either. They were obviously watching her. If they followed her back to Lansing, still thinking she was Meg, would sensible Jeff protect her? For no reason he could pin down, he didn't have a good feeling about Lauren's fiancé.

Speak of the devil.

Lauren walked in, and Drew patted a spot on the floor beside him. She settled into a cross-legged position and leaned forward with her elbows propped on her knees, watching him sort through papers. She didn't seem angry, so he assumed he'd been forgiven for insulting her lame excuse for a fiancé.

"What are we looking for?" she asked.

"I have no idea. Anything that strikes us as odd."

"Like a threatening note that says, 'Give us the money or we'll kidnap your wife'?"

"Yeah, like that." That would actually be too good to hope for. Then he might have a clue to what in the hell was going on. Sorting through piles of insurance policies and tax records had so far revealed nothing. "If you have a better idea, I'm open to suggestions, but this is all I can think of."

She shook her head and looked about as hopeless as he felt.

"Okay, then I guess we do this. Help me look through these." He glanced at another stack of investment statements and set them aside, making no effort to angle them her way. She scooted closer and peered over his legs, examining the papers. He was about to tell her they weren't important but was distracted by the light floral fragrance of her hair. It seemed at odds with her "practical through and through" personality. Selecting another folder from the pile, he pretended to peruse it closely, making her bend her head near his own to see it. Lavender? He was no good at these things, but the scent was definitely feminine. He inhaled deeply.

She was giving him a puzzled look. Jerking his attention from her hair, he frowned as if she had interrupted his concentration. "What?"

"You sighed," she said.

"I did?"

"Yes. Am I missing something?" Her gaze went to the folder, then back to his eyes. "It just looks like a thank you letter from President Carter."

"It is." He looked at the letter and blocked out the sensory input that made him think of the springtime meadows around his house. "It's from my dad's first term in Congress. I was just . . ." Just sniffing your hair, like some sort of pervert. ". . . remembering."

"Oh." She watched him carefully.

This would work better if she weren't leaning so close to him. He hefted a stack of folders and set them in her lap. "Here, hold these. You look at each one first, then pass it to me."

It hadn't been smart, having her sit next to him. She was attractive and spirited, which aroused a feeling he'd normally follow up on, but there was little point in pursuing it with Lauren. They were going to end up hating each other if she wasn't there already. He already despised the social climbing tramp who'd married his father, and despite an instinctive faith in Lauren, she was the tramp's sister. Better to keep things impersonal, allowing everyone to enjoy their mutual distrust later. Besides, whether what's-his-name was a poor choice or not, she had a fiancé.

Lauren scrutinized each paper before passing it to him. He glanced at the vehicle registration she'd just examined at length and suppressed an amused snort as he set it aside. "You're taking this search pretty seriously, aren't you?"

Her eyes flashed disapproval. "Of course I am. My sister suddenly married a notorious playboy twice her age, has dirty pictures of herself hidden away, and two men with guns are trying to kidnap her. I want to know why, and I intend to examine every detail of her life I can find." She slapped a paper in his hands. "Here, see if everything looks normal on this statement. I wouldn't know."

He scanned the annual report from an investment firm. "I wouldn't either. You aren't suggesting I look for suspiciously large withdrawals of cash, are you?"

"Or deposits," she said seriously. "We don't know what we're looking for, so we have to look everywhere, for everything."

He should probably snap back in his dad's defense, but since her doubts about Harlan Creighton were no different than his low expectations about her sister, he let it go. Besides, he didn't want to argue with her. If she got all huffy, she might not let him sit beside her and catch whiffs of her hair, or notice the way she caught her lip in her teeth when she concentrated.

She was doing that now, as she stared at another financial report. "Diligent, aren't you?" he said. She ignored him. Her hair had fallen forward as she bent over the next folder, and he couldn't see her face. He liked it better when she looked at him. "Good work ethic. I'll bet financial management requires all sorts of rules and procedures. No room for creativity."

It was like poking a caged animal just to see what it would do. Not nice, but it got a reaction.

She brushed back her hair, fixing him with a regal, I-am-not-amused stare. "Are you calling me anal?"

Her eyes looked gray in this light, but not the least bit dull. They still had a nice, sparkly quality when she was annoyed. "*Are* you anal? Not that it wouldn't be useful. I'll bet being thorough comes in handy with whatever it is that financial managers do."

She squinted at him, probably trying to decide if telling him was worth the effort. "I do cost analysis for an engineering firm," she said.

"Uh-huh," he said agreeably. "Interesting."

"It is," she told him, instantly defensive. He didn't give a damn what she said about cost analysis. He watched her eyes, trying to decide between gray or green. "I look at the projected cost of a job and determine how much the company can afford to bid. It's a very responsible position, and I'm very good at it."

Drew smiled and took the folder from her hands. "I believe you."

Her look said he probably couldn't tell a profit-loss column from a grocery list. "What do you do?"

"I ski." He flipped through the folder he held, then set it aside, letting her grapple with the concept of skiing as a career before he elaborated. "I run a small ski resort in Colorado, which is an excuse for doing what I like best—climbing and skiing." He left it at that, knowing she'd assume the worst.

"You're a ski bum?" Her disbelief was mixed with an equal amount of disdain.

"I prefer to think of myself as a small business owner who skis."

"And climbs."

"Yup. Whenever I can."

Her brow furrowed and he could tell she was trying to decide whether a recreational activity qualified as a job. Her eyes were downcast, but her surreptitious gaze swept his body, lingering on his chest and the thigh that nearly touched her own. If she was trying to think of all the ways a winter of skiing followed by a summer of climbing was a bad idea, she wouldn't find it there. But he didn't mind her looking.

Drew watched her lift another folder from the stack; he stared at what lay beneath it. "Damn," he said softly.

He noticed Lauren's gaze shift to her lap, and she sucked in her breath as he lifted the light blue envelope. It was identical to the one they had found at the

bank, the one that contained compromising, embarrassing photos of Meg and the blond Viking look-
alike.

He met her wide-eyed gaze, his raised brows questioning whether she wanted him to open the clasp.
Lauren nodded, then rested a pink polished fingertip
between her teeth. When she caught him looking at it,
she dropped her hand to the stack of papers in her lap.
Both hands gripped the edges of the pile tightly, braced
for a shock. "You open it."

Drew worked the clasp and tipped the envelope,
catching the single paper that slipped out. Lauren
flinched as he turned it over, probably expecting another X-rated photo.

He sighed with relief and held it out for her to see.
"It's my parents' marriage certificate."

Lauren relaxed and leaned closer. She read aloud,
"Kathryn Amelia Shay. Pretty name."

She was too polite to ask, but he could see the question in her eyes. "They were divorced," he told her.

"Oh, I'm sorry."

"No need to be. I was in high school and Miranda
was in college, so it's not like it traumatized us. Things
were better after they split up, and they were pretty
good friends by the time my mom died a few years
ago. I think she always loved him, she just couldn't put
up with his constant affairs."

"I imagine you were surprised when he married
Meg, then."

Drew snorted. "Surprised is putting it mildly. I was
flabbergasted. He said he'd never marry again, and in
my opinion he never should have been married in the
first place." He gave her a rueful smile. "You were

dead on when you called him a tomcat, you know. Fidelity is not in Harlan Creighton's nature."

"Hmm." She motioned toward the envelope. "Let's see Meg's marriage license. Is it in there?"

He glanced in the envelope and shrugged. "Nope."

Lauren looked surprised. "Why not? Isn't this where he keeps all his important papers? Where else would it be?"

"I have no idea." He had even less interest, but it was obvious that she did. "What's the big deal? You don't think your sister and my dad lied to us about being married, do you?"

"Well, no . . ." It didn't sound convincing.

"Dad's office even announced it to the press," he said, citing what for him was proof. Seeing her doubtful look, he tried for a lighter touch. "What's the matter, don't you want to be related to me?"

She seemed oddly unsettled by that comment, and he made a mental note to come back to it later.

"It just seems like it would be here, with the other one. If Meg changed her name, would she need to have it for ID purposes?"

"Only if they left the country. But we don't know if she changed her name. Let's keep looking."

They examined every folder and document in the safe before finally admitting it wasn't there. He couldn't have cared less, but Lauren had begun nibbling on a new fingernail. He already recognized it as the first sign that she was anxious. Reaching for her hand, he pulled it away from her mouth and examined the fingertips. All five were short, with chipped, ragged ends. She looked guilty and tried to pull her hand away, but he held on.

"Nervous habit?"

"I know it looks awful. I'm trying to stop, but I've had a relapse ever since all this with Meg."

He ran a finger over the short pink nails. He could have sworn a small quiver trembled through her hand just before she jerked it away and shoved both hands behind her back. "D-don't do that," she stammered. "I'm self-conscious about how they look."

"Then stop biting them."

Her smile lacked sincerity. "Why didn't I think of that?"

She seemed a little more unnerved than what simple embarrassment called for, which he found fascinating. He wanted to take her hand again, maybe massage his thumb along her wrist, just to see how she reacted.

"Where else can we look for their marriage certificate?" she asked, apparently intent on following up this new concern.

"I don't know." He stood and ran a hand through his hair as he turned in a slow circle, scanning his father's den. Lauren stood, too, rocking on her toes impatiently while he thought. "I've checked everything here," he mused. "Maybe his bedroom."

She perked up. "Good idea. Meg might have left her briefcase there."

Unless she had a file of threatening notes from her would-be abductors, Drew wasn't sure what helpful information might be in Meg's briefcase. Or, for that matter, in her underwear drawer. He wasn't sure what he was looking for at all, since the police were already following up with his dad's appointment logs and address books. But he couldn't just sit and wait.

He led the way upstairs, aware that Lauren walked

a few feet behind him, hands tucked firmly in her pockets. Self-conscious about her nails, or simply avoiding his touch? Not that he had any reason to reach for her, but she'd turned skittish again since he'd held her hand. He wished he didn't find that attractive, but skittish looked irresistible on her.

He stopped at the bedroom door, forcing her to stand beside him to look into the room. He didn't move, enjoying her nearness and refusing to examine his feelings further.

The bedroom was still very much his father's, masculine in furnishings and decoration. He supposed that would change, now that his father shared his space with a woman. Those fancy perfume bottles would appear on the dresser, along with family pictures in pretty frames, or flowery pillows and curtains. All things that weren't evident yet.

"That's odd. It doesn't even look like Meg's been here," Lauren said, obviously thinking along the same lines.

"Maybe she hasn't. They just got married a few days ago, right?"

She rolled her eyes at him in an expression of disbelief that he might be naïve enough to think Meg and his dad hadn't shared a bed until then. He smiled and shrugged. He had no doubts about his father's over-active libido; he just didn't know if Lauren had been deceiving herself about Meg's sex life. Apparently not.

"Meg made it sound like they'd just been married," Lauren told him. "And Gerald said she left here Tuesday morning, so she must have spent at least one night here recently." She crossed the room as she talked, heading for the closet. "Maybe Harlan is a good influence on her. Meg usually has clothes and shoes lying around, and half the time her bed isn't made . . ." Her voice trailed off as she entered the walk-in closet. He heard clothes rustle, then hangers being forcefully shoved aside. After several seconds of furious activity, she appeared, frowning. "Something's wrong here."

"What?" He joined her as Lauren marched back inside and grabbed a random handful of shirt sleeves, shaking it at him. "This. Nothing in here belongs to my sister. No business suits, no blouses, no shoes, not even a bathrobe. This doesn't make sense. Check the drawers."

They opened every drawer, including the nightstand beside the bed that held tissues, a box of condoms, and a bottle of Viagra. Lauren lifted the tissue box, revealing a pile of sex toys. Drew slammed the drawer shut before he could think about it. "Nothing. You're right."

"No briefcase, either," she said, obviously disappointed. "I think we should check Meg's apartment first thing in the morning."

"I agree."

He saw her hand go to her mouth and start on another nail, then with a quick glance his way, she transferred her hand to her hair and began twirling a strand around her finger.

"You're nervous again."

"I'm confused." More twirling. "Okay, I'm worried, too. And I'm starting to wonder if we can't find that marriage certificate because it simply doesn't exist."

He raised an eyebrow, pretending to consider whether she could be right. "You mean I might not be your nephew? And I was so hoping for a nice Christmas gift from my Aunt Lauren."

She almost smiled, but the worry won out. "Don't joke. Your dad and Meg are conveniently gone, and someone tried to abduct me thinking I was my sister. This sudden marriage has something to do with it, but I have no idea what." She bit her lip, then admitted: "It's scary."

Her concern sobered him quickly. "Hey. I'm sure they're all right, Lauren. They're not even in Washington any more." Without thinking about how she'd react, he walked to her and put an arm around her shoulders. And for a moment, she seemed to forget to be nervous about her sister—and about him. She leaned against him, closing her eyes with momentary relief at the sympathy. The next second they snapped open and she stiffened, taking a step away from him. Damn, just when he'd begun to be aware of what a good idea that instinct to comfort her had been.

She watched him warily. "What makes you so sure they're all right? That tape we saw was recorded earlier. Maybe they were abducted, then forced to call us so we'd quit looking for them."

She had quite an imagination. "Because Meg sounds as smart and resourceful as my dad," he said, not sure if it was true, but hoping it would make her feel better. "And think about it. If someone tried to abduct you this evening, it's because they *don't* have Meg. If they did, they'd know you couldn't be her."

A look of hope gradually replaced the fear in her eyes. "You could be right."

He smiled. "Don't look so surprised. I sometimes am."

Her mouth softened into the beginning of a smile, the shapely upper lip parting slightly from the full lower one. His focus narrowed on those soft lips, and he was struck by the sudden, crazy urge to pull her toward him and see what it would feel like to put his mouth against hers. The compulsion was so unexpected and strong he started to reach out to her, but her wide-eyed stare made him hesitate long enough to come to his senses.

With a reassuring smile, his hand detoured cautiously toward her hair, mindful of the punishment his shin had suffered the last time he'd touched it. Gently capturing the wavy strand she'd been twisting, he smoothed its length and tucked it behind her ear, turning his frighteningly intimate impulse to kiss her into what he hoped was a harmless gesture.

And a strange thing happened.

Huge greenish-gray eyes blinked several times and she caught the rosy swell of her lip between her teeth. It eased out as her sexy lips parted again in an expression of amazement. For several seconds she simply stared at him.

"Uh," she began, stepping backward. "Um," she tried again, taking another step, obviously searching for words and having a difficult time finding them. Lauren motioned toward the door. "I think I'll just"—she stepped backward again, bumping into the dresser—"turn in early. We'll want to check Meg's apartment in the morning."

"You're turning in?" he repeated, half amused, half disappointed.

She nodded, hands feeling for the dresser behind her. "Early."

"It's only nine o'clock."

She took a couple steps sideways. "I brought some work with me. In my briefcase," she added.

"Okay." He knew what the problem was, but he also knew she had to figure out the answer for herself.

"I really should fax it in by tomorrow, so I'll get started on it. I mean, I'll finish it." Words were coming faster now, and she seemed to realize how flustered she sounded. "Good night," she said quickly, and fled.

Drew listened as her footsteps hurried down the hall, encouraged by what had just happened. The first time he'd touched her hair, she'd kicked him soundly. The second time, she'd turned into a stumbling, babbling simpleton. He'd felt enough energy arcing between them to know exactly what her panic meant. Lauren was seriously conflicted.

He hoped she figured it out soon because next time he wasn't going to let her run away.

Chapter Five

Lauren slammed the bedroom door behind her and leaned against it, breathing hard. Damn, she'd handled that one like a silly freshman schoolgirl with a crush on a senior.

If she was lucky he'd think she was incredibly immature. But Drew wasn't naive and he probably knew the truth, that proximity to him made her heart race and that his touch sent tiny shocks through her body. Every last one of them shot toward her lower abdomen where they sizzled and popped and sent off so much heat she thought she must be glowing. What the hell was wrong with her?

Men didn't affect Lauren this way. God knew, Jeff certainly didn't. When Drew had run his hand across her fingers she'd felt so feverish she'd actually thought she was coming down with something. Then he'd pulled her against that broad chest, so close to his amazingly expressive mouth that she felt his breath on her hair, and she'd nearly groaned with desire and molded herself against him.

Lauren slid down the door and sank to the floor, holding her head in her hands. What was wrong with her? She was acting like an idiot. A silly, emotional— she nearly gasped at the sudden realization—she was acting like Meg!

Well, damn it, she had a good excuse. Her nerves were frazzled. She had repressed her worry about her sister's marriage, then stepped into the chaos of Meg's life, complete with compromising photos and a near-abduction. And a sexy as hell nephew.

She took a deep, fortifying breath. She needed to regain her emotional stability. A warm bath and a good night's sleep would put things in perspective. By morning Drew Creighton would probably look as ordinary as any man, and be as easy to resist.

Her theory was smashed to pieces as soon as she entered the kitchen the following morning. Gerald sat at the table eating cereal, but her smile skidded right past him and stopped dead.

Shirtless and barefoot, Drew lounged in a kitchen chair as he sorted through a pile of mail, one jean-clad leg propped on the chair beside him. A mesh of dark hair sprinkled his upper chest, but did nothing to hide the well-defined muscles. Even his sleep-tousled hair reminded her that he'd just stepped out of bed and into those snug jeans, probably because they were handy and he'd been sleeping in nothing at all.

Now, there was a thought to make her pause.

Her gaze traveled back over his chest. Skiing and mountain climbing, huh? If this got out, it could put the health clubs out of business.

Lauren caught Gerald's curious look and did her

best to channel her sudden hunger into a desire for food. "Hi!" She tried to sound perky and oblivious to finding a half-naked hunk in the kitchen. "What's for breakfast?"

Gerald used his spoon to point at the kitchen counter. "Cereal, muffins, bagels, and fresh fruit. Coffee and tea next to the fridge."

"Sounds good. No wonder you eat here."

"I'm usually here before six and stay until nine at night. You bet I eat here." He flashed a smile.

She prepared a bowl of cereal topped with strawberries and blueberries, conscious of Drew's gaze on her the whole time. Daring a glance from under her lashes, she saw that the mail had been set aside and she had his full attention, he watched every move she made, his elbows propped on chair arms and hands entwined lightly over his bare abdomen.

Lauren's stomach fluttered, which only made her annoyed—with herself and with him. The longer he watched, the more irritated she became.

He waited to speak until she was at the table. "I've been thinking," he announced.

She raised her eyes to his, making sure to skim right past his impressive chest. "Was it difficult?"

Genuine amusement flashed in his eyes. Damn, he wasn't the least bit offended. How was she going to keep this man at a safe distance?

"I *am* out of practice," Drew agreed. "A life spent chasing after snow bunnies doesn't lend itself to deep thinking."

Lauren nodded. "I imagine it's strenuous at that altitude."

"Exactly."

He was toying with her. She'd tried not to judge his lax lifestyle, but calling him a ski bum had probably given her away. If she was that easy to read, she was in big trouble.

"Actually, I was thinking about you."

For one second her spoon froze over the cereal bowl before she willed it to scoop up a strawberry, as casually as if her heart hadn't just tripped over itself. "How nice for you."

He grinned, and she wondered if sarcastic defiance had been the wrong move. He seemed to love it every time she rose to his challenge.

Gerald stopped eating, looking between them with a puzzled expression. "Did you two have a fight after I left last night?"

Drew's eyes never left hers. "Of course not," he assured Gerald. "I adore my aunt Lauren."

She gave him a tight smile. She wasn't going to touch that one. Instead, she answered Gerald. "I spent several productive hours in my room last night, catching up on my work." It was a blatant lie. She'd barely been able to concentrate on the fashion magazine she'd bought at the airport, much less the weighty budget reports in her briefcase. "But I'm curious to hear what thoughts my nephew has labored over."

Drew tilted his chair onto the back legs, and cocked his head thoughtfully, as if he'd given his idea long and careful consideration. "We need to cut your hair," he said.

She didn't deliberate nearly as long over her response. "I hope you didn't waste too much time thinking about my hair, because I like it the way it is." Actually, Jeff liked it that way, long enough to wear down during the day, in a pony tail for playing tennis, or in a twist for dining out. Three different looks from one cut—a practical hairstyle.

"The way you like it isn't important. It has to look exactly like your sister's. Gerald said hers is now shorter than yours."

"And layered," Gerald reminded him. "With wispy bangs."

Drew nodded. "Can't forget the wispy bangs."

She chewed longer than necessary, stalling. "And why would I want my hair to look exactly like Meg's?" she finally asked, feigning disinterest, even though she was afraid she was not going to like the answer.

"So you can pretend to be her tonight when we attend the party at the Watergate Hotel."

She lowered her spoon and gave him a suspicious look. "When we what?"

"It's a fundraiser. There's an invitation on my dad's desk, and he never misses an opportunity to work his contacts. Does he?" Drew turned to Gerald for confirmation.

"That's true. He planned to go."

"And since he was unexpectedly called out of town, his son is filling in for him, and escorting his father's new wife."

"He wasn't called out of town. He just told all of Washington he's on his honeymoon."

"He came back," Drew told her, apparently inventing a new scenario. "Because of an important issue that just came up. Now he's tied up in meetings with the big money men back in Texas, and Meg—that's you—is stranded in Washington, with no escort to the party. Fortunately, her considerate new stepson is visiting and would love to accompany her."

Lauren didn't like it. There would be too many questions. Besides, she wouldn't recognize anyone, and wouldn't know what was expected of her. "Why?"

"Why not? To see what happens." Drew reached for his coffee cup, cradling it on his flat stomach. "To see how people react to this marriage, or whether someone tries to get you alone and steer you away from the party. We might learn something. More than we would sitting here, anyway."

She frowned. "You mean you want to use me as bait."

"You'd be perfectly safe. As your escort, I'll be close by you all night."

She refused to indulge the appealing mental image of Drew dancing her across a crowded ballroom and ignored the flush that crept to her cheeks. "No."

Gerald's mouth turned up in a smug, I-told-you-so smile. Drew must have run this idea by him earlier with the same result.

Drew seemed mildly irritated, but she couldn't tell if it was with her or Gerald. "Why not?"

"Because it's stupid," she told him. Gerald bit his lip and raised his coffee cup in front of his spreading grin. "Did you forget someone tried to kidnap me?"

"We were taken by surprise. They've lost that advantage now."

"Not good enough. Besides, a prominent senator doesn't suddenly disappear on his honeymoon, then rush back to town a day later without causing a lot of questions. And we don't know how to answer them.

We'll cause so much of a stir we won't know what's gossip and what's important." She met his frown and tilted her chin up stubbornly. "And I think Jeff is right. We need to be sensible and let the authorities deal with whatever is going on."

Gerald lowered his coffee. "Okay, tell. Who is this Jeff?"

"Some guy she knows," Drew said with a dismissive wave.

"My fiancé!" Lauren held her left hand up and wiggled her ring finger significantly to display the modest diamond.

Gerald rolled his eyes. "Oh, him."

She narrowed her eyes. "You don't even know him."

"Meg told me about him. Mr. Perfect with a stick up his ass. Sounds dull to me. But whatever works for you, honey."

Drew choked on a laugh and she turned her glare on him. "Jeff is a responsible person who wants what's best for me. Maybe you two find common sense funny, but I intend to follow his sound advice. Meg and Harlan asked us to stay out of whatever is going on. That's what I'm going to do."

"You're going to sit here and wait while your sister has armed kidnappers looking for her and God knows what else?"

Lauren pressed her lips into a firm line. "Yes. Or maybe I'll fly home and wait there. With *Jeff*."

Drew assessed her as he sipped his coffee. "I thought you might be a little more . . . adventurous. My mistake."

His disappointment in her cut deeply. She wanted

to object that there was nothing wrong with being sensible and that she could be every bit as adventurous as the next girl, when adventure was called for. The words actually formed in her mind, but it was Jeff's voice saying them.

In the disgruntled silence the phone sounded louder than usual. Lauren stiffened, remembering the last call from Meg and Harlan, and slid an expectant look at Gerald.

He shrugged and dug into his cereal. "I'm the senator's personal assistant, not his butler. That's the house line. Besides, it's Saturday. I'm off."

Her gaze shifted to Drew. He had tensed, also.

"I'll get it," she volunteered. Lauren rushed across the kitchen. If it was Meg, she intended to get a lot more information from her sister than their four-way conversation had imparted last time.

"Senator Creighton's residence."

A relieved gasp sounded on the other end and a male voice with an eastern European accent said, "Meg! I am so glad I found you! I've been calling everywhere!"

"I'm sorry, but you didn't. I—"

He cut her off. "There's no time for old arguments, darling. We are both being watched. Meg, you are in grave danger. More than you realize. I must talk to you."

Lauren's intended correction died on her lips. Information was information. Hesitantly, she asked, "What do you know?"

"Not on the phone. You must come to the embassy tonight."

The man sounded like he knew Meg well, but she

had no idea what embassy he was talking about and didn't know how to ask without giving herself away. "I don't think I can."

"You must!" Urgency made his words more clipped, his accent more pronounced. Something Slavic? "There is a party. An invitation has already been delivered to Senator Creighton. Please, Meg, whatever unresolved issues we have, you must trust me. I fear for your life. There are things you don't know, things that could kill you!"

Blood drained from Lauren's face and hands, making her shiver. "Where will I find you?"

"The usual place."

Oh, good, that was helpful. "I don't recall—"

"Be there, darling. I'll see you then." The click that ended his call was abrupt. She laid the phone on its base and turned around.

Both men were staring at her.

She cleared her throat. "Gerald, was there also an invitation to some embassy function tonight?"

He thought for a few seconds. "There's one for a party at the Romanian Embassy."

A Romanian accent? Yes, very likely.

She took a deep breath. "Drew, I've reconsidered. In light of the fact that a strange Romanian thinks my sister's life is in immediate danger and wants to meet with her tonight, I think your little fable about a one-day honeymoon might work after all."

His eyebrow lifted. "Who was that?"

She shook her head and returned to the table. "I have no idea. But he seems to be on familiar terms with Meg, and he's worried sick about her. That makes *me* worried. I'd rather risk kidnappers than miss a chance to meet with him."

"You don't think he knows her well enough to know you're not Meg?"

"I'm sure he does. But maybe by the time he figures it out, I'll be able to convince him to give me his information." She gave a hopeless shrug. "It's worth a try."

Drew watched her for a moment and then nodded. "Right. Gerald can take care of your haircut."

"Me?" Gerald aimed his spoon at Drew. "I'm an administrative assistant, not a friggin' hair dresser. Just because I'm gay doesn't mean I know anything about cutting hair."

"Gee, no kidding," Drew said, with a look of mock disgust. "Gerald, you're the only one here who saw Meg's hair. Since you seem to have such fantastic powers of observation, you'll have to tell someone how to cut it."

"Oh." He dug back into his granola. "That makes sense."

"Not her regular hairdresser. Someone who won't blab about giving the senator's wife a new hairstyle just a few days after someone else did."

"I can ask Steven. He used to cut hair before he went into computer programming."

"Is he good?"

"He does mine," Gerald said.

Drew glanced at Gerald's perfectly styled hair and smiled. "Great. Can he to do it today?"

"Maybe." His eyes focused on some invisible point as he considered the request. "He's probably out jogging now, but he'll be home in an hour or so."

Drew turned a satisfied smile on Lauren. "Don't worry. We're making progress already, and we haven't even checked out your sister's apartment yet."

She chased down the last blueberry in her bowl. "There's just one thing. I didn't bring anything to wear to an embassy party."

Drew hesitated at that one, but Gerald brushed her protest aside. "Meg has several dresses that will work. Check her closet for the black silk sheath. That's her best piece, very flattering. Especially in the bust area." He wiggled his eyebrows.

Drew gave her a speculative look, his eyes straying to her chest long enough to make her blush. "Black sheath. Can't wait."

Lauren picked up her empty bowl and carried it to the sink, as if establishing a distance from Drew could reduce his effect on her. She felt warm every time his gaze lingered on her for more than two seconds. Despite her concern over Meg, she might spend the entire embassy party in a state of flushed excitement. Resisting Drew would be easier if she'd avoid him rather than date him, but she didn't have much choice. The Romanian had information and he wanted to talk to Meg. Drew was the logical escort.

And if someone *did* make a second attempt to abduct her. . . . She glanced across the kitchen, taking in approximately six feet three inches of toned, muscular manhood draped across the chair. Yes, Drew was the man she'd want protecting her.

"If you're afraid, you don't have to go," he said, misreading her look. "I'll find the guy somehow."

"No," she insisted. "I want to be your date."

Flustered as he lifted an eyebrow, she corrected herself. "I mean, you may escort me to the party."

If she didn't die of embarrassment first.

They still needed to search Meg's apartment for any hints of what she'd been involved in lately. Lauren wore sneakers, jeans, and a sweatshirt, and pulled her hair into a ponytail. Her sister's distaste for house-keeping could turn this job into dirty work.

They headed straight across the lobby toward the elevators and nearly made it before an authoritative male voice barked out, "Excuse me!" Even if she didn't speak English, she would have known by his tone that he really meant, "Hold it right there!"

She turned with a broad smile, hoping the ponytail disguised the actual length of her hair, whatever he expected it to be. "Hey!" She was too far away to read his name tag, so she settled for a wink, a gesture Meg threw out liberally to men. "How ya doin' today? It's just me, and this is Senator Creighton's son, Drew."

"Oh. Miss Sutherland. I didn't recognize you, dressed like that."

Shoot, she hadn't thought about that. If her fashion-conscious sister ever wore jeans, it would be with a smart leather jacket and to-die-for boots. She probably didn't even own sneakers. Lauren heard uncertainty in the guard's voice, but Drew didn't give him time to think about it.

"Hi, nice to meet you." He stepped closer and read the name tag, using it like the son of a politician should. "Daniel. Do I need to sign in or something?"

"No, sir, I'll make a note in the log."

"Okay, thanks." They both turned, eager to be gone.

"I saw you on TV, Miss Sutherland. They said you got married to Senator Creighton."

She guessed the unspoken part was, *So what in hell are you doing with his son?* She talked as they kept walking. "I did. Surprise, huh? Drew's helping me move a few things out." She pressed the button for the elevator.

Daniel trailed them. "The TV said you left on your honeymoon."

She heard the ding and stepped inside before the elevator doors were fully open. "That's just what we told the press. Can't have them knowing our real schedule, after all." She gave him a mischievous smile and wagged her finger. "I'm counting on you to keep our secret."

Daniel raised his voice as the doors closed. "Of course, miss!"

Lauren and Drew looked at each other as the elevator made its silent ascent. "Nicely done, Mrs. Creighton," Drew said.

They got out on the fifth floor and followed the hallway to number 532. Drew inserted the key Gerald lifted from the household key ring, and the door opened easily.

Drew stopped dead on the threshold.

"Shit. Someone's already been here. They tossed the place."

Lauren brushed past him, stepping over the shoes that spilled from the open front closet. "No, they didn't. This is how Meg keeps house. Now you can see why I doubted she was ever in your dad's bedroom."

Drew followed, cautiously avoiding a twelve-pack

of empty Pepsi cans and a six-pack of beer bottles. "You may have a point there," he murmured.

Lauren ignored him, letting him pick his way through the mess while she zeroed in on the stack of mail on the kitchen table, then the pile of papers on the open rolltop desk. Tossing her coat on the couch, she spent the next fifteen minutes flipping through the stacks, looking for anything that seemed out of place, leaving Drew to explore on his own.

No luck.

She turned to Drew, who stood by the coffee table, sorting through a bunch of newspapers and magazines. He hadn't removed his leather jacket, and he looked slightly uncomfortable handling Meg's possessions. "Anything suspicious?" she asked.

"Not unless you call three TVs, about a hundred video tapes and DVDs, and subscriptions to four different papers suspicious."

"Meg's a news junkie."

"And a slob. How can she be so organized at work, and live like this?"

Lauren sighed, familiar with the sentiment, since she'd expressed it so many times herself. "Meg says being organized *is* like work for her. She can do it as part of her job, but she doesn't want to bother at home." She nodded toward the bedroom, where she'd heard Drew poking around a few minutes before. "Was there any sign that your dad's been staying here?"

He shrugged. "I didn't see any suits or men's shoes in the closet, but I didn't open any drawers."

"Did you check the bathroom?"

"Not yet."

Drew followed her, watching while she went through the vanity drawers. She did her best to ignore him, but in the bathroom filled with lotions, potpourri jars, and scented candles, Drew Creighton seemed overwhelmingly male. He was close enough that his clean smell cut through the cloying sweetness of the candles, causing Lauren's nostrils to flare like a mare scenting a stallion. Alarmed, she moved as far from him as she could.

It was probably the potpourri that was making her lightheaded.

Lauren pointed at the wall beside Drew. "Check the medicine cabinet," she instructed. She wasn't about to reach across his chest to do it herself.

Drew flicked open the mirrored door. She spotted the evidence they sought two seconds later. On the shelf above the pain killers and cold medicines, a man's razor, shaving lotion, aftershave, and comb lay neatly lined up along the glass shelf. Lauren felt something like relief.

"I guess your dad's been staying here after all."

"I don't think so." Drew picked up the comb and examined it closely as he spoke. "That's not his brand of shaving lotion or aftershave. And this," he pulled something from the teeth of the comb, "is definitely not his hair."

Lauren peered at the short brown strand Drew held out, recalled Senator Creighton's full head of silver hair and felt suddenly queasy. In a voice filled with apprehension, she asked, "Could it be from the man in the pictures?"

Drew's thin smile was too tight to be sincere. "You tell me, you had a better look at them than I did."

"I guess not," she told him weakly, recalling the

pale blond hair in the photos. Lauren sighed at the thought of another sleep-over lover in addition to Senator Creighton and the X-rated Scandinavian stud. She'd wanted to believe the pictures had been faked. And for Meg's sake, she wanted Drew to believe that her sister was not the type who could have posed for those pictures. But it was getting harder to defend her.

"It's not what you're thinking," she told Drew.

"What am I thinking?"

"That Meg is some sort of slut who sleeps around and indulges in kinky sex fantasies."

"That's not what I think." Before Lauren could exhale with relief, he continued, "I think she's the sort of"—he hesitated before carefully amending the word—"woman who sleeps her way to the top, and who's more than willing to indulge other people's sexual fantasies if it helps her get there."

In a flash, her relief turned to jaw-clenching fury. "That's so unfair! You don't even know her."

"Really?" He put the comb back and gave her his full attention. "Here's what I know about your sister." He thrust his finger in front of her face. "One. She's worked in my dad's office eight months and is already his personal staff secretary, a brilliant little bureaucratic coup on her part."

"She's very good at what she does," Lauren spat back, her eyes scrunched to narrow slits that she hoped he found evil and dangerous.

"Two." A second finger flipped up under her nose. "She has had at least three love affairs during those eight months, not counting the Scandanavian photo stud—don't look so surprised, I told you Gerald knows everything—all of whom were flush with money and on the way up the political ladder."

Lauren adroitly skipped over the number of Meg's affairs. "What do you expect? The only men she meets are in government."

"Three." His three fingers made a reversed Boy Scout salute in front of her face. She barely refrained from batting them aside. "She is quite willing to date her boss, a traditional no-no for any secretary who wants to keep her job, except for the ambitious ones who want to promote themselves to Mrs. Boss."

That one really got her steamed. "Why does Meg get the blame for that? That is such a chauvinistic, male point of view, Creighton. Maybe the lecherous old bastard went after *her*."

He wasn't the least bit offended. "Yeah, I'll admit that could happen, except for number four." She got a close-up view of all four fingers as both his hand and his face moved in, driving home his point. "Just two weeks ago Dad was dating some divorced socialite in Virginia who had his favorite qualification—she's a former centerfold. Yes, you can thank Gerald again. Then he was suddenly getting calls at home from Meg, and having late night meetings with his dedicated secretary, who probably felt threatened by Miss Fuck of the Month and decided to make her move."

"That's ridiculous!"

"*And* who's young enough to flatter him into thinking he's a young stud again himself, because she's pretty and ambitious, and too damned sexy for her own good."

"And how the hell would you know that?" Lauren snapped.

They glared at each other as the answer sank in. He

didn't know Meg. He did know her look-alike sister. Any physical impression he had of Meg would have come from Lauren, or from his brief glance at the nude photo of Meg, who they both knew was identical to Lauren in every pertinent respect.

Too sexy for her own good?

Lauren felt her face go blank.

Drew's anger faded to a cautious look, and he backed away as far as he could before he hit the wall, which was about one foot. He was still too close for Lauren's comfort, judging by the fluttering in her stomach, especially since he didn't look the least bit embarrassed by the implications of what he'd said. Instead, he seemed to be assessing its accuracy and looking far too interested in his conclusion.

Lauren stepped back and stared, grappling with the concept. On her best days, she felt pretty. She would never have put herself in the sexy category. Even sweet, smitten Jeff, who called her beautiful and smart, had never called her sexy. Before she could wonder about that oversight, she had to wiggle out from under the fascinated gaze of her *nephew*, who was making her feel distinctly un-auntlike.

Since he hadn't actually said she was sexy, she decided to pretend she'd never taken it that way.

Using her best haughty voice, she said, "Excuse me, I need to get clothes from Meg's bedroom for the embassy party."

He moved all of three inches. Lauren squeezed past him, so close she felt his breath on top of her head and detected a scent that was both spicy and warm, which made her realize how rattled she was, since warm was not a smell.

She went directly to Meg's closet and scanned the racks for her sister's best dresses.

It wasn't like shopping at Lord & Taylor, but pretty damn close. Meg obviously had a busier social life than Lauren, judging by the number of cocktail and evening dresses, most black, and all more daring than Lauren would have preferred. Nothing had a decently high neckline or a hint of sleeve.

She pulled out the black sheath Gerald had recommended, a figure-hugging line of clingy silk with tiny spaghetti straps.

"Sexy," Drew said behind her.

He lounged in the doorway of the tiny walk-in closet. His smug smile was aimed at her, not the dress.

That one word was enough reason not to wear the dress. Lauren arched an eyebrow, stuck the dress back on the rack, and blindly selected the one next to it. "Too bad. I'm wearing this one."

The smile broadened to a grin.

Lauren looked at the dress in her hands. A form-fitting strapless top dipped in a low heart shape, hugged tightly to the curve of invisible hips, then flared into a long skirt. Perfect for dancing, preferably a sizzling hot tango. Lauren's mouth went dry.

Choking back a laugh, Drew said, "Excuse me. I need to order a long-stemmed red rose." He left before he could even appreciate her fuming scowl.

Lauren sighed and considered the dress. She could select a different one, but Drew would know she'd been intimidated by his reaction. Better to be intimidated by a dress than by Drew.

Another worried look at the plunging neckline assured her that she was not overstating the problem.

She wouldn't have to search Meg's underwear drawers for a strapless black bra; the crisscross lacing on the back of the dress showed too much skin for that. Her modest bosom was on its own. She would have to hope the heart-shaped curves of the bodice offered adequate enhancement.

At least she could pilfer some black nylons from Meg.

Several minutes of searching made it clear that panty hose were out. Meg's preference was obviously thongs, black garter belts and stockings. It was either wear the racy underwear, or stop at a drug store for her usual package of cheap pantyhose.

Lauren ran the silk stockings across her hand thoughtfully. No one would know but her, and it might make her feel daring enough to be comfortable in the dress.

What the hell.

Shaking off a shiver of anticipation, she gathered them up and left before she could change her mind.

Her last hope for a demure look ended with Steven.

"Are you sure you want me to cut it?" he asked, standing back to give Lauren's hair a critical eye and speaking to Gerald. "She has enough length and volume to do a loose, wavy fall. Very feminine and pretty, especially if I weave some tiny flowers into the top."

Lauren looked up hopefully.

Gerald shook his head. "Can't do it. It has to look exactly like Meg's. Razor cut along the bottom so it curves in, feathered through here and here." Fingers lightly fluffed Lauren's hair. "And wispy bangs down to here."

Steven shrugged. "Okay. It's a flattering style, but not as sexy."

She was getting used to the idea of sexy and thought it sounded fine.

"Of course it isn't. She can't go to the embassy like that!" Gerald look horrified. "After you cut it, you'll have to do some sort of upsweep." His fingers danced over the crown of Lauren's head in demonstration.

"No," Drew interjected from across the kitchen, chair tipped back in what must be his usual pose. "Don't change it from the way Meg was wearing hers the last few days. We want her to be recognized. She's supposed to be Senator Creighton's wife, remember?"

"Okay," Gerald agreed reluctantly. "But it needs *something* to make it look special. This is an embassy party."

"I didn't bring any accessories, Gerald." Steven stepped out from behind the kitchen chair so Lauren could see him without twisting around on her stool. In blue jeans and flannel shirt, Steven couldn't look more different from Gerald, who wore his standard vest and tie even though it was Saturday. "Did you bring anything with you that we could use?" he asked her. "Ribbons, silver combs, jeweled barrettes, anything?"

Lauren mentally reviewed her meager grooming supplies. "I have a velvet band I use to tie my hair back," she said doubtfully.

Steven rubbed his neatly trimmed beard as he studied the top of her head. "I could work with that. What color?"

"Red."

Gerald smiled. "Perfect. She has a black dress, Steven. It'll be great. Very sexy."

The world was conspiring to make her sexy. Lauren warmed to the idea and flicked her gaze toward Drew. He looked entirely too detached and carefree, and she felt too exposed in her bathrobe, even though it covered her from head to toe. "Why aren't you getting ready?" she asked him. "What are you going to wear?"

"I have a tux upstairs. Dad usually ropes me into attending these things when I'm in town. He keeps hoping political aspirations will rub off on me." His cynical tone said it was a vain hope.

Like a typical man, he'd probably devote all of ten minutes to getting dressed, and look perfect. But letting him watch while Steven transformed her into something sexy made her squirm. She'd already caught his gaze on her a bit too often this afternoon.

"Shouldn't you check with the police? I thought they were going to keep us updated on their search."

It was the right diversion.

"Yeah, you're right." Drew's chair dropped. "I'll give that cop a call."

"Detective Rasmussen," Gerald supplied, keeping a critical eye on Lauren's hair as Steven began snipping.

"That's the guy. I'll be right back."

"Take your time," she muttered to his back.

Lauren closed her eyes, prepared to sink into the luxury of being pampered, when Gerald crossed his arms and planted himself in front of her. "Okay, time to review your homework."

She stiffened. This was the scary part. "There's no way I can learn all those names and faces in the next few hours. Can't I just smile politely at everyone and avoid using names?"

Gerald scowled. "No, you cannot. You could end up being too remote to one of Senator Creighton's best friends, or worse yet, flashing a smile at Callista Featherstone and giving the whole thing away." He narrowed a sharp stare at her while wagging a finger. "I can not emphasize this enough. Callista is a petty, jealous witch-with-a-B and hates Meg with a passion. Once you open your mouth, it will take her all of ten seconds to realize that you are not your sister. Ten seconds after that, the whole room will know."

Lauren swallowed but couldn't get rid of the lump that had suddenly developed in her throat. "How am I supposed to recognize her? Can't you come with us?"

Her desperation softened Gerald's glare. "No, I can't. Just stay away from any tall blondes with a crash-test front end."

"A what?"

"Air bags, sweetie," he said, holding his hand up to support giant, invisible breasts. "Fully inflated. Avoid any women matching that description, especially if they have a nasty little predatory glint in their eyes." He shrugged. "That should eliminate most of the strumpets. You can be polite to the rest."

Lauren's shoulders sagged with defeat, causing Steven to poke her back to an upright posture. She moaned, "I'll never remember all those people."

"Andrew can help. He knows some of the men." A wicked grin swept across his face. "And probably most of the women."

Somehow that was more irritating than reassuring, which was probably the reaction Gerald intended. While she concentrated on looking disinterested, Drew walked into the kitchen.

"The police are off the case," Drew said, not looking very happy about it. "Orders of the Secret Service. I couldn't get hold of whoever's in charge of it now."

"Is that normal?" Lauren asked.

"Probably," Gerald told her. "The Secret Service provides protection for senators and representatives if it's needed. They have a full investigative staff." He squinted critically at the side of her head. "More layering," he directed Steven. "It has to swing when she moves her head back and forth." He demonstrated, swishing imaginary layers of hair across his collar.

Lauren wasn't sure she liked the way their case had been passed around. "The Secret Service hasn't even talked to us about what happened."

Drew frowned. "Rasmussen said they have his report, and they'll contact us when they know something."

She glanced at Gerald, who seemed more concerned with supervising Steven's every snip than he was about the Secret Service. Fine. If he wasn't concerned, she wasn't either. Worrying about Callista Featherstone was enough to keep her stomach in knots.

Drew's thoughts might still be on the investigation, but she doubted it. He was leaning against the kitchen counter, watching with interest as her new hair style evolved.

Lauren shifted uneasily under his unwavering gaze. She adjusted her robe, uncrossed her legs, re-crossed them.

"Hold still," Steven ordered.

She tried, but ended up swinging her foot to a nervous beat. With three men hovering around, she felt like the main exhibit at a museum. Gerald had to be there to advise Steven, but Drew didn't.

"Don't you have something to do?" she asked him.

"Me? No."

She caught Gerald's eye with a pleading look. He glanced at Drew and said, "Ladies only, get lost."

Behind her, Steven muttered something and snipped perilously close to her neck.

Drew raised an eyebrow, but Gerald had already turned his back. Lauren smiled sweetly and said, "'Bye."

"Just be ready by seven," Drew told her, and left.

She threw a grateful smile at Gerald. "Thanks."

"The big guy makes you nervous, huh?"

"Shut up, Gerald," Steven said mildly as he created wispy bangs with his razor. "And if you stereotype me one more time you're sleeping in the garage."

Gerald grinned and winked at Lauren. "Isn't he adorable?"

She wasn't sure if he meant Steven or Drew.

Steven's skills were magical, and Lauren loved the way her new hairstyle feathered down to swing just below the line of her chin.

The dress was more than magic. Her mind skidded away from the word sexy, but she was quite sure she'd never looked this good in her life. The fake red fingernails she'd applied were the finishing touch. If Meg felt this way about herself all the time, Lauren might have to consider investing in a few new dresses.

Lingerie, too. There was no getting around the effect the skimpy panties and lacy elastic garter straps had on her attitude, even concealed beneath the long dress. Posing in front of the mirror so she could admire the way the tight bodice persuaded her average-sized breasts to scrunch into rounded mounds with honest-to-God cleavage, Lauren felt a surge of confidence.

It dissipated into quivering shyness as soon as she saw Drew.

He was as stunning as she'd expected in his tuxedo. He greeted her at the foot of the stairs with a warm gaze that lingered in all the right places, and a low, sensual, "Very nice."

He reached for her hand as she descended the final tread, drawing her as close as he would for a dance. Too close for comfort. Even in heels she had to tilt her head to meet his eyes, and as soon as she did, his gaze slid down to her mouth, then lower to her breasts. Her pounding heart was probably adding significant tremors to her cleavage.

His sparkling blue gaze returned to hers. One side of his mouth curved into a mischievous smile. "I think our bodies will fit together quite well." She nearly melted under a hot, liquid rush of emotion before he added, "When we dance, that is."

"Oh," she said, stupidly letting him know that she'd assumed he was referring to another way they might fit together. She winced.

When she dared to look at him again, he drew his free hand from behind his back and brought it into the small space between them. She looked down at a single, long-stemmed red rose.

"I couldn't resist." He grinned, a devilishly charming little boy's smile that nudged her heartbeats into a gallop. Damn, that mouth was sexy. "You don't have to hold it in your teeth. I'll find a bud vase so you can leave it here."

She nodded, wondering what it was about Drew

that kept knocking her senseless. It wasn't like she'd never been given a rose before. In fact, she'd received hundreds. Jeff sent them in all colors, by the dozen, on a regular basis. Of course, they were delivered, not handed to her personally. And he'd never looked at her quite like that.

She had taken the rose from Drew and now she didn't know what to do with it. Simply holding it was dizzying, like being sucked into an emotional whirlpool with Drew at the center. Her panicked mind sought a way out.

Thrusting the rose back, she blurted, "I forgot, I have to call Jeff before we go."

"Great," he muttered. "Sounds like a real buzzkill to me."

That was the point. As quickly as she could manage in three-inch heels and a floor-length dress, she fled the room.

Jeff was safe. He was stable and dependable, and he never made her feel quivery inside. At least he never had before that misguided phone sex incident, which was *never* going to happen again. He was also suspicious.

"What do you mean, you were searching Meg's apartment? What for?"

"That's what I've been trying to explain, we don't know. Anything that might relate to the photographs, or to why someone might try to kidnap her. But we didn't find anything." Lauren decided not to mention the short brown hair in the comb; Jeff was already disapproving enough of Meg's "misguided morals."

"Lauren, I told you to leave that stuff to the police."

"Yes, I remember. Jeff? I . . ." She hadn't planned to bring it up, but suddenly his answer seemed important.

He waited through her hesitation, then said with exaggerated patience, "You what, Lauren?" He sounded impatient today, maybe a reaction to how vulnerable he'd sounded during the phone sex incident. If he was still embarrassed about it, she was sure the blame was going to shift back to her.

Lauren had to remove an immaculately manicured fake fingernail from her mouth to speak. "Would you be willing to come to Washington and help me?"

"Help? I don't think interfering with a police investigation would be helpful, Lauren. I'm sure the police would rather have you stay out of it, and I'm certain they don't need my help."

"The Secret Service," she mumbled.

He couldn't have heard her, because he spoke over her. "Besides, I have that Board of Directors meeting for the Downtown Development Project, and you know how important it is that the mayor have a good impression of Duchaine Properties."

"Yes, I suppose your family's business is more important than my sister."

"Of course it is," he assured her, then seemed to realize the trap he'd fallen into. "Not that Meg isn't important to you, honey, but she has a husband to take care of her now. I have to think about us. The success of Duchaine Properties will ensure our financial future. It's my job to look out for our welfare."

"Uh-huh." Lauren knew he expected her to be pleased with his response, but only felt numb. Money was important to him; Meg wasn't.

Jeff's voice became hearty and encouraging,

probably in response to her lack of enthusiasm. He hated it when she was worried or tense. "So what did you do with the rest of your day? Did you get a chance to visit Aunt Betty and Uncle John?"

Damn, she'd forgotten all about them. "No, I got my hair cut. I think you'll like it."

She heard several seconds of silence before Jeff's voice came back, sounding cautious. "I suppose a few hours at the beauty salon might make you feel better."

"I didn't go to a salon, one of Gerald's friends did it here. His partner, actually."

"Gerald? What do you mean, his partner? Are they police officers? For God's sake, why would a policeman be cutting your hair?"

She'd thought talking to Jeff would make her feel safe and secure. Instead, she was feeling more reckless every minute, like she'd been confined and needed to break free. Since she'd already admitted to half of today's irresponsible behavior, she ignored his questions and blundered on with the rest of it. "It wasn't to make me feel better, it was so I could look exactly like Meg when we go to the party at the Romanian embassy tonight." Confession was supposed to be good for the soul.

"The Romanian . . . ? We? Lauren, what are you talking about?"

Nothing he would approve of, she was certain. Why make him worry? "Gosh, Jeff, I just realized how late it is. Drew's waiting. I'll talk to you tomorrow, honey, okay?"

"Lauren, wait—"

"'Bye." She clicked off, then slowly raised one of her remaining endangered nails to her mouth before remembering it was protected by an acrylic one. Her nail got a reprieve as she considered the brush-off she'd just accomplished. She wasn't used to hiding things from Jeff, but sometimes men just didn't understand the bond between women, especially between sisters.

Except Drew. He understood.

But Drew didn't have an important job to worry about back home. He had skiing dates with snow bunnies. That was one big difference between him and Jeff. If she wanted to bother comparing them, that is. And she didn't.

In fact, she'd like to forget about Drew altogether. That would be difficult, however, if he intended to spend the next few hours on a dance floor, fitting their bodies together.

She stubbornly blocked Drew from her mind and concentrated on the socializing she would have to do. Callista Featherstone hovered ominously in every imagined situation.

Lauren's gaze strayed to the sherry on the bar built into Senator Creighton's bookshelves. Perhaps a little liquid courage would help.

Chapter Six

Drew tucked Lauren's arm through his as they entered the embassy ballroom. He would have loved to touch more than her arm; he had wanted to ever since she'd appeared in that dress, but for tonight she was his new stepmother, not the tempting, head-strong bundle of nervous energy who both liked and despised him.

He dipped his head so Lauren could hear him over the buzz of the ballroom. "If we get separated, don't leave this room with *anyone*, even if he turns out to be your mysterious Romanian."

She looked panicked. "You said you'd stay with me."

"I won't let you get far, and I won't take my eyes off you. But he might not approach you if I'm right beside you." He scanned the crowd for familiar faces. "Do you think you can remember all those people Gerald drilled you on?"

She shook her head firmly. "I don't think so. Sometimes people don't look like their photographs—"

"Meg, you sexy devil! I haven't seen you in ages."

Lauren was whirled from Drew's arm and into the embrace of a tall, sandy-haired man. "I told you to marry me, but did you listen? No, you married that old coot, instead. He might have more money, sweetheart, but I have more stamina."

Drew crossed his arms and regarded the man tolerantly. "Hello, Senator Pierson."

"Drew Creighton! Nice to see you! Where's that old man of yours? I must challenge him to a duel for the hand of this fair maiden."

Drew worried for a moment, but Lauren freed herself from Senator Pierson's embrace and picked up on his hint without hesitation.

"Paul, who are you kidding?" Lauren said, kissing the man's cheek. "You don't give a damn about fair maidens. And if you thought I qualified you wouldn't have your lecherous paws all over me."

Very good. She'd done better than he hoped.

"Ha! You're right about that. I like my women bold and experienced. So where is that sly old man of yours? I can't believe I had to hear about your wedding on the news."

"He was called away on business," Drew said.

Pierson's eyes never left Lauren. "Is that so? Well, it'll serve that irresponsible son of a bitch right if I steal his woman. Come on, Meg. Let's do a round on the dance floor before I get too loaded to see straight."

Lauren allowed herself to be swept off without as much as a backward glance. Drew frowned, grabbed a drink from a passing waiter, and found a spot where he could watch from the sidelines.

She was easy to keep track of on the dance floor. His eyes were drawn to her smooth, flowing movements no matter how many couples came between them. He wasn't the only one watching, either. Word of Senator Creighton's new wife passed quickly through the room, and Drew noticed several heads turn her way. Or maybe they were as mesmerized by the attractive, laughing young woman as he was.

She looked more relaxed every second. What had happened to no-nonsense, sensible Lauren? He took a long drink of champagne and clenched his jaw, noting which people seemed most interested in Lauren.

After watching several minutes of close dancing and Senator Pierson's hand sliding down Lauren's back to rest irritatingly close to her swaying bottom, Drew left his glass on a table and crossed the dance floor.

"Excuse me, Senator. I'm afraid I promised to stick close to Meg tonight." He forced his way between Lauren and Pierson, pulling her close and continuing the dance. Senator Pierson acquiesced, but leaned close to Lauren and said, "If you ever get tired of the old man, Meg, you know where to find me. Just be sure to ditch your babysitter here first." He clicked his tongue twice while winking at Lauren, punched Drew on the arm, and left.

Lauren watched him go with a bemused look. "Are you sure he's a good friend of your dad's? He sure put the moves on me."

"Did he?" Drew aimed a hard stare at Pierson's back. The man was probably no more than fifty, young and handsome enough to be a serious threat. "He's probably all talk, but only because he values my dad's friendship. Otherwise you'd be fair game."

"But I'm married! That is, Meg's married—"

"Meg Sutherland!" a woman interrupted. "But I

hear it's Meg Creighton now. How very romantic, the secretary marrying her boss." Drew turned in time to see the woman give him a head-to-toe glance that could have chilled a blowtorch before addressing Lauren again. "I suppose your husband isn't able to fulfill his obligations tonight," she said, leaving no doubt that she was referring to more than accompanying his wife on the dance floor.

Anger gathered inside Drew, but before he could let fly with a nasty retort, Lauren moved closer to Drew and said, "Isn't it wonderful that my stepson is so willing to help out? He's such a good—" She hesitated as she fixed Drew with a coy look. "—dancer."

Just when he thought she was going to be able to pull this off. Drew whirled her away before she could say more.

"Do you have any idea what you're doing? That woman is the president's chief advisor on domestic affairs," he said through clenched teeth.

"Really? Good for her. She seems to hate my sister." Lauren darted evil looks over his shoulder in the woman's direction. "Why is that?"

"I don't know. She's too old to have been one of my dad's former lovers. Maybe she just hates beautiful, young women like Meg who take a shortcut up the power ladder. Especially if they belong to the other party." He took a close look at Lauren's gray-green eyes, still flashing with aggression. "And where the hell did this other side of you come from?"

"I don't know." She gave him a bemused smile that made his heart skip a beat. "I was nervous, but then I just started being Meg. My sister has an outgoing personality. Effervescent."

"I'm sure Paul Pierson found you effervescent. Doris Atherton probably thinks you're a bitch."

Lauren shrugged. "She already did. Besides, I kind of like speaking my mind. Where can I get another drink?"

Drew wasn't sure she needed to loosen her tongue, but he couldn't complain. For the most part, Lauren was following the script, being conspicuously social and provocative. He just hadn't expected her to be so good at it. It should have confirmed his suspicion that she was just as phony as all the others, but Lauren's phoniness had nothing to do with flirting. He was beginning to think the phony part of Lauren was the controlled, practical woman who met all her parents' expectations. The woman who was engaged to the ever-so-sensible Jeff.

Drew steered them to the side and snagged two champagne flutes. He took a hearty gulp, but Lauren only had time for one genteel sip before a medallion-covered Romanian dignitary demanded an introduction. He appeared to be at least a couple decades older than the man they were looking for, the one Lauren described with an irritating smile as sounding "cultured and sexy."

"Ahh, Mrs. Creighton," the man said. "I thought this was you. I saw you and your new husband on the news."

"Did you?"

Lauren sounded genuinely charmed by the fact that the man watched TV. Drew nearly snorted at her lame attempt to flirt but was surprised to see that she was on target. The man beamed like a full moon. "I must hold such a beautiful woman in my arms, if only for a few short minutes," he said. "Immediately."

"Gag me," Drew muttered, but Lauren smiled at the dignitary. She tossed back the rest of her champagne and handed the empty glass to Drew. "I'll be right back," she assured him happily. Drew was left holding two empty glasses as Lauren glided off in an embrace that held her conspicuous cleavage far too close to the Romanian's chest.

Drew stuffed down hors d'oeuvres and exchanged quick greetings with his father's friends while keeping an anxious eye on the dance floor. Just when he'd had enough of the Romanian's snug hold on Lauren, the dance ended and she was appropriated by a handsome, dark-haired man who held her even closer and executed moves that made Lauren's dress flair and flip alluringly as he spun her across the floor. Drew moved closer. If that was their sexy Romanian, he seemed to have recovered from his concern for Meg. By the time Drew cut in, Lauren's face was flushed with pleasure and her partner's was alive with interest.

"Hi, Mom," he said, surprising the man into releasing Lauren to Drew's waiting arms. "Thanks for keeping my stepmother entertained," he told him. "I'll take over now." The man offered Lauren a gracious, if confused, bow as Drew danced her away.

He remembered to hold her at a respectful distance, despite the possessive feelings that made him want to crush her to him. He frowned at the sparkle in her eyes and the exposed swell of her breasts that rose and fell with each excited breath. Looking at them, he became a bit excited himself, which only irritated him more.

"Enjoying your new social life?" he asked dryly.

"Very much. Why, aren't I supposed to?"

"You're supposed to be getting information, not whisker burns from tangoing cheek-to-cheek with every Don Juan on Embassy Row."

She laughed. "How can I do that if you keep cutting in? Is my stepson jealous?"

The fact that she'd hit it exactly on the head didn't make him more cheerful. "Was that him?"

"No, David's an attaché with the British Embassy, and he's not a Don Juan, either. He was very sweet."

Sweet David made his jaw clench. "And I suppose the Romanian field marshal was holding you close so he could whisper state secrets in your ear?"

"His medals were cold," Lauren giggled. "I thought that long dangling one was going to drop right down my dress."

"So did I," Drew grumbled.

"Mrs. Creighton!"

Lauren released him as she turned, and a large, florid man pumped her free hand with both of his own. Draping an arm over Drew's shoulder, he said, "And you must be Harlan's son. Glad to meet you, boy."

Drew tried to step away, but the beefy hand was locked onto his shoulder, while whiskey fumes indicated that somewhere there were drinks more bracing than champagne. "And you are?" Drew prompted.

"Bud Childers. I've known your dad for years. We—hey, smile for the camera!"

Drew turned in time to catch the flash straight on. One of the ubiquitous photographers snapped several shots of the three of them while Bud squeezed the group together and beamed at the camera.

"Always good to be seen with a beautiful lady," he told Lauren. "Gotta run. You be sure to tell Harlan I said hello."

Drew scowled with annoyance and directed Lauren to a more secluded corner near the orchestra. It was also close to the kitchen door, and Lauren released him as a young man passed by with a tray of champagne.

"I'm so thirsty! It must be all the dancing." She selected one, then turned to Drew. "Want one?"

"No, thanks." He waved the man off and waited impatiently while Lauren took a long sip. He started to speak, but stopped as he saw her face pale and her eyes widened with alarm.

"Hello, Meg," a cool feminine voice said behind him.

Drew turned and nearly bumped into the protruding assets of a beautiful, tall blonde woman. Her low-cut gown barely confined her cleavage, giving him a close-up view of her firmly rounded breasts.

He raised his eyes to meet a frankly curious stare.

"Callista Featherstone?" he guessed.

The woman's perfectly fringed eyes blinked in surprise, and red lips opened with a childish innocence completely out of character with the rest of her body. "Have we met? Surely I'd remember."

"No, I haven't had the honor." And if he played it right, he wouldn't have to. Drew took another deliberate look at her suspiciously large mounds and tried to sound sincere. "But I had hoped to meet you. I've heard so many wonderful things about you."

Callista's chest swelled proudly. At least he'd taken her attention off Lauren.

"I'm already intrigued, Mr. . . . ?"

"Oh, let's not spoil the mystery so soon," Drew replied, making sure to let his gaze slip again to the obvious invitation she displayed between them. He smiled. "There will be that much more for us to discover about each other. Perhaps you could meet me near the bar in ten minutes? I would love to buy you a drink and," he slid another lingering look over her curves, "get to know you better."

Callista's eyelids lowered in sultry satisfaction as she flicked a glance past him to Lauren. From the corner of his eye Drew saw Lauren lift her glass and take another quick drink, hiding behind the only thing available.

Callista smiled. "I'll see you there," she purred. "Come alone."

Lauren lowered her drink and watched Callista strut away. "Wow. You're good with sluts. You must get a lot of practice."

She looked so genuinely impressed he nearly laughed. "Not that much."

"How are you with good girls?"

His amusement died in a rush of heat, and he took a closer look at her. He didn't know if it was the alcohol or the dancing that had raised the pink glow in her face, but he found himself suddenly imagining what it would be like to press his mouth to her flushed skin and lick the champagne off her wet lips. The flirtatious look she was giving him wasn't making her easier to resist.

"Stop looking at me like that," he whispered harshly.

"Like what?" The pink tip of her tongue ran over her upper lip and wide eyes blinked innocently at him.

"Like you're not married to my father!"

"I'm not." The champagne must have dulled her reactions, because it took a moment for her to wonder aloud, "Exactly how am I doing that?"

Damned if he knew. Maybe it was his overheated imagination, reading something into the lively green eyes—they were definitely green now—that wasn't really there. He needed to cool off. Fast.

"Come on." Taking her free hand, he led her behind the orchestra, where French doors opened onto a sheltered patio. Even though the March night was clear and mild, it was still no more than fifty degrees, and the patio was deserted. Perfect. A good dose of cold air might chill his overactive hormones into submission.

Lauren followed willingly, but as soon as the doors closed behind them, she shivered, hugging herself for warmth.

"What are we doing out here? It's freezing!" She tipped a long gulp of champagne down her throat.

"Alcohol won't help." He took the glass from her, setting it on a wide cement ledge. Removing his jacket, he draped it over her bare shoulders and pulled it together in front. Shirtsleeves still felt plenty warm after the heat she'd raised in him.

Lauren stuck her arms into the oversized sleeves and clasped the lapels together. "I don't see why we have to stand out here," she complained again.

"We need to reevaluate our plan, and I don't want to be overheard." To assure that they weren't seen either, he led her around a large marble statue of a naked woman garlanded by marble flowers, holding a bowl of marble fruit.

Lauren raised her eyes as they rounded the statue.

"Look, even she's cold. Her nipples are all puckered and hard." She snickered at her choice of words. "I guess all of her is hard, isn't it? But her nipples look like they're frozen stiff."

Drew peered closely at Lauren. That comment about nipples sounded a little glib for a woman who'd been reluctant to wear a form-fitting strapless gown. "Are you feeling all right?"

"I feel great. I also feel cold. Why are we reevaluating our plan? I thought people were supposed to approach me, and they are."

"Yes, and you look like you're enjoying the hell out of it. You're going to make it look like my father married a little tramp, flirting with half the men in Washington while your new husband is out of town."

"Oh, phooey," Lauren said.

"Phooey?"

"Phooey, as in you're full of it." She poked his chest with a finger that barely extended beyond the long sleeves of his jacket. "Meg always flirts with men. All men. Old, young, married, and single, in three languages. I can't do French," she said, then lowered her voice confidentially, "but if I meet the German ambassador, I know a few risqué phrases that'll knock his socks off." She winked at Drew.

Drew leaned closer.

"Lauren, are you drunk?"

"Nooo," she explained in slow, carefully distinct words. "I keep telling you, I'm cold." Before he could figure out how that related to not being drunk, she raised her hands to his face and clasped each cheek with icy palms. "See? I'm cold."

Drew blinked with surprise as she tilted her head and smiled.

"My, you're nice and warm." One hand trailed down his shirtfront and nimble fingers flipped a button open. He made a grab for her hand, but her fingers were already plastered against his chest. "Oh, God, are you ever warm," she murmured.

He shivered from more than her cold hands. Grasping each wrist, he pushed her hands away and held them in front of her. "You *are* drunk. You have no idea what you're doing."

In the space of a second, the innocent eyes grew sultry. "I know *exactly* what I'm doing," she purred. "I'm not some silly little schoolgirl, you know."

The schoolgirl analogy puzzled him, allowing her to take advantage of his momentary lapse in concentration. Slipping her hands from his, she reached for his neck and pulled his head toward her.

"Your upper lip has the sexiest little curve, did you know that?" She whispered the information bare millimeters from his startled mouth, then delicately traced the outline of his lip with her tongue.

Drew's brain stripped several gears as it came to a full stop. There was something he should do here, quickly, but he couldn't think what it might be. All he could focus on were those sexy, smiling lips and the pink tip of her wet tongue. This was more than any man could be expected to take. When her mouth moved toward him again, he didn't hesitate. Capturing her full lower lip between his, he pulled her against his chest and melded his mouth to hers.

Lauren was ready for him. She slipped into his

embrace with a hunger seemingly equal to his own, parting her lips and meeting his tongue with a moan.

Drew was nearly staggered by the sensory overload. A hot champagne blow to the head, with undertones of perfume. And cold hands or not, the rest of her was warm and willing. For several incredible seconds, he allowed his entire body to experience the fiery sensations of Lauren's mouth on his, her body molded against him, and his hand cupping the full roundness of her bottom beneath the maddening folds of her dress.

Their tongue-tangled explorations trailed off to small, lingering kisses before Drew regained enough sense to push her away. He stared at Lauren's flushed face. She was a temptress. It was all he could do to keep from diving back into another kiss. This was not the time or place, but damn, that had been one hell of a kiss; he was definitely going to find a way to do that again.

Lauren's dazed eyes focused on his mouth, while her own lips parted in a dreamy smile. "You do that sooo well," she assured him in tones only the seriously sloshed could manage. "Do it again."

Lauren's eyes closed and her mouth aimed at his. Drew's hands caught her shoulders just in time. "Ask me later," he said, holding her back and hating himself all the while.

The full lower lip he'd just ravished to perfection pushed itself into a seductive pout. "I've waited long enough already. Months and months." She leaned against his hands, pushing closer and lowering her voice. "Confidentially, it's been years. I *need* to be kissed like that again. *Right now.*"

Now, there was some truly useful information. If sensible old Jeff couldn't muster enough passion to ignite this sexy little tinderbox, Drew had no qualms about taking his place. But he preferred his women alert and sober.

"This is an interesting side of you, honey, and I'd love to explore it further, but I can't take advantage while you're drunk."

"Pssht." She waved away his objection with the swish of a hand. "You have my permission." Her hands pulled at his shirt, bringing her lips closer to their goal, as her eyes fluttered shut.

"Christ, Lauren," he groaned, taking a step backward. "I'm not made of stone. You have to stop this. If you don't despise me two hours from now, I'll be more than happy to kiss you. In fact, I'll kiss more than your mouth. I'll kiss the soft spot below your ears, I'll kiss the tips of your toes, and I'll kiss places in between that'll make you blush to the roots of your hair and melt into a pool of wet desire."

He had her breathless attention. Her eyes blinked once as she considered it, then once again. "You will?"

"I promise."

"Oooh," she said, her voice barely audible as she considered the offer. "Okay."

God, if she remembered this, she was either going to hate him or give him the most memorable night of his life.

Meanwhile, he had to find a warm, quiet place where Lauren could sober up. They didn't need someone taking a photo of Senator Creighton's inebriated new wife doing the town while he was away.

Or doing her stepson, either.

* * *

Lauren allowed herself to be ushered along the edge of the ballroom, acutely aware of Drew's hand on the exposed skin of her back. It was as warm and firm as the rest of him, and she wondered what it would feel like against more sensitive parts of her body. Maybe another drink would give her the courage to find out.

She wasn't drunk yet. Not drunk enough, anyway.

The light buzz from the champagne had been enough to loosen some inhibitions, to free her from her studied propriety. She'd known exactly what she was doing when she'd kissed Drew. She'd known she shouldn't do it, known she would lose control if she did, and still couldn't stop herself. Dancing with him, being held in those strong arms, had been wonderful. But it wasn't enough. She wanted more.

His kiss had ignited a burst of desire that rushed through her body and settled into a wonderful, throbbing heat in her pelvis. Her arousal slammed into her when his hand gripped her bottom and pressed her against him close enough to know that the feeling was mutual. His promise of more intimate kisses had her head spinning far more than the champagne did. If she was drunk, it was on Drew Creighton, not champagne.

He directed her through an archway into a wide passage, strolling casually along it while testing each locked door they passed. The third one opened just as someone ahead of them called, "Drew Creighton! Is that you?"

He pushed her inside and shut the door behind her.

Alone, Lauren blinked at the black room and felt for a light switch. Her hand connected, and a table lamp across the room flared into a soft, yellow glow.

She barely had time to take in the small sitting room filled with couches and chairs, when a hand spun her around and pulled her into an embrace.

"Meg! Oh, thank God, you're safe!"

The voice and the body were distinctly male, and the accent was the same as the man on the phone. Lauren was crushed against the silk lapel of his tuxedo jacket, inhaling the faint spiciness of an unfamiliar aftershave. A hand stroked the back of her head while the other held her tightly against a broad chest. She drew her head back to look at the man's face, but only caught a glimpse of a straight nose, black eyes, and even blacker hair before he murmured, "Megan, you are driving me crazy," as his lips closed over hers.

Startled, she made a *mmmf* sound against his lips and pushed on his shoulders, but he held her fast. Apparently, Meg knew him well enough to kiss him back. Lauren didn't, and she froze, not knowing whether she should reveal her identity so soon.

The man's hand cupped her cheek gently, and stroked a soft thumb along her jaw in a distracting, re-assuring way. It wasn't like kissing Drew, but it wasn't like kissing Jeff, either. This man's kiss lacked the crackling heat that Drew emitted with every touch, but was still more thorough and tender than any kiss she'd ever had from Jeff. Either the men of Colorado and Romania knew a different technique they weren't shar-ing with the rest of the planet, or Jeff was a romantic underachiever. While her fogged mind struggled to figure out which it was, the man's lips were jerked forcibly from hers.

"Hands off, buddy," Drew growled.

The transformation from gentle lover to angry

combatant was instantaneous. While Lauren steadied herself, the man whirled, throwing a punch at Drew's face. Miraculously, it didn't land. Drew dodged, then swung back, a jab that was expertly deflected with a forearm as the man's right fist darted out.

"Stop!" Lauren yelled, as Drew moved quickly aside, grabbing the man's arm and twisting.

They stood still in a deadlock, each man trying to leverage the other into letting go.

The Romanian's handsome face scowled with concern and probably a considerable amount of pain. "Run, Megan!" he ordered.

"She's with me, you goddamned idiot," Drew said in a strangled snarl.

Lauren shoved her arm forcibly between the two men, prying them apart as they reluctantly let go of each other. Doubt crept into the Romanian's face, and he peered closely at Lauren. "Meg? No, it can't be. Meg's lips are as full, but her taste is a little more—"

"Watch it," Drew warned.

"Different." His face cleared as he stepped back from Drew. "Ahh. Then you must be Lauren."

"Yes," she said, surprised. "How do you know my name?"

"Megan told me, of course." He turned an amazed look on Drew. "Are you Jeff?"

"Hell no," Drew spat out. "I'm Drew Creighton."

"The senator's son? Yes, that makes more sense. From what I've heard, I didn't think Jeff would"—he glanced at Lauren—"be here," he concluded, which Lauren thought was not what he'd been about to say. "Where is Meg?"

"In the Virgin Islands," Lauren said. Then,

considering the steamy kiss she'd just received, she emphasized, "On her honeymoon."

He made a negating motion with his hand. "I have heard that rumor. So you don't know where she really is?"

Lauren frowned at his easy dismissal of Meg's claim, but before she could question it, Drew said, "Why don't you tell us why you think she isn't where she says she is, and why you think she's in danger. And start with your name."

"Forgive me. I am Michael Dragos." He shook hands with Drew, then smiled warmly at Lauren. "I think we have already greeted one another," he told her.

Drew scowled.

Lauren smiled back self-consciously. It occurred to her that in the past ten minutes she'd been in a passionate clinch with both men, neither of whom was her fiancé. Maybe she really was a bit drunk.

"How do you know Meg?" Drew asked. At least one of them was thinking clearly.

"We have dated for the past two years."

"Meg has dated several men during the past two years," Drew told him. "And she married my father."

Dragos waved Meg's marriage aside. "No, that is what they want you to believe. She is in love with me."

Lauren exchanged quick glances with Drew. The man sounded like an obsessed ex-lover. "She never mentioned you," Lauren told him cautiously.

Dragos nodded, unfazed. "Michael is the American-ized version of my name. Meg would have referred to me by my real name, Mihaly. That is what she calls me."

"You're Mihaly?" She turned to Drew. "There is a Mihaly, a guy she keeps going back to between other men. She seemed pretty hung up on him."

Drew looked at him skeptically. "Doesn't sound like love to me."

"Meg is in denial," Mihaly told them, shaking his head with regret. "She has difficulties with the concept of love but, fortunately for her, I am a patient man. However, she is putting herself in danger, and *that* is straining my patience."

Lauren watched him run his hand through his dark hair and decided that her sister was an even bigger idiot than she'd suspected. Meg was skittish about love, but if her sister was risking the devotion of this gorgeous hunk of a man by fooling around with other guys, even rich United States senators, she was out of her mind. Anyone who would tolerate Meg's flings while patiently waiting out her "difficulties" with commitment was either crazy or truly in love with her.

Lauren decided she trusted Mihaly. She also decided that he would never learn of the photos of Meg and the blond stud.

In a burst of sobriety, Lauren remembered their reason for their meeting. "When you called you told me Meg was in danger. Why do you think that?"

He gestured at the chairs and they all sat, but no one looked comfortable. Mihaly was on the edge of his seat, leaning toward them as he spoke.

"I returned from Bucharest yesterday and discovered that someone had broken into both my embassy office and my apartment. Believe me, these are impressive feats. Nothing was taken, but someone went through all my personal papers—letters, pictures, expense accounts, anything having to do with my personal life. It was a professional job, bypassing alarms and opening deadbolt locks."

Drew listened impassively. "If nothing was taken, how can you be sure someone broke in?"

Mihaly gave him a direct look. "I know these things."

Drew narrowed his eyes, and Lauren realized what Mihaly had meant—he had more than a passing acquaintance with espionage.

"I don't see how breaking into your apartment puts Megan in danger," she said.

"They disabled the alarms, but they didn't bother with the security cameras," Mihaly said, his accent making each word precise. "The man entered with his gun drawn and checked the rooms before he searched the place. He spoke into a wireless microphone and said, in English, 'She's not here.' Before he left, he asked his partner if he'd found anything in the Maxima."

Lauren bit her lip. "Meg drives a Nissan Maxima."

Drew seemed not to hear her. "You have security cameras *inside* your apartment?" he asked. "And audio?"

Mihaly turned an expressionless gaze on him.

Drew stared back, his eyes hard and calculating. "Perhaps the danger to Meg has something to do with your profession," he said.

"Perhaps," Mihaly admitted. "But I don't think so. The man seemed to be interested only in things pertaining to Meg."

"What did the guy look like?" Lauren asked. "Did he have a large, hawkish nose? Or wear a trench coat?"

Mihaly looked confused. "No, no trench coat. He wore a ski mask, so all I could tell was that he was a tall white man with long hair, possibly blond. Some of it stuck out from beneath the mask.

Her gaze darted to Drew's in alarm. He shook his head, and she stayed silent, but felt chills creep over her back. If it was the same blond guy who had co-starred with Meg in the photos, then they obviously knew about Mihaly and her sister *had* been set up. Meg might be in more danger than she realized.

Mihlay had reached a similar conclusion. "I didn't recognize him, but that only means he's probably not CIA, because I know most of them. Meg is still in danger. And if Lauren is mistaken for Meg," he paused to look directly at Drew, "she is in danger, too."

Suddenly, enjoying the Washington social scene while passing as Meg wasn't as much fun anymore.

Drew apparently had the same thought. "Let's get you home," he said, offering his hand.

Mihaly stood too. "You will call me if you hear from Meg?" He offered Drew his card.

"If you'll do the same," Drew agreed. "Or if you learn anything about Meg and my father."

They left Mihaly standing with his hands jammed into his pockets, a worried look creasing his brow and tightening his mouth. His distress seemed sincere; Lauren flashed a sympathetic smile before the door closed. The possibility that her sister might have a future with Mihaly Dragos intrigued Lauren and made Meg's marriage to Senator Creighton look even more like a lie.

"Do you think Mihaly is a spy?" she asked Drew.

"Ssh, not so loud." He pulled her against him as they walked through the people mingling in the wide corridor. "The term is intelligence agent, and yes, I think he is. Or was. I don't know what his position with the embassy is now." He steered her to the coat check room. "Now that we've talked to him, I think we should get out of here. I don't like the idea of you posing as Meg when those guys have already zeroed in on her connection to Dragos."

He was being protective again. Since she seemed to need it, she wasn't about to object.

With a light wool cape over her shoulders, the night didn't seem as chilly. "Let's walk to the car," she suggested.

"In those heels? It's several blocks."

"I know. The night air will clear my head."

He chuckled. "I hope it doesn't clear everything from your head. I'm interested in pursuing a couple of the thoughts you had back there."

Uh-oh. Perhaps Lauren had been a little *too* uninhibited on the embassy patio. She hadn't meant to offer an open invitation—had she? She tried to move away but Drew tucked her arm firmly against his side as they started down the sidewalk.

He didn't say anything as they walked, just hummed to himself under his breath. Lauren winced. He thought she'd meant something with that silly little kiss. Well, okay, maybe it was a steaming hot kiss, and it had been fun, but it didn't mean she wanted more than that. This was exactly why Jeff was right about never veering from a sensible, prudent lifestyle. As soon as you did, someone was bound to misinterpret your harmless intentions.

"Are you warm enough?" Drew took her hand in his as they stepped off the curb at the end of the first block. "Your fingers are cold. Don't worry, I know how to warm them up." His smile promised incredible heat.

Oh, damn. If only he wouldn't look at her like that. His eyes glinted dark blue in the lights from a car pulling out of a parking spot down the street, and his smile had the lopsided, devilish curl of a little kid with a naughty idea. She shouldn't have met his hungry gaze, because now she couldn't look away, and her body vibrated with anticipation and her heart pounded, until the roar of blood rushing in her ears drowned out everything else . . .

Drew's rough embrace dragged her off her feet. It wasn't until they were falling sideways that she realized the noise in her head was the roar of an oncoming car, bearing down on their position in the center of the street. Drew's pull swept her out of its path a mere inch from the blur of metal and tires. The car fishtailed through the intersection, squealed as it laid a strip of burnt rubber, and sped off. The roar died out, along with shouted obscenities from other distant pedestrians, and Lauren was left sitting on her butt beside a parked Land Rover on the dark street, with Drew sprawled motionless beside her.

Chapter Seven

"Are you all right?"

They said it together, but Lauren answered first. "I'm fine, just a sore tailbone." Between dodging cars and falling on slippery sidewalks, that part of her body was getting quite the workout. He hadn't moved, and she laid her hand on his head, lying still beside her. "You're injured," she said, her voice wavering.

"No, I'm fine."

"Then why aren't you moving?"

"I'm enjoying the view."

Lauren looked down. His face was turned toward her, less than a foot from her fully exposed thigh.

"Stockings and garters." He sighed. "God, I love an old-fashioned girl." His hand reached toward her.

She slapped it, then yanked the full skirt down with a swish. Embarrassment, and maybe something else, gave her a warm flush.

"Spoilsport." He sat up, brushed dirt from his jacket, then eyed her critically. "You're really okay?" He pushed a strand of hair behind her ear and leaned close, examining her face by the weak light of the street lamp.

She nodded. "Thanks to you. That idiot could have killed us both."

His voice was low and serious, his eyes watching her closely. "I think that was the idea, Lauren."

She sucked in her breath. "Because he thought I was Meg?"

Drew didn't answer, but his expression was hard as he got up and helped her to her feet. "Come on, you're going home. No more role-playing."

She wasn't about to argue. Whatever Meg had gotten herself into was far more than Lauren could get her out of.

She was silent on the ride home. Between the cool air and nearly being flattened against the Washington, D.C., pavement, the effects of the champagne had evaporated. It didn't take her long to discover that even acrylic nails could be chewed off, and her last decent fingernail was history before they hit the quiet streets of Georgetown.

Drew parked in the driveway and came around to open her door. With a rueful glance at the hand he held, he said, "I'm glad your fingernails were the only casualty tonight."

"I don't care about my nails. I just want Meg to be safe."

"And I'm not worried about Meg. No, wait!" He held up his hands. "Before you start shooting laser beams from your eyes, listen. She's with my dad, and he has all sorts of resources in this town. I'm more worried about keeping you safe. I'll feel better once you're home."

"We are home." Concern made her glance up and down the dark street. "Do you think someone might try to kill me between the car and the house?" She moved closer to him.

"No," he said, but put his arm around her anyway and kept her close as they walked to the front door. "I meant I'll feel better once you're home in Lansing. You'll be safe there."

She looked at him in surprise. "You want me to leave?"

"As soon as possible." He unlocked the door and took her arm to guide her inside, since she was too stunned to move on her own. "You can call your boyfriend in the morning. I'm sure he'll approve."

My fiancé, she thought, but didn't say aloud. She was distracted by the realization that, even though Drew was probably right, she wasn't looking forward to seeing Jeff. She'd much rather stay with Drew.

It hit her like a blow to the head.

"I'll miss you, though," he told her with a mischievous smile as he locked the door behind them and set the alarm. "I hate to let you leave without giving me a chance to fulfill my promise."

"What promise?"

"Don't tell me you forgot." He leaned close and ran a finger from her ear, down her neck, over her collarbone, to the rise of her breasts. She shivered, not sure if it was from his finger or his gentle breath on her ear. "The promise I made to kiss you all over your body until you were breathless and hot and yearning and . . ."

And wet, her mind finished eagerly. Part of her brain was stumbling in shock, but the part that controlled her physical responses was keeping up just fine.

Drew's finger stopped right above her cleavage. "But I guess attempted murder spoils the mood, doesn't it?"

No, it doesn't, her overheated libido fairly screamed.

"Too bad," Drew said, pulling back enough for her to see that he looked truly regretful. "I'd bet it would be phenomenal."

Phenomenal? She'd had good sex before, but never anything she'd call phenomenal. It could have been an arrogant boast, but she believed it.

Lauren hadn't moved a muscle, including her eyes, which couldn't seem to leave his face. They nearly crossed as his mouth moved toward hers.

"Good night, Aunt Lauren," he murmured, and pressed a soft kiss to her cheek. While she blinked stupidly, he turned and headed upstairs, humming the melody from one of the songs they'd danced to.

She carefully felt for the door behind her and sagged against it.

The feather-light touch Drew had placed beside her mouth was playing as much havoc with her nerve endings as their soul-searing kiss at the embassy. That wasn't good. Jeff should be the one shorting out her neurons, not her sexy nephew, whom she'd known all of three days.

She'd lied to Drew about not having been kissed like that in years. She'd *never* been kissed like that. Even under the liberating influence of alcohol, Jeff's kisses didn't compare to the heated rush of passion Drew could ignite with one touch of his lips. Jeff's kisses left her content and confident of his love. But not once had she felt pierced to the soul, restless with desire, and heaven help her, eager to wrap her legs around him and do it again.

And she was about to walk away from the one man who did.

Tomorrow she would go down to breakfast, change her airline reservations, and tell Drew good-bye.

Lauren exhaled a deep, shaky sigh.

It would help if this time he wore a shirt.

Drew tucked in his long-sleeved T-shirt as he descended the stairs, perking up at the bottom when he heard the low sound of Lauren's voice. His interest died when he saw her in the den, talking on the phone. She would either be making arrangements with the airlines or giving the good news to stuffy, proper old Jeff. He didn't care to overhear either conversation.

The smell of coffee led him to the kitchen, where Gerald sat at the table reading the morning paper.

"What are you doing here? It's Sunday."

Gerald lowered the business section. "I wanted to hear how it went last night at the embassy. Besides, Steven's painting the kitchen and if I stay he'll make me help." When Drew merely nodded, Gerald prodded, "So what happened?"

Drew poured a cup of coffee and carried it to the table. Stirring in cream and sugar, he considered the best way to summarize their night. "Lauren charmed half a dozen dignitaries and got tipsy on champagne, and I nearly punched out our contact before we found out he was Meg's ex-lover and some sort of Romanian spook. He has a pretty convincing story about a couple of professional types who are seriously looking for Meg, one of them being the guy who co-starred in

Meg's porn collection. Then we left and someone tried to run us down and kill us. Are those jelly donuts?"

Gerald's eyes went wide behind his glasses as he passed the box of donuts. "So not much, huh?"

"Right."

"Holy shit," Gerald muttered. "Pardon my French." He sipped his coffee and thought for a minute. "Lauren can't go around posing as Meg anymore. She can't go out at all."

"I know. I'm sending her home today."

"Good." Gerald watched him closely. "You don't look too happy about that."

Drew turned a sharp glance his way but didn't answer. He'd already lost hours of sleep over Lauren, and it wasn't open for discussion. The need to keep her safe outweighed the odd, unsettled feeling he got in his chest whenever he looked at her. Not to mention the eager tightening in his groin.

They sat silently for a few minutes until Lauren wandered in. She gave Gerald a distracted greeting, then looked at Drew and bit her lip as she sat down.

At least she wasn't being perky about leaving. "What's wrong, isn't Jeff glad you're coming home?" Drew asked.

She looked up, apparently having a hard time focusing. "Hmm? Oh, yes. He is."

Drew frowned. "Lauren." He waited until her gaze cleared and settled on his. "What's wrong?"

She chewed her lower lip. "Nothing. Well, maybe something. Jeff said a man has been at his apartment twice, asking for me. He didn't leave his name, he just said it was personal."

Drew tensed. "Is he still there?"

"This morning? I don't know. Jeff drove by my apartment and said the guy was parked in front of the building for several hours last night."

Drew's thoughts were momentarily sidetracked. "Your apartment? You don't live with your fiancé?"

She looked embarrassed. "What's wrong with that? I like my independence."

She liked being able to get away from the man she was going to marry. He'd come back to that one later.

"What was Jeff's impression of the guy?"

She brushed it off impatiently. "He thought I must have won a sweepstakes contest, or something. The guy was friendly, but said he couldn't leave a message, he had to talk to me personally, so Jeff thinks I have to sign a big check."

"Or receive a summons," Gerald suggested. "Is there any reason you might be served? A car accident? A liability issue at work? A medical lawsuit?"

Lauren shook her head to everything. "No, none of those. Believe me, I lead an uneventful, dull life. No summons."

He set his cup down. "Okay, change of plans. I don't know what in the hell Meg and my dad are involved in, but you can't go home, Lauren. Now they're looking for you *and* your sister, and no offense, but Jeff doesn't sound like he'd provide much protection."

She didn't deny it. "But why? I don't have information, I didn't see anything, and I don't know why Meg and Harlan disappeared."

"Maybe those guys think you do."

Her eyes looked gray, all shadowy and somber. "This is getting too scary."

"I agree," Gerald said.

"Damn right. That's why you're going to have to stay in this house, at least until we know what's going on," Drew told her. If he could keep her out of the way, he might be able to contact some of his dad's friends without drawing attention, ask a few discreet questions, and—"

"No."

Drew and Gerald stared at her.

"Pardon me?" Gerald said.

The gray eyes were cool with disdain. "You are not keeping me locked in this house while you go running around on some manly quest for the truth. How do you know that car wasn't aiming at you last night? How do you know that the guys in black suits and black cars aren't searching the Colorado caves, or wherever the hell you live, looking for you, too?"

Gerald choked on a laugh. "Caves? Have you seen—?"

"Not now," Drew cut him off with a wave of his hand. He narrowed a thoughtful glance at Lauren. "Good point. I'll call some people and check." He smiled. "The neighbors in the cave next to mine."

"Go ahead."

He looked at his watch. He might wake someone up, but oh well.

The first call to the lodge manager got no results outside of a grumpy request to get home before the ski season was over, but a call to one of the counselors told him what he didn't want to hear.

Lauren and Gerald looked up expectantly when he returned to the table.

"You're right, a couple guys were asking for me.

They said they were with some alternative school back east, but Duane said they didn't seem to know much about our programs."

Lauren's brow creased. "What programs? You have classes on how to be a snow bunny?"

"That's not important," he said, brushing her question aside, but noted the way Gerald watched with interest. Damn, that man picked up on everything. "The point is, they're looking for me, too. After our close call with the car, we have to assume they aren't interested in asking a few polite questions."

No one spoke. Gerald appeared lost in thought, which meant he was in problem-solving mode. Having his father's assistant as a resource was reassuring, but Lauren still looked scared. Her fingernails were now in danger of being gnawed to their nail beds, and her gracefully arched brows were drawn flat with concern. Drew resisted the impulse to reach across the table and smooth a finger over those creases, to coax the spirit and determination back into her eyes. For some reason he had to keep fighting the urge to protect Lauren, even though she seemed perfectly capable of taking care of herself in most respects.

Except in love. In that area she seemed remarkably obtuse, deluding herself into believing she loved a man who was obviously wrong for her. He'd spent the night thinking of nothing else and was pretty sure he understood her problem. In her determination to be the family paragon of virtue, Lauren had tied herself to a man certain to keep her that way. A sensible, safe life with no adventure, no daring, no fun. Drew longed to show her what she was missing, to make those intriguing eyes sparkle with excitement.

His pulse quickened at the thought. And since she wouldn't be leaving now, he might get the chance to make it happen. Hell, he would make sure he got the chance. Sparkling eyes weren't nearly enough; he wanted to see her glow with desire. Make her heart race, her breath catch, and her body convulse with—

"We need a plan," she said.

He raised an eyebrow at her and smiled. He was already formulating one. "Oh, I agree."

A suspicious twitch made her eyes narrow before she nodded and relaxed. "Good. It'll be better if we can work together on this."

"Absolutely."

His easy agreement seemed to have her puzzled. She asked cautiously, "Do you have any ideas?"

"I certainly do."

"Great." She folded her arms on the table, leaning closer. "Let's hear it."

He lowered his voice confidentially. "It involves that dress you wore last night. Except without all the people and a lot less champagne." His glance slid toward Gerald, then back to her. "Are you sure you want me to get specific right now?"

"Yes," Gerald cut in. "We do."

Her eyes widened with shock, then turned stormy.

He smiled. If he couldn't have heated passion, he'd take heated anger. Not like that predictable, emotionless excuse for romance she was used to. Lauren didn't know it, but she was about to be liberated.

She should have seen it coming. The man was incapable of rational thought.

"Shut up," she snapped.

"I'm trying to help."

"I'll do without it. You're impossible."

Drew's lips slid into a crooked smile and her mind went fuzzy. "On the contrary. I intend to be very easy."

She pictured him being *very easy* while she had her way with him again, and her nude fantasy returned with full force. Wonderfully sensitive parts of her grew hot with anticipation.

"Ooh, my, this is an interesting development," Gerald said.

Lauren started. She'd forgotten about Gerald.

Removing his glasses, Gerald huffed a quick breath on each lens, polishing them with a napkin before returning them to his face. He scooted forward. "This is good. Don't stop now." He made an encouraging wave at Lauren. When she just stared, he looked between them. Considering the standoff, he smiled happily and wagged a finger at them both. "This time I'm pretty sure you two didn't have a fight."

"We didn't," Drew told him, his gaze still locked on hers. "In fact, Lauren was very friendly last night."

"Bite me," she said.

Drew grinned and wiggled an eyebrow. The heat spread to her fingers and toes.

"You don't say," Gerald said thoughtfully. "Details. Give me the details."

"No," they said in unison.

Gerald waited, but when they continued to ignore him, he sniffed his disappointment. "Okay, I can take a hint. I'll give you two fifteen minutes to come up with that plan, or I'm going home to help Steven paint the kitchen. Let me know if you figure out how to play nice with each other." He grabbed a muffin and left the room.

Lauren looked at Drew. On the positive side, she was so annoyed that she wasn't the least bit tempted to kiss him again. On the negative side, she was lying to herself; she was aching to kiss him again. She wanted to throw herself at him, lick his mouth all the way back to his tonsils, then open his shirt and work her way down his body. Her vision blurred just thinking about it.

"Are you hungover?"

"What?" She jolted back to reality. "Of course not."

"Because you look a little out of it. And you were awfully drunk last night."

"I wasn't the least bit drunk."

Damn. It was out of her mouth before she realized what she was saying.

Drew grinned, his direct gaze holding hers, before roaming over her hair, her face, her breasts. "So you remember *everything* that happened. That's good to know," he said.

She sucked in a shaky breath. "Why are you doing this to me?" It came out more whispery and pathetic than she'd intended.

"Because we both want me to."

She had no response to that. Groaning, Lauren propped her elbows on the table and dropped her head into her hands, clutching her hair. "We are *not* talking about this. We are going to come up with a plan to find my sister and your father, and figure out what's going on."

He sipped his coffee and considered her demand. "Okay."

"Okay?" She looked up suspiciously. "You mean you'll help me come up with a plan?"

"Not exactly." He held up a hand when he saw her temper flare. "I won't try to talk you out of it, because I understand how you feel. I feel the same way. But we start by talking to the Secret Service. That keeps you out of the line of fire, and they might have some leads by now."

"Fine." Now he was being sensible.

Drew leaned forward. "*Then* we talk about it."

From the intensity of his gaze, she had no doubt what "it" was. Her insides squirmed, and she looked away. "I think it would be best if we forgot it," she mumbled.

"Not possible."

She refused to meet his eyes, afraid of the way they made her heart flutter and her body want to do inappropriate things. A desire to run for safety, to call Jeff again, rose like panic in her chest.

"Don't run from me, Lauren," Drew said, his voice soft and low as he read her thoughts.

She looked up, startled. This was not fair. Her engagement ring was supposed to ward off advances from other men, but Drew wasn't following the rules. And she wasn't nearly as disinterested as she was supposed to be. Before she could figure out why, her thoughts were interrupted by an urgent shout.

"Hey! Get in here, quick!"

They turned in alarm, then pushed back their chairs and dashed toward the living room. Gerald stood before the TV, his half-eaten muffin on the coffee table.

"Look at this!" His finger jabbed toward the TV screen. "You neglected to mention this."

Lauren's eyes widened with surprise. "Hey, that's me! Why am I on TV?"

Drew stepped closer. "And me. And that's the fat guy we met, what's his name, Childers. What—"

"Shhh!" Gerald flapped his hands at them for silence.

A woman's voice narrated, "—was arrested as he left the Romanian Embassy last night. Police say he is charged with bribery and fraud, and is currently being held without bail." The picture disappeared and Lauren recognized Dana Zamecki, the blonde reporter who had waylaid Meg and Senator Creighton at the airport. Behind her, power cables snaked across the front lawn of a quiet residential neighborhood.

"Hey, that's your front yard," she said. She started toward the window, but Drew grabbed her arm and held her in place.

"But I want to see—"

Gerald waved her quiet again, as Dana continued, "Mr. Childers has been a major contributor to political campaigns, most notably that of Senator Harlan Creighton the third. The senator's wife and son were partying with Childers last night shortly before his arrest."

"Bitch," Gerald said.

"Vultures," Drew muttered.

Outraged, Lauren shushed them and stepped closer to the TV.

Dana looked excited about her news. "Police sources tell us they are investigating Mrs. Creighton's rumored ties to a political action group suspected of being a front for illegal campaign contributions."

"Uh-uh." Gerald shook his head vigorously. "That's

an outright lie. Meg didn't have ties to any local PACs. I did her background check."

Lauren ground her teeth. She was getting tired of hearing her sister insulted, criticized, and second-guessed. Reporters got away with too much simply by adding the word "rumor" to their accusations; Dana deserved to be confronted about that lie. Lauren glanced at the window. Conveniently, Dana was standing on the front lawn at this very moment. Lauren turned away with sudden determination.

"Hey," she heard Gerald say as she stalked toward the door. "Where are you going? You can't go out there!"

Alerted, Drew swore and yelled, "Lauren, don't!" but she had enough of a head start. She flung the front door open and had one foot on the porch before Drew grabbed her arm from behind.

"Get back inside," he hissed in her ear.

She shook him off. "I will, just as soon as I set that woman straight."

Crowding next to Drew, Gerald grabbed a handful of her sweater. "Don't talk to them," he pleaded.

She reached behind her to swat at his hand. "Let go."

Something jabbed her chin. As she turned, Dana pulled the microphone back a scant inch and said, "Mrs. Creighton! Could you comment on Bud Childers's arrest?"

Lauren could have taken a bite out of the microphone, it was so close. As she parted her lips to snap out a response, Miss Blonde Ambition hit her with the next question.

"What does your husband have to say about Mr. Childers's claim that you and the senator's son accepted a fifty thousand dollar bribe on Senator Creighton's behalf just last night?"

Lauren blinked at the woman, stunned. "What?"

Before she could utter more, Drew's hand landed on her shoulders and yanked her back inside. Gerald slammed the door behind them, nearly crushing the microphone.

The foyer wall was at her back, and Drew's face was in front of her. Anger flattened the sexy curve of his lip, although it was still attractive enough at this close range to keep her attention. Even when he ground his teeth like that.

Gerald didn't bother fighting for control. He waved a finger under her nose and scolded, "You nearly broke the first commandment, young lady: Never speak to the press without consulting me first." His voice grew menacing enough for scary bedtime stories. "Remember this: Reporters will eat you alive, then fight over your bones. They are bad, bad people. Do you understand?"

She nodded, then looked warily back at Drew.

"Gerald's right," he told her firmly.

"I remember. Gerald's always right."

"And don't you forget it," Gerald harrumphed. She nodded again, meekly, which seemed to pacify him. "Excuse me while I get rid of the Evil Witch of the Potomac," he grumbled, pushing past Drew to slip out the front door.

Drew still held her shoulders to the wall, and Lauren squirmed under his gaze. If he meant to intimidate her with his size, it wasn't working, because she was getting a hot tingle of awareness that had nothing to do with intimidation.

"I'm sorry," she said.

"Good."

"You can let me go now. I promise I won't talk to the press." He didn't move. She wasn't even sure he heard her. "Drew?"

He squinted thoughtfully. "What color are your eyes?"

"What?"

His brows puckered. "Sometimes they look green, and sometimes they look gray, like now. What color are they?"

"Hazel."

His deep stare softened, and so did his mouth. "Yeah?"

Geez, how could he do that with one word? A pleasant pressure built between her thighs and her temperature soared along with her pulse. Not that her mind wasn't still capable of composing a brilliant response. "Yeah," she said.

He seemed to find that wonderfully incisive. His lips curved even more, and her lungs collapsed with a deep sigh. God, the things she wanted to do to that mouth.

"I like them."

"Huh?" Had she actually suggested something aloud?

"Your eyes. They're pretty."

"Oh. Thank you."

Her sparkling conversation was having an effect; his smile grew even wider. He moved closer.

Lauren flattened against the wall, but Drew's forearms did too, framing either side of her head and bringing his face inches away from her own. She struggled to remember why she was supposed to resist him. It had something to do with morals. With one tiny move she could have her lips sealed against his. Her breasts picked up the warm tingle from below and arched toward him. If he would just lean a little closer . . .

He did, his chest brushing exquisitely against her nipples and his mouth grazing the side of hers. She closed her eyes and waited, breathing heavily and trying to resist temptation.

"You know what I think you should do?" he asked against her trembling lip.

"What?" she asked, her voice tremulous.

His lips brushed her cheek as he whispered in her ear, sending shivers down her neck, all the way to her toes. "I think you should call Jeff."

Her fantasy crashed. "What?"

His face drew back enough for her to see his dark blue eyes and feel the warmth of his breath. One hand lifted off the wall and his fingers caressed her cheek, then trailed a fiery line down her neck. "If you're about to cheat on the poor man, the least you can do is break up with him first."

Just because he was dead on target didn't mean he wasn't an arrogant ass. "Cheat? Why, you insufferable—" she began, but her words were smothered by his mouth as his lips covered hers and his tongue plunged right into her startled open mouth. His hands left the wall and cupped her face, holding it still as his tongue sought hers and his chest pressed her against the wall.

She maintained her indignation for a full second, then melted under the heat building inside her.

Whether her mind consented or not, it seemed her body was more than willing to follow Drew's lead.

She stopped resisting.

With a moan that hummed from her mouth into his, she reached up to pull him closer, an effort that was physically impossible. Lauren heard herself make urgent, happy little sounds as she raised her knee against the side of his leg. He responded, pressing her to the wall so firmly that she felt the hard line of his erection. Just as she was trying to devise a way to slip a hand between them, the door burst open, then slammed shut again.

They parted like guilty teenagers.

"Ha! I dispersed the vile hordes," Gerald gloated, "and I threatened their evil queen with a lawsuit if she so much as implied bribery without hard evidence . . ." His voice trailed off as he looked at them. "What's wrong?"

"Nothing." Drew propped one hand on the wall and half turned toward Gerald, keeping the front of his pants from view.

"We were just talking," Lauren said. "Arguing, actually." That sounded more realistic.

"I see. Well, continue. I have to check out her report, then contact the Secret Service and light a fire under someone's ass. They haven't told us a thing about their investigation, and it seems to be more complex than we knew." He took a few steps, then glanced back. "By the way, Andrew, that shade of lipstick really isn't you. I'd go with more brown tones."

"Damn," Drew muttered to Gerald's back. "That man knows everything that happens around here."

She stifled a nervous giggle. "We made it pretty easy." Lauren used her finger to wipe lipstick from his upper lip. When his interested gaze settled on her, she withdrew her hand. "I think I'll go see what Gerald can find out about those men who tried to kidnap me."

He smiled as she edged away. "It's not me you're afraid of, you know. You're afraid of yourself."

She didn't bother responding, because this time she knew he was right. She was scared to death of the powerful attraction she felt for a man who was all wrong for her.

He was right about something else, too. She needed to call Jeff.

Chapter Eight

"For heaven's sake, Lauren, I'm at work. Is this important?"

Jeff's dedication to Duchaine Properties was admirable and she'd never infringed on his work time before. "Yes, it's terribly important. I'm having doubts, Jeff." Scooting the senator's office chair closer to the desk, she clutched the phone in a white-knuckled grip, waiting for his reply.

"Why would you have doubts? I thought we already decided you're coming home." He hated indecision, and she could hear it in his voice.

"Not about that. About us."

"What do you mean, us? Our plans? Oh, I see. This is about not being able to visit Uncle John and Aunt Betty, isn't it? That's a good point. Maybe you should go there before you come home."

"No, no," she cut in. "I'm having doubts about our relationship."

After a moment of tense silence during which she heard his desk chair squeak as he sat down, he spoke cautiously. "I don't think I understand. What sort of doubts?"

Lauren instantly recalled the blinding hot desire that had ripped through her at Drew's kiss. "Don't you ever feel that something is missing between us, Jeff?"

"Does this have something to do with that embassy party? It must have been glamorous, maybe seductively so. Are you dissatisfied with our social life?"

She sighed. "No, Jeff. I'm not talking about our social life." Although now that she thought about it, there was room for improvement there, too. "I mean, don't you feel something is missing in our personal relationship? Something spontaneous and passionate?"

"We aren't teenagers, Lauren." His words came out in a careful, slow cadence, as if she had become too dense to comprehend his regular speech pattern. "We are mature adults who know how to exercise control. Passion fades. You need a steady, dependable relationship."

"I thought I did," she murmured.

Jeff's voice was soothing. "We do have passion, darling. It's simply not something one indulges outside the proper time and place. You know I have always been impressed with the example you tried to set for your sister, showing her that it was possible to build a strong, steady relationship rather than hopping from one bed to another." He paused. "Is this about Meg? Does something about her wild life in Washington actually seem appealing to you?"

"No, it has nothing to do with Meg or Washington."

There was a longer hesitation this time. "This isn't about phone sex again, is it?" When she didn't answer right away, she knew he'd made the leap to something even more worrisome. "Lauren, please tell me there's not some other technique you want to try."

She rubbed the frown lines that crossed her forehead. "No, it's not about phone sex. It's about *us*. It's about *me*. I didn't realize I could feel a passionate attraction to someone else, Jeff. An attraction I don't want to resist. But it turns out that I can, and that means something must be missing in our relationship."

"Who is he, Lauren?" Jeff's voice had gone flat with anger. Controlled anger. "That philandering son of Meg's boss? Does he seem appealing to you and your new, liberated sexual ideas?"

"It doesn't matter who. What matters is that I don't feel that with you, and I want to feel it."

"Are you talking about breaking up?" His voice rose with disbelief. "That's absurd, we have plans. Do you know how much that will disappoint our families? My mother has already arranged for you to be invited to join the Luncheon Ladies at the club."

"The what? Jeff, I'm not interested in that kind of stuff."

"Why? Because you're more interested in phone sex?"

"For God's sake, forget the phone sex." She sighed. "I'm not the right woman for you. Staying engaged, keeping you from someone else, would be selfish. You deserve to find someone who can be as"—*don't say dry and colorless,* she cautioned herself—"as mature and controlled as you are."

"I did find someone like that. Or at least, I thought I did." His voice became bitter. "But I guess I was wrong. Do you really want to throw away three years of our lives?"

I already have, she thought. *I just don't want it to be more.*

"I'm sorry," she said with honest regret. "This won't work. I gave in to whatever you wanted for three years. I'm done."

She'd expected that admission to hurt, but it felt surprisingly good.

Irritation crept into his voice. "What's happened to you, Lauren? You've always been so levelheaded. I don't know what's gotten into you." He used what he thought was his worst threat. "Do you want to turn into Meg?"

Did she? Did she want to follow her impulses instead of worrying about what was sensible and practical? Did she want to be like her sister and wear black stockings and thong underpants? Did she want to have a passionate affair with a man who was interested in her uninhibited, impractical side? Visions of Drew wearing nothing but her bedsheets and kissing her into that promised pool of wet desire scorched her mind.

"Yes, that's exactly what I want."

"Fine." It had only taken him a few seconds to adjust to it. "Then I guess it's best that we break up because I don't want to be married to a woman like Meg. I certainly couldn't have a woman like that hosting dinner parties and taking tennis lessons at the club, so I guess I should thank you for admitting this to me before it's too late."

He made marriage to him sound like a death sentence, which was probably pretty accurate.

"You know, my mother warned me about you."

She sighed, knowing what was coming.

"She said Meg was proof that you had bad genes,

and that you'd turn out to be like your sister. I should have listened."

Lauren smiled. "Tell her I said thanks for the compliment."

He made a disgusted *tsch* sound. "That's just immature, Lauren. God, I should have seen this coming when you suggested that perverted phone sex." His voice took on a dark edge. "This is a phase, you know. You're going to get over it, and you're going to realize what you've lost. But it'll be too late to get me back."

It was probably a good thing he couldn't see her careless shrug. "Then I guess I'll just have to live with that, won't I?"

"You're damn right you will, and I'm sorry to say this, but I hope you get everything you have coming to you."

She actually had to bite her lip to keep from adding her eager agreement. If she got half of what Drew had promised, she figured she would come out ahead. In a voice tight from holding back a giggle, she said, "That's fair. 'Bye, Jeff."

The phone clicked on the other end, followed by a dial tone.

Sitting back in the chair, she did a quick assessment of her feelings. No sadness, no regret. Just the sense that a huge weight had been lifted off her chest.

That was good, because there were more important things to worry about right now. Like what the half-drunk, disreputable Mr. Childers had been up to. By now, Gerald had probably figured it out.

"I don't know how they did it, but it's there. Fifty thousand dollars, deposited into the senator's account on Friday." Gerald pointed to the computer screen.

"How did someone get his account number?" Drew asked.

Gerald shrugged. "Maybe someone has connections at the bank. Or enough power to bypass them."

"We didn't even meet Childers until Saturday night, though. The deposit was made Friday." Drew looked at Lauren. "Someone wanted to make it look like my dad had accepted a bribe, and their plan was in motion before we even got there. Getting our picture with him was just a bonus."

"But we still don't know who's doing this and why." Frustrated, Lauren dropped into one of the leather wingback chairs facing Gerald's desk. His office was small, but tidy and well-appointed. "In fact, we don't know *anything*. We don't know who wants to kidnap Meg, or why she has X-rated pictures of herself, or even why one of the president's advisors hates her. We don't even know if they're really married."

Gerald looked confused. "Why would you think they aren't married?"

"Lauren thinks it's significant that we can't find their marriage license."

"I didn't know you were looking for it," Gerald said. "I have it."

Lauren mentally cuffed herself on the head. "Can I see it?"

He shrugged and opened a desk drawer, pulled out a file folder, and retrieved the document. He passed it to her, and Drew leaned over her shoulder while she fingered the official State of Maryland seal.

"Looks real enough to me," Drew said.

It did to her, too, darn it. Megan Colleen Sutherland married Harlan Andrew Creighton III in a civil ceremony on the seventeenth day of. . . . Startled, she looked up. "Hey, according to this they were married two weeks ago!"

"Let me see." Drew reached for it over her shoulder, surprising her as his hand brushed her breast. Her nipples tingled and tightened. Boy, was she a goner.

"You're right. But Dad didn't call me until four days ago, and I got here the next morning."

"Me, too." She looked at Gerald, who shifted uncomfortably.

"Hey, don't blame me, it wasn't my decision. I'm just his assistant."

Gerald was too competent to ever be "just" an assistant. She lifted an eyebrow and stared him down.

He threw his hands up in the air. "I told them to call you guys, and the senator said they would as soon as they got back from their honeymoon. He didn't tell Miranda, either. Still hasn't, as far as I know."

Apparently, Drew's sister didn't follow political gossip any more than he did if she still didn't know about her father's marriage.

"I would have told you if I thought it made a difference. I swear!" He raised his right hand as if taking a solemn oath. "But it doesn't." He looked at Drew. "Does it?"

"I don't know," he growled. "It's just one more weird thing, and I don't like it."

"I agree," Lauren said. "They waited ten days before telling us, we get here on day eleven, and they sneak out of town on day twelve without even seeing us." She shook her head. "It doesn't make sense."

Gerald raised his shoulders helplessly. "I know. Maybe they just wanted some time to themselves."

Drew cocked his head suspiciously. "Really? Were they living together? 'Cause it didn't look like it to us."

Gerald put a hand to his chest and blinked innocently. "How would I know?"

Drew's mouth twisted. "Am I supposed to believe that? Come on, you know everything."

"Okay, okay." Gerald gave up easily, assuming a haughty expression. "I pay attention to details, and sometimes I overhear things that maybe I'm not supposed to hear. It's part of my naturally inquisitive nature." He ignored Drew's snort. "But I couldn't find out anything about their living arrangements. They weren't around much during those two weeks; I don't think either of them slept here."

Lauren looked from one to the other. "Why not? Where were they?"

"A hotel?" Gerald speculated.

Drew shook his head. "That doesn't make sense. They could have all the privacy they wanted here or at Meg's apartment. All Dad had to do was tell you to take some vacation time." When no one else offered an explanation, he slapped the marriage certificate onto the desk."

"I know. But what can we do?" Gerald asked.

"Lauren says we need a plan, so we'll put our heads together and come up with one. Go paint your kitchen with Steven. We'll call if we hear anything."

"Shoot. Okay," Gerald agreed, dejected. "But you have to talk to the FBI and find out what they're doing to catch those two guys. They said they'd send someone over."

"The FBI? What are they doing in this?"

Gerald made a face. "It's the appearance of bribery. Very serious stuff, and everyone wants a piece of the action."

"Okay, don't worry, I'll handle it."

Gerald seemed reluctant to entrust them with interviewing the FBI, but he left. It wasn't until he was gone and silence descended on the house that Lauren realized her situation: She was alone with Drew.

She was still in the senator's office when Drew returned from seeing Gerald out. She raised her eyes cautiously. He leaned on the doorjamb, arms folded, direct gaze seeming to take her measure. Warm pressure built between her thighs the second her eyes met his, and she felt her cheeks flush. Arousal seemed to have become a conditioned reaction.

The corner of his mouth quirked in response to her discomfort. "So, Lauren, what's the plan?"

His eyebrow did a tiny, suggestive jump. Obviously, he wasn't referring to a plan to find blackmailers, kidnappers, and missing persons. The smug bastard.

"Don't get your hopes up, Drew. It has nothing to do with me ravishing your naked body." What a lie.

"You, me, what's the difference who does the ravishing, as long as we're both naked."

Her body tingled. "Degenerate."

"Lucky you, just what you need."

Lauren nibbled a fingernail. It was what she wanted, too. Desperately. And since she'd melted all over him like hot butter during that last kiss, he knew it, too.

He had a risky sort of appeal, the kind that sucked the air out of her lungs and shot tracers of liquid fire through her body. If a kiss could cause that sort of spark and sizzle, making love with him would probably short-circuit her whole body. She'd never experienced that sort of electric jolt when she kissed Jeff. If she'd known it was possible, she wouldn't have spent the last three years trying to convince herself that his sedate, steady influence was what she needed. She'd take a thrilling zing in her neurons over Jeff's anesthetized version of life any day.

She and Jeff had been more committed to strict principals than to each other. It was a mistake she didn't want to make again. She obviously needed to do some serious reflecting before venturing into a relationship again.

But a fling. That didn't require common sense or commitments. Just infatuation and desire, qualities she had in abundance every time she got close to Drew. The man created itches deep inside her that urgently needed scratching.

She was weighing her desires against her common sense when the doorbell rang. Drew glanced toward the front door, back to her, then released a resigned sigh as he straightened. "Don't lose your place," he said, and went to answer the door. As if he'd been reading her mind.

The FBI agent was earnest, professional, and driving him crazy.

Drew had repeated all the information they'd given Detective Rasmussen, heard all the assurances about the FBI's experience with missing persons investigations, and listened to the reasons they should sit tight and let the federal agents do their jobs. He didn't even bother to mention that it was all redundant with the Secret Service already on the case. Now if the man would just skip the hand-holding part and get the hell out, Drew was confident he could reignite that flame in Lauren. He couldn't wait to kiss her again and remind them both of the incredible attraction that sizzled between them. He felt it every time they made eye contact, and from the slightly dizzy look in Lauren's gray-green eyes, he knew she felt it, too.

What he couldn't tell was whether she felt the same emotions he did, crackling beneath that current of desire. He wasn't ready to examine it closely, but he felt it humming every time she defended her sister or smacked down his cocky remarks. She was spirited and loyal and willing to do whatever it took to find Meg. He was falling hard, and he didn't care. Between his feelings and their chemistry, this promised to be the most explosive sex he'd ever had.

And Mr. Important Government Agent was getting in the way.

He had finally tapped into the instinctive, passionate Lauren who kissed like fire and responded to his touch like a wild inferno. Now the careful, sensible Lauren was probably wondering if she should put out the flames he'd ignited.

After nearly two hours of reviewing their case Drew was yawning with boredom, and even Lauren had excused herself to order a pizza. She'd come back, but stood near the door, looking like she might bolt any second. The fed was totally killing the mood.

"Well, I'm impressed," he told the agent. "It looks like you've got it under control. Thanks for stopping by."

The agent nodded, not taking the hint. Glancing around the living room, and into the adjoining study, he said, "Nice place Senator Creighton has here."

"Yes, it is." Drew stood, but the agent was either too obtuse or too intent on his job to follow Drew's lead.

"Good security system?"

"The best. We'll be fine."

"Hmm." The man finally rose, but instead of heading toward the front door, he walked to a window where he checked the latch and security sensors. "Looks pretty good."

Drew ground his teeth. "Like I said, it's the best."

"Silent alarm?"

"No, it's loud enough to wake half of Washington."

"How about a guard dog?"

Drew frowned. "Is there some reason you think we aren't safe here?"

"Just being thorough." He gave a reassuring smile. "How about—"

"Look, the house is secure," Drew interrupted. "And we have every confidence that you'll keep us safe." He strode across the room and offered his hand in an obvious invitation to leave. "I know you need to concentrate on finding Senator Creighton and Meg, so I'll let you go. Thanks for your time."

The agent reluctantly shook hands. "You're welcome, Mr. Creighton. Like I said, it's no trouble for me to stay if you two feel insecure about your safety—"

"No need. We feel absolutely safe and secure, don't we, Lauren?"

She angled a heavy-lidded glance his way. "For the moment."

Drew slapped the man on the back. "Miss Sutherland likes to take life moment by moment. She's the impulsive, thrill-seeking type." Drew grinned at Lauren as he propelled the man toward the door, and saw an amused twitch at the corner of her mouth. Good: She was still with him.

"As long as you're sure . . ."

"Positive. Call us if there are any developments." Drew handed the agent his coat and ushered him out before he could think up any more questions. The man had been amazingly inquisitive, considering Gerald had to demand this meeting. Next time they'd settle for a phone update. He slammed the door and bolted it.

"I feel better now that I've talked to them, don't you?" Lauren spoke from the wide entryway to the living room. "Knowing those two men who attacked us might be the same ones they've been investigating for bribery and fraud. It sort of ties the whole thing together."

"Yeah, I feel better, too." A whole lot better, in fact, now that the eager beaver agent was gone.

He tried to assess her mood, but he couldn't read her. With her jeans, T-shirt, sneakers, and casual-but-perfect hairstyle she looked like the wholesome girl next door. He could easily picture her skiing the slopes with him or curled beside him in front of his fireplace while the snow piled up outside. But with a simple tilt of her head, her eyes took on a sultry look and the homey scene in his imagination altered abruptly. He saw the same fireplace, but now she was stretched out on the rug before it, naked and glowing from the flames licking behind her. Or maybe the flames were inside him, he wasn't sure. The same way he wasn't sure why he kept picturing her in his house.

She bit her lip as she watched him. "With the Secret Service and FBI taking over, I suppose we don't need to make a plan now."

"That's ironic, because I just made one," he said.

He noticed the startled flicker of awareness before she settled a confident gaze on him. "Really?" Her lashes lowered as she assessed him. "What are you going to do?"

Good question. "That depends," he said, moving toward her. "Which Lauren am I talking to?"

She didn't back away, just arched an eyebrow. "There's more than one?"

He nodded. "Oh, yes. There's the proper, sensible Lauren, the practical financial manager, and there's the more daring, spirited Lauren who's been hiding behind the first one, who follows her passions."

"How do you know that second one is there?" Her voice was teasing, but he sensed a real curiosity behind the question.

"If you have any doubts, I'll be glad to introduce her to you." He brushed a lock of hair aside and looked into her eyes. "Which one am I talking to?"

She gave it careful consideration. "I'm the unattached Lauren."

She followed his gaze down to her left ring finger and seemed surprised to see the diamond there. Embarrassed, she twisted and tugged until she had the ring off. Without a backward glance, she tossed it over her shoulder. Drew watched it bounce off the living room sofa and land on the carpet. "*Completely* unattached," she repeated.

He pulled her into his arms, no more than two steps from where he'd pinned her to the wall that morning. "I'm developing a fondness for this particular part of the house," he murmured against her mouth, before sinking into a kiss that felt as hot as molten lava and as natural as coming home.

Lauren's arms locked around his neck, one hand gripping his shoulder and the other fisting in his hair, while her mouth opened for him with eager passion. Her tongue was warm and wet, actively matching each of his strokes, as her fingers massaged his body. Sexy little sounds rose from her throat and were smothered against his mouth. She seemed helpless to fight the desire that gripped her and that turned him on even more than the wild excitement of her mouth.

His hands roamed down her back to her soft bottom, pressing every part of her to him. Her body squirmed against his, rubbing purposefully across his erection. Drew groaned and backed her against the wall. They hit with an awkward thump, but their kisses never missed a beat. He leaned against her, pressing into every curve. If they got any closer he'd be inside her, which was exactly where he wanted to be.

One hand rose to find her breast and she arched into it, whimpering when his thumb passed over the hard nub of her nipple. He sucked on her lower lip, kissed her firmly once more, then moved his mouth away from hers just long enough to utter a succinct, "Upstairs." No other words seemed necessary.

"Mmm," she replied against his lips, licking and nibbling and driving him insane. "That sounds like a good idea."

He dragged her into one last deep kiss, then whispered

harshly, "Let's go," just as the doorbell chimed over their heads. He jumped like it had been a gunshot.

"What the hell?"

Lauren's foggy expression cleared. "Pizza delivery."

"Let's ignore him."

She grabbed his arm. "Wait, I want food. Besides," her eyelids lowered seductively, "you're about to work up a very big appetite. I promise. Take ten seconds to pay the man and I'll demonstrate."

He growled with a different sort of hunger.

"Damn." He reached for the wallet in his back pocket, shifting uncomfortably as he pulled against the snug fit in the front of his jeans. He pulled out bills while she opened the door. A crack of sunlight and cool air entered, then disappeared in a whoosh as she slammed the door shut. Panic widened Lauren's eyes as she stood with her back to the door.

"What's wrong?"

"It's Trenchcoat," she whispered, as if the man could hear her through the heavy door.

"Who?"

"The guy in the Burberry trench coat who hangs out with Hawknose, the guy with the gun."

Drew froze. "The man who tried to kidnap you is standing at our front door?"

"He's delivering our pizza," she squeaked. "He's wearing the pizza place's jacket and he's holding my extra large with mushrooms and green peppers, but I know it's Trenchcoat. I recognize him."

"Shit." He stuffed the wallet back in his pocket, his arousal already flagging. The doorbell rang again as he gave hurried directions. "Step back as you open the door, so he has to come inside. And talk to him so he keeps looking at you." He positioned himself to be behind the arc of the opening door, waiting tensely. "Go."

Lauren's face was still flushed and her hair slightly tousled. Drew hoped Trenchcoat found the sight as incredibly distracting as he did. If the man kept his eyes on Lauren, Drew felt confident of his ability to take him down.

She didn't question him, just turned to do what he asked. The door opened, forcing Drew backward. Following directions, Lauren stepped away, saying "Come on in," with such a slight quiver in her voice that he was sure the other man never detected it. Past the edge of the open door, Drew watched a red-jacketed man step into the foyer, a large pizza box in his hands. Trenchcoat.

Drew moved forward silently, stopping behind him. Reaching out, he tapped the man on the shoulder. Trenchcoat gave a startled jump and turned his head. Ready for the move, Drew aimed his fist at the man's jaw and threw his hardest punch.

Trenchcoat grunted and crashed against the open door. The pizza box dropped. Lauren darted forward, caught the box, and stepped back again as the man teetered like a drunk and fell to his knees. Raising a confused face, Trenchcoat tried to focus on the person before him. "Mrs. Creighton?" he asked, blinking dizzily. Drew caught him with a second punch, snapping the man's head sideways. His body followed, crumpling to the slate floor.

"Wow," Lauren said.

Drew grimaced and shook the pain from his hand. "Please tell me you're still sure that's the same man."

She bent over the unconscious figure. "That's him."

"Good." He noticed the pizza box in her hands and smiled. "Nice save."

She smiled back, losing some of her tension. Stepping over the man on the floor, he put his hands on her shoulders. He couldn't get closer while she held the pizza box between them. "Hey, I'm sorry I made you put yourself in front of him like that, even for a few seconds. I didn't think about how scary that might be for you."

She shrugged. "It was, a little, but I'm okay."

He smiled. "That's all I care about. Let's find out who this jerk is." Bending over the still form, Drew unzipped the red jacket and felt around. He found what he was looking for in the man's shirt pocket. Standing, he flipped open the thin leather ID holder.

And froze. "Oh, shit."

"No kidding," Lauren said, peeking inside the pizza box. "They gave us olives instead of green peppers."

"Not that, sweetheart." He held the open ID for her inspection. "This."

Her face paled. "Oh, shit," she agreed. She met his eyes. "Secret Service?"

Drew ran his hand through his hair. "We've captured a Secret Service agent. Swell."

Lauren didn't trust the man, even in his unconscious state. She stood several feet away, clutching the pizza box. "Maybe we should tie him up."

Drew was one step ahead of her. He had already yanked off his belt and was using it to fasten the man's hands behind his back.

"How can he be Secret Service?" she asked. "That man and his partner tried to kidnap me. At gunpoint! I thought Secret Service were the good guys."

"It's probably a fake ID," he said, cinching the belt around the man's wrists.

"That FBI agent told us the guys who tried to kidnap us were probably part of the bribery scam. He didn't say they might be Secret Service agents."

"That's what I'm saying, it's probably a fake ID. Or else that twerp didn't know what he was talking about, which wouldn't surprise me either."

Drew rolled the guy over, reached inside his jacket and came out with a gun. Lauren bit back a gasp, but Drew handled the gun confidently, looking it over before tucking it into the back of his waistband.

He folded his arms and surveyed the trussed agent. "Whoever he is, let's hope he's not the real thing. I could probably get several years in prison for knocking out an agent and a few more just for tying him up."

"No you won't, you were just protecting me." Drew hauled the moaning Secret Service agent to a sitting position and slapped his face. "Come on, fella, you're messing with my love life. Wake up."

His groggy eyes gradually opened. The man squinted first at Drew, then Lauren. Jerking his arms and finding himself bound, he aimed a nasty look at Drew, who gazed back, unmoved. With only the pizza box between her and her attempted kidnapper, Lauren moved closer to Drew and felt his arm come around her waist. That was much safer.

Gingerly, the man licked a drop of blood off his puffy lower lip and raised his eyes to Lauren. "Mrs.

Creighton, I give up," he said in a weary voice. "I'm tired of chasing you. Would you please just tell me why you don't want me to protect you?"

Lauren's mouth dropped open. "Protect me? You tried to abduct me! And I'm not Mrs. Creighton."

"I did not—" He paused with a frown, appearing to doubt what he'd heard. "What do you mean, you're not Mrs. Creighton?"

"Mrs. Creighton is my sister, Megan. My name is Lauren." She didn't see any harm in telling him. At least he might stop trying to kidnap her.

The man's voice sounded confused. "Sister? I was told to pick up the Senator and Mrs. Creighton and take them to a safe house. I wasn't told about a sister."

"Who didn't tell you?" Drew cut in. "Who are you working for?"

"Secret Service. The name's Agent Chapman."

"Yes, Dwayne Chapman." Drew flashed the ID he still held. "I see that. But can I believe it?"

"Why wouldn't you believe it? Oh, yeah, because you get your kicks out of attacking agents and smashing them to the ground. Thanks a lot for that." He took a few moments to get his sneer under control. "Listen, I don't know what's going on with you people, but if you don't untie me and let me call my partner, you're going to have a whole team of agents storming this house in five minutes." He tested the belt confining his arms again and must have noticed the missing bulk behind him. He shot Drew a hard look. "And give me my gun."

"No," Drew replied. "First you make the call. Then I make a call, and if I'm satisfied you're who you say you are, you get the gun."

Their staredown lasted several seconds. "Goddamn it," Chapman finally grumbled. "Okay. But hurry up."

When Drew released his hands, Agent Chapman called someone Lauren presumed to be Hawknose, explaining in clipped words that he was talking to the subjects and would be out in fifteen minutes. He disconnected and wordlessly handed over the cell phone. While Drew called a number he got from Gerald's desk, Chapman tested the movement in his jaw, wincing with each motion. Lauren hoped he didn't expect an apology. The man had scared her to death, and Drew had obviously reached his limit of tolerance with Secret Service agents.

When Drew's call ended, he flipped his phone shut and told her, "The agency confirmed his identity. He's authentic."

She didn't know whether to be relieved or not. That meant they had a legitimately pissed off agent on their hands.

"Damn right I'm authentic," Chapman said. He stuck his hand out, fixing Drew with a cold stare until his gun and ID folder were handed back. He tucked them away and looked only partially mollified as he said, "So now do you want to explain what the fuck's going on here?"

"I think all of us have some questions," Drew told him, folding his arms. "How do you feel about mushrooms and olives?"

He'd declined the pizza, but it was well past lunch time and Lauren quickly put away two pieces while Agent Chapman complained about his sore jaw.

"Damn, you hit me hard. I think I have a loose tooth."

"Sorry," Drew said, not looking sorry. "If I'd known Secret Service agents were dressing in Gino's Pizza jackets these days, I would have restrained myself."

"I needed a cover. When you ordered the pizza, it gave us an opportunity to get in the house without drawing attention."

Lauren lowered her third slice of pizza. "You heard me order pizza?" Her voice rose with outrage. "You tapped our phones?"

He seemed surprised that she asked. "Of course we did. We couldn't get bugs planted, and we had to know if you were being threatened by someone."

Having her phone conversations overheard could be embarrassing. Thinking back, she decided it was more embarrassing for Jeff than her; someone must have had a good time listening to his stilted attempt at phone sex. That one could become a department classic.

Drew, on the other hand, couldn't seem to have a conversation with her without throwing in a sexual innuendo. Her gaze skimmed his shoulders and legs, and she remembered stroking a hand down to clutch that tight, muscular butt. Hell, his whole body was sexually suggestive. Taking a thoughtful bite, she considered some of the possible results of exploring those suggestions.

"Lauren? Are you listening?"

"Hmm?" She focused on Drew's concerned face. "Yeah, he tapped the phones."

"Because Dad and Meg volunteered to help them catch whoever has been blackmailing senators."

"They did?" She frowned at Agent Chapman. "Is that what this is about? Where's my sister? Is she okay?"

He shrugged. "I don't know. Until a couple minutes ago, I thought you were Meg."

A tiny flutter of panic tightened Lauren's chest. "What do you mean, you don't know? I thought you were Secret Service. I thought you were experts at protecting people."

She'd obviously hit a nerve. Before Chapman could snap out a defensive reply, Drew diverted his attention.

"Why did you let them help you? My dad and Meg are civilians, and catching blackmailers sounds dangerous."

The agent relaxed slightly at hearing a question he could deal with. "We didn't have much choice. They're targeting senators, and we couldn't exactly put someone undercover, pretending to be a senator. We were lucky Senator Creighton was willing to do it. These guys are using sexual indiscretions as blackmail, and he's impervious. The senator is, um"—he glanced hesitantly at Drew—"he's known to date around."

"You mean he's a womanizer," Drew said in a flat voice.

"Well, yeah. You can't blackmail someone who looks at a picture of himself in bed with a woman and asks for enlargements." At Drew's cool look, Chapman cleared his throat and continued. "Senator Creighton came to us when another senator, a friend of his, received some revealing pictures, along with instructions on how to vote on an upcoming bill. That senator wasn't willing to risk an otherwise solid marriage to catch whoever did it. Senator Creighton wouldn't tell us who the first victim was, but he and his secretary volunteered to make themselves potential targets to help us catch these guys."

The pieces fell together. "You mean they pretended to get married so someone could attempt to blackmail Senator Creighton when he continued to see his current girlfriend," Lauren said.

"Exactly."

"Then they aren't really married!" she exclaimed.

"Not exactly. Sort of." Seeing Lauren's impatient look, he explained, "There wasn't a ceremony, but we filed a real certificate with the state of Maryland. If the press tracked it down, it had to look real. So officially, Maryland says they're married."

"Get to what happened," Drew said. "Someone took pictures of my dad and tried to blackmail him?"

Chapman shifted in his seat, looked away, then back at Drew. "We don't know. He received something, an envelope, we think, but that's when they both panicked and ran. We never saw what it was."

Lauren thought of the pictures in the safe deposit box, and her alarmed gaze flew to Drew. He shook his head, warning her to be silent. "Why? Where did they go?"

"I wish to hell I knew. We think they must have received a threat to their lives. My partner and I were watching the house so we could take them into protective custody as soon as they received the bribe. But apparently the bribe went to the senator's office in the regular mail delivery and they didn't tell us. Tuesday morning Meg left for work and never came back. Senator Creighton checked in to say she'd made an overnight trip for him, but then he disappeared the next morning so he must have been covering for her until she got away. That's when you arrived, Miss Sutherland, and we thought you were Meg. We tried to get you away from this guy," he nodded at Drew, "when he seemed to be forcing you to go places with him. The bank, the senator's office. We thought he was holding Senator Creighton somewhere until he got what he wanted from you."

"Well, he isn't." He didn't have to. When she risked a glance at him, the amused lift of his eyebrow made her falter. God, she loved when he did that. It also distracted the hell out of her. She fastened her gaze on Agent Chapman. "What's the problem? Everyone knows where they ran to. They're somewhere in the Virgin Islands. Doesn't the government have ways of tracking them down?"

"Yes, we do," Chapman snapped, obviously resentful at having to explain his whole case. "That's how we know they aren't there. They were at the airport, and they obviously wanted us, or someone else, to think they left, but they never boarded a flight. They disappeared, and we don't know why."

She put down her half-eaten slice of pizza. "You lost them? Do you mean to say you have absolutely no idea where they are?"

He didn't seem to care for her wording. "Ma'am, people generally want our protection. We aren't used to people running from us, and we can't protect them if they don't cooperate. Senator Creighton and his secretary didn't do what they were told."

That was his excuse for allowing an endangered United States senator and his wife to disappear? She stared, unable to speak. Drew knuckled a spot on his forehead, as if talking with Chapman was giving him a headache. "Do you know anything about the money that was deposited into my dad's account last Friday?" he asked.

"Yeah, I do. That was another attempt to pressure the Senator into doing what they want, and you two made it simple, showing up at that party. All they had to do was pay some idiot to pose for a picture with you, then make sure the D.C. police pick him up on trumped up charges. *Bingo,* Senate bribes are headline news, and you guys provide the perfect proof that Senator Creighton is involved. Nice going."

Drew became still—too still. Lauren noticed the tiny muscles clench in his jaw. Remembering the surprising effectiveness of his first attack on Chapman, she hurriedly said, "We're sorry about that. We never would have done it if we'd known what was going on. You could have informed us, you know."

Drew's hard gaze never left Chapman as the agent slid a sour look her way. "We didn't know who you were."

"You do now. Did you find out which bank employee deposited the money into the senator's account?"

Chapman shot her a close look. "What makes you think it was a bank employee?"

She shrugged. "It's the logical way to do it. Anyone else making a deposit would be on camera. An employee could access the account anytime, and move money from one account to another. But you'd be able to tell who it was from their access code on the computer terminal. So have you found the person who did it?"

"How do *you* know all that?"

"It's basic banking procedures. Doesn't everyone know it?"

Drew's look threatened violence. "Don't go there, Chapman. Lauren's on your side."

"Hard to tell with you two," Chapman grumbled. "Yeah, we have a name, a financial advisor at the senator's bank. We're looking for him. The guy seems to have disappeared."

"I would, too," Drew said.

"We'll find him. In the meantime, we'll expect you to confine yourselves to this house until we find Senator and Mrs. Creighton, and resolve this mess."

"Gladly." She looked at Drew. "Right?"

He shifted his eyes toward her. "Right," he replied in a flat voice.

She smiled pleasantly at the agent. Chapman frowned at each of them, then stood and slapped a business card on the table. "Call me if there's a problem."

"We will," she assured him.

"I'll see you out," Drew said, rising.

He stood close enough to Chapman that she couldn't help noticing the difference between the two. Both were tall, probably six-two or -three, with a solid, athletic build. But Chapman's moves were abrupt and jerky, the motions of someone who spent too much time in a business suit, riding in cars, and sitting behind a desk. Drew's movements had the fluid grace that implied a well-conditioned body, used to physical exertion and tests of strength. Besides the fact that looking at him heated her from the inside out like a blowtorch, she wouldn't bet a dime on Chapman in any physical confrontation against Drew. Which looked to be about one sentence away from happening if the agent didn't leave now.

"Don't bother," she said, stepping between them and taking Agent Chapman by the arm. "You sit and eat, Drew. I'll see him out." She placed a hand on Drew's chest and shoved, which had no effect but to make him to look at her. She narrowed her eyes in a threatening glare, then tugged Chapman toward the foyer. Before she could get him out the door, Drew called out from behind them.

"Hey, Chapman."

The agent turned with a suspicious look. "Yeah?"

"We're going to make a trip to the grocery store to stock up before we lock ourselves away here. Just wanted to give you notice in case you don't trust us, and want to follow."

Chapman returned his steady look. "I'll do that."

"Whole Foods, in thirty minutes."

"See you there," Chapman sneered, and left.

As soon as the door closed, Drew's expression turned innocent. "What?"

"Only a man could make grocery shopping sound like a showdown at the O.K. Corral."

He smiled. "Do you have a coat with big pockets?"

It was probably easier to play along, rather than ask him to explain. "Yes, my raincoat. But it's sunny today."

"That's okay. Put a few changes of underwear in those pockets and any other necessities you'll need for the next few days. Maybe a T-shirt if there's room."

"The next few days? That's an ambitious shopping trip you're planning."

He took her hand and led her back to the kitchen. It was a simple thing, having his hand around hers, but it felt good. Natural. She closed her fingers around his.

"How much confidence do you have in our young Agent Chapman?" Drew asked.

She made a face. "Not much. He lost track of probably the most recognizable man in the country after the president and vice president."

"Right, and you can take the vice president off that list; he hasn't been around Washington as long as my dad. So do you want to sit around here and wait while those two goons chase their tails, or do you want to get in on the action?"

It seemed he already knew her well enough that he didn't have to wait for her answer. Picking up the phone, he punched in a series of numbers and waited.

"Gerald! What are you up to?"

While he listened, Drew smiled at Lauren and ran a finger along her cheek, seemingly more intent on her face than on whatever Gerald was saying. She shivered with pleasure.

"Why don't you wash that paint off? I want to ask you for a favor. By the way, did you know the Secret Service has our phone tapped?"

This time his finger went around her ear, then slid through a lock of hair. More shivers.

"Neither did I. Anyway, they want us to lie low here for a few days. So I was thinking I might be able to borrow that hot Swede of yours."

Hot Swede? Was he asking to borrow pornography?

She'd known he'd be more sexually adventurous than Jeff, but it had seemed like she was all the stimulation he'd need.

While Gerald answered, or thought about his answer, Drew held the phone away and leaned close to her ear. "That's what he calls his Volvo," he whispered, then licked her earlobe while he was there. Her head tilted involuntarily with pleasure, rubbing against his.

"We're going to make a quick trip to Whole Foods to stock up. You could meet us there." His finger traced the line of her jaw, then traveled down her neck, hooking into her crew neck collar and pulling slightly. She wanted to rip it off.

Drew chuckled into the phone. "Yeah, I can pay in euros, you elitist snob. I'll see you there in half an hour. Thanks, buddy."

He hung up. "He won't trade for the Taurus. Paying in euros means we have to give him my dad's Mercedes," he told her absently. His wandering finger came back up to tilt her chin toward his face as he captured her gaze and sent her pulse racing. She held her breath in anticipation.

Drew's voice lowered passionately. He murmured, "If you stuff any sort of nightgown into those pockets I'm going to be very disappointed."

She shivered deliciously. A nightgown? Perish the thought.

Chapter Nine

They found Gerald lurking among the melons, driving cap pulled low over his eyes, appearing to be in deep deliberation over which fruit to buy. When he saw them he lifted a melon in front of his face and whispered furtively around it.

"Are you being followed?"

Drew took the melon from him and placed it in their empty shopping cart. "No, they waited in the parking lot. They're parked next to the Mercedes."

Gerald looked disappointed. "Who are they?"

"It's Hawknose and Trenchcoat," Lauren told him, nodding sagely to emphasize the significance of her information.

His mouth dropped open. "Those two incompetent idiots are Secret Service?"

"Yes, and they're expecting us to buy a cart full of groceries," Drew told him, "so give us a good twenty minutes or so before you go out to the car."

Gerald snorted. "You can add another ten onto that while I berate that big clod for ripping my topcoat.

The federal government owes me a refund, and by God, that clumsy oaf is going to get the bill."

"Just don't forget to buy some groceries first," Drew said.

"Yeah, yeah, don't worry."

Drew dangled the keys to his dad's Mercedes in front of Gerald's face.

"Oh." Gerald pulled a set of keys from his pocket and made the switch. "I parked by the loading dock in back. And if that ape in the produce truck got so much as a speck of dirt on my car, call the cops. I already have his license plate number."

The side of Drew's mouth quirked upward. "Will do."

They started to leave when Gerald called out, "Hey, where are you going? How can I find you if something comes up?"

"I'm not sure where we'll be, but we'll check in with you."

Gerald leveled a finger at Drew. "You be careful with Lauren."

Drew's arm went around Lauren's shoulder and pulled her close. "Don't worry."

She broke away to go back and kiss Gerald's cheek. "You're sweet," she said.

He smiled. "It's one of my best qualities. Hey, what's with the pockets?"

She followed his gaze to the bulging pouches on each side of her jacket. "Clean underwear."

Gerald's eyes darted to Drew, then back to her. He leaned close and said in a confidential whisper, "The skimpy, sexy kind, I hope."

She shoved a hand into his shoulder. "I take it back. You men are all alike."

A wicked grin crossed his face. "When opportunity knocks, be prepared. And girlfriend, you've got a huge hunk of opportunity standing over there."

She bit her lip. "'Bye, Gerald. Don't be too hard on the feds."

"Sorry, a man's gotta do what a man's gotta do. You take care, now."

He set off purposefully toward the dairy section as Lauren rejoined Drew. Exiting through an "employees only" door, they found the rear loading dock. Lauren followed Drew's direction down a short flight of cement steps to the oil-stained pavement behind the store, and stared at the sleek silver sports car gleaming in the spring sun.

"*That's* a Volvo?"

"Volvo C-Seventy. Nice, huh? Gerald's a car snob."

She gave it a long, appreciate look. "Bet it goes fast."

"Bet we aren't going to find out." They took a side driveway, then slipped into midday Washington traffic.

Lauren hadn't questioned Drew's escape plan, probably because her mind became muddled every time he touched her, and he'd made his plans while stroking her and her brain cells into rapturous confusion. With both of his hands on the steering wheel, she had a better chance at holding an intelligent conversation.

"Now tell me why we're playing hide and seek with the Secret Service," she said, tossing her raincoat into the back seat. "We're not the ones Chapman and his partner were supposed to protect. Do you really think they'll waste their time looking for us?"

"I'm more concerned with avoiding whoever followed us to the embassy and tried to turn us into road kill. And as for the Secret Service, they did follow us to

Whole Foods. Maybe they think the best way to find Dad and Meg is to stick close to us, in case they try to contact us again."

She liked the idea of eluding whoever was trying to kill them, but Lauren had been hoping Meg would call again. "If they do try, we won't be at the house. What if we miss a call from them?"

His mouth set in a grim line. "I don't think we will. Something spooked them, Lauren, and they ran from the people who were there to protect them. They took a chance and called once just so we would think they were safely out of the country. I don't think they'll risk it again."

She nodded, thinking. Who was her sister so afraid of? "I wasn't enchanted with Agent Chapman, but when he thought I was Meg he seemed honestly frustrated that I wouldn't let him take me into protective custody. I don't think he was lying, Drew. He doesn't know why they ran from him."

"I know, I don't get it, either. But if we want to find them, I think our chances are better if we stay away from the Secret Service. And since the Secret Service might think their chances are better by staying with us," he patted the dashboard fondly, "we use Gerald's hot Swede to sneak away."

"Makes sense," she said, settling back in her seat. And by the way, we could get there a lot faster if you'd give this baby some gas."

He shot her a puzzled smile. "Is this a glimpse of your wild side?"

She didn't know what it was. She felt suddenly free, like she'd just been sprung from a cage and was eager to see how far and how fast she could go. "I like fast cars," she said, even though she was pretty sure her feeling had nothing to do with cars.

"Sorry to disappoint you, but we don't want to attract attention."

Too bad. But she could indulge that impulse another time, since she had no intention of going back in that cage. "So where are we going?"

"Take your pick. We could check the last place we know they were—the airport. If they never left for the Virgin Islands, we can assume the Secret Service made sure they didn't get on a different flight, either. And if they didn't fly out of there, they must have driven. We could try the rental car companies and taxis, which would take days. I'm guessing the Secret Service is already on that, and doing a better job than we could. They could also have called a friend for a ride. We could contact the most likely suspects and see if they know anything."

She nodded. "Time consuming, but it might work. What else?"

"Dana Zamecki, the TV reporter. How did she happen to be there with a camera crew exactly when Dad and Meg were trying to run from the Secret Service?"

She thought for a few seconds. "You think someone tipped her off. Who? Meg and your dad?"

"I think either Dad and Meg set it up to make the Secret Service and everyone else think they were leaving the country, or the bad guys tipped Dana off, just to cover that avenue. If Meg and Dad tried to fly out of town, it would be news, and they'd hear about it."

"Agent Chapman said another senator was being

blackmailed first. If we could figure out who it was, maybe he'd have some idea who might be doing it, or where your dad and Meg are hiding."

He smiled and reached over to gently squeeze her thigh. "Good thinking. Now where would you like to start?"

Right there's good, she thought as her brain cells scrambled again. *Or a little higher*. The warmth of his hand spread up her leg to settle between her thighs.

Closing her eyes, she willed his hand to move upward.

"Lauren? Are you thinking?"

"Yes." She peeked at him.

Comprehension sparked the moment their eyes met. For one second Drew appeared startled, then his gaze shot into her like a laser, clean and purposeful. "Jesus," he muttered, jerking his hand back as if he'd been burned. "Tell me where we're going right now, before I pull into the nearest Marriott."

She nearly asked how close the Marriott was, but an irritating thread of common sense held her back.

"Let's start at the beginning, with your dad's friend, the other senator who was being blackmailed."

Drew released a sharp breath. "Okay. That means we go see Paul Pierson, the octopus you danced with at the embassy. He and Dad aren't in the same political party, but they've both been in Washington a long time and no one knows my dad better." He took a sharp right turn and began working his way back toward the Capitol area.

Lauren thought she did a credible job of looking calm and collected, even though her heart pounded and her pelvis throbbed. The connection between them was only growing stronger, and it shocked her every time she felt it. It wasn't just sexual—she admired Drew's resourcefulness and intelligence, and the way he kept his sense of humor in a crisis. But she wasn't about to downplay the sexual part. It was new and powerful, and best of all, mutual. She intended to explore it in languorous detail, not in the desperate collision of bodies that this new, outrageous side of her seemed prone to.

Although they could try that, too. Lauren looked out the passenger window, chin propped in her hand to hide her grin.

Drew silently thanked Gerald for his Eagle Scout preparedness. The BlackBerry in the glove compartment contained every conceivable phone number, from the Georgetown dry cleaner to the president's secretary. Combined with IDs and passes for nearly any government building in D.C., they were inside Senator Pierson's suite in the Dirksen Senate Building with barely enough time for Drew to lose the persistent erection he suffered whenever he touched Lauren.

Paul Pierson met them in the deserted corridor with open arms. "Meg, you luscious temptress, you decided to leave the old fart after all! You've made the right choice."

Drew inserted his arm between them as the senator attempted to wrap Lauren in an embrace. "Sorry, Senator, not this time. You can flirt all you want with Dad's wife, but this is her sister, Lauren. I wouldn't want her to think you're as lecherous as you pretend to be."

Pierson dropped his arms, but looked intrigued, staring first at Drew, then Lauren. "You're kidding."

Lauren shook her head. "I'm sorry about deceiving you at the embassy, but we had a good reason."

"That was you?" After another long, interested look at Lauren, Pierson asked, "Does Meg know about this?"

"No." Lauren shook her head.

"Harlan?"

"No," Drew answered.

"Huh. This should be good. Come on in and sit down. It's Sunday and the Senate recessed for a week, so we have the office to ourselves. I can offer you a drink, if you'll settle for Pepsi, 7-Up, or Nestea."

Drew caught Lauren's surprised glance as they followed him to his inner office, and smiled. "The senator's not the lush he appears. He also has a wife and six kids, so I hope he's not an adulterous lech, either."

"Hey now, son, don't give away my secrets. Just tell me why you two are going around Washington impersonating my favorite lady. Right after my wife and four daughters, that is."

Drew watched Lauren succumb to Pierson's charms and felt a twinge of jealousy. They weren't even lovers—not yet, anyway, an oversight he planned to correct soon—and already he felt proprietary. Lauren seemed to bring out all sorts of new feelings in him. But he had other important things to worry about now.

"This is confidential information, Senator. You can't talk about it with anyone, because we don't know yet who Dad and Meg are hiding from or why."

"Hiding from?" Pierson's expression grew serious. "Tell me."

They told the story the way Agent Chapman had related it to them, beginning with Senator Creighton's report to the Secret Service that someone was attempting to use another senator's indiscretions to buy votes, his idea to "marry" his secretary and continue seeing his current girlfriend in order to make himself a target, followed by Meg and Harlan's abrupt disappearance when the apparent blackmail was received.

They left out the X-rated photos in the safe-deposit box. Drew was fairly certain the pictures were what had been offered to buy Senator Creighton's silence, although he didn't understand how his father might be intimidated by proof that his wife had had a previous lover.

Pierson's sharp mind hadn't missed any of the implications. "That's an incredible story, son, but I don't see why you're so desperate to find Harlan and Meg. Why not wait for them to show up on their own?"

"Because they're so afraid of something they don't even trust the Secret Service to keep them safe," Drew told him. "Whoever tried to blackmail them must be pretty powerful if they don't feel safe with that level of protection."

"And they tried to convince us to stay out of it, to keep *us* safe," Lauren added.

"So naturally you want to get right in the middle of it."

"Someone has to," Drew told him.

He regarded them over his soft drink as he took a long sip, then set the can on his desk. "Okay, how can I help? I assume that's why you've told me about it. I'll do whatever I can."

"We're hoping you can give us a name," Drew said. "We have very few clues to go on. Maybe if we know which senator confided in my dad, it would help us figure out who might be trying to blackmail them."

"You mean tell you who might be cheating on his wife, so you can confront him?"

"Do you have a better idea?" Drew asked.

Pierson eyed him speculatively for several seconds, then shook his head. "No."

The senator rose and stood at the window, staring at the street below. Lauren gave Drew a worried look and he took her hand with a gentle, reassuring squeeze while they waited for Senator Pierson to decide how much he could trust them.

Finally, Pierson turned. "I heard something recently that I discounted at the time. It may be nothing, but there is one person who could be in that sort of situation, and who would probably confide in Harlan before anyone else." Drew waited, while Pierson struggled with his reservations. "It has to remain strictly confidential."

"Of course."

"And remember, this is only speculation."

Drew nodded impatiently.

Pierson took a deep breath. "It could have been Senator McNabb."

Whatever name he expected, it wasn't that one. "Senator *Charlene* McNabb?"

"Yes, Charly. And I'm not going to tell you why I think so. If she wants to talk to you, she'll tell you. If not, well, rumors aren't always true."

What Drew knew about Charlene McNabb was the image she showed the entire country—a conservative wife, mother, and politician who fought hard for the very family values she personified. He couldn't imagine confronting the woman about possible sexual dalliances, but if she was their only lead to finding his father and Meg, he'd have to do it.

They shook hands with Senator Pierson and promised to keep in touch. Guiding Lauren back through the empty corridors, Drew took an impulsive turn away from the elevators.

"This building connects with Hart. Let's stop by my dad's office while we're here."

"Why, will someone be there?"

"Probably not, but maybe if they wanted to get in touch they'd leave a message on his private phone, thinking no one else would get it." He shrugged. "It's a long shot, but we're already here, so why not check?"

They passed a few people and saw several offices with doors open and lights on, but Senator Creighton's office was locked. Drew had never before used the key Gerald insisted he carry, but he silently blessed his dad's secretary for his obsessive precautions. He locked the door behind them while Lauren went to her sister's desk and replayed a droning string of phone messages.

"Nothing here. Try your dad's phone."

He bypassed the light switch for the inner office and turned on the small desk lamp instead. It provided more than enough light to see that the assistant office manager must have taken care of any messages that had come in. Nothing was on the machine.

Lauren's obvious dejection was a good excuse for him to wrap a comforting arm around her shoulder, and her disappointed sigh aroused his protective instincts. "Don't worry, we'll find them," he said, turning her toward his chest so he could run his other hand through the silky hair that lay against her cheek.

For no reason he could name, his brain conjured an image of Lauren among the wildflowers on the slope below his house and laughing in the bright sunshine that filled his Colorado kitchen. It must be some scent in her shampoo, one of those herbal concoctions with fanciful names like "Spring Breeze" or "Mountain Sunshine," that triggered memories of home.

Lauren cuddled closer, her head falling softly against his chest. He went from protective to predatory in two seconds, and it seemed impossible that she could keep up with that electric jolt of lust.

He used both hands to cup her face as he whispered, "Lauren?"

The eyes she raised to him were hazy green in the yellowish lamp light, clouded with desire. Drew's heart rate shot up. She wanted him as much as he wanted her.

When he lowered his head to kiss her, she met his mouth willingly, slipping her arms around him and pressing her breasts against his chest. His hands slipped beneath her thin cotton shirt, thumbs stroking the sides of each soft mound. The satisfied little "Mmm" sound she made only excited him further. Desire escalated to frantic need. He wanted to touch her all over, then sink into her hot center and never leave it. He wanted her naked, now.

"Lauren," he said, breaking away from her mouth and murmuring into her hair as he kissed her neck, her ear. "This isn't the best place."

Her voice was breathy, words catching in her throat. "I know. It's the office of a United States senator. It's not the best time or place, but I can't wait." Her voice dropped to a near moan and she pressed her forehead against his chest, as if bracing herself against pain. "Oh God, Drew. I want you now."

He groaned with anticipation. "Good, but I meant we don't have to do it here. There's an adjoining room with a bed."

"A bed?"

"A place for my dad to crash during long sessions and committee hearings. It's not big, but then I don't think we'll need much room. We're going to be very close together."

"Hmm."

It sounded so ambivalent he feared she'd just lost interest. He'd probably been stupid to propose using his father's bed, especially after she'd said it felt wrong to want him while they were in a Senate office. Damn. He suspected she wasn't as proper as she pretended, but he'd pushed it too far. He should—

She gave his shoulders a shove and he fell back into his father's desk chair. "I think I like it better right here."

"Huh?" He looked up into eyes sparkling with mischief as she straddled his knees and leaned into him, hands braced on the chair arms.

"I don't want to use your father's bed. You bring out something different in me, Drew." She lifted a hand to trace random lines across his chest, sending messages straight to his groin. "Something a little wild. Uncaged. A bed would be all wrong for that image, don't you think?"

"Absolutely. What was I thinking?" He might have made one stupid assumption, but he was a fast learner.

Her secretive smile was turning him on as much as anything else. Right now the anything else was her breasts, which arched toward him as she twisted to look around the office. "This place is so stuffy and proper. It makes me want to break a few rules."

He smiled and ran his thumbs across the tips of her breasts, delighting at the feel of her nipples hardening through her clothes. "Lauren, I can't believe how badly I've underestimated you."

"Mmm, well, don't worry, I'm about to let you make up for that." She backed up a step, out of his reach, her hands closing over the hem of her top. In one smooth move she whipped it over her head and dropped it to the floor.

He took a deep breath and groaned, his desire growing by the second.

She smiled, serene and confident. The only hint of excitement lay in her rapid, shallow breaths and flushed cheeks, and he knew they only hinted at the energy beneath the surface.

He was hard as a rock. He should have guessed there were hidden depths here. She was too intriguing, too contrary to be the responsible, proper woman she wanted the world to see. And Drew was curious as hell to see just how improper Lauren Sutherland could be.

Part of her couldn't believe how bold she'd become, stripping her top off and propositioning Drew in the office of the most powerful senator in the country. Another part of her reveled in the surge of power she felt every time she saw lust flare in his eyes. The irony didn't escape her—after years of being the good girl and setting the right example, it turned out she was as sex crazed as Meg.

She was fine with that. She was done with a sex life that was planned in advance down to every boring day and time. Spontaneity was her new mantra. Like the impulse she'd had when she looked at Senator Creighton's expansive desk with its neat stack of files at each end and all that lovely, uncluttered space in between.

All she could think of was grabbing Drew, spreading her legs over some pending legislation and having wonderfully inappropriate sex.

She took Drew by surprise, but he was catching on fast. Pulling her back against his knees, he slipped his fingers inside her bra, popped out one eagerly swollen breast, and lowered his mouth.

Silky, wet heat surrounded her and she swayed dizzily. The man knew how to use his mouth, and wanton impulses flooded her pelvis with each tug on her nipple. She moaned happily.

"Good?" he murmured, switching sides.

"Incredible." The pressure between her thighs turned into a tickle that made her wiggle against his knees. Drew seemed able to get her from interested to panting a lot faster than she'd expected. She reached behind her back and unfastened her bra. Slipping it free from between their bodies, she flung it aside, the bra catching on the corner of the picture frame behind Senator Creighton's desk. Thomas Jefferson now had a lightly padded B-cup tilted rakishly over one eye. But he didn't seem to mind, and knowing Senator Creighton's reputation, she thought it might not be the first bra tossed in that room.

"Nice one," Drew said. "Try the jeans next." His fingers worked at her zipper.

She grabbed a handful of shirt and pulled him out of his chair. "Not until you catch up."

"No problem." He had his shirt off in seconds and went back to her zipper, pulling jeans and panties down in one swipe. She laughed, trying to toe her shoes off and getting tangled in her jeans. "Help."

He boosted her bare ass onto the desk, her butt

cheeks resting squarely on cool, polished mahogany. "Stop kicking," he said, and knelt to pull off her shoes, then finished stripping off her jeans. He rose, eyes holding hers as he stepped out of his own shoes and unfastened his pants. All that eye contact was heart-fluttering and romantic, but there was no way she was going to miss her first close-up of that lean, hard body.

His mouth slid into a crooked smile. "Let me know when you're done looking."

"We don't have that long. I'll look some more later." Hooking her legs around his thighs, she pulled him close until his erection ran into her abdomen. "Almost," she croaked. "A little lower."

"Not yet."

She sucked in her breath as a thought occurred to her. "You're right, I forgot all about protection. I hope you brought something."

"Are you kidding? I brought several somethings. And I'll put one on just as soon as you get ready."

"Now would be good."

He chuckled. "Patience." One hand moved from her hip to caress between her legs, releasing a hot rush of need as she nearly collapsed onto the desk. She propped herself on her elbows, breathing hard. He leaned over her, stroking her into a blissful, preorgasmic haze.

"Right on the desk, eh?" he asked.

She nodded, then gasped as his finger slid deep inside her, making her shiver with pleasure. When he drew it out and traced a wet line upward, she closed her eyes and panted in shallow, shaky breaths.

"Jesus, Lauren," he murmured, lowering his mouth to hers, kissing her between words. "You're more than ready."

She looked into the blue eyes so close to her own. "Legislation turns me on."

His eyes sparkled. "Really? In that case, maybe I should recite the Bill of Rights. Or should I just"—his finger moved lower again, slipping inside her as his hand pressed and circled—"do this."

"Do that," she croaked, then bit her lip as a second finger joined the first. She wanted to tell him to stop, to put himself inside her, that he was going too fast, but seconds later waves of ecstasy rolled through her, and her muscles tightened around his fingers until she went limp. She opened her eyes.

He was smiling. "I think you're ready now."

"I think you missed it."

His fingers left her as he searched his jeans pocket for a condom and put it on. "I'll catch the next one."

"I hate to tell you, but one is all I get."

"We'll see," he said.

He pressed himself against her, smiling as her eyes widened, and she began to think he might be right. She spread her thighs wider and hooked her heels behind him, aching for him to complete the penetration. She'd just reached orgasm on a senator's desk, which seemed appropriate for her new wild and uncaged life, and she was about to do it a second time. She felt liberated. In fact, if she had the chance, she'd do it in yet another inappropriate location . . .

"Wait!" She sat up, nearly bumping heads with Drew.

"What's wrong?"

"I changed my mind. I want to do it on the floor."

He squinted like he was having a hard time focusing on her words. "You want to move *now*?"

"Yes." She slipped her hand between them and

cupped his scrotum, massaging while she nibbled at his neck. "Please?"

He closed his eyes and groaned.

"I want to try another new place that I've never tried before." She moved her hand higher, stroking the hardness with her fingers. "Humor me."

"You're killing me here." He kissed her once, hungrily, then pulled her against him and lifted, her legs still encircling his waist. He stopped on a thick pile rug between brown leather chairs. "How's this?"

"Perfect." She slid from his arms and pulled him to the floor on top of her. "Now where were we?"

"I know where I was just about to be." He found his place and without hesitation slipped inside her.

Warmth flooded outward from her center and she arched up against him, asking for more. He lowered himself until his dusting of chest hair rubbed against her breasts, hardening her nipples to tiny buds. Nuzzling her neck, he moved inside her slowly, teasing and brushing until the pleasant tingle in her lower body became an inflamed need. Within a minute she was panting and arching her back to pull him deeper with every thrust of his hips.

Just a little more . . . She pushed against him, closing her eyes and reaching for what was just beyond her grasp. If he would just go a little faster . . .

His movements slowed. She opened her eyes to find his face hovering just above her own, watching, smiling with every deliberate thrust that increased her need without fulfilling it.

"Close?"

She nodded, breathing hard.

He moved hard against her, prolonging the contact. "More?"

"Yes!"

"Sure you don't want to change places again?"

She tried for a threatening glare, but he moved again and it felt so good she laughed, the sound rumbling from deep in her chest. "Please," she managed between panting breaths.

He chuckled softly, sounding a bit strained. Taking her mouth in a deep kiss, he pumped his hips faster. Seconds later she gasped against his mouth and wrapped her legs around his hips, hanging on tightly as pleasure rocked through her in hard waves.

As the final paroxysms eased, she stroked the cool dampness on his back, too drained to move more than her hands. "Oh my God, Drew," she said on a groan.

He eased his weight up, propping himself on one elbow as he stroked a lock of hair off her face with is other hand. He made a small, deliberate movement inside her. *Hello there.* She automatically squeezed back.

"You're amazing," he said softly.

"And a little weird."

"Adventurous," he corrected with a kiss. "My kind of woman."

His heavy-lidded eyes look so aroused that Lauren decided it might be a good thing to be a little weird.

She'd never felt this way with Jeff, not even close. Apparently having the right kind of sex required the wrong man. And career-less, aimless, philandering Drew Creighton was *definitely* the wrong man.

Chapter Ten

Drew retrieved Lauren's bra from the Jefferson paint-ing, even though he preferred her standing there without it. He could get used to indulging her penchant for inappropriate sexual behavior. Several more possibilities had already come to mind, and Drew was determined to use them. One time with Lauren was not nearly enough.

"What do we do now?" Lauren asked as she bent to retrieve a tennis shoe from under a chair.

Drew eyed her elevated bottom speculatively, but refrained from saying the first thing that came to mind. "Now we find Senator Charlene McNabb before she goes home during the Senate recess."

"Where's home?"

He shrugged. "I have no idea."

"Fort Myers, Florida. She left last night."

Senator McNabb's office manager seemed unimpressed with their claim to have urgent business with the senator once she learned they were not from her state. "I can give her a message."

"We have to talk to her in person," Drew insisted. "It's personal."

The woman shrugged. "Can't help you then. She'll be back a week from tomorrow, if you want to make an appointment."

"It can't wait."

"It never can."

Drew clenched his jaw muscles and kept his temper in check. The woman was just doing her job. "Can you at least give us her phone number?"

She sent him a withering look. "The senator's home phone? Yeah, right."

"How about you dial the number, then let us talk to her in private?"

"How about you make an appointment like everyone else?"

She didn't notice his narrowed eyes because her attention was back on her computer screen, ignoring him. Drew ran a hand through his hair and looked away until he could get his irritation under control.

"Senator McNabb doesn't actually live in Fort Myers, does she? Isn't she on Sanibel?"

Drew shot an incredulous glance at Lauren. Where did she get that idea? And why was she making small talk while the Queen of Proper Procedures threw roadblocks in their path?

She sat on one of the empty desks in the deserted office, swinging her legs and watching the office manager with interest.

."Lauren," he began, when the woman looked up from her screen in surprise.

"Yeah, Sanibel Island. How'd you know that?"

"My parents have a condo there. They pointed out the senator's house once. It's on the Gulf side, right?"

The woman nodded, looking pleased. "Right."

"North end of the island, isn't it?"

She hesitated. "Well, I'd say more middle than north."

"Yeah, I suppose you're right. You'd know, since you've probably been down there quite a few times yourself."

"Not that often."

Drew stood still, afraid to distract the woman and fascinated with Lauren's questions.

"Oh, you should be there now. This is the perfect time of year. Isn't that little beach near the senator's house? I don't know the name but you know which one I mean, don't you?"

The woman smiled. "Yeah. I don't know the name either."

Lauren braced her hands on the desk and leaned forward, an eager light in her eyes. "This is the perfect time of year to leave D.C. You really should find some urgent reason to see the senator. Just drive right up to those big white gates and—"

"Black gates."

"Black? I was sure they were white. Maybe they painted them since I was there. Anyway, you should find some excuse to get down there. It sure beats Washington in March."

The office manager sighed wistfully. "Yeah, I wish."

Lauren hopped off the desk abruptly. "Well, you

work on it. You could always find some urgent business you need to discuss in person, right? We'll see you when the senator gets back next week, and I expect you to have a tan by then."

They laughed and waved good-bye. Drew let Lauren take his hand and pull him out of the office. She didn't speak until they were several doors down.

"Think you can find it? Gulf side of the island, north of middle, black gates out front."

"How in the world did you know she lived on Sanibel Island?"

"Just a guess. The family has money, and that's the best oceanfront real estate around those parts."

"Your parents have a condo there?"

"Ha. My parents couldn't afford a mobile home on Sanibel, if they allowed them there, which they probably don't."

"But you've been there before?"

"We drove around it once when I was a kid. Sightseeing."

He grabbed her by the upper arms and kissed her. He put an arm around her shoulders as they walked toward the elevators. "You're pretty terrific, Lauren Sutherland, you know that?"

"Even with my clothes on?"

"Terrific with them on, amazing with them off."

Her eyes sparkled and she leaned into his side as they walked, and he thought that maybe terrific and amazing were understatements.

They could get two tickets to Fort Myers if they were willing to leave at six the next morning and pay an exorbitant amount for first class fare. Lauren groaned;

Drew offered a credit card number without blinking.

"I'll pay you back," she said, wondering if she even had that much in her savings account.

"It's taken care of. I just won't be able to put that addition on the cave this year." He winked.

She wasn't stupid. She'd begun to suspect he didn't live in a cave after all.

"Won't the Secret Service be able to trace us by watching for activity on your credit card?"

"Not unless they look for charges on Steven's card." He grinned and held it up for her inspection. "Found it in the glove box. Gerald must have left it for us. That man thinks of everything. I'll pay Steven back before he even gets the bill."

They chose a hotel near Reagan National Airport, and at Drew's insistence they sat in the Volvo for twenty minutes, watching cars come and go until they were sure they hadn't been followed.

Lauren was relieved. "I'll sleep better knowing that guy who tried to run us over doesn't know where we are."

"You were planning to sleep?"

Lauren's impulse to break her engagement to staid, dependable Jeff in favor of a few exciting flings was looking like the right move. And having that first fling with Drew was the best idea ever.

She couldn't wait to find Meg, if only to tell her sister that she'd been right all along, that tying herself to one uninspiring but dependable man forever had been a horrible mistake. And it was not one she intended to make again.

The hotel room was dominated by a solitary king-sized bed, making it difficult to think of anything but possibilities. Lauren tried to block it out by concentrating on her other appetite; unfortunately, ordering food only killed five minutes.

She set the receiver back in its cradle. "Room service said it'll be twenty minutes. I don't know if I can wait that long. I'm starving."

Drew pulled her into his arms. "Maybe I can take your mind off it." He kissed her with a slow, deep passion that left her heart pounding and her body begging for more.

"That'll do it," she managed to get out.

He smiled, looking as dazed as she felt. "Sorry, but it's not nearly enough." His hands went under her shirt and directly to the clasp behind her back, flicking it open and out of his way in two seconds. A hand covered each breast, stroking her nipples into hard pearls, while his mouth trailed kisses along her neck. She could get used to this.

Lauren shivered with pleasure, but he broke off suddenly with a groan, resting his forehead against hers. "I don't believe how badly I want you again, but I refuse to watch the clock while we make love," he said.

Make love sounded so much nicer than *have sex* she hoped he'd used those words deliberately. And while making love boded well for the after-dinner entertainment, right now he was driving her crazy.

"Then stop teasing." She shoved his chest, causing him to plop back onto the bed. "Distract me with conversation. Tell me about your cave in Colorado." She turned a chair to face him and sat down. Watching him wasn't as good as touching him, but it wasn't half bad.

"Okay," he agreed, settling back. "My cave is actually a little cottage behind the ski lodge. I run a year-round operation as—" He faltered as she slipped her arms out of her shirt long enough to pull her unfastened bra off, then tugged the shirt back down. Drew smiled. "That's nice."

She glanced down at her white T-shirt; it did little to hide the dark circles of her nipples. "Stick to the story," she ordered, trying to sound stern even though his obvious interest only made her more aroused.

He licked his lips. "Um, yeah. As I was saying, the lodge is open year-round."

"You manage the place?"

"I own it. I bought it five years ago in pretty run-down condition, and it's been in operation the last three years."

"As a resort where snow bunnies can cavort on the slopes." And in your bed, she was tempted to add, but didn't. She couldn't criticize while she was doing her own cavorting with him.

"Well, no. That was your embellishment. There are no snow bunnies."

She frowned. "You said you ski—"

"And climb. I do. With the groups of teenagers who stay at the lodge for three or four weeks at a time, challenging themselves physically while they work on their self-confidence and the basic social skills no one bothered to teach them at home. It's an alternative education program for troubled teenagers."

Lauren had expected some sort of ski resort job that helped support a self-indulgent life style, but that sounded nothing like what he described.

"That's . . . that's an admirable career," she said.

He smiled. "You really thought I was a shiftless ski bum?"

"I'm sorry." She felt herself flush, even as she squinted suspiciously. "But you let me think that. You could have told me you had a proper house and an actual job."

"I thought it would be better if you didn't like me much."

"Why?"

He leaned toward her, his fingers straying through her hair as he talked. "Because you were apparently my aunt, you were engaged to another man, and all I could think of was getting you in my bed." He grinned, then his expression grew thoughtful as his gaze roamed her face, lingering on her mouth. "How much time until room service gets here?"

The knock on the door answered his question. As he got up, he dropped a kiss on her mouth and whispered, "Eat fast."

She didn't. It was sweet torture, but she took her time, meticulously cutting the chicken strips in her salad and taking leisurely bites, aware of his gaze following every pull of the fork through her lips, every deliberate lick of her tongue. She couldn't remember ever having this effect on a man, and she intended to savor it.

She sipped her chardonnay, meeting his mesmerized gaze with a raised eyebrow. "You have an oral fixation."

"Quite possibly," he agreed. "Finish your wine and let me do something about it."

Two more sips of wine seemed to push Drew's patience past its limit. Taking the nearly empty glass from her hand, he set it aside and pulled her onto the bed, rolling her beneath him. He took her mouth with a rough growl that softened as he pinned her wrists beside her head and he gradually deepened his kiss. She cooperated fully, yielding to his tongue and spreading her thighs to make room for his body between them. His weight pressing her to the bed was enough to start the familiar longing between her legs. She hooked an ankle around his leg, raised her pelvis firmly against his, and rubbed.

Drew groaned and lifted his mouth from hers. "Damn, woman, it's hard enough to hold back without you doing that. I want to make it last longer this time."

Longer sounded good. "How are you going to do that?"

"By keeping your hands off me for now. And by not stimulating your deviant imagination with anything improper. You'll get nothing more aberrant than watching yourself in that mirror."

Lauren glanced to the side and saw a reflection of Drew lifting her shirt over her breasts in the mirror behind the narrow counter that served as a bar. She watched his image fondle one breast while his mouth nipped at the other, and caught her breath.

He looked up. "What, don't tell me you never watched yourself before?"

She shook her head.

"No?" He looked amazed. "Have you ever done it anywhere but a bed?"

She pretended to think, because it didn't require any thought at all, then shook her head again.

"Honey, you're making this too easy for me." He pulled her to a sitting position, and she let him take off her shirt, then lay her back on the bed. "You just lie still and enjoy yourself."

She licked her lips and nodded, already flushed with heat. What woman could object to that? "But you have to undress first," she told him. When he looked surprised, she said, "If I can't participate, at least give me something to look at."

Drew smiled and climbed off the bed. "That's fair."

She watched as he shed every bit of his clothes, boldly staring at his engorged penis when it popped from his pants and longing to put her hands on it. She wanted to taste him too, a thought that came from no where and surprised her. She wanted Drew in every way she could have him.

Maybe he felt the same way. When he climbed back in bed, his mouth followed his hands everywhere, sucking her breasts into hard peaks and licking shivers across her stomach. When he parted her thighs and dipped his head she tensed. This was something Jeff didn't care to do, something she'd never have been bold enough to ask for, but Drew didn't hesitate. His tongue slid down her folds, then up again to explore her hidden nub with excruciating, slow circles that made her fist her hands in the bedspread and gasp, "Oh!" Releasing her breath, she said, "*Ohmygod*," which came out as one long moan.

Lauren cracked an eye open and peeked at the mirror. Her thigh hid the most significant part from view, but just the sight of Drew between her legs with his head bent over what had become the throbbing center of her universe, sent a surge of lust through her body, trembling down to her bare bottom where his hands gripped her.

She moaned aloud, riding a building pressure.

"Please, Drew," she said, not even sure what she was asking for, then couldn't manage to finish the request as the pressure crested and she arched against him, whimpering and shaking, and finally collapsing limply on the bed.

When she opened her eyes he was grinning at her from between her legs, which was erotic enough to send residual tingles rippling through her.

"How are you doing?" he asked.

"Terrific." She took a deep breath and ran her tongue across her dry lips. "Also thirsty. Let me up."

"Stay there." He stood and handed her the rest of her chardonnay which she sipped while looking out of the corner of her eyes.

There it was, right in front of her, jutting out proudly and putting all sorts of daring thoughts in her mind.

She lifted the empty glass. As he took it from her, she grabbed him, pulling so he had no choice but to step forward. Drew uttered a groan of pleasure that turned into an indrawn breath as she ran an experimental lick down the length of him. He pulsed against her palm.

"I hope you know that thing could go off."

"Not yet," she told him sweetly. She was going to put him through the same intense pleasure he'd given her while *he* trembled and gulped deep breaths. A minute later the empty wineglass hit the carpet with a small thud and Drew uttered a strangled, "Lauren."

She looked up. "Yes?"

"This is great, but I want to be inside you. Now."

It was easy to convince her. They lay entwined on the bed, touching and stroking until Lauren was once again swept up in the incredible waves of desire she always felt with Drew. His hands found all the right places, and the pressure kept building, rushing in her ears and swirling through her brain until she lost the ability to focus on anything but the glorious feeling of him moving above her and inside her. She met his rocking hips in the cradle of her own until all the pressure gathered into one tremendous tidal wave that crested and broke, crashing through her pelvis and clenching muscles all the way down to her rigidly curled toes, before easing back to tiny ripples of contentment.

Lauren sighed but didn't move, luxuriating in the weight of Drew lying, warm and damp with sweat, on top of her. Next to her ear where his face was buried in her hair, she heard a mumbled, "You're fantastic."

Not *that* was fantastic, *you're* fantastic. The difference probably meant nothing to him, but it made her blink hard to clear the excess moisture from her eyes. "So are you," she said softly, and he raised his head to smile and kiss her before going to dispose of the condom.

He called out from the bathroom, "Next time I promise we'll make love in some completely inappropriate location, someplace sure to warm your perverted little heart."

But they didn't. The next time was when the alarm woke them at 3:00 a.m., and it made no difference to her newly awakened desire for inappropriate sex that they were in bed with the lights out and curtains drawn. Making love with Drew was mind-blowing, no matter where they were. That realization was profound enough to make her shove him out of the shower while she stayed under the pounding stream of water, biting the stub of her fingernails and contemplating the recent oscillations in her emotional life.

She hadn't expected her attraction to Drew to be this overwhelming. But it was, and it had nothing to do with his lean, mountain climber's body or his dark, hungry gazes. That was just the bonus part. It was because of who she was when she was with him. She was herself. Not the Lauren who made herself into someone else's idea of what she should be, but the person she really was. The one who liked sexy dresses and impractical sports cars, and dangerous men who didn't follow all the rules. And probably a lot of other things she didn't even realize yet.

She was looking forward to finding out what they were.

She emerged from the bathroom in clean underwear and yesterday's jeans to find Drew at the window with the lights off, frowning at the dark parking lot three floors below. He motioned her over and pointed to a black car below, parked in a shadowy corner away from the bright halogen lights.

"See those two guys? They've been parked there since we woke up."

A chill replaced the warmth in her stomach. The men had a clear view of their Volvo across the parking lot.

"They must have figured out that we switched cars," Drew said. "It didn't take them long."

"You think they're Secret Service?" That wouldn't

be so bad. Better than if it was the guy who'd tried to run them down.

"Must be. They look official."

"Why are they waiting for us in the parking lot? Why not come to our room?"

"For one thing, they don't know where it is. I paid with cash. They couldn't know that Mr. and Mrs. Grabowski from Phoenix are the people they want. Also, I'm not sure they want to stop us. They might think we'll lead them to Meg and my dad."

Part of her wished she could do just that. She didn't understand why Meg and Harlan would run from the Secret Service, the very people who were best equipped to protect them.

"You paid for the plane tickets with Steven's credit card. Do you think they made that connection?"

He shrugged. "Maybe. Probably. They must have the legal authority to access credit card information."

She turned to him. "So what do we do?"

"We call a cab. We aren't sure it's Agent Chapman, and I don't see any reason to make it easy for them." He looked her over. "You stay here. I'm going to bribe the desk clerk into opening the gift shop downstairs. They should have some clothing."

What they had wasn't her style, but she supposed that was best. The Grabowskis met their cab in polo shirts featuring the Capitol dome and baseball caps with "Washington, D.C." embroidered above the bill. Lauren tucked her hair under the back, the best she could do to achieve a different look.

The crowds at the airport helped her feel anonymous, but they also allowed anyone who might be following them to be anonymous, too. Since they couldn't expect to be welcomed by Senator McNabb if they showed up trailing the very agents she'd tried to avoid, Lauren kept scanning the crowds for familiar faces.

There were more than a dozen men she'd seen when they entered the terminal. At the ticket counter, at security, and at the boarding gate they saw the same group of people who were traveling to Fort Myers on their flight. It was useless to try guessing which of them might be agents.

Lauren fidgeted as they sat at the gate across from theirs, trying to look inconspicuous. "These polo shirts are kind of tacky attire for meeting Senator McNabb," she told him.

"We'll buy something else when we get to Fort Myers."

She kept her voice low. "How much money did you bring?"

"A couple thousand, emergency money from my dad's safe. I think we can afford a few items of clothing."

"Do you think I should buy some hair dye?" she asked.

He laughed. "I think we can skip that for now."

She looked toward their gate as first class passengers were called to begin boarding. "I'm going to the ladies' room before we get stuck on the plane for a couple hours. I'll be right back."

Drew rose. "I'll wait outside the door."

"Don't be silly, I'll be fine. It's right over there, see? No one could force me to leave without you having a clear view of the whole thing."

He sat down with obvious reluctance. "Hurry up."

Lauren shouldered her purse and walked briskly toward the restrooms. Her timing was unfortunate—several women waited in line ahead of her. Ten minutes later, she dried her hands under the blower and hurried out the door just as the final section of her plane was called to board.

The gentleman exiting the opposite door was also in a hurry. Lauren was so intent on spotting Drew that she didn't see the man until she slammed into him.

"Oh!" she exclaimed, grabbing his arm for balance. "I'm so sorry. I wasn't watching where I—" Lauren's voice caught in her throat and stuck there as she lifted her eyes to his.

She stared, open mouthed.

His long blond hair was combed straight back but she'd know his perfect features and aloof gaze anywhere.

The man's irritated gaze met hers, and his hand shot out, binding her wrist in a powerful grip. When she gasped, his mouth twisted into a knowing smile.

The same smile she'd seen in Meg's X-rated pictures.

Chapter Eleven

——

Fear washed over Lauren like a wave. She took an instinctive step backward, and the man's hand turned, twisting her arm and shooting pain through her wrist. She couldn't break his grip, but if she screamed and made a scene he would have to release her. Before she could try it he stepped closer.

"If you struggle, I'll handcuff you. No one will interfere with the arrest of a fugitive," he whispered harshly.

Her panicked gaze flew past him, searching for Drew.

"Lauren!"

The man turned, saw Drew rushing toward them, and hesitated. In that moment of indecision, his grip eased. Lauren wrenched her wrist free.

She'd taken the man by surprise, but he recovered quickly. He did the only thing he could to stop Drew from tackling him.

The man forcefully hit her in the center of her back,

shoving her off balance. Her injured wrist crumpled on impact with the floor of the concourse. She flattened less than gracefully, her stomach smacking the carpet as air rushed out of her lungs.

Drew's knees hit the floor in front of her nose.

"Son of a bitch! Easy, honey."

Before she could move, Drew's hands were on her, gently lifting as he questioned her anxiously about scrapes, sprains, and broken bones.

Lauren shook her head and muttered "no" to everything, not sure if she was telling him that no, she wasn't hurt, or no, she was not all right. When he wrapped her in his arms she decided it didn't matter.

"Damn it," Drew muttered in her hair. She looked up, following his angry glare down the concourse where the fair-haired man had sprinted through a cluster of businessmen and disappeared into the crowd around a boarding gate.

He was gone.

Drew smoothed her hair back. "Are you sure you're okay?"

The palms of her hands stung, her wrist ached, and her knees burned, but Drew was holding her close against his firm, broad chest. "I'm fine," she said.

More than fine, but she didn't say that part. She hadn't even realized it until he'd asked. But sitting on the floor of the concourse, emotionally shaken and moderately rug-burned, his simple question had made her look inside herself for the answer. It was an odd way to find out just how important he'd become to her, but "fine" only skimmed the surface.

Drew kissed her forehead and pulled her into

another fierce, protective hug. He guided her past staring people to the end of the boarding line. Using both hands, he lifted her wrist and examined it closely. Even though the red marks were fading, Drew frowned as he smoothed his fingers over her skin. He probed gently, flexing and massaging, causing her to flinch a couple times but going a long way toward soothing her rattled nerves.

"Nothing broken," he concluded with obvious relief. "Maybe sprained. Can you move your hand?"

Lauren flopped her hand up and down, testing. "It still works."

Drew smiled, then pulled his brows together in a worried frown. "I didn't see the guy well, but that hair—"

"It was him," she confirmed, shivering at the memory. "The same guy who was in the pictures with Meg. Why would he be here?"

"He's probably one of the guys following us."

It was the only logical answer. But it didn't fit with the suspicions Drew had voiced about the photographs. "I don't see any reason why one of Meg's ex-boyfriends would follow us," she said, thinking aloud. "I bet those photos really are faked."

Drew tipped his head, acknowledging the possibility. "Your faith in your sister is touching, honey, but keep in mind he could have seduced her in order to blackmail her. Blackmail seems to be the name of the game for everything that's been going on."

Lauren wanted to jump to Meg's defense, but in truth she was no longer sure just what her sister would do or with whom she would do it.

"Maybe we're jumping to conclusions," Drew said.

"Just because he had long blond hair doesn't mean he was Meg's—" He hesitated. "—*partner* in those pictures."

She recalled the man's perfect features, cold eyes, and emotionless smile. "No, it was him. I saw his face."

Her revulsion must have shown. "Hey," Drew said softly, stroking a hand through her hair. His gaze grew tender with concern, and she mentally added that to his list of good qualities. Damn. They were beginning to add up for someone who was just a fling.

He tilted her chin up and smiled. "I guess I should be glad it was his face you were looking at in those pictures."

"As opposed to?" Then she got it. "Very funny. It's not like I could have been looking at anything else, since it was usually buried in . . ."

She broke off, aware of curious glances from a nearby couple. "Never mind," she muttered.

She was still worried, but Drew's joking had calmed her, and his arm around her shoulder was reassuring. She snuggled closer as the line inched forward.

He seemed to relax, too, while they boarded the plane and found their seats. As Lauren buckled her seat belt, she felt him watching her, an odd look on his face.

"What?" she asked.

He shook his head and smiled. "Nothing. Just thinking."

He'd been giving her odd looks like that lately, sometimes so intense she thought he would drag her off for a quickie, and sometimes so preoccupied it was like he wasn't there at all.

* * *

Drew's mind was wandering again. Somehow his thoughts had gone from worrying about Lauren and how to keep her safe, to envisioning her safe and happy at his Colorado home. Maybe he was just homesick.

Lauren was quiet as she looked out her window. Washington and the eastern seaboard dropped away below them. He spoke gently, reluctant to cause her more worry. "His being there wasn't a coincidence, you know."

She nodded, turning a concerned gaze on him. "Do you think he was one of the guys in the hotel parking lot?"

She was surprised when he shook his head. "No. That would be an easy solution, but the clerk at the front desk said two guys with Secret Service ID asked for us. So they were the two guys in the car. Blondie has to be one of the bad guys."

It was enough to make his head ache. How many people could be following them?

Lauren frowned. "He said he'd handcuff me if I didn't obey. Doesn't carrying handcuffs mean he's someone official?"

"Did he say he was?"

"No."

"Then he wasn't. A real agent would have announced who he was. Anyone can buy handcuffs. And he took off as soon as I stepped in. No matter what he said, I don't think these people want to create a scene. From now on, stay close to me. They won't try anything if we're together."

At least he hoped not. If it was the same guy who'd

tried to run them down after the embassy party, he wasn't adverse to taking risks.

She looked doubtful. "Do you think they'll follow us to Florida?"

Yes. "Maybe."

She sighed and turned back to the window.

She wasn't fearless, but she was brave in spite of her fear. Good. He wouldn't have to worry that she would be too paralyzed to act quickly if necessary. But he was starting to worry about something else—that this would get a lot more dangerous. They were making someone very nervous.

Lauren's spirits improved when they landed in Fort Myers and discovered the weather was a sunny eighty-five degrees.

"Let's ask the rental company if we can get a convertible," Lauren said.

The sparkle in her eyes made him smile. "I don't know. That sounds pretty impractical."

He'd been teasing, but she looked surprised. "Yeah, it is. Can we do it anyway?"

He laughed. "Honey, we can do whatever you want."

Her brilliant smile sent an arrow right into his heart.

As the day went on, his elevated mood persisted. He'd been cautious and alert, but hadn't spotted anyone following as they wandered around the airport and lingered over lunch. No doubt someone would catch up with them later. And if Agent Chapman decided to waste Secret Service money by sending some flunky to tail them around southwest Florida, he'd consider it added protection. He wouldn't let it interfere with the pleasure of being with Lauren.

He had her to himself for the next day and night.

Drew found himself humming under his breath while he waited for Lauren outside the ladies' room at the car rental agency. He recognized it as one of the tunes they'd danced to at the embassy party. The music seemed to have gotten stuck in his head, but he didn't mind. For a hunted man, he felt incredibly carefree.

Still humming, he checked his cell phone for messages: one. Punching in the retrieval code, he expected to hear Gerald's voice, but the angry growl in his ear was far too low to belong to his father's assistant.

"Goddamn it, Creighton, call me."

Agent Chapman. Drew dialed and waited for the familiar snarl on the other end.

"Creighton, I told you to stay put."

"Yes, you did," Drew answered pleasantly.

His cheerfulness didn't help Chapman's attitude. "Did you hear from your father?"

"No."

"Because if you did, and you two idiots are trying to handle this on your own—"

"Relax, Chapman. I said no. We're tracking down a lead."

"What lead?"

"I'd rather not say. It's based on a rumor, and it's highly personal. Politically sensitive information."

"Oh, I see. You wouldn't want the Secret Service to hear something like that." Sarcasm practically dripped from the phone.

"Glad you agree." As much as he enjoyed jerking Chapman's chain, he couldn't blame the man for being angry. No one was as privy to the private lives of politicians, and as discrete about it, as the Secret Service. Grudgingly, Drew threw him a bone.

"If it turns out to be true, you'll be the first to know. I just want to check it out."

A few seconds of silence followed, during which Chapman was probably seething and kicking puppies. Drew's gaze was distracted by Lauren as she exited the ladies' room and walked toward him. Long, shapely legs moved in a provocative rhythm, and her hips swayed sensuously beneath her new sundress. Allowing Lauren time to change into her new clothes had been well worth the delay.

He kissed her cheek and lifted a finger.

"Chapman? You still there?"

"Yeah," the gruff voice rumbled. "Listen, Creighton. We found that bank employee who deposited the bribe money."

It could be the break they were looking for. "Excellent! Did he tell you who put him up to it?"

"He couldn't. We fished him out of the Potomac last night. Took a bullet to the head, execution style."

He tried not to let Lauren see the panic that twisted his gut into knots. "Shit."

"Yeah. These guys aren't playing nice and you're out there taking too many chances. Just tell me where you are."

"You know where we are. You followed us."

"The hell I did. How important do you think you are, Creighton?"

Despite the warm sun, an icy tendril wormed its way down Drew's spine. Keeping his voice calm, he asked, "You didn't have anyone follow us to the hotel and the airport?"

"What? The airport? Hell, no. I can't spare agents to follow some dumbass civilian when I've got a U.S.

senator missing and possibly in danger. Are you telling me you left Washington?"

Drew sucked in a deep breath, and let it out slowly. "We're in Florida. Two men were watching our car in the hotel parking lot. I thought they were your boys."

The anger was suddenly gone, and Chapman's tone was clipped and professional. "How do you know someone was watching your car?"

"I didn't go down and ask them, but two guys sat in a black Ford for a couple hours this morning with a clear view of our car."

"Your car. That would be the Volvo?"

Drew thought he detected a bit of taunting behind the question. "Yeah, congratulations, you caught me. Forget the car. Who were the two guys, Chapman?"

"Did you get a plate?"

"No." Damn. "I didn't think I had to. The guy at the front desk said they flashed Secret Service ID."

Drew listened to a couple seconds of silence before Chapman responded. "I don't know, but I'll look into it."

It was all he was going to get for now. "Make it quick," Drew said, then broke the connection and shoved the phone in his pocket. Having an unidentified tail in addition to the blond guy was worrisome. And if the two guys *were* Secret Service, wouldn't Chapman know about it?

"What's wrong?" Lauren asked.

"Nothing. Agent Chapman doesn't know who was watching us at the hotel. It's probably just a couple of low-level agents his boss sicced on us without telling him. He's going to find out, just to put my mind at ease." He downplayed it, satisfied that he wasn't lying.

She watched him closely. "You wouldn't be one of those guys who'd keep stuff from the little lady as part of some misguided protective instinct, would you?"

Drew smiled. He didn't want her to worry, but he liked that she read him so well. "Yes, I would."

"That's sweet. Don't do it, okay?"

He considered carefully before nodding. "Okay."

"Is there anything else you're not telling me for my own good?"

He hesitated, then said it. "They found the bank employee. Dead."

She swallowed, then nodded. "Anything else?"

"No."

"Is the car ready?"

Drew tossed her the keys. "Red, like you wanted. It's over there."

She turned, the first hint of a smile returning to her face. It might be forced, but he was glad to see it.

He hadn't wanted to tell her about the murdered bank employee. He hadn't wanted to cause those worry lines on her forehead as she steered the car onto Daniels Parkway. But he respected her need to know the truth. The Mustang convertible couldn't take away the worry, but for a short time he could at least pretend they were carefree. He relaxed in the passenger seat, enjoying his view of Lauren as much as he enjoyed the hot Florida sun on his bare arms.

An hour later they were on Sanibel, cruising slowly past Senator McNabb's front gates for the third time. With a security fence and heavy vegetation screening the house, they couldn't see much more than the garage. But at least no one in the house could see the red Mustang prowling back and forth either.

A man they assumed to be the senator's husband had loaded up golf clubs and driven off earlier. Ideally, they should talk to Senator McNabb while her husband was gone, but she still wasn't alone. For the past hour, two teenage boys had been hanging out near the open garage, washing a Jeep Cherokee and cleaning its interior.

Lauren smacked her hand on the steering wheel. "Why didn't we think of this? I pictured her being alone down here. Naturally, her family would be here, this is their *home*. How can we talk to her while they're around?"

"Awkward." Drew agreed. " 'Hello, Mr. McNabb. Is your wife at home? We'd like to speak with her about her marital infidelities. Won't take but a minute.' That would put him off his golf game for sure."

"Damn, those boys are meticulous. Must be picking up a couple girls," Drew added, admiring the clean Jeep as the boys finally started the SUV.

"Well, I hope they get out of here it's soon. We can't keep cruising around like this. Someone's going to get suspicious."

"We can say we're checking out property, considering buying a vacation condo."

"In my dreams."

Lauren parked a quarter mile down the road, where Drew pretended to consult a map. Ten minutes later, the two boys blew past them in the shiny black Jeep.

"About time," he said, folding the map. "Let's go."

Lauren pulled a U-turn and drove back, slowing as she neared the senator's property. The tall iron gates had just come into view when they swung open, and a small station wagon pulled out with two women in the front seat. Drew craned his neck to see the logo on the driver's door.

"Gulf Breeze Clean," he read aloud. "Looks like the cleaning service is done for the day. That makes the husband gone with his golf clubs, at least one kid gone with his friend, and the maid service gone. I say we try our luck."

Lauren nodded and pulled up to the imposing black gates, now closed again.

"Press the button on the call box," Drew instructed, moving as close to her and the speaker as the gear shift allowed.

"We should have switched places," she said, leaning back in the bucket seat to give him room.

Drew braced an arm on the dash and edged closer to her side. "I like it better this way." It was actually damned uncomfortable, but worth the risk of impaling himself on the gear shift in order to brush against Lauren's breast and inhale the scent of suntan lotion rising from her warm skin.

"Yes?"

The tinny static from the box was marginally better than a fast food drive-up. Drew spoke loudly.

"Drew Creighton to see Senator McNabb."

"Do you have an appointment?"

"No. I'm here on urgent, personal business. Tell her I'm Senator Creighton's son."

"One moment, please."

He shifted position while he waited, rubbing against Lauren breast.

She smiled. "Enjoying yourself?"

"Yes, thanks. Are you?"

"You're insatiable," she said, pursing her lips in a

way probably meant to look prudish. It made him want to tug her pouty lower lip into his mouth and run his tongue over it.

He dropped his eyelids seductively and murmured, "You're right, I am," just to watch the flush spread up her neck to her cheeks. Damn, he loved it when she blushed like that. It made him want to lock them both in a bedroom for a week and—

The box rattled to life. "I'm sorry, Mr. Creighton. Senator McNabb is unable to see you."

"What?" He'd assumed his father's name would arouse the lady's curiosity, if not outright concern. "Tell her it has to do with my father's recent marriage," he said, then added pointedly, "And with his rather sudden departure from Washington." If she was the one who had been blackmailed, she would have to know he was referring to the Secret Service sting operation.

This time only a few seconds passed before the man's fuzzy voice replied, "Senator McNabb sends her congratulations on Senator Creighton's marriage, but she is not available at this time."

The pause had been too brief for the man to have left to consult Senator McNabb. She was either beside him, listening, or her security man was making presumptive decisions for her. Drew gambled on the former.

They'd risked their own safety to track her down and he wasn't leaving without seeing her. If Paul Pierson was wrong about Senator McNabb having a secret worth protecting, she wouldn't respond to threats. But if she was the one who'd been blackmailed, he had to talk his way inside those gates.

In a hard voice, he said, "Tell her it's about some highly sensitive personal information she gave my father. Tell her I'd prefer to discuss it with her, but if she's unavailable I will be glad to question other government officials about the matter in order to confirm—"

The box crackled with a staticky, "The senator will see you, Mr. Creighton." The gates began their slow swing inward.

Lauren sucked in a breath and looked at him with pain in her eyes. "It *is* her," she whispered. "How awful for her."

"Thank you," Drew muttered to the box and eased back to his side of the car. He slumped in the bucket seat. "I have a feeling we're not going to receive a warm welcome."

Drew's prediction was an understatement.

They sat on a patio behind the house, sipping lemonade and watching the Gulf of Mexico roll onto the senator's white sandy beach for nearly fifteen minutes before the woman appeared.

Drew stood to shake her hand, suffering a cool stare and an even cooler hello.

"Thank you for seeing us, Senator McNabb," he said.

Sharp brown eyes assessed him. "I agreed to see you as a courtesy to your father, who is a friend and colleague."

He understood; she would not concede without proof. "Senator, this is Lauren Sutherland. Her sister is—"

"Meg Sutherland, Harlan's secretary. A charming

young woman." Charlene McNabb tilted her head as she shook Lauren's hand, her short hair gleaming in several expertly tinted shades of blonde. "But I suppose I should refer to Meg as Harlan's wife now."

"No, you shouldn't."

Lauren's soft reply seemed to startle Senator McNabb. She studied Lauren as they settled back into chairs under the filtered shade of the patio umbrella. "Why shouldn't I?" she asked carefully.

Drew closed his hand over Lauren's and answered for her. "Because they aren't really married. But you already know that."

The senator's piercing gaze shifted to him. "What makes you say that?"

This was where things got messy. He pinned her with a hard stare, willing to be as blunt as necessary. "You're the one who went to my father with a story about blackmail, so naturally you would know that his marriage was a ruse. You know he and Meg announced their marriage in order to draw whoever had blackmailed you into another attempt. My father must consider you a good friend, Senator, if he was willing to put his reputation in jeopardy to save yours."

Something flickered in the steady brown eyes, but her lips remained pressed tightly together. He'd told her what she already knew, and she didn't intend to admit to it. It was what she didn't know that might get her to talk.

"The Secret Service was supposed to catch whoever tried to blackmail them, but it didn't work. Something went wrong."

Her eyebrows jumped with a tiny twitch. "What went wrong?"

"We don't know. But the story about my dad and Meg leaving on a honeymoon was obviously a diversion. They ran from both the blackmailers and the Secret Service, and we don't know why. They're even hiding from us to keep us safe. Except it's not working. We started asking questions, and two nights ago someone tried to run us down and kill us."

That seemed to crack her composure a little. "Perhaps if you would just let the Secret Service do its job—"

"I'd love to, Senator, but the Secret Service doesn't know where they are or why they disappeared. And more important, they don't know where to look for answers, because my dad refused to give them your name."

She did a credible job of looking skeptical. "Are you saying he gave it to you?"

"No, he didn't. Someone else did."

That one shook her. Senator McNabb whispered, "Someone else told you I was being blackmailed?" She swallowed and made her voice stronger. "Who?"

"I'd rather not—"

Lauren squeezed his fingers. "She needs to know," she said before turning to Senator McNabb. "Senator Pierson told us there were rumors about you and another man."

The senator's face crumpled and Drew watched her break. As a seasoned politician, Senator McNabb would know how to draw on composure she didn't feel, but it required a coolness that seemed to have escaped her. She closed her eyes tightly as if in pain. "I hoped it would never . . . I didn't think anyone would . . ." Senator McNabb's hoarse voice failed altogether.

"I'm sorry," Drew told her gently, knowing that the woman was seeing her political and personal future going down in flames. As sleazy as it made him feel, he leaned forward and spoke intently, determined to push his advantage. "Please understand why we are here. You were the first target. We're hoping you know something that will help us find out who's doing this before there are any more victims."

And before they kill us. He didn't say it because she was already nodding dully.

Adding the only reassurance he could, Drew said, "We have no interest in making this public, Senator, and rumors are only that. They don't have to destroy you. Believe me, if you know anything about my father, you know he has survived several unsavory escapades."

Her smile was bittersweet. "I am not Harlan Creighton. I'm a woman. A *married* woman who stands for family values and morality in government. The public will not forgive me." Her voice broke. "I don't deserve forgiveness."

He couldn't respond, couldn't judge her, and couldn't reassure her. He also didn't know how to get useful information while Charlene McNabb floundered in self-pity.

Lauren's fingers slipped away from his and Lauren leaned forward, her feminine concern all but dismissing him from the conversation.

"Senator, I don't know how this happened, but I don't believe you would be careless enough to risk exposure. Do you have any idea how someone obtained photographs of your . . . affair?"

Charlene McNabb sank back in her chair and

covered her face with her hands, shaking her head as she spoke. "No. I don't know. I can't believe it happened. It wasn't even an affair. It was a spontaneous thing, just one night, while I was on vacation in the Bahamas." She raised her eyes in a pleading look. "I don't even know his last name, and I know he doesn't know mine. I lied about it." She clenched her eyes shut and pounded her fists onto the table. "God, I sound so pathetic. I don't understand this. I swear there's no way anyone could have known, much less taken those pictures." She choked up.

Drew hardly dared breathe while Lauren gave the senator several seconds to collect herself.

"Who was he?" Lauren asked.

Senator McNabb shook her head. "I don't know. Just a guy on vacation. He approached me at the bar. We talked, and he invited me to have dinner with him. I was there alone, feeling sorry for myself because my husband . . . well, we'd been having difficulties over our careers, with both of us being out of town a lot and the kids acting out, needing more supervision." She waved her hand as if brushing aside her concerns. "We were working it out. But I was angry, feeling rejected, and Tony was so sympathetic, so understanding."

Senator McNabb took a deep breath and seemed to make an effort to pull herself together. Her back straightened and her expression grew determined. "I have no excuse. I was vulnerable, but I knew what I was doing. But those pictures . . . I've thought about nothing else for the past month. And as impossible as it seems, I can only conclude that I was set up."

Drew couldn't suppress his sudden flare of interest. "What do you mean?"

"It's not like we were out on a beach. We were in his hotel room. Blinds closed, door double-locked—I was rational enough to be paranoid about being recognized. Yet there were pictures. It had to have been a hidden camera."

For one swift second he caught Lauren's glance and knew they were both recalling the pictures of Meg. "Were the photos high quality? Like they were professionally done?"

She shook her head. "No, the room was dim. They were just clear enough that you could tell it was me. Why?"

"Never mind, it doesn't matter." Maybe it didn't, he couldn't sort it all out now.

"Did you ever hear from Tony again?" Lauren asked.

"No. I didn't even stay the night, I was so ashamed of what I'd done. And like I said, he didn't know my real name. At least, I didn't think he did." She laughed, a bitter, harsh sound. "I'm not even sure I know his. I remember I laughed when he told me it was Tony, because it didn't fit. Tony sounds so stereotypically Italian, that dark, olive-skinned look, you know? But he was so fair and blond, almost Nordic."

Drew felt his skin go cold despite the clammy Florida heat and knew from Lauren's wide eyes that she felt the same thing. Her voice was weak when she asked, "Did he have long, straight hair? About to here?" She indicated a line just above her collar.

Senator McNabb looked surprised, then suspicious. "Yes. How did you know that?"

"There are similar pictures," Lauren said, her voice shaky. "Of my sister and . . . and a man of that description."

Color drained from Senator McNabb's face. "Oh my God." Drew saw her hands tighten into white-knuckled fists and felt the same tense response in his gut. "For them to have planned that . . . my trip to the Bahamas was a last-second decision. Someone had to have known my schedule, followed me, have the whole seduction planned in advance." To her credit, she didn't waste much time on self-pity. "If they were that organized, this could be huge. And dangerous." She turned her gaze back to him. "Are you aware of what they used those pictures for, Mr. Creighton?"

"I know you were asked to vote a certain way to keep the pictures secret."

"Yes, I was told to vote against my party's position on the offshore drilling bill." She paused, shame obvious in her flushed cheeks and downcast eyes. "God help me, I did. It passed by four votes, close but far more than anyone expected." She looked up. "It wasn't expected to pass. Do you see? With that margin I thought my vote didn't matter, that it would have passed anyway, but how many of those four votes were coerced like mine was?"

Drew didn't have to be in politics to understand the enormity of what she was suggesting. New laws, appropriations, taxes—all were decided by the House and Senate. Many passed by only a few votes. If some-one gained control of more votes, whole political agen-das could be changed.

One powerful person, with enough political black-mail behind him, could control the course of the coun-try. One powerful, *corrupt* person.

"Who wanted the offshore drilling bill passed?" he asked grimly.

"All of the opposing party pushed for it, but it was the president's baby." Senator McNabb watched Drew's shocked response and shook her head, following his thoughts. "No, it can't be him. I don't agree with the president's agenda, but I know and respect the man. I'm certain he'd never be involved in something so immoral."

Drew didn't argue, but he couldn't help recalling the evil glare and snide remarks Lauren had received at the Romanian embassy. The president's domestic advisor had not bothered to conceal her disdain for both Meg and Harlan Creighton. Even if the president were too principled to have done it, that didn't rule out any of the ambitious sycophants he employed.

Drew's mind whirled with scenarios of presidential advisors sneaking around Washington, luring senators into sexual traps, then forcing them to vote for the president's pet programs. It was a plot far beyond the scope of Watergate, and he couldn't believe it. For one thing, it was too complex. To break into Mihaly's apartment, trail Senator McNabb to the Bahamas, and deliver the blackmail photos to Meg and his dad right under the nose of the Secret Service all required incredible resources. And skill. And inside information. Almost like the Secret Service itself.

Drew stiffened.

It was so obvious. Why hadn't he seen it sooner?

He stood abruptly, pulling a surprised Lauren up with him. "I'm sorry, Senator McNabb, but we must be going. Don't worry, your name won't come up. I'll do my best to see that this doesn't affect your career."

The senator's mouth pulled into a tight, regretful

smile. "Thank you, but it doesn't matter. I'll be resigning my seat."

"No, please don't make a hasty decision—" Drew began.

"I'm not. I've given it a lot of thought, and I have to leave. Those pictures will be used against me again and again, and I refuse to violate my office and my constituents by voting against my conscience again. I'll be resigning when the Senate resumes session next week."

At their stunned looks, she shook her head wearily. "It's not your fault. If they want to use the pictures to destroy my marriage, they can try. That's my problem. But I won't let my mistakes influence the course of domestic and foreign policy. I hope Harlan and Meg are okay, and I'm sorry I couldn't help."

"But you did," Drew told her.

"I did? I don't understand."

He wasn't going to explain until he had proof. "If I learn anything, I'll keep you informed, Senator McNabb. Thank you for seeing us." He hustled Lauren toward the walk that led around the house to the driveway.

As soon as they rounded the corner and plunged into the senator's landscaped jungle of banyan trees and flowering hibiscus, Lauren tugged at his arm. "Will you please tell me what in the world is going on?"

Drew looked around, then pulled her into the deep green shade of a tree, sending several small lizards scurrying up its branches. As isolated as they seemed on the shaded path, Drew no longer trusted his sense of security. He leaned close to Lauren's ear.

"We have to return to Washington as soon as

possible. I think we'd better call Mihaly, too," he said, grimacing at the thought.

Lauren lowered her voice conspiratorially. "Why?"

"Because I know why Dad and Meg disappeared. I just figured out who tried to blackmail them."

"Who?"

Even saying it aloud seemed dangerous. Instead, he put a finger to his lips and asked for the car keys.

When he was behind the wheel, squealing the tires as he sped out of the senator's driveway, he told her.

He knew she heard him over the noise because she stared in disbelief. "The Secret Service? That's impossible!"

"No, it isn't."

"How can the Secret Service possibly be blackmailing senators? They're the ones who set up the sting in the first place."

"Some of them did," he corrected. "But I think some others, maybe only one or two, pulled off this blackmail scheme. Think about it. Why else would my dad and Meg run from the Secret Service? They must have figured out who was behind it, and didn't know who to trust."

"How? How did they figure it out?" She frowned, obviously not convinced. And she wasn't blinded enough by love to believe him without proof.

The idea that Lauren might love him was intriguing, and worth exploring, but not now.

"I can't be sure how they figured it out. Maybe it was the blond guy in the photos. Maybe my dad recognized him." Anticipating Lauren's objection, he added, "Or if the pictures were faked, maybe Meg recognized him. Anyway, the timing fits. Chapman said an envelope was delivered to them just before they ran. I agree with him that it had to be the photos. Realizing who the blond guy was would have been enough to spook them into disappearing. He's got to be Secret Service. It's the only reason they would run from the people who were supposed to protect them."

He dug the cell phone out of his pocket and handed it to Lauren. "Here, the airline's number is in the directory. See if we can get on a flight back to D.C. today."

She looked worried as she dialed, so he knew she was at least partially convinced. With the phone to her ear, Lauren asked, "Why would the Secret Service care about how anyone voted on the offshore drilling bill?"

"They wouldn't. It's not the agents, it's whoever they're working for," he told her grimly. "Senator McNabb swore it couldn't be the president. But those agents have to be doing this on behalf of someone, someone who cares about the outcome of that bill."

That was the missing piece of the puzzle. Who had the most to gain by passing that legislation? Drew didn't keep up with politics well enough to know. His father's office staff might be helpful, but he didn't want to involve more people, especially people he didn't know. But Senator Pierson was already involved, and he would know who would benefit.

While Lauren spoke to the airline, Drew devised a plan. He was so lost in thought, he hadn't even noticed the sedan that zoomed up from behind and shot out on their left until it was beside them. It was too close. Drew swerved sharply to the right. The Mustang fishtailed, tires sliding on the crushed shells and sand of the shoulder, throwing up stones that banged against the windshield and sheet metal. Drew swore, fighting the wheel. The car rocked to a stop as the speeding sedan roared past more cars until it was out of sight.

"Goddamned freakin' idiot, he could get someone killed!" He looked at Lauren, who was rubbing her shoulder. "Are you all right?" He undid his seat belt and gently grabbed her arm, turning her toward him.

"I'm fine, I just bumped my shoulder on the door, and dropped the phone. Did you see where it went?"

Her eyes searched the floor but it was something else that grabbed Drew's attention. Gazing past Lauren, he stared at three neat, round holes in the passenger door and glove box.

A chill swept over him. The banging sound had been bullets, not stones. He swore again, his grip inadvertently tightening on Lauren's shoulders.

"What's wrong?" She followed his gaze, looking at the holes in confusion, then dawning horror. Her voice was weak. "They shot at us?" She turned to him, eyes clear gray and wide with fear. "Why?"

The terror in her gaze sent a hot bolt of anger ripping through his gut.

"Maybe because we're getting too close to the truth."

Wedged between Lauren's seat and the center console, Drew spotted the cell phone. He called 911, reporting the shooting in terse words, and hung up only when he heard approaching sirens.

White and shaken, Lauren watched him. The urgent need to pull her into his arms left him frustrated—the damn gear shift was in the way. He held her hand, keeping her cold fingers wrapped in a reassuring grip, no longer questioning the part of him that knew he would never let go of her.

Or the sobering realization that went with it: He'd brought her here, exposed her to this. This was his fault. His first responsibility was to get her to safety.

"Were you able to get us on a flight to Washington tonight?" he asked.

She nodded, then found her voice. "Yes."

"Good." In Washington, he could make sure she was safe.

From the opposite direction, a squad car raced toward them down the center line. "When we're done here, I'm going to make sure we get an escort back to the airport. As soon as we do, call Mihaly and have him meet us at the airport. I don't care how late it is."

"Okay. But why?"

"Because he's the only one who knows what he's doing with this spy business, and he doesn't have conflicting allegiances. I'm sure he doesn't give a damn about the Secret Service; he only cares about Meg."

As the squad car did a U-turn behind them, he glanced at Lauren. She wasn't going to like this. "There is one problem."

"What?" she asked cautiously.

"If we want him to believe us, we're going to have to tell him how we made the connection with the Secret Service. We have to tell him about the photos of Meg and the blond guy."

Chapter Twelve

They not only had to tell him, they had to *show* him.

Lauren didn't like it; she was certain she was betraying Meg. But when Mihaly met their plane at 2:00 a.m. and heard about the X-rated pictures, his face became stern and cold. He insisted on seeing them. She offered to describe them, but Mihaly wouldn't budge.

Meg was going to kill her.

Lauren was at the bank when it opened, bleary-eyed after only two hours of sleep and sunburned after forgetting to reapply sunscreen for the drive back to the airport. With minimal conversation, she retrieved the envelope from the safe deposit box and hurried back to the car.

"Not here," she said, holding the envelope away from Mihaly's grasping hands.

"I'll be very quick," he said, reaching again.

"No. When we get to the house." If she had to let him see the photos, at least it would be someplace private.

Neither Drew nor Mihaly objected, and neither said a word as they drove back to the Creighton home.

Mihaly followed impatiently as Lauren led the way into the living room. The lightweight envelope felt heavy and ominous in her hand. She thrust it at Mihaly.

Lauren hadn't planned to look, but Mihaly collapsed onto the sofa across from her and dumped the photos on the coffee table. She glanced, then looked away, blushing. It wasn't the sex she found embarrassing. It was that they showed Meg with a man whose only interest was victimizing her. She wished there'd been a less brutal way to convince Mihaly of the blackmail scheme.

Drew stood nearby, his gaze also avoiding the photos as he watched the Romanian.

Mihaly spread the photos out, studying each one with a grim expression. Lauren ached for him, doubting any man's love could hold up to that sort of betrayal. Certainly she would never be as stoic as Mihaly if she were to see compromising photos of Drew. The pain of that thought was so intense she shuddered and blocked it from her mind. It was not her love life that was crumbling here; it was Meg's.

Mihaly's jaw tightened, his dark eyes unreadable as he gathered the photos and stacked them facedown on the table before leaning back against the sofa.

"These are fake," he pronounced.

Lauren shared a sympathetic glance with Drew.

"I thought so, too," she said carefully. "At first. I just couldn't picture Meg doing that. I mean, I could, but not with some guy who . . ." She was making a mess of it. "But I'm pretty sure that's Meg. I mean . . ." She glanced at Drew. Oh, what the hell, he'd already seen everything. "I'm sure it's her, Mihaly. And the man is the same guy another senator described, probably the same one who broke into your apartment. Meg had to be set up."

Mihaly's mouth twitched into an odd smile. She wondered if he was trying to hide his pain, but his eyes were definitely twinkling with amusement.

"You thought I meant that wasn't Meg?" He chuckled. "No, that is most certainly Meg. But that is not our young Scandinavian friend. It is *his* picture that has been faked."

Confused, Lauren glanced from Mihaly, to the stacked photos, then back to Mihaly. It was a tempting idea, but made no sense. "What makes you think so?"

"Because it is me." He actually seemed to be enjoying her discomfort. "I am the man in those pictures."

She realized her mouth was hanging open, and closed it. "How, um, I mean, what . . . ?" She gave up.

"They were obviously stolen from my apartment. You must realize they were meant to be private, only for Meg and me."

Numbly, Lauren nodded. If she learned any more about her sister's love life she'd never be able to look her in the eyes without blushing.

Drew cleared his throat, probably no more eager than she was to know the details of Meg's private life. "Why would they change them?" he asked. "They couldn't work as blackmail, since Meg would have recognized them."

"I suspect your father was the intended target, at first. If their marriage were real, these might have been very effective blackmail."

"At first? What are you talking about?" Drew demanded.

"Imagine the situation you described to me," Mihaly explained. "Senator Creighton and Meg announce their marriage. They wait for someone to contact them with some sort of blackmail. They are prepared for this type of photo, but they aren't worried. If the pictures are of Senator Creighton and some woman, he would expect that they can not damage his career. It is well known that he has dated, and been intimate with, many women in this town. Am I correct?" he asked Drew.

"Correct," Drew muttered.

"In his home state, it is known he is like this. It is also known he is a good senator, so they re-elect him. If these photos show up, so what? He says, 'I am appalled, I did not know she took them.' Then maybe the woman looks bad, that's all. They would not influence his vote. He doesn't care, so he is immune."

Mihaly watched both of them to see if they followed his reasoning. Lauren nodded. "We get that much. Senator Creighton can't be blackmailed with dirty pictures of himself. But they would expect him to want to keep similar pictures of his wife out of the press."

"Yes, quite likely," Mihaly agreed. "It is the nature of politics, at least in your country. Wives are expected to be pure, a good influence on the man. The people are more likely to forgive his indiscretions if his wife does."

His assessment of American politics sounded right on target to Lauren. "So why change the pictures? Why aren't they just as effective with your picture on them? It shows his wife fooling around with another man."

Mihaly rubbed his chin thoughtfully. "This is the troubling part. I believe the pictures are more than blackmail. They are a warning."

"How? For whom?" Drew said it, but Lauren was glad he asked. She was starting to wonder if she was the only one getting lost in the tangled web of lies.

Mihaly assessed them before answering, debating how much information to share. Finally, pointing to the pictures, he said, "Do you understand what this means? They broke into my apartment to get them. The blackmailers know who I am and what I do, and they were *still* able to get into my apartment. Meg knows what that says about their level of competence."

Drew was nodding, but Lauren wasn't about to let him off that easily. "That's not good enough," she said, surprising both men. "I want specifics here. We're talking about my sister, who apparently means something to you."

"I love Meg," Mihaly said, as if that should have been obvious. "And she loves me."

"So you said. And I'm beginning to believe it, at least your side of it. So I think I have a right to know exactly who you are. Are you a spy? Have you involved Meg in something dangerous or illegal?"

"Lauren, he can't—" Drew began. Mihaly cut him off with a raised hand.

"It's okay, she has a right to ask." He smiled at her. "Spy. That word has a certain panache, no? Perhaps more than I deserve. I am the Romanian Deputy Ambassador to the United States. But I also provide information to certain people in my country. Sensitive information. I do not meet with agents in dark alleys or sneak into government buildings to steal documents. Usually. But what I do is not always legal. Technically."

Lauren frowned. "Yeah, that's real specific."

"I think you can say he's a spy," Drew said.

Mihaly shrugged.

She wasn't happy with the answer, but realized she wouldn't get any more out of him. "And Meg knows this?"

"Yes."

"But all this blackmail stuff isn't related to who you are and what you do?"

"No."

Lauren didn't think so either, but she wanted to hear him say it. "So how is altering pictures to put someone else's face on your body a warning?"

"These people are not being subtle. It means they have eliminated me. Removed me. It is a threat, in case Meg wants to turn to me for help. Obviously, they do not want me helping her. So they would expose her affair and my identity along with it. She won't contact me, because it would put me in danger."

"And she won't put you in danger because she loves you."

"Yes. She is wrong to do this, of course, but she is acting out of love."

His confidence in Meg was amazing, and Lauren was beginning to believe it was justified. She bit her lip while she thought it through. Mihaly Dragos was at the very least a close friend of Meg's and probably the person best qualified to help her deal with threats from government agents. Yet, she hadn't contacted him. Meg must care a great deal for the Romanian man if she chose to protect him when she needed his help the most.

"All right, so the pictures aren't sexual blackmail," Lauren said. "They're a warning that Meg shouldn't contact you. Which explains everything except why Meg and Harlan ran from the Secret Service agents they were supposed to be working with."

Mihaly considered the problem. "On that, I agree with Drew's conclusion. One of them recognized the blond man as a Secret Service agent. It is the only answer. Some of these men act like they are invisible, you know, but they are not. Maybe this one made that mistake."

He leaned forward, more intense than he'd been before. "You must let me help you. We have to find them before these rogue agents do."

Lauren thought "rogue agents" was a good term for them. She also thought it sounded dangerous as hell. "What do you think we should do?"

"Is there someone who might know a place Senator Creighton would consider safe? Or anyone he might contact if he needed help?"

"I wish it were us," Drew complained. "But he won't let us get involved, so my only guess would be Senator Pierson. Their politics may differ, but they've been friends for years."

"Can you trust him?"

"Yes. If he were part of it, he could have removed us from the picture before we went to Florida. Plus, he already helped us once."

"Then perhaps he will be able to help again."

Drew nodded and looked at Lauren, including her in his response. "We'll talk to him."

"And this Agent Chapman you mentioned. He is expecting to hear from you?"

"I'll contact him again," Drew offered. "Maybe he already knows something about the guys who followed us to the motel yesterday."

"Yes, we will have to involve him. Perhaps he can find out who the other Secret Service agents are, the ones Meg and Senator Creighton ran from, if they really are agents." He scowled at the facedown photos. Lauren had half expected Mihaly to propose some clandestine operation right out of the pages of an espionage novel and was mildly disappointed that he would run straight to the authorities with their story.

"And perhaps he will recognize the blond man in the pictures. I would especially love to be present when we find him." From Mihaly's expression, he was not going to be forgiving about someone else having seen his private photos of Meg.

But exactly how private were they? Lauren recalled her initial assumption that Meg had been unaware of the camera. A hidden camera wouldn't be a surprise in Mihaly's electronically enhanced apartment. Lauren had to consider the other possible explanation for the pictures. If Meg hadn't known she was being photographed, she might have been appalled to discover that her lover had taken advantage of her that way. She might have avoided contacting Mihaly because she no longer trusted him.

She should have thought of it sooner. Lauren eyed Mihaly suspiciously. "I'm surprised Meg agreed to let you take those photographs," she said.

He looked up, dark gaze sparkling as he assessed her. "Meg can be rather uninhibited," he said, watching her closely. "The photos were her idea, Lauren. Perhaps there is more to your sister than she lets you know."

Lauren blinked. He sure had that right.

Mihaly slid the pictures back in the envelope, folding the clasp. "I would prefer to keep these, if you don't mind."

She minded only if he was lying about being the man in the pictures, and about Meg being aware of the camera. She had a feeling he wasn't.

Lauren nodded, and watched him fold the envelope before fitting it into an inner pocket of his suit coat. The photos would be creased, but she imagined he had negatives. Or maybe it was Meg who had them. Suddenly recalling the rows of video tapes at Meg's apartment, she flushed, glad they hadn't decided to look through them. Who knew what else her sister had decided to record.

Drew used the tapped house line and put Agent Chapman on speaker so Lauren and Mihaly could hear.

"What do you want now?" Chapman's voice barked.

"Hello to you, too."

"What state are you in now, Creighton? Or have you left the country?"

Drew grinned, beginning to enjoy ruffling Chapman's feathers. "We're back in Georgetown."

"Be still, my heart." The words were flat and lifeless.

Lauren stifled a giggle and whispered to Drew, "Be nice, I like this guy."

For a second Drew felt a stab of jealousy toward

Chapman, wishing she'd said that about him. Not that she hadn't demonstrated how much she liked him in several ways over the past few days, but he hadn't actually heard the words. He was surprised to realize how much that mattered. Shrugging it off for now, he groused to Chapman, "Hey, don't I get points for keeping you updated?"

"You're a bit late. I got word last night about three a.m. that you were home. I really enjoyed that wake-up call, by the way, 'cause I've been getting way too much sleep lately."

Drew didn't hide his surprise. "You have someone watching the house?"

"We're not totally incompetent, Creighton." The agent's voice was sharper now, and not the least bit friendly. "We even know that you visited your father's safety deposit box. Again. I might overlook that bit of identity fraud on Miss Sutherland's part if you want to tell me what it is that's so important in there."

He glanced at Lauren before answering. "Come on over, and we'll tell you all about it."

A moment of silence followed. "Are you saying you're ready to cooperate?" He could hear the caution in Chapman's voice.

"Fully." He waited to see if the agent would believe him.

"Let me guess. You have something important and you need help."

"Yes."

"I'm an hour away."

"Then we'll see you in an hour." Drew hung up the phone and looked at Lauren and Mihaly. "One down, one to go."

Pierson seemed even more eager for an update than Chapman. "Come on over, I'm at the apartment. You need the address?"

"I have it in Dad's book. Be there in ten," he said, clicking off.

Lauren looked confused. "He has an apartment?"

"Pierson's from Pennsylvania," Drew explained. "That's not too far from Washington for him to get home on weekends, so his family stays there and he lives in an apartment when he's in town. A lot of senators and representatives do that. It's not far from here. You want to come?"

"Are you kidding? Just try to stop me."

He loved it; she was always ready for a new adventure. How this woman ever led a structured, uneventful life was beyond him. It sounded like she had a lot of cautious living to make up for, and he was just the man for the job.

"I'd better stay out of it," Mihaly said, jerking his thoughts back to the moment. "Just be back by the time Chapman gets here."

"No problem. And I'll get Gerald to come over, too. He'll kill me if I leave him out of this."

The visit with Pierson would be quick. All he needed to do was prod the senator into examining his memories. Maybe he could shake something loose, some tidbit of information like the one that led them to Senator McNabb.

Pierson ushered them inside his small apartment and showed them to the single couch while he pulled up a chair. His face was paler than normal, and his anxiety was anything but subtle, with his hands on his knees, looking ready to spring into action at a moment's notice. "Did you talk to Charly? What did you find out?"

He and Lauren had already discussed how they would answer this one. Even though Pierson had given them that lead, Drew saw no reason to tell what they'd learned. He'd promised Senator McNabb to leave her out of it if he could, and he intended to do that.

"That's no longer important, Senator Pierson."

"It's not? I don't understand. I thought you needed to find out who the blackmailer is."

"We think we know. At least, we have enough information to track him down." An exaggeration, but close enough.

Pierson looked ready to go after the blackmailers himself, right now. "You do? My God, tell me what you found out. Have they tried to compromise other senators? Do you realize the implications here?"

"We do." He should have guessed that Pierson would see how the blackmail scheme would play out. The man wasn't stupid. Naturally, he would fear the very scenario that Senator McNabb confirmed.

Drew glanced at Lauren and raised an eyebrow. She nodded, agreeing they would have to fill Pierson in on some of what was happening. He couldn't hide a quick smile, enjoying the fact that they were thinking alike. They worked well together. They did everything well together. He squeezed her hand.

Since Pierson was aware of the possibilities, Drew didn't try to play it down. "Someone is trying to control votes on key bills, Senator. And this won't be the only time. Senators, and maybe congressmen, will be repeatedly pressured into voting a certain way. We don't know how many, but it's possible it's already happening. I don't even want to think about how it would upset the balance of power. Someone has a very large, very frightening agenda."

"Damn straight! And if it's already started, this is more urgent than I thought. We have to find out who it is and stop them."

It felt good to know they had someone from the inside in their corner willing to help.

"We agree, Senator," Lauren chimed in. That's why we're turning over everything we know to the Secret Service, who can contact the FBI and whoever else they need to track the culprit down."

Pierson's eyebrows went up. "Well, that's a change. The last time I talked to you, you didn't trust them because Harlan and Meg gave them the slip."

"We can't do this alone; we need help," Drew admitted.

"Hell, I'll help however I can. Just don't get the authorities involved if you don't know who you can trust."

"They already were involved," Lauren reminded him.

"But they don't know shit! Why not keep it that way?"

Two days of thinking about it had obviously gotten Pierson pretty worked up. Drew held up a hand. "Don't worry. We've been talking to an agent we're pretty sure we can trust."

"Who?"

"He's the guy in charge of the task force my dad was working with."

Pierson gave him an incredulous look. "The guy

Harlan and Meg ran away from? *That's* the guy you trust?"

It sounded like a pretty lame move when he put it like that. Drew ran a hand through his hair in frustration, but Lauren jumped to Chapman's defense.

"This guy expended a lot of effort trying to keep me safe when he thought I was Meg. We're not just going on instinct. You'll have to trust *us* on this."

Pierson gave them each a long, hard look before nodding. "Okay, it's your call. Let's just get moving on this thing. You gave this guy the information?"

"We will as soon as we leave," Drew assured him.

"Good. I hope you'll keep me informed."

"We will. But Lauren and I were hoping you could do something else for us. You know my dad as well as anyone in Washington. Can you think of any place he might go to hide out? Maybe he mentioned some private cabin he used on occasion or maybe he has some friend who would give them a place to stay where no one would spot them."

Pierson sat back with a thoughtful look. "Are you asking me about some private hideaway where Harlan might have taken a lady friend?"

Was he? Why else would his dad sneak off somewhere, except for one of his notorious trysts? "I suppose so. If he might have mentioned that to you."

"If he mentioned it?" Pierson chuckled. "I've heard a few stories from him over the years. Let me think, there must be someplace . . ." Pierson began pacing the small area between the kitchen and living room, eyes on the floor and mouth pressed into a firm line.

They watched quietly, then glanced at each other as one minute turned into two. Lauren leaned toward him, whispering, "How many incidents can there be?"

Drew grimaced. "A lot." He doubted that his dad had talked about most of them, but if he'd just mentioned a hideaway where he'd been able to avoid the press for a few days . . .

"I might know of a place."

Pierson's sudden announcement made them both sit up straighter. "Where?" Drew asked.

"Maryland, out in the sticks. There's this place Harlan told me about years ago that's about as remote as you can get. It's a small vacation cabin, way off some back road. He pointed it out once when we drove by it. It might be nothing, but it's the only thing I can think of."

"That's great," Lauren said enthusiastically. "It's a place to start. Can you give us the address or tell us how to get there?"

"Sure, let me write it down. I can tell you as much as I remember, which might be enough to get you there, seeing as how there's not much else out that way. I don't know why I didn't think of this place before." He found a pen and paper and began writing down directions, explaining them aloud as he did.

Drew put the folded paper in his pocket and rose, pulling Lauren up with him. "Thank you. We'll let you know if we find them."

"You'd damn well better, son, because I won't sleep a wink until you do." He trailed them to the door. "You'll check that out soon, won't you?"

"As soon as we can, probably by tonight," Drew reassured him.

"Great. And if I think of anything else, I'll call."

They thanked him again and left. Drew took Lauren's hand as they walked to the car, aware that he was just looking for a reason to touch her. He was fine with that.

"He sounded as worried as we are," Drew said.

"I know." She was silent for several seconds, and Drew thought she must be thinking about Pierson. "You know what?" She smiled up at him.

"What?"

"Jeff didn't approve of public displays of affection like holding hands."

It seemed to him that her hand was doing as much clasping as his was. "What do you think about it?"

"I like it." Her smile became a grin. "I like you."

He smiled back, pretty sure that what he felt for her was more like *I love you.*

She watched Drew driving, studying the features she'd become so familiar with the past few days. She could look at him forever. "Drew?"

"Yeah?"

"I've been thinking about the photographs of Meg and Mihaly."

"What about them?" He turned at a stoplight, his attention on the road.

"When we first found them at the bank, I couldn't believe Meg would let someone take photos of her like that."

He chuckled. "You *were* pretty embarrassed."

"But I understand it now."

That got his full attention. He looked at her, eyebrows arched in amused surprise. "You do? You understand someone taking pictures of herself having sex?"

"That wasn't sex. She was making love with Mihaly, which must have been very special and emotional for her. She wanted to preserve that feeling. I think he's right; she really does love him, whether she admits it or not."

"Huh." He thought about it as he switched lanes. "What made you think of that?"

"It reminded me of when we were at the hotel and you told me to watch in the mirror. It was exciting, and . . . beautiful."

He gave her a long look. "Well, one of us was beautiful."

"Have you ever taken photographs of yourself like that? You know, making love with someone?"

"No. Have you?"

She smiled. "Not yet."

He stared, darted a look at traffic, then back to her before grinning like a fool.

They arrived at the Creighton home before Chapman. Mihaly was there, in the process of fitting together an array of metal pieces that lay on the coffee table before him. It took Lauren about three seconds to realize he was reassembling a gun. She sobered quickly.

"Where did that come from?"

He jammed two pieces together. "What?"

"That gun."

"What gun?" He tucked the completed weapon into his back waistband and covered it with his sweater.

She narrowed her eyes at him but said nothing. There were about to be a lot of government agents involved, all carrying guns. She'd better get used to it.

Mihaly turned to Drew. "Tell me what you think of this Chapman. Do you trust him?"

Drew curled his lip in distaste as he threw his coat

over a chair. "He's officious, arrogant, and rude. And he's young. But as irritating as I find him, yes, I trust him."

Lauren felt obligated to defend him. "He's not irritating. He's just another dominant male butting heads with you over who's in charge."

Drew looked at her, eyebrow raised. "A dominant male?" He smiled. "I didn't know you financial types dabbled in psychology."

"All women dabble in psychology," she answered sweetly. "We're forced to."

He snorted, then said to Mihaly, "He's competent, but a bit on the surly side. I should warn you, Mihaly, he's not fond of us. We ambushed him then skipped town. When he finds out we've been withholding this information, he won't be happy."

Agent Chapman leaned forward on the sofa and cradled his head in his hands. The man appeared to be in actual pain. The clenched eyelids and the circles he massaged into his temples indicated the beginnings of a migraine.

"Let me get this straight," Chapman said, squinting up at them. "Compromising photos of Miss Sutherland that you refuse to show me were delivered for purposes of extorting votes from Senator Creighton?"

Seated on the sofa across from him, Lauren nodded. She had volunteered to be the bearer of bad news, hoping he'd be less likely to explode. Gerald sat beside her for moral support. Standing behind them, Drew and Mihaly simply stared back at Chapman.

The agent pressed two fingers against what appeared to be a particularly painful spot on his temple. "The pictures were also meant to warn Miss Sutherland not to involve her boyfriend in the scheme. A boyfriend who is quite possibly a foreign agent operating in the United States."

Lauren nodded again.

"I am the Romanian Deputy Ambassador," Mihaly corrected.

Chapman's eyebrows drew together as he scrutinized Mihaly. "Yeah, right."

"He checks out."

Hawknose, who had been introduced as Agent Renke, tossed the ID holder back to Mihaly before flopping into an arm chair. Lauren noticed that he kept a wary eye on Gerald sitting beside her with arms folded, glaring holes into the man's skull.

"No espionage activity?" Chapman asked his partner.

"If there is, the CIA isn't sharing it." Renke gave Mihaly a final hard stare before shifting his gaze to Drew. "The senator's son, however, has training in several martial arts disciplines and is licensed to carry."

Lauren turned a surprised look up at Drew, but he kept his calm gaze on Chapman and Renke.

"I carry a handgun back in Colorado when I have to transport checks and cash into town. I've never used it."

"And the martial arts are to guard against bear attacks?" Chapman asked in a cynical tone.

"I work with juvenile offenders who are often ex-gang members. I find it best to be prepared for all contingencies. What does this have to do with finding Meg and my father?" Drew asked.

Chapman's headache appeared to stab harder as he bristled at Drew. "You're the one asking us for help here, Creighton. I'll decide what's relevant and what isn't." He included Lauren in his fierce scowl, then rubbed at his forehead again before stating the part he apparently liked least. "And you think one of our agents is behind all this?"

"At least one. Has to be," Drew said.

"He's right," Mihaly added, earning him a glare that clearly said the opinions of foreign intelligence agents weren't welcome.

Lauren tried to explain without giving too much away. "We know which Senator first approached Drew's father about the blackmail scheme. The, uh, compromising incident occurred during a spur-of-the-moment trip, and only the senator's secretary knew the destination. And she only told one person, a Secret Service agent who asked to see the Senator during that time. We asked the senator to check that part out."

"You just said the secretary knew," Chapman pointed out. "What makes you think she didn't have a partner who propositioned your senator?"

Lauren paused. They hadn't even considered that. She thought about the woman in Senator McNabb's office. Efficient, controlling, and maybe a tad resentful at being left behind when her boss went to Florida. But a little too careless with information to be a successful criminal.

"Gut instinct," she told Chapman. "And because whoever is behind this must have a significant stake in the result of the vote, probably a financial stake. That means someone with power and influence, not a secretary. And most of all, because there's only one reason my sister and Senator Creighton would run from the

Secret Service agents who were supposed to protect them—because they knew they might be the same people who were threatening them."

Chapman chewed on the inside of his cheek while he considered it. "Which one of you wants to tell me about the senator you visited in Florida?"

"I just did," Lauren pointed out.

"The senator's identity is privileged information," Drew said.

"Come on, Creighton, there are only two senators from each state. I'm gonna figure it out. Save me some time. You found out something down there that convinced you, and I want to know what it is."

"You're right. We found bullet holes in our car. I found it very convincing."

Lauren tried to defuse what promised to become a messy distraction. "Look, we gave our word and the information is irrelevant. The senator was photographed in a compromising situation with the same man who appears in my sister's doctored photos and who broke into Mihaly's apartment."

"I can show you my security tape for identification purposes," Mihaly interjected.

"You have a good picture of the guy?"

"Not his features, just his blond hair sticking out from under a face mask."

"Uh-huh," Chapman mused. "So I will assume that either the distinguished Senator McNabb is hiding an adulterous affair, or the equally distinguished Senator Stockton is hiding a bisexual double life."

Through clenched jaws, Drew said, "Assume what you want, it doesn't matter. We told you what you need to know—the blond guy is a major part of the scheme, and it's likely that either my father or Meg recognized him as an agent. Are you going to help us out here or not?"

The two men stared at each other for several seconds before Chapman growled at his partner, "Get the pictures together for them to look at. All the white male agents in D.C. under forty, no matter what their hair color. He could have dyed it. And don't advertise what you're doing. We don't know how many people might be involved."

Lauren breathed a small sigh of relief. Despite Chapman's stubborn attitude, he was going to help.

Renke stood. "You gonna bring these guys in to look through them?"

"No. Someone's obviously worried enough to want them dead. Bring the pictures here. These two can look through them," he said, pointing at Lauren and Mihaly. "They got the best look at the guy."

"While he does that, I'll check out the location we got from Senator Pierson."

Drew's announcement made Chapman look up. Lauren turned to look, too. Drew stood behind the couch with arms folded and feet planted, an intimidating presence. Chapman must have felt at a disadvantage, because he stood before answering. "We'll do that later."

"If I go now I'll still have some daylight."

"If you go now, you won't know who to watch out for or who might take the next shot at you. We identify the blond guy before anyone goes anywhere."

Drew was obviously unhappy with Chapman's order, and the two men spent several seconds staring each other down. Lauren was getting a crick in her neck, trapped between the two posturing males. She jumped to her feet, smiling sweetly at Chapman. "We just want to help any way we can. Isn't that right, Drew?"

She didn't turn around, waiting with her smile in place and praying that Drew would take the opportunity to back down. Finally, she heard him say, "That's right."

Chapman dropped an equally cool stare to Lauren. "Good. Right now you can help most by waiting for Renke."

"Sure thing." And by keeping Drew and Chapman on opposite ends of the house.

It was more than two hours before Renke returned with a pile of printouts on the agents, concise one-page resumes with pictures. Chapman split the pile, sending Lauren and Mihaly to separate rooms to look through the stack. Two-thirds of the way through her stack, Lauren felt her stomach flip at the sight of the familiar, perfectly cut features. The man had short, brown hair and the serious, unwavering gaze typical of all the agents' photos. But she knew it was the same face she'd seen hovering with passionless perfection over her sister, the same face that had shoved close to hers at the airport, threatening her with cold disdain.

She didn't want to touch the page. Sitting back in her chair, she pointed and told Chapman, "This one."

He took a long look at the photo and copied some of the agent's personal information in a notebook while he motioned toward the stack. "Keep looking."

"But I'm positive that's him."

"Humor me."

She shrugged and did as he said, then did it again

when he exchanged her stack with the one Mihaly had examined. No one else looked even vaguely familiar. She shoved the pile away. "No question. The one I pointed out is the blond in the pictures."

"The Romanian said the same thing," Renke said from the doorway.

Chapman nodded. "Run the info and see where he's been assigned for the past two years. His contacts could be a clue to who recruited him for these dirty little tricks. And don't call me, just get back here as soon as you can."

"Can we order something to eat now?" Lauren asked as soon as Renke disappeared.

"No. No one leaves, and no one comes to the door. Find something in the house."

She supposed she should be glad for Chapman's caution, but she took a lot more pleasure in finding that Gerald had made an impressive haul when they'd left him at the grocery store two days ago. The five of them ate without talking, Chapman, Drew, and Mihaly all with serious, remote expressions. She imagined they were all working out various plans for outing an agent gone bad or for finding Meg and Senator Creighton. Grateful that someone at least had an idea, she left them alone and leaned against the counter next to Gerald.

"I see you and Renke haven't kissed and made up."

Gerald made a strangled sound and coughed something into his hand. "Please, sweetie, I'd like to chew this apple, not suck it into my lungs. Mind your metaphors."

She grinned. "Sorry."

He brushed an invisible speck off his vest and glared

across the room at Chapman, a surrogate target since Renke wasn't there. "The boorish brute is unwilling to take the blame for ripping my coat. Raise your hand if you're surprised."

"You already asked him?"

"Politely but firmly. He went off like a phaser on overload."

She snickered at the *Star Trek* reference. "Ooh, I saw that once. Those things are dangerous."

"My point exactly. Probably 'roid rage."

"Hmm." She let it go. Her opinion wasn't going to count, anyway. "So he refused to reimburse you?"

"I believe that was the gist of his profanity."

Knowing Gerald, that couldn't be the end of the story. "So?"

Gerald flashed an evil smile and chewed his apple as if it were a piece ripped directly from Renke's leg. "You know me so well, already. And you are so right. I've drafted a detailed letter to his superiors about Agent Renke's uncalled-for aggression, along with a bill for the coat, which they *will* pay for in full. And let me tell you, I don't buy cheap sweatshop knockoffs."

"I could tell." Lauren gave a solemn nod.

"Fortunately, I have the receipt."

"Of course you do."

"And witnesses. That's you. These people don't know who they're messing with."

Lauren's smile was as much from admiration as amusement. "I guess you know how to deal with bureaucrats, huh?"

"Honey, I deal with AGAs every day. I could eat these guys for breakfast."

"AGAs?"

"Arrogant Government Assholes. Can't throw a stone in this town without hitting two of them." He bit into the apple for emphasis.

Lauren let out a small laugh.

Gerald pointed his apple at her. "Take some advice from the master, sweetheart. If you're going to play with the big boys, the only way to beat them is with their own rules. And they'd better not try turning it into a paper chase. I can bury those pencil pushers in paperwork, if that's the game they want to play."

"I'll remember that."

Even though she didn't expect to need it. She was almost done playing with the big boys. They'd identified the blond guy, and when Renke found out what he'd been doing for the past couple years, they might know who hired him. No doubt an AGA of the first order. And once they knew who it was, Meg and Harlan wouldn't be the only ones in possession of that deadly secret. They would be out of danger.

She wished Renke would hurry up.

He arrived minutes later, looking rushed and smelling like greasy fast food.

Chapman grabbed a folder from him and headed toward the living room. "What took so long?"

"I stopped for a burger." He shrugged out of his jacket as Chapman opened the folder. "Doesn't matter, I didn't find anything helpful."

Lauren exchanged concerned looks with Drew as they all followed Chapman.

They stood around while Chapman shuffled a few papers, pausing to read while everyone remained unnaturally silent. It took half a minute. "Shit," he spat out, shoving the papers at Renke. "The guy, Marlow, has been detailed to the White House for the past year. He's worked with all levels of staff from the president down."

Renke nodded. "That's what I mean. He could have had contact with almost anyone. Senators, congressmen, cabinet members, you name it. Any one of them might want to set their own political agenda. This is a dead end."

Chapman nodded, his gaze focused on nothing as he thought. When his eyes finally sparked with determination again, Lauren was surprised to see him turn to Drew rather than Renke. "We need to identify Marlow's partner. That's our only chance to narrow things down. And as far as I can tell from your story, we only know of one person who got a good look at him."

Drew's eyes caught the same spark as he nodded. "The desk clerk at our hotel. The kid said he wasn't blond, so I didn't ask him to identify the man. But it must be him, the blond guy's partner."

Mihaly was apparently thinking along the same lines. "Maybe one of these men recruited the other. But maybe they were both recruited by the same man. Perhaps there is some official they both had contact with. If we get an ID, we can compare assignments with Marlow."

Chapman didn't seem excited to have so many self-appointed assistants, but only asked, "What time did you talk to the desk clerk?"

"It was about three thirty in the morning, just before we left for the airport."

"Night shift. Okay, I'll call the hotel, get his home address. Maybe we can catch him before he goes to work."

He was back within five minutes. "No go. The kid

lives with his mother. Mom says he's out with friends and won't come home before going to work. She suggested I look for him at Gamer's nightclub in Arlington or a nearby McDonald's," he reported dryly. "I say we wait until his shift starts at eleven."

Five hours. Crime solving was getting duller by the minute. Lauren could think of a fun way to pass the time but stealing away upstairs with Drew would be rather conspicuous. Disgruntled and tired from being up all night, she went upstairs alone to nap.

No one seemed to have moved when she came downstairs four hours later, except Gerald. While the others sat silently behind magazines or newspapers, he had resorted to dusting the furniture to keep busy. On hands and knees, he squinted through his wire-rimmed glasses as he polished the clawed foot of an end table. Sighing, Lauren picked up a magazine and joined Drew on the sofa.

Two minutes later she was startled by a yell.

"Ouch! Holy effin' hell! Darn it!" Holding his knee, Gerald rubbed vigorously, then picked up something from the carpet. The object in his fingers caught a tiny glint from the table lamp. "Someone lost a diamond ring."

He looked directly at Lauren.

"Not mine," she said, shrugging.

Gerald's gaze drifted to her ringless left hand and his eyebrows rose.

Hearing a soft snort from Drew beside her, she caught his smile as he kept his attention on his newspaper. "Finders keepers," he murmured, as he shot her a hot glance from behind the pages.

Lauren felt heat rise in her cheeks, wanting to believe Drew referred to more than just her ring.

"Now, that's a new one," Renke said. "Guess it shows how much money you have when you find diamond rings in the carpet. If I found a ring in my carpet, it woulda come from a gum machine."

Chapman leaned over to see it better. "I don't know, doesn't look like much of a diamond. You sure it's real?"

With Renke and Chapman bored enough to take an interest in her ring, Lauren did a frantic mental search for any territory they hadn't covered. Anything to keep the conversation off that ring. "So what happens if you identify this other agent?"

Chapman instantly lost interest in the ring in favor of protocol.

"With two positive suspects nailed down, we bring them in. If they're still working as agents, they shouldn't be too hard to locate."

"What if they don't talk?"

Chapman's tight expression indicated how unfortunate a choice that would be.

"Then it just takes a little longer. We might be able to narrow the list by connecting them to the same official, like he said." He jerked his thumb at Mihaly. "But from the beginning we've been checking out anyone who might have an interest in the outcome of the offshore drilling bill. It's a long list." He smiled grimly. "So I plan to make sure they talk."

Mention of the bill reminded Lauren of the partisan battle in Congress that had caused the forced votes. Privately, Lauren wondered how much the president's chief advisor on domestic affairs might care about the outcome of that bill. The woman's comments at the

Romanian Embassy party had been particularly biting. Although jumping from a dislike of Meg to black-mailing United States senators seemed too much of a stretch to even mention to Chapman.

By the time Agent Chapman pulled out his car keys at ten thirty, they all responded like dogs eager to go along for a ride. Renke was the first to get shot down.

"You have to stay here with these guys."

Renke frowned at his babysitting duties. "You can't go out alone. Once you look like you're investigating a decent lead, they're gonna go for you."

"I'll go," Mihaly volunteered quickly. "I have experience with this sort of . . . diplomacy."

Chapman obviously knew what he meant, jingling his keys thoughtfully while considering it. But it was Drew his gaze finally settled on.

"Creighton can come. Seeing him might help jog the clerk's memory. Besides," he scowled at Lauren and Drew, "The last time I left you two alone with orders to stay put, you were gone within thirty minutes."

"Fine," Drew agreed. "But Lauren goes too. She stays with me."

"Miss Sutherland stays here." Chapman was equally firm. "She's a target, and I'm not parading her around D.C. where someone can shoot at her again."

Drew frowned, considering it. For a moment Lauren was touched by his obvious concern, until the implications of what Chapman had said hit her. With an anxious start, she jumped to her feet. "That means Drew's a target, too."

Her worried gaze met his. Through the shared danger of the past two days, she'd never considered the possibility of losing him.

Unspoken emotions churned inside her, stirring up feelings she'd tried to ignore. Feelings she shouldn't have for a man intended to be nothing more than a casual fling.

"I won't be nearly as much of a target without you." Drew's calm words cut through the turmoil inside her.

Chapman sneered. "Especially if you're not bombing around town in a bright red convertible that practically shouts, 'Look at me!'"

Lauren ignored him. Watching Drew, she bit her lower lip to keep from blurting out the words that tugged at her heart.

"Mihaly," Drew began.

"Don't worry," he said. "I will stay with Lauren."

"So will I," Renke muttered. "But I'm only an experienced Secret Service agent, so you might not find that reassuring."

Gerald stood, hooking his arm through Lauren's. "So will I. You just run along and play cops and robbers, Andrew. We'll hold down the fort."

A hint of a smile showed on Drew's mouth. "Thanks."

Chapman studiously ignored Gerald. "Let's get going."

Lauren watched him go without saying what she was thinking, hoping she'd get a chance to say it later.

Waiting was torture. Lauren couldn't avoid the feeling that something big was about to happen, that they were on the verge of finding the person behind the blackmail photos. And, consequently, on the verge of finding Meg and Senator Creighton. And she was stuck at home, waiting, while Drew got to act.

After half an hour of leafing through magazines, Lauren decided one more minute on the couch would drive her crazy. "How long do you think they'll be?" she asked Renke.

"Don't know. Maybe an hour and a half."

"Fine. I'm taking a shower."

The prospect of warm water and fragrant soap sounded like the best thing she'd done all day. The best thing she'd done, in fact, since yesterday morning when she woke up beside Drew in the hotel, snuggled against his naked body, which had been one of the best things she'd *ever* done.

Lauren stripped off her jeans and T-shirt, recalling Drew's hands on her, touching her, teasing her, kissing her until she was dizzy with an emotion that felt suspiciously like love.

Lauren sucked in her breath at the thought. That wasn't supposed to happen. She wasn't—

Gerald's shriek carried up the stairs. Hastily wrapping a robe over her bra and panties, she ran downstairs.

Gerald stood in the living room, red-faced with anger, glaring at Renke's back. Seeing Lauren he huffed, "These federal boys wave their substitute penises around at the slightest excuse, just to scare the citizens."

She scrunched her brow. "Huh?"

"The gun," Gerald sniffed.

Lauren followed his gaze to the front window and finally noticed the dull black Sig Sauer in Renke's right hand as he peered around the curtains.

"Mr. Macho could have shot my head off the way he whipped that thing out. All because a car pulled into the driveway. Sheesh."

"Quiet." The order came from Mihaly, who peered out another window, gun in hand.

"He's coming up the walk, fast," Renke reported, as he switched to a two-handed grip, moving to stay out of view.

When the doorbell rang Lauren looked at him. Renke motioned at Gerald with his gun, stepping around to the foyer. "Get it."

Casting a nervous look at Renke's gun, Gerald eased past Renke to check the peep hole. He looked at Lauren in surprise. "It's Senator Pierson."

"Let him in," she said.

"Just one damn minute!" Renke stomped forward, the gun held against his side, but his other arm pointing at Gerald. "Don't touch that door. Miss Sutherland does not decide who comes in this house. I do."

"Oh, for Pete's sake," she said, pushing past him. "Senator Pierson knows about Meg and Harlan, and what's more, he's the only one who's provided any help so far. We're letting him in."

Renke dropped his arm, his face blank with confusion. "The only one . . . ? Does anyone even wonder what the government pays me for?"

Lauren pushed past Renke, reaching Gerald just as he opened the door.

Pierson startled her, bolting inside, slightly disheveled and breathing hard. "Gerald! Where's—" Seeing her, he started again without a pause. "Lauren! I just got a phone call—"

Pierson made a gargling sound as he spotted Renke,

gun drawn and aimed at him. He jumped back. "Jesus Christ! What's going on here?"

Lauren pulled him all the way in as Gerald shut the door. "It's okay, he's a Secret Service agent." To Renke she hissed, "Would you put the gun down? This man is a family friend."

Renke didn't obey and neither did Mihaly. Gesturing at Pierson with the gun, he barked, "Hands above your head."

Pierson did as ordered, rolling alarmed eyes at both of them. The Romanian's gun remained leveled at the Senator's chest while Renke frisked him.

Renke stepped back. "He's clean." Lauren thought he almost sounded disappointed. The agent straightened, tucking his gun into a shoulder holster. Mihaly's gun disappeared in a similar manner.

Pierson ran a hand through his slightly mussed, short hair, eyeing the two men with caution. "Gerald, is everything okay here?"

"Yes it is, sir," Renke responded before Gerald could open his mouth. "Could you tell me why you're here?"

"I was asked to deliver a message to Drew Creighton." He turned to Lauren. "And you."

Prickles of fear ran up her arms. "Drew's not here, but he'll be back soon. Who is the message from?"

"Harlan and Meg." His uneasy glance darted to the men, then back to her. "Maybe it's a good thing they're here," he said. "We need help."

Only a determined effort kept her from grabbing him by the arms and shaking him. "You heard from Meg? What was the message?"

"They called me. Told me to find you and Drew,

have you bring whatever authorities you know you can trust. I don't know what in the hell they meant by that, if they meant the police, or Secret Service, or—"

"Don't worry," Lauren interrupted, suddenly as edgy and anxious as Pierson. "What did they want us to do?"

"Meet them." He grabbed her arms, squeezing with startling force. Fear seemed to run like an electric current from his hands into her body. "But you can't go, Lauren. It could be a trap. Harlan sounded afraid, and in all the years I've known him, I've never heard that kind of fear in his voice."

"Why did they call *you*?" Mihaly's harsh question interrupted him. "And why now?"

Pierson kept his alarmed gaze on Lauren as he answered Mihaly. "They said they know who the blackmailer is."

Chapter Thirteen

M ihaly swore fiercely. "If they made that known, they must be in danger. Where are they?"

Pierson looked from Mihaly to Renke, suspicion mingling with confusion on his face. "Are you both Secret Service?" He peered at Mihaly. "What was that accent? Are you even an American?" Without waiting for an answer, he turned to Lauren. "I don't understand. Why are these men here? Why do you need protection?"

Before she could answer, Renke spoke up. "Why did they call you when they could have called us?"

"They said this phone was tapped." Pierson frowned. "I'd like to see some ID."

"Yes, sir." With an efficient flick of his wrist, Renke flipped open a leather folder. Pierson glanced at it, grunted, and nodded his head at Mihaly. "You, too."

Lauren didn't see what Mihaly showed him, but Pierson looked up and said, incredulously, "*Romania*?"

"Deputy Ambassador," Mihaly said dryly, supplying

the title no one seemed to believe. "Also a good friend of Meg's. Please tell us what they told you."

"In detail, from the beginning," Renke added.

Pierson took a deep breath and nodded. "Harlan called me at home about half an hour ago. He started to give me some story about hiding out from the press, but I told him I knew about the blackmail scheme. He wasn't happy about that." Pierson gave Lauren an apologetic smile. "He seemed concerned that I would be in danger, too. And he gave me an address where Drew and Lauren can meet them. He said someone spotted them yesterday and they think the area is being searched. They're afraid to come in on their own." With another hesitant glance at Lauren, he added, "They said to hurry."

Mihaly swore again.

"Where are they?" Renke demanded.

The Senator handed over a slip of paper. "It's in Maryland, about forty-five minutes from here." To Lauren, he said, "My hunch was right. It's the same place I told you and Drew about earlier."

A sense of urgency shot through Lauren. Forgetting she wore little more than a robe, she rushed to Mihaly, grabbing his arm. "We can't wait. Come on, we'll go now and Drew can meet us there."

She started for the door, but Mihaly didn't budge. Renke's hand shot out like a stop sign in front of her. "No."

She stared. "What do you mean, no? You heard him, Meg is in danger. We have to go *now*!"

"Not you. My partner said you stay here, and I agree."

"They asked for me and Drew," she insisted. "At

least one of us has to show up, or they'll think it's a trap."

"No. He's right, Lauren." Mihaly's voice was softer, but no less firm. "I promised Drew you would be safe."

"Where is he?" Pierson interrupted. "He's supposed to be there, too."

"He and Chapman are checking out a lead, but we can call him. He'll be there," she assured him. "And so will I," she told Mihaly.

"No, you stay here. I will go. Meg will trust me."

"And me." She'd practically forgotten about Gerald, who was apparently as bored with sitting around waiting as she was. "If I can't go home, then at least I can help." He stuck his hands on his hips and faced Renke. "But I won't carry a gun, so don't ask."

Renke gave him a withering look. "Never occurred to me. In fact, taking you along never occurred to me, either."

"Too bad." Gerald pushed past him. "You need to create a presence, and they both know and trust me. I'm not doing anyone any good here. Don't just stand there, let's get moving."

Renke turned a skeptical look on Mihaly, who shrugged. "He's right. The more of us, the better."

When Renke's gaze swung to Lauren, Pierson moved to her side. "I'll stay here with Lauren," he offered. "Please, just find Harlan and Meg, and get this whole thing over with."

"Damn it," Renke muttered, looking at his improvised posse. "Okay, let's go."

"Hey!" Lauren objected.

The door shut in her face. She kicked it, almost glad of the pain that distracted her from her frustration.

Pierson watched silently out the window as Renke's car drove off, then pulled a cell phone from his pocket. An awkward sense of propriety that Lauren thought she'd overcome compelled her to quote the rules as he dialed a number. "The Secret Service didn't want us making calls, even on cell phones. The wrong people could listen in."

He flashed a cool smile, holding the phone to his ear. "I don't think it matters anymore." He may have been right, but before she even had a chance to argue he spoke to someone on the other end. "They're on their way."

At Lauren's puzzled look, Senator Pierson flipped the phone shut, raked her with a head-to-toe appraisal and held an arm out toward the couch. "Shall we make ourselves comfortable while we wait? It won't be long."

Something in his smile made her shiver.

Drew ground his teeth as the desk clerk flicked another piece of lint from his blazer. In about ten seconds Drew was going to leap over the counter, grab a fistful of that nifty red blazer the clerk seemed so fond of, and stuff it down the little twerp's throat.

"Yeah, I remember the badge," the twerp said. "It was really cool. Star shaped, just like in the movies, ya know? But I didn't really look at the guy's face."

Chapman's patience looked to be fraying, too, but it was still more stable than Drew's. "You must have noticed something because you said he wasn't blond."

The clerk nodded thoughtfully. "That's right, I did. And I'm positive about that. So I guess I am kinda observant, huh?" He stood straighter and adjusted the jacket.

Drew's jaw was beginning to hurt from clenching

it so hard. The kid at the desk had actually spoken to the man who was their best lead, and he couldn't remember a thing about the guy, except that he wasn't the man in the picture they'd shown him. Drew would have loved to knock the kid's memory back into place, but since Chapman's method was more likely to get results, he ground another millimeter of enamel off his molars and kept quiet.

"Maybe he was older," Chapman suggested. "Maybe he had gray hair."

"Fu . . . I mean, heck, no. The guy wasn't that old. I woulda noticed that, for sure. Secret Service guys are never old, right? Say, what do they do with you guys when you get too old to take down some bad guy?"

Chapman's eye developed a tic, and he looked like he wanted to demonstrate his proficiency at that skill right now. "So he didn't have gray hair?"

"No way. Hey, I remembered that! I'm pretty good at this. Ask me another one."

Drew massaged the pain between his eyes and resigned himself to a long interview as Chapman ground out, "Any tattoos?"

"No! That's another one! You and me make a good team, man."

Tension settled in Drew's neck. Tuning out the kid, he tilted his head upward and to the right until he heard a tiny crack. Much better. Tilting to the left, he repeated the process, concentrating on the stiff spot in his neck as his gaze drifted along the upper corner of the wall. And stopped.

Without moving his head, he tapped a knuckle against Chapman's shoulder until the agent turned with an irritated, "What?"

Drew pointed. Chapman's gaze followed, then froze at the upper corner of the wall behind the clerk.

"You have a security camera," he said.

The clerk glanced at the object of their fascination and shrugged. "Yeah."

Drew exchanged cautious looks with Chapman before addressing the kid. "Does it work?"

"Sure. Wouldn't do much good if it didn't." His expression said they were going to have to be brighter than that if they expected to find their man.

Chapman leaned over the counter and grabbed the kid by his bright red lapel. "Find the tape from the night before last. Now."

The clerk's blank, open-mouthed stare gradually took on the glimmer of intelligence. "Hey, good thinking! The dude is probably on there, isn't he?"

"Let's hope so," Chapman muttered as he released the kid. "We deserve a break."

They got more than they expected. Watching the flickering TV screen in the manager's office, Chapman kept his finger on the remote's fast forward button until Drew ordered, "Stop. There he is."

On the silent, black and white film, a man showed his badge and spoke to the desk clerk.

"Hot damn," Chapman exclaimed, leaning closer to the screen. "I know this guy. Tough attitude, chip on his shoulder. He got himself messed up pretty bad in a car wreck and was off work for close to a year. He can't have been back more than a few months. If he's been assigned to any of the same officials as Marlow, it should be easy to find out. Someone had to have recruited these guys."

"The sooner we find out, the better," Drew said.

Chapman already had his phone in his hands when it rang. Frowning at the readout, he answered with a growled, "I said no calls. This better be good."

Drew listened with disinterest until he heard the agent's startled, "You're *where*?"

Curiosity turned to caution as he saw Chapman's posture stiffen. Something had happened. Drew drummed his fingers on the manager's desk until Chapman hung up.

"Your father and his secretary phoned Senator Pierson," Chapman summarized as he began dialing another number. "Said they know who the blackmailer is. They're in danger, so Renke and your friends went to get them." He held his hand up as he snapped out a fax request to someone on the phone, then hung up. "We'll join them as soon as I get the fax on this guy."

Drew struggled to absorb the sudden developments. Somehow, his father had figured it out. The case was about to split wide open with his dad caught in the middle, holding the dangerous information that would expose some high-level government official. If the blackmailer knew, he would panic. His dad's life was in danger, along with the lives of anyone with him.

His mind reeling with information, Drew focused on the part that mattered most —Lauren.

"Lauren's with them?" The thought of her heading directly into a confrontation with the agents who'd shot at them hit Drew like a punch to the gut. He couldn't put her in danger again.

"No, they left her at the house. Pierson volunteered to stay with her."

Relief eased through him. Pierson wouldn't be his first choice, but Lauren would be safe enough until he

could get back to her. The worst he could say about
Senator Pierson was that he was a lecherous ladies'
man. But unlike Senator Creighton, Pierson's leering
propositions were just an act. Probably.

"I have to get back to Lauren," he said.

Chapman squinted at him in disbelief. "You did
hear what I said, didn't you? Your father is in danger.
So is your girlfriend's sister. Your girlfriend is safe."

His girlfriend? Drew tested the word in his mind.
No, Lauren wasn't his girlfriend. She was far more than
that. Somewhere along the way his instinct to protect
her had slipped into a need to never let her go. And
right now, rescuing his dad from certain danger took
second place to assuring himself that Lauren was safe.

Like it or not, Chapman was going to have to drop
him off at the house before rescuing Senator Creighton.

Drew held out his hand. "Give me the keys. I'll have
the car waiting at the door as soon as you get that fax."

Chapman leveled a hard stare at him. "You're not
driving. And if you take off with a government car I'll
put you in jail."

"I'm not stupid. I need something to do." All he
needed to do was put himself behind the wheel. Chapman could go to Maryland, but he'd be stopping in
Georgetown first.

"I know the feeling." Chapman tossed him the
keys. "But don't think I'm kidding about jail."

Drew let the big, black Ford idle by the entrance,
pondering the problem of how he could convince Lauren to commit herself to one man after showing her
all the fun she'd missed by doing that very thing. To
plan a future together after scoffing at her fondness for
plans and procedures.

The irony was difficult to appreciate at the moment.

Drew's thoughts scattered abruptly as the passenger door jerked open, then slammed behind Chapman.

"Drive!"

The edge of fear in Chapman's voice was new. Without thinking, Drew responded to the urgency, ripping the car into gear and slamming his foot on the accelerator. Tires squealed as he barreled out of the driveway, barely pausing to check oncoming traffic. Still rocking from the turn, Drew drove his foot to the floor. Chapman reached down below the glove compartment and came up with a flashing red light. Lowering his window, he slapped the light onto the roof.

Damn. Drew blew through the next light.

Traffic was light this close to midnight. Swerving around an SUV, Drew spared a glance at Chapman. The agent's mouth was set in a grim line as he reached for his seatbelt. Drew had a feeling the detour to Georgetown wasn't going to go over well. Maybe he should just call Lauren to reassure himself.

"Turn here," Chapman ordered. "We're going to Georgetown."

Cold knifed into him, then twisted in his gut. The emergency was in Georgetown.

"What happened?" he demanded.

He felt Chapman's gaze from the passenger seat. "Look, I might be wrong. It could be nothing."

If that was meant to be reassuring, it didn't work. Drew knew enough about the methodical, organized Chapman to know the agent didn't react like this to "nothing."

"*Goddamn it.*" Drew growled. "*What's wrong?*"

"The fax." Chapman brandished the wrinkled

paper he'd tossed on the seat next to him. "Our guy has spent all his time working in the identity theft department. He's only had contact with one high-level official since he returned to work. And it's a name that shows up repeatedly on Marlow's résumé."

They did it. They'd found the common denominator, the one person most likely to have selected the agents to aid him with the blackmail scheme.

Drew eased up on the accelerator until the car slowed to ninety, then took his eyes off the road long enough look at Chapman.

Chapman's lip curled with distaste. "Senator Pierson."

Drew swore. And floored it.

Pierson's hand on her thigh made her skin crawl right through her robe. She jumped to her feet, tightening the flimsy belt as she did. "This is terribly inappropriate, entertaining company in my robe. If you'll give me a moment, I'll just go put some clothes on."

She started toward the stairs, but a tug on the end of her belt reeled her back like a leash. "I disagree. You'll be a lot more entertaining in your robe. Sit." He patted the couch beside him and pulled on her arm firmly enough that she had to either sit or fall into his lap. She sat.

He was too close and his hand was back on her leg, just above her knee. It might have been a fatherly gesture if not for the avaricious gleam in the senator's eyes. She wanted to slap his hand away, but had a bad feeling it would only be a signal to play rough.

She cleared her throat and steadied herself so her voice wouldn't shake. "Senator, what's going on?"

"What does it look like, Lauren? We're finally

getting to know each other without your watchdog getting in the way."

Watchdog? "You mean Drew?"

"Nice boy but a bit too possessive. Too bad his father didn't teach him to share."

She tried to concentrate on what he was saying, but his hand had begun massaging her thigh. She reacted, pushing his hand away and smoothing her robe with short, nervous strokes. "You've been, uh, sharing with Senator Creighton?"

"Let's just say he never seemed to mind when I dated his ex-girlfriends. Harlan's not the possessive type." His hand settled back on her leg, a little closer to her inner thigh than before.

Too many things were wrong with this situation. She lifted his hand this time, setting it firmly on his own thigh while giving him a direct look. "I thought you were married."

He chuckled. "I know you're not that naive, Lauren. Your sister certainly isn't. But don't worry about my wife causing problems. She's glad I have my little distractions."

"Ah. Thank you for clearing that up." Oh God, what had Meg been doing? She remembered how Pierson had made no secret of his attraction to Meg, but she'd thought it was all a flirtatious act. "Senator, I'm not like Meg." It was easy to make her voice firm when she was this sincere. "Not at all."

His lips curved up. "That's good to hear." His voice was silky, and his mouth close enough for her to smell the nicotine on his breath. "Meg's a tease, always putting me off. She's been making me wait for too long. I'm glad to hear you're not like that." His hand was back, sliding into the curve of her thigh, as far as the robe permitted him to go.

Even without touching her skin, the move was far too intimate. She bolted from the couch like a horse from the starting gate, thinking fast. The only option was to play along until she could devise a way out.

She faced him, eyes hooded, smile deliberately calculating. Stalling. "I'm beginning to understand, Senator. So let's set some ground rules."

"The only rule is I'm in charge, and I'm going to fuck your brains out."

Her heart lurched and her mouth went dry. It was hard to think when he said stuff like that but talking was better than doing. "Oh, yeah. Talk dirty to me." She lowered her voice to a confidential whisper. "Tell me what you're going to do."

"I just did. Now let's do it."

A city full of blowhard politicians and she got the one man of action. Her mind was frantically clawing for escape when the cell phone on the table beside her startled her with a loud ring. Before Pierson could stop her, she snatched it up. "Hello?"

"Lauren! Thank God!" The relief in Drew's voice was a contrast to Pierson's scowl. The senator didn't seem to like her being on the phone, which was all the more reason to stay on it.

"Hi, Jeff," she sang out happily. "I was hoping you'd call." She thought Pierson relaxed marginally, his eyes showing a flicker of suspicion.

Several seconds of silence crackled over the cell phone while she prayed Drew had enough confidence in her to know something was wrong.

"Is Senator Pierson in the room with you?"

"That's right!" She smiled brightly, hoping Pierson couldn't detect her sigh of relief. She couldn't hide the nervous edge in her voice, but maybe that was a good thing. "How did you know?"

Pierson watched intently. She rolled her eyes for his benefit and mouthed, "My boyfriend," as if slightly embarrassed to have one. His eyes narrowed, and she realized that making him think help was nearby could make it hard to stall him. "In Michigan," she added, hoping distance would ease his mind.

"Renke told us about Pierson coming over. I know you're alone with him." She listened through another pause and realized Drew was choosing his words carefully. "Is everything okay there?"

Smiling at Pierson, she told Drew, "No, not at all!"

Drew swore. "Has he hurt you?"

"No." She heard the blare of a horn followed by a screech that sounded like a car braking too fast. Chapman swore loudly in the background, making Lauren's heart race.

"We identified the other agent," Drew said, his voice as steady as if nothing had happened. "And there was only one official both agents had worked for—Pierson. We think he's the blackmailer. I'll bet he's the guy who tried to run us down outside the embassy, too."

"That's not surprising." She didn't know how to explain herself in front of Pierson. They'd obviously misjudged him, but it didn't seem like the blackmailer would tell them about Senator McNabb.

"Honey, I think he's been using us to find them, but now we're getting too many people involved and he has to stop it."

She bit her lip and glanced at the Senator. "Oh." Oh

God. Suddenly Pierson's phone call about Renke and the others being on their way, and his constant clock watching, took on new meaning. "Yeah, I think you're right about that, honey."

Pierson watched her closely. Every part of her. His gaze made a leisurely trip down the center of her terry-cloth robe, all the way down to her bare feet. He might be the blackmailer, but she was certain that right now his crime of choice was adultery.

Pierson was fit and barely past fifty. She had no hope of fending him off if it came to force. Playing along would be risky, but it might keep him under control until one of the five men who'd been so determined to protect her showed up.

Stalling wouldn't be enough. She could only think of one course of action, and it scared the shit out of her. Forcing a nonchalance she didn't feel, Lauren sat on the arm of the sofa across from the Senator and crossed her legs. The robe fell open, revealing her bare legs from the upper thigh down. Pierson's gaze fell and stayed there. She pretended not to notice his interest as she listened to Drew.

"Lauren, listen carefully, but don't be scared. If we're right, sending the others away was probably a trap. He needs to get rid of them in a way that won't be connected to him."

"Can't you do anything about that?" She tried to make it sound like an unsightly mole that should be removed rather than three men who were most likely driving into an ambush.

"We're working on it." She could hear the frustration in his voice, and for a moment she felt bad for the situation Drew was in, torn between crises in two different directions. But just for a moment. She had her own crisis to worry about.

"Okay, honey."

"Look, I don't want to alarm you. You may be safe. He's probably waiting for a call telling him they've been taken care of. Until that happens I don't think he'll touch you."

"I don't agree."

Pierson looked at his watch, then checked the signal strength on his phone. Letting him get restless was not good. Swinging her leg, she allowed the robe to shift, exposing more thigh and giving Pierson a view that stopped a bare inch from her panties. He stared intently. He seemed to enjoy taking a good, long look before touching. In Drew, she would have appreciated it. In Pierson, it was disgusting. But the longer she kept him watching, the longer she avoided his hands on her.

"You don't agree with what?" Drew was stuck on her last response. "That it was a trap?" When she didn't answer, he tried again. "That he's waiting for a call? That he won't touch you?"

"That's the one," she told him.

"If that bastard lays one hand on you, I'll kill him." She heard a deep breath followed by one long exhalation as Drew made an attempt at control. "I'm calling for help."

Lauren imagined the police arriving with sirens blaring. Afraid of pushing the senator into a violent reaction, she said, "That sounds noisy." Scrunching her nose at Pierson, Lauren whispered, "He's in a rock band. Very noisy."

"Right," Drew said. "No sirens."

Pierson lifted his gaze, locking it on hers. Deliberately, he licked his lips. Lauren nearly gagged.

The last two inches of thigh must have been too much. He rose suddenly, walked to the window, and pulled the drapes closed. Then walked to the next window and closed those too.

Making her voice cheery, Lauren said, "So when will I see you again?"

"Fifteen minutes," Drew growled. "Less if I can help it."

She estimated Pierson to be ahead of Drew's schedule.

"Lauren, Chapman's calling for more agents right now. They'll probably get there sooner than I can."

Finished with the drapes, Pierson stood in front of her, close enough that her bare leg touched his pants. "Tell him you have to go now," Pierson growled.

She could refuse, but he looked prepared to enforce his order. "I have to go now, Jeff," she said brightly. "I'll see you soon."

Tires squealed through the phone again. Drew's grim voice said, "Damn right you will, sweetheart."

"Hang up," Pierson ordered.

Playing along was harder when he towered over her and every instinct told her to fight or run, neither of which would work. She took a shaky breath and smiled as if nothing were wrong, as if he weren't standing close enough to hear her heart hammering beneath her breast.

" 'Bye," she said into the phone and disconnected. It felt like standing on the deck of the *Titanic* and throwing away the last life preserver. She was on her own.

Pierson took the phone from her hand and put it in his pocket. "We don't want any more interruptions."

His finger traced the edge of her robe from the collar to between her breasts. "Do we," he added, not making it a question.

"Mmm," Lauren hummed, because her mouth had gone so dry with fear she couldn't form words. Time to kick up the action if he was going to believe her.

Gerald had told her how to win against Arrogant Government Assholes, and Pierson certainly fit the definition. All she had to do was play by his rules. But since Pierson's rules seemed to include having sex with him, winning this one was going to require a lot of risk. And a lot of confidence.

She never would have attempted it before knowing Drew. But he'd given her something Jeff never had; he'd made her feel desirable. Sexy. Confident of her ability to drive a man insane with lust, then satisfy him to the point of exhaustion. She just needed to trust her instincts.

Sitting on the arm of the sofa put her at eye level with Pierson's tie. Taking a deep breath, Lauren pasted on a smile and made herself stroke the tie, because that was far better than stroking him. "I don't think there will be any more interruptions."

"I'll make sure of that." He didn't stop her from fondling his tie, but he watched her skeptically.

She lifted her gaze and came embarrassingly close to batting her lashes. "Sooo," she crooned, "what kind of women do you like, Senator? Adventurous? Dominant? Submissive?" None of the above was probably too much to hope for.

"Which kind are you?" Dodging the question, typical politician.

"Maybe I'm whatever kind you want me to be," she purred.

That sparked enough interest to make her regret leaving the choice up to him. "Willing and ready would be nice." He fondled her hair with a thoughtful expression. "But not necessary."

That about covered it all. She tried not to flinch from his hand as it brushed her cheek. "Willing and ready is easy. I was hoping we could get together from the first moment I saw you," she murmured.

"Were you." It was too cynical to be a question.

"I even fantasized about it. But not on a couch. I was thinking a bed might be better, and there's several to choose from upstairs."

"Honey, I hope you weren't planning on the standard missionary position. There's a lot you can do on a couch. I'll show you."

His leer sent her stomach into free fall, and she sincerely hoped this little stunt didn't ruin her appetite for any of the plans she had for inventive sex with Drew. "It's not so much the position I was thinking of. It's the toys."

"Sex toys?"

"Senator Creighton has a drawer full of them."

He grinned. "That sly dog. I should have guessed." He took her roughly by the shoulders, turning her toward the stairs. "Lead the way." Before she could move he pulled her back against him, nuzzling her neck and growling, "I can't wait."

He grabbed her bottom for a pinch, which was all she needed to make her rush up the stairs and into Senator Creighton's bedroom.

Pierson was right behind her. "Where are they?"

"Right here." She opened the nightstand drawer and moved the tissue box, exposing the collection.

He looked. "Interesting. How did you know about these?"

She folded her arms because it put something between them and gave an illusion that she wasn't one item of clothing away from naked. "Drew and I were, uh, looking for something to do."

He gave her a wolfish smile. "Damn. You should have called me."

"Well, you're here now, Senator. And Drew's not."

And if her idea didn't work, she was going to be wolf food.

His lip curved into a smug smile. "If we're going to be *friends*, Lauren, you can call me Paul." He emphasized friends in a way that gave it a whole new definition.

Lauren tipped her head and pretended to give it careful consideration. "Paul . . . hmm. I think I'd rather call you 'senator.' It's so . . . commanding."

It was a sickening performance, all coy and sweet, but he went for it. Unfortunately, he went for more, grabbing her by her upper arms and pulling her close. "That's what you like, eh? A commanding lover?"

He'd been preparing; the scent of breath mints nearly knocked her out. "Yes," she said, not having to try for a breathless whisper, since she was trying not to inhale. "But there seems to be a problem."

He frowned. "What problem?"

"Look at you." She patted his lapel, then stroked down his arms so he'd have to let go of her. "You're wearing a suit. You're fully dressed, and I'm . . ." She glanced at her robe before giving him another playful smile. ". . . not."

He raked a hot look to the sash at her waist. "I noticed." She anticipated his move for the belt and pushed him away. "Uh-uh, Senator," she said, wagging her finger at him. "You first. I gave you a preview while I was on the phone, and now I want to see what I'm getting. After that," she fondled her belt, "I'll show you what you're getting." She purred seductively.

Yech. She was disgusting. Revolting. Afraid she'd overplayed the scene, Lauren prepared to laugh at herself.

She stopped just in time.

He was mesmerized. Staring at the loosely tied knot at her waist, he began unbuckling his belt. Dragging his shirt out of the way, he fumbled with the button on his pants, clumsy in his haste to get out of his clothes.

Too fast! At this rate he'd be naked and pawing at her robe before her posse of rescuers could even MapQuest the address.

"Whoa there, sugar, slow down." Sugar? Lauren felt like she was channeling a hooker.

Pierson leered at her. "Just trying to show you the goods, doll. And once you see it, you're gonna want it. Bad."

"I'm sure I will." Remarkably, she didn't choke on the words. "But you have to tease a lady, take your time." She wiggled a finger, indicating his chest. "Start with your shirt."

He yanked his tie off in a couple quick moves. Starting in on the shirt buttons, he cocked his head at her. "I was kinda hopin' you weren't a lady, if you know what I mean."

She didn't, and preferred to leave it that way, but gave him a promising lift of her eyebrow.

The buttons were undone, and Lauren silently thanked God for the cuff links that slowed him down for half a minute before the shirt hit the floor. His undershirt fell on top of it.

Pierson took a moment to inhale deeply, puffing his densely furred chest at her. She supposed a compliment was expected.

"Very nice," she said.

The side of his mouth curled in a roguish, James Dean way. "Women like a man with a hairy chest. You can touch it," he invited.

"Mmm, that's tempting, but I think I'll wait and touch everything at once." *Where in the hell were those Secret Service agents?*

"Then get ready to touch something special," Pierson growled, and dropped his pants.

Lauren couldn't miss the bulge in his boxers, and snapped her eyes shut before she blushed. Women like whoever she was pretending to be probably didn't blush at the evidence of a man's arousal. They probably gave it a frank stare. So she cracked her eyelids, hoping her slitted gaze resembled heated bliss, and looked at Pierson's hip as he lowered the boxers.

She gave it a full five seconds, then met his eyes. And smiled. *And the Oscar goes to Lauren Sutherland.*

He grinned back, teeth bared. "Your turn," he said.

Chapter Fourteen

D rew took another corner at something approaching Mach 1, sending the Ford into a sideways slide. Brakes squealed and Chapman cursed as his shoulder hit the window.

"Goddamn it! This is government property, Creighton!"

The car rocked, then steadied, and Drew spared a glance at his passenger. "You or the car?"

Chapman sent him a scorching look. "Both. Do you think you can keep all four wheels on the ground long enough for me to make this phone call?"

At least he hadn't told him to slow down, not since his call to Lauren. Drew gave him credit for that, especially since Chapman realized his partner was heading into an ambush, along with Gerald and Mihaly. It had to be making him crazy. All they could do was call and warn Renke. Drew wasn't about to change course, and Chapman hadn't asked him to.

Speed turned the dotted white lines into one continuous white line. Drew's gaze darted between the road and Chapman as he waited for the call to go through. "Come on, what's taking so long? Call them!" he snapped, as tense as Chapman.

"I did! He isn't answering!" He muttered a litany of swear words as he hit end and redialed. After a few more nerve-racking moments, he straightened with a jerk. "Renke! Speak up, I can't hear you."

Drew listened with growing anxiety as Chapman yelled, "Who?" then added in alarm, "What the fuck's going on there?"

"What? What's wrong?" Drew demanded.

"Hell if I know. I've got your dad's fuckin' assistant answering my partner's cell phone, and I can't think of any good reason why that would happen. Then he tells me to hang on 'cause he can't talk right now, like I'm calling during his fuckin' lunch break. What the fuck!" Chapman yelled the last part into the phone so Gerald could appreciate his anger, too.

"Give it here, let me talk to him," Drew said, holding out his hand. At the same time he made a quick, one-handed correction with the wheel, which translated to an eighty-mile-an-hour lurch into the next lane.

"Fuck that. You're barely keeping us alive as it is." He flicked the phone to speaker mode and held it between them. "Talk to him."

"Gerald? What's going on?"

A few seconds of silence followed, and Drew was about to repeat his demand in a testier tone, when they heard rustling. "Damn it, keep your panties on," Gerald said in a hoarse whisper. "I'm turning the volume off. Stand by."

Chapman almost looked pleased at Drew's frustrated swearing. "You see? I swear to God, if that stupid little jerk took Renke's phone and is playing amateur secret agent, I'll wring his scrawny neck. He could be putting my partner in danger! The guy gets a hair up his ass just because he got his precious coat ripped when he interfered with an agent acting in the line of duty, and now he's acting out some petty vendetta against government agents—"

"Hey, whoa, back off, Chapman," Drew said. He figured he already deserved credit for not telling the guy to shove it up his ass. "You don't know Gerald. Petty, maybe. But stupid? Never. He's one of the brightest people I know. He's not playing at anything. Shut up and wait until we find out what's happening." If Gerald really was doing something just to annoy Renke, Drew would personally hold him down while Chapman wrung his neck.

Another quarter mile of highway flashed by before they heard more rustling from the phone, followed by Gerald's low voice. "Okay, I think it's safe. Talk to me. But keep it down."

Chapman snarled at his phone, but followed directions. "*You* talk to *me*. Start by telling me where Renke is."

"Certainly. Your dumbass partner is about sixty yards away from me, stalking through the woods like friggin' Davy Crockett."

"Well, get him!" Chapman kept his voice down, but Drew thought he might be close to rupturing an artery from the effort.

"I can't get him," Gerald hissed back. "We're in the middle of a covert operation here. We don't have time for chitchat."

Chapman stared at the phone in his hand as if it

had suddenly turned into something rank and slimy. Drew snatched it away, at the same time cutting off a semi and getting a blast from its horn in return. If Gerald was in full officious mode, Drew would have more patience for it than Chapman. "Gerald!"

"Ssshhh!" he scolded. It sounded like he had his mouth directly on the speaker. "Do you want them to hear you?"

Gritting his teeth, Drew adjusted his voice to a low rumble. "Them who? What's going on? Start at the beginning, and keep it short and sweet."

"Fine. We're in the middle of godforsaken nowhere, with no street lights or houses, much less malls and spas. But we think we've found Senator Creighton and Meg. We passed a car on the side of the road with its parking lights on, like it's just waiting for someone. Renke stopped around the curve, and he's walking back toward it through the woods. Mr. Official Agent says it's always best to be safe. Mihaly is walking back down the center of the road, because if it's them, Meg will see him and recognize him. I should be the one doing that, because they both know me, but Mr. Bigshot told me to wait in the car while they did their hero stuff. And he left his phone, so now I have it."

Drew relaxed marginally. "So you're in the car?"

"Of course I'm not in the car. What good would I be there? You think I'd do something just because some government-trained twit tells me to?"

Of course not, what was he thinking?

"Give me that," Chapman growled, grabbing the phone back with one hand while using the other to brace himself against the dash as Drew cut lanes and swerved into a right turn. "Listen carefully," he ordered. "That's not Senator Creighton in that car. In all likelihood it's the two agents who have been blackmailing senators. It's a trap, and they're going to try to kill all three of you. You got that?"

Gerald paused. "How do you know?"

Drew answered, knowing Gerald would be less apt to doubt him. "Because the blackmailer is Pierson."

"Holy shit," Gerald breathed into the phone.

"Where exactly are you?" Chapman asked.

"I'm getting up close and personal with Mother Nature, on the other side of the road from Agent Renke. I stepped in something highly questionable, and probably snagged my hand-tailored pants that I— Oh, shit!"

"What?" he and Chapman blurted out together.

Gerald's voice went an octave higher. "They just spotted Mihaly and turned on their headlights. He's totally lit up, so now he probably can't see the car or anyone in it. Oh, that's not good."

Chapman brought the phone closer to his mouth and spoke in urgent, clipped tones. "You've gotta tell Renke and Dragos to back off, now."

Drew hit narrower city streets and was forced to slow down to navigate parked cars and frequent turns. The squealing tires were the only sound in the car as they listened for Gerald's response.

"I can't see Agent Renke. Mihaly's a sitting duck, completely blind. They're just waiting for him to get closer."

"For God's sake, call them off!"

"If I do that, the guys in the car will start shooting, won't they?" Gerald said, sounding more contemplative than Drew would have been at that moment.

"They're going to start shooting anyway. Just do it!" Drew bet if the light had been better Chapman's face would be deep purple.

"Ssshhh! Shut up, I'm thinking."

Drew frowned in confusion, unable to imagine Gerald not going for the scream-and-run plan.

Chapman was more direct. "What's to think about?" he asked, his voice vibrating with stress. "Rule number one, stay out of harm's way. Get the fuck out of there!"

"Will you hush or do I have to turn you off?"

Chapman gave Drew an incredulous look and tossed the phone onto the console, apparently giving up. "The man's a control freak! But only an idiot would think he can control this situation. He's going to get everyone killed," Chapman said.

Drew wasn't sure he could defend Gerald on that point.

"Let's see," Gerald mused from the dashboard, sounding as if he were deciding which suit to wear and not how to prevent three people from getting shot. "The car windows are up. They won't shoot at us through the windows."

"Right," Chapman muttered, although Drew doubted Gerald was waiting for his opinion.

"They must be wondering where Agent Renke and I are."

"How do you know they're both in the car?"

Chapman's question stopped him. "Good point," he conceded. "One of them could be waiting for us in the woods."

Chapman nodded vigorously, obviously pleased that he was beginning to get through to him.

"So I'll have to check that out."

"No!" Chapman yelled it, and Drew could almost see the agent's blood pressure shoot back into the red zone. All Drew could do was grip the steering wheel in frustration,

With the Ford's engine roaring in his ears, Drew barely heard Gerald's soft murmur from the phone on the dash. "I have the volume low and I'd like to keep this phone on in case you have any useful advice, but if you two don't keep it down"—he emphasized the last three words—"I'm turning it off. *Capisce?*"

Neither bothered to respond. They'd come up behind a slow-moving car whose driver either hadn't spotted the flashing light behind him or wasn't impressed. Drew laid on the horn until the car edged over, then shot past it with a roar.

"That does it, the volume is going off."

Chapman looked at Drew in disbelief. "I don't believe this. He turned me off." Processing that information must have been difficult, because he didn't even comment as Drew oversteered a corner, jumped the curb, and scraped the car's back bumper against a tree. "If anything happens to my partner, I'm gonna kill that little prick," he announced.

The phone went silent for a full minute, so it surprised them both when a low voice spoke from their dashboard.

"They're both in the car. I'm sneaking around the back. If I'm on the other side, our dumbass agent in the woods should see me. Even he should be able to figure out something's wrong if I'm crawling around on the ground."

"What in the hell is he doing?" Chapman grabbed the phone again.

"I don't know, and I can't worry about it now." His dad's house was only a couple miles away. All Lauren had to do was keep Pierson at bay for a few more minutes.

"Okay, I made motions to indicate danger, so I hope dumbass saw them."

Gerald's voice was so low he must have had his mouth directly on the phone, but Chapman still held it near his ear. "What'd he say? Something about making motions?"

"How should I know?" One crisis at a time would be nice, but if Drew had to make a choice, Lauren's safety was more important than anything else. Lauren was more important.

Chapman yelled at the phone. "Get away from the car!"

Since he couldn't hear them, Gerald's voice never paused. "I'm going to have to trust your brutish friend to cover this side of the car. I'm crawling back to the driver's side now. Mihaly's getting close and they're going to open those windows soon. Damn it, this gravel is killing my trousers. The government is for damn sure going to get another bill from me."

Chapman had gone still. "My God, he's waiting for them to lower the windows."

"Why?" Not that he had time to care. Pierson probably felt pressed for time and wouldn't allow Lauren to stall for long. He had to hurry.

Chapman barely seemed to notice the trash bin that went flying as Drew dodged a car nosing out of a driveway. He stared at the phone. "He must have some lame-brained idea that he can overpower them when they stick their guns out the window to shoot at Dragos. That's insane. Even if he surprises the driver from behind and manages to knock the gun out of his hand, there's still the other guy to deal with. Renke doesn't know what's going on, and Dragos has no idea *anything's* wrong. They could shoot him before—"

He broke off at a whispery sound from the phone and held it to his ear.

Drew tore his eyes from the road long enough to see the worry on Chapman's face. "What'd he say?"

"He's going to leave the line open, but he can't talk anymore. Holy Christ, what's he think he's going to do, twist the guy's arm until he yells 'uncle'? Hit him with a stick? Punch him?"

"Gerald's a biter." Drew managed one terse sentence. The house was only two blocks away now. Lauren might still be okay. She was smart and resourceful . . .

Drew slammed on the brakes as a man walking a dog started across the street. Their headlights raked parked cars on both sides of the street as they fishtailed, then straightened out. From the corner of his eye Drew saw the man and dog scamper to safety and he gunned it.

Chapman grabbed the dash again and swore, but Drew wasn't sure if it was for his driving or for the tense silence from the phone. He couldn't worry about it. His heart and mind were full of Lauren. Besides, Gerald had always been able to take care of himself.

Screaming erupted from the phone, startling them both. A second later a different voice yelled out, followed by a confused mixture of noises and screams. Chapman stared at the phone. Drew stared straight ahead, eyes on the road while acutely aware of every sound coming from the small speaker. Men yelling. Bumping and banging. Then a sound that sent fear ripping through him—a gunshot, followed by a high-pitched shriek. He strained to hear more, but the garbled mixture of noises cut off abruptly.

The phone went silent.

Chapman threw it to the floor. "Fuck!"

Drew clenched his jaw and refused to think about what might have happened. Only one thing mattered: *Lauren.*

Chapter Fifteen

Panic shot through Lauren. It must have been at least ten minutes since she'd talked to Drew. Someone should be here to save her by now. Anyone. A surreal sense of exasperation followed. Did she have to do everything herself?

Things like this didn't happen in her former well-planned, evenly paced, dependable life. No blackmail plots, no shootings, no extraordinary man making love to her. And certainly no naked senators intent on having sex with her. She had no experience to draw on. Meg might know how to deal with a randy, naked senator, but Lauren was going to have to wing it.

She blinked at the pants around his ankles, then up at him. Her own newly realized desire to make love in inappropriate places had been an incredible turn-on. It was probably too tame for Pierson, but she hoped he had a few fantasies of his own.

Your turn, he had told her.

"Okay," she said, as seductively as she could manage. "But I have a favor to ask first."

Pierson didn't look happy about anything that might postpone his raunchy plans.

"What?"

"I like things a little . . . kinky."

His suspicious look cleared and turned lascivious. "Yeah? How kinky?"

"I want you to tie me up."

A smile spread slowly until his teeth showed. "You surprise me, Lauren. In the best way possible."

She pretended to be flattered. "Good. Because I have one more surprise."

"What?" His voice had gone gravelly with passion.

"Uh-uh. Tie me up first."

His hairy chest heaved as he blew out a deep breath. "Damn, I can't wait to give it to you." He nodded at her terry-cloth belt. "We can use that."

"No!" she blurted, refusing to let go of the only thing keeping him from ogling her body.

"You're right. Leather is much better." He whipped the belt off his trousers and kicked them aside. "Put your hands together and I'll lash you to the rails on the headboard."

Holy shit, it was hard to stay ahead of this creep. "I was thinking you could use handcuffs. That's why I wanted to come up here." She dug through the drawer and pulled out the silver handcuffs she'd spotted a few days ago, before Drew slammed the drawer closed. She dangled them in front of Pierson.

If snakes could smile they would look exactly like the senator, only less slimy and without all those teeth. "You bad girl. Give me those."

She hopped onto the bed and scuttled to the other side. "No need, I can do it." She pulled the key from the lock and wasted a few seconds fumbling with the cuffs. His actions were getting ahead of her words and she needed more time. "I hope you have plenty of stamina, Senator, because you're really going to love what we do after this."

She paused to close her eyes for a delighted shiver, and he quit rummaging through the drawer to give her a curious glance. "After what?"

"After we handcuff me and you enjoy that for a little bit, then it's your turn to be handcuffed."

"Not my thing. You sure you don't need help?"

"No, I've got it." She clicked one cuff closed and tugged it so he could see that it was fastened securely to the headboard. If he got hold of the cuffs now, it would be all over for her. But if she could play on his fantasies for just one more minute . . .

She made a show of opening the other end and placing it on her wrist while she talked. "Oh, I could change your mind about that. You have no idea. My boyfriend taught me this game and Drew was too straitlaced to try it, but Jeff says it gives him the most mind-blowing orgasms he's ever had."

She let the cuffs encircle her wrist as if she were trying them on for size, and peeked at him. He'd become still, his cautious gaze on her, not the cuffs. "Creighton's too straitlaced?"

"He's a prude compared to Jeff." Since she was trying to appeal to Pierson's deepest perversions, Drew probably *was* too straitlaced for what she was about to suggest. Jeff would faint dead away just listening to it.

"He has me cuff him to the bed, and I pretend I'm a sex-starved nymphomaniac who's going to force him to service me again and again." She let the cuff dangle, unfastened, while she talked. It didn't matter, because he wasn't looking at her hand. He was waiting to hear more, and she was making herself dizzy trying to think up an erotic scenario on the spot. "Jeff rattles the cuffs and pretends he wants to get away, just to turn me on. You won't have to do that because I'm already so hot for you." She smiled, trying to ignore the taste of bile. "And then I start *doing things* to him."

His mouth hung open as he listened. "What things?"

"Oh, I imagine there are a few things in that drawer I could play with." Except Pierson obviously wanted specifics and she wasn't sure what some of that stuff even was. "But he likes it best when I use my mouth."

"Uh-huh." He licked his lips.

"And my tongue." She licked hers, too, while he watched intently. "And of course, my hands. Jeff says he's never been harder in his life, and I go on and on while he moans in ecstasy."

Pierson was fondling himself as he listened, which was probably a good sign, but not something she wanted to see. "Then what?" he croaked.

"Then he starts begging for me to finish it, but I don't, I keep him close to the edge and torture him with pleasure. I lie on top of him and slide my body along his, focusing on certain parts of him, and finally—this is Jeff's favorite part—I use this special technique I learned from a woman I know."

"What kind of technique?" he panted.

"Oh, I can't give it away." She smiled, doing a mental search for something that sounded exotic. "She used to be a geisha in Japan. She gives lessons, and you have to pass certain proficiency levels before you can learn the best stuff." She winked. "I was an excellent student."

She was so impressed with her own story she nearly forgot to finalize the deal, and from the dazed look in his eyes, it was time. "I'd really love to show you that. I promise it's like nothing you've ever experienced. But we can do my stuff later because I'm sure you can do me twice. We have time, don't we?"

He licked his lips nervously. "Maybe not a lot of time. Let's do your thing first." He climbed onto the bed beside her, and she scooted to the far edge, forcing herself not to bolt. Not yet.

"Are you sure?" Protesting seemed realistic, but tiny ripples of panic were swirling in her stomach, making her queasy. Time to end this. "But if you really want me to do you first . . ." She lowered her voice and did her best minx impression. "I can give you the best, longest, hardest orgasm you ever imagined."

"Me first." He yanked the cuff off her wrist and snapped it over his own. Leering, he said, "I'm ready. Show me what you've got, honey."

She exhaled, a drawn-out, shaky breath that released all the fear and tension she'd been holding back. She slipped off the bed, tossing him a regretful look as she backed toward the door. "Sorry, gotta run."

Whirling, she gathered her robe and charged toward the door. Behind her, Pierson yelled, "Hey! You goddamn little prick tease, get back here!" She heard a crash, then a string of swear words as she tore down the stairs, the key pressed tightly inside her fist. The cuffs had looked strong, but for all she knew they were just a toy, made to pop open under enough force. He could be seconds behind her. She didn't look back to find out. Pulling the front door wide, she bolted into the night.

And tripped over the crouched body of a man.

Somersaulting head over heels, she ended up flat on her butt on Senator Creighton's front lawn, staring at the man. Staring at his gun.

Dark hair. The blond man's partner?

"Miss Sutherland?"

Breath seeped back into her lungs as she recognized the respectful tones of the Secret Service. "About time," she said, sagging.

She'd been rescued, mere seconds after rescuing herself. Lauren closed her eyes with relief, then tensed as a distant vibration rapidly turned into the roar of a car bearing down on the house.

Rubber screamed against cement, a long, high-pitched noise that raised the hairs on her neck at the same time as it thrilled her heart. The car flung itself into a ninety-degree turn in front of the Creighton house, rocking to rest on the grass, headlights blinding.

"Lauren!" A yell came from behind the lights.

"Drew?" She stood, squinting, holding her arm up to shield her eyes from the glare. It didn't help. Two circles of white filled her vision, with black to either side. She couldn't find him. Uncertain, she stared into the light, waiting.

Hurtling out of the darkness beside the headlights, Drew scooped her into his arms, crushing her to him.

"Lauren! Thank God, you're safe!"

Frantic kisses brushed her brow and pressed against the side of her head. Choking on a sob of relief, she tucked her face beside his neck, clinging tightly while aftershocks of fear trembled through her. For a few seconds she simply breathed in the smell of him, thrilled that she could know him by just that one sense, that the feelings he stirred were so familiar and so safe.

Drew's hands touched her face, coaxing her head back so he could look at her. In the bright light, she watched as the last jagged edge of worry disappeared from his eyes.

"Oh, God, Lauren," he moaned and took her mouth in a fierce kiss. She fell into it, opening to him, soaking in the need that seemed equal to her own. She wrapped her arms around Drew's shoulders, and gave back in passion what she didn't dare say in words.

Words like *I love you.*

"Creighton!"

They parted as Drew looked toward the house. Chapman stood in the doorway, motioning at Drew to come inside.

"Get over here. You gotta see this for yourself, or you'll never believe it."

He gave Lauren a puzzled look. "Do you know what he's talking about?"

"Well, um, maybe."

Her admission appeared to cause concern. Taking her hand in a firm grip, Drew pulled her along as he followed Chapman inside and up the stairs.

She had to admit to being curious. There had been that crash behind her as she'd fled, and the headboard had looked awfully sturdy . . .

She bumped into Drew as he came to an abrupt halt at the entrance to his dad's bedroom, staring. Paul Pierson stood beside the bed, naked body pale except for the livid red of his face, furiously tugging at the cuffs holding him to the headboard. The overturned nightstand had spilled a variety of sex toys across the carpet.

Chapman smirked. "Seems your girlfriend had a little fun at the senator's expense."

Drew turned amazed eyes on Lauren. "You did that?"

Lauren stared, then tried to hide a smile. She wouldn't have called it *fun*, but she couldn't deny responsibility. "I guess I did."

Pierson looked up at their voices, his scowl turning darker as he spotted Lauren. "You! You'll pay for this, you little bitch. Trying to humiliate a United States senator—you won't get away with it."

Drew dropped her hand and stalked toward Pierson. "I beg your pardon, *Senator*," he said, his voice dangerously calm. "What did you call Miss Sutherland?"

Pierson turned on him, aiming his fury at a new target. "You heard me. And you're both going to hear from my lawyers."

Lauren couldn't resist a glance at the withered remains of his arousal. Muffling her giggle with a snort, she looked away quickly.

Her amusement didn't improve Pierson's temper. Heedless of his nudity and the handcuffs holding one arm back, he faced Drew with defiance. "I see what's happened here. The two of you have apparently conspired to embarrass one of your father's political opponents. If you and your little slut girlfriend think you can—"

Pierson broke off with a flinch as Drew stepped into

range, drew his fist back and aimed at the senator's jaw.

Chapman caught it before the punch could land. With Drew's arm in a lock, he turned a cool look on Pierson. "You have a point, Senator. This incident is sure to have political repercussions. Perhaps we should take pictures to document it. Your wife could so easily misunderstand the situation, based solely on the facts."

Pierson's face drained of color.

Drew spoke through gritted teeth. "One punch, Chapman. You can say he hit his head on the night-stand."

"Sorry, no." Chapman released Drew's arm. "But I trust you'll understand when I send Miss Sutherland a large bouquet of flowers to thank her for this memo-rable moment. It more than makes up for your death-defying drive over here."

"Yeah, sorry about that last tree." After a glance at Lauren, Drew asked Chapman, "You mind if I take Lauren to her room so she can get dressed?"

"Go ahead. But don't take long, I have a few ques-tions for her."

"Yeah, so do I."

Lauren had forgotten she was dressed in a robe, with only underwear beneath it. When Drew left she'd been fully clothed. Seeing Senator Pierson's condition, she supposed he did have a few questions.

She explained it to him briefly while she got dressed, then again in more detail for Chapman when they con-vened in the living room. Drew listened quietly at first. When she mentioned Pierson's hand on her leg he nar-rowed his eyes, and when she got to the part where he grabbed her arms, Drew jumped up and paced. By the time she finished she was glad Pierson had been taken away, because she didn't think Chapman could have prevented the beating Drew was ready to give.

He was furious with Pierson. She understood, was flattered, even. But the more distance she had from the event, the more excited she felt about her part in it. The proper and perfect Lauren Sutherland who had come to Washington, D.C., would have handled things differently.

Drew was the one who'd seen the potential for change in her; he even encouraged it. It was part of why she loved him. That, and the way he cared about standing up for what was right and correcting what was wrong. And his tight butt and amazing shoulders. She might tell him about that part.

But not the rest. She didn't want to be one of those women he hated, the ones who used men for what they could get out of them. Because that sure was how it looked. She broke out of her self-imposed prison and wanted an adventure, and she'd grabbed the first man who offered one. But wanting to keep him hadn't been part of the plan.

"We still don't know where Meg is," she said aloud, not even knowing who to ask about it. The house had been crawling with FBI and Secret Service agents, a few of whom were still there.

Chapman looked up from his notes. "Doesn't matter. As soon as this hits the news tomorrow morning, they'll come in, you can count on it. They'll know it's safe."

The front door opened behind her for what might have been the thousandth time that night, but the voice she heard in the foyer was one she'd been waiting for.

"All you had to do was shoot him." Gerald was lec-turing someone in a superior tone. "That shouldn't be difficult to figure out, even for someone on your rung of the evolutionary ladder. Don't you Neanderthal types excel at those basic skills—eat, sleep, and kill things?"

"You're the only one who came close to killing someone," Renke growled. "That shot could have hit your Romanian friend if it had been any higher."

"Not likely, Bozo, since I knew exactly what I was— Lauren!" Spotting her in the living room as she jumped up, he complained, "I've had the most awful night, consorting with emotionally stunted G-men and gun-wielding thugs."

Lauren looked appropriately shocked. "You poor thing, it sounds terrifying."

"You have no idea. You came alarmingly close to losing me."

She led him to the sofa where she sat down next to Drew, patting the cushion beside her. "Where's Mihaly?"

"Gone already. He took off in his car to scout some areas looking for Meg. It's driving him crazy that she's out there, probably scared, and with some other man." He grinned. "Isn't love wonderful?"

Not when it was one-sided. She was sure Meg's feel-ings for Mihaly went beyond fondness and friendship but was less sure of Drew's feelings for her.

"Hey," Drew greeted Gerald. "Glad to see you're alive. We've been waiting to hear from you."

Chapman laid his notes on a bookshelf and folded his arms. "Yes, tell us about it. I'd be fascinated to know why you ignored my direct orders and risked the lives of two other men."

Gerald leaned close to her, rolling his eyes. "These law enforcement types think no one else can plan an operation or capture a criminal. Like it's rocket science." Peering around her, he said, "Andrew, I hope that associating with these men hasn't damaged your good nature and sense of decency."

Drew gave him a wry smile. "I think I'm okay."

"That's a relief." He squeezed Lauren's hand. "Sometimes he may act like one of them, but he's worth hanging on to."

Somehow, she kept smiling. Hanging on to Drew was not a topic she wanted to think about right now. A premature sense of loss pierced her heart at the thought of him leaving. He would go soon enough. She wasn't ready to accept it graciously and didn't know how she ever would be.

"I'd like to hear what happened," Drew told him.

Gerald settled into being the center of attention. "Well. You know we thought we were going to meet Senator Creighton and Meg. And when we drove by the area Senator Pierson had told us about, there was a car on the side of the road with its parking lights on. We thought it was them."

"Not exactly." Renke's voice came from behind her, and Lauren realized he'd followed them into the living room, probably to hear Gerald's version of what happened. Judging from his sour tone, he found it a bit inaccurate. "Not all of us were so trusting and naïve."

Gerald clutched his chest in mock alarm. "Forgive me. Agent Renke, with godlike foresight, sensed a trap and saved the day."

Renke snarled, "I followed procedure and took precautions, which turned out to be a smart move."

"Yes, it worked out well when you surprised the bad guys and wrestled that gun away, saving Mihaly's life. Oh wait, that was me."

"Asshole," Renke muttered.

Chapman pinched the bridge of his nose, then waved his hand at Gerald. "Just get on with it. Skip the part we know and get to what happened after you decided to run amok."

"Huh. You'd think they'd be more appreciative," he confided to Lauren.

"I'm sure they will be when they hear they hear what happened," she assured him.

He patted her cheek like an elderly aunt. "That's so sweet, hon. You have faith in people." He peeked around her to turn his fond smile on Drew. "What'd I tell you? This one's a keeper."

"Gerald . . ."

Drew's warning snapped him back to storytelling mode. "Right. The guys Agent Chapman has been trying to track down are sitting right in front of us, and what does Mr. Big Government Agent tell me to do?"

He obviously wanted a response, so she shook her head. "I don't know. What?"

"Run away! Can you believe it? Of course you can't. Neither could I. I knew we had to catch these guys or Meg and Senator Creighton would still be in danger, and so would you."

"That's bull. We would have caught them," Renke began, but stopped at another hand gesture and head shake from Chapman. "Forget it," he grumbled. "Tell it in your own special way."

Gerald seemed to take it as a compliment, and continued. "I have to tell you, Agent Chapman was no help.

Apparently he gets a little tense in a crisis situation."

She stole a look at Chapman. If he kept grinding his jaw like that, he was going to end up with another migraine.

"So I turned the volume off on the phone and took matters into my own hands. I crept around the back of the car to the other side where Agent Renke could see me. And you know me, if I'm creeping through the undergrowth, something must be seriously wrong with this picture. Even a moron would know that, so I thought there was a chance he would figure it out."

"Which he did," Lauren said. Renke deserved at least one positive comment.

"Sort of, but don't get ahead of me." He brushed off Renke's part in the story. "I had to crawl back around the car, and I mean on my hands and knees. Look at the dirt on these trousers! It's—"

Drew cleared his throat.

"Right. So I waited behind the driver's door. I knew they would roll down a window so they could shoot Mihaly, who was getting close. That would be our only chance to take them by surprise. Which was exactly what happened. Simple deductive reasoning."

He looked at Chapman and Renke to make sure they appreciated how right he was and how dense they were not to figure this plan out themselves. "The guy's hand came out holding a gun, and I grabbed it and twisted. The gun went off, but he didn't drop it. So, I bit him. Works every time. The guy screamed like an enraged bull and opened the door, which knocked me down, which knocked the cell phone out of my pocket, where he stepped on it and broke it." Gerald looked at Renke. "You might want to bill the government for that."

Renke's lip curled with disgust.

Gerald shrugged. "Your loss. Anyway, I grabbed the guy's ankle and knocked him down. That's when Mihaly ran up to us, stuck a big black gun in the guy's face, and I let him take over."

"You let him take over." Chapman shook himself out of his mesmerized state and turned to Renke. "What happened with the other guy?"

"The man in the passenger seat jumped out when the cat fight started on the other side. I had my gun on him before he could turn around."

"Because he'd seen me creeping around the car earlier and he knew something was wrong," Gerald said. "Right?"

Renke gave him a resentful stare. "Right."

Chapman looked slightly ill. "I'm glad you'll be writing up that part, not me," he told Renke.

Lauren imagined the whole report would be a masterpiece of creative writing.

Beside her, Gerald gave a slight gasp and grabbed her hand. "I just realized you were alone with that despicable Senator Pierson. Did he try to hurt you?"

"Um, not exactly."

Drew moved his arm from the back of the sofa, slipping it around her shoulder to pull her closer. "Don't worry," he told Gerald. "She handled it."

She had. She wasn't sure how Drew felt about that, but she was pleased with herself. She credited Drew with helping her find her new confidence, but she owed a little to Gerald, too.

"AGAs," she told the senator's secretary with a wink. "You just have to know how to handle them."

Chapter Sixteen

By the time Chapman, Renke, and Gerald left at 3:00 a.m., Lauren was physically exhausted and emotionally drained.

She didn't give much thought to the fact that Drew became more quiet and introspective with each rehashing of events. He'd been up a full forty-eight hours by then—no wonder he seemed so pensive.

"You're going to bed," she ordered.

"Shower first," he corrected. "Then bed." He pulled her against him, thoughtfully touching her cheeks and tracing the shape of her eyebrow. "I hope you'll take this the right way, Lauren, when I say you're looking awfully dirty."

She figured it sounded good either way she took it. "You think I need a shower?"

"Desperately." He kissed her.

She hadn't thought he'd have enough energy left for a session of hot, steamy sex in the shower, and he didn't. But slow and tender lovemaking, pressed against a cold shower wall, turned out to be just as good. When he pulled her into his bedroom afterward, Lauren was so satiated she fell asleep within moments of curling against his body, a deep dreamless sleep that she woke from to the sound of pounding on the bedroom door.

She squinted at the bright sunlight blasting through the window, then at Drew as he propped himself up beside her with the same disoriented expression.

The door vibrated again under four hard knocks. "Andrew! Wake up!" Gerald's voice continued in lower tones to someone in the hallway, a half-whispered, urgent conversation. As they listened, it grew more agitated.

"I said I'd get him," Gerald hissed. "Wait downstairs."

Lauren and Drew exchanged confused glances.

The other voice, female and just as agitated, protested his order in words Lauren couldn't make out.

"Andrew!" Gerald pounded on the door again. "It's past noon, for Pete's sake. Open the door."

"Let me." She heard the woman's suspiciously familiar voice, along with the unmistakable sounds of a scuffle.

Lauren turned alarmed eyes on Drew. "Is it locked?"

"Yes." He ran a hand through his hair and sighed. "But it doesn't sound like they're going to go away." Grabbing a wool throw off the chest at the foot of the bed, he wrapped it around his waist and walked to the door.

"Hang on," Drew grumbled. Turning the lock, he cracked the door open. "Gerald. Why aren't you home sleeping?"

Lauren couldn't see Gerald, but she heard him clearly. "Because your father called me when no one answered the phone here."

Drew straightened. "He's back? I never heard the phone."

"Obviously," came the dry response.

"Where's Lauren?" the woman's voice demanded.

"Who are—" Drew's voice cut off, apparently having realized the answer to his question.

Stunned, so did Lauren.

"You must be—" Drew began.

The door banged open as she barged past him into the bedroom.

"Meg!" Lauren held the blanket to her chin and stared at her sister.

Meg stopped dead. "Lauren?" She stared, incredulous.

Lauren gave her a sheepish smile. "I broke up with Jeff."

"Obviously." Meg looked from Lauren to Drew, then back to Lauren. "I'd say we have some catching up to do. I'll be downstairs." Turning toward the door, she looked Drew over. "You're Drew, huh? I should have guessed."

Drew smiled pleasantly. "Hi, Mom."

Meg narrowed her eyes at him while Lauren groaned and ducked her face into the blanket. She'd run through several happy scenarios for her reunion with Meg. This hadn't been one of them.

Wearing only the wool wrap at his waist and a smirk, Drew held the door as Meg turned to leave. He'd nearly closed it behind her when she turned around.

Braced for a caustic comment, Lauren was relieved when Meg gave her a wry smile. "Thanks for coming, Rennie." She winked. "Nice haircut."

Lauren and Meg lay in lounge chairs on Senator Creighton's secluded back yard patio, talking and soaking up the last rays of a beautiful spring day.

Drew frowned at them from the kitchen window.

"How long you going to stare out that window? You look like a peeping tom," Harlan said, stirring the large pot of chili on the stove. "Why don't you slice some of that bread to go with the chili, and leave the girls alone."

Drew grudgingly left the window but figured he was too preoccupied to be trusted with a knife. Slouching against the refrigerator, he brooded as he watched his dad add chili powder to the bubbling pot.

"Nice girl," Harlan said.

"Who?" He looked at his father's patient expression. "Oh, Lauren? Yeah, she is."

"She seems to like you, too."

"Hmm." His father hadn't been in the house when he and Lauren had gone downstairs, and Drew saw no reason to tell him about their sleeping arrangements. "She hated me at first. Thought I was a shiftless ski bum. And being your son wasn't a point in my favor. "

"A discerning girl. It seems like she got over that."

"Gradually." With a few nudges from him. Not that he felt guilty about Lauren dropping her dud of a fiancé. That was something she should have done a long time ago.

"Guess you two got pretty well acquainted while I was gone."

Drew reassessed his dad's expression. Harlan Creighton didn't usually take an interest in his son's personal life. Drew didn't know why his dad would be fishing for gossip now, but he wasn't going to offer any. "I suppose."

Harlan stirred the chili in silence, then said thoughtfully, "Gerald said they found Lauren in your bed. I'd call that well acquainted."

Drew shot a threatening look toward the office where Gerald was working. "Aw, hell," he muttered. "I didn't want this to become an issue. Yes, we were sleeping together. So what? Believe me, Lauren and I are a lot better acquainted than some, no, most of the women you've been in bed with."

Harlan raised an eyebrow at him, which was enough to make Drew regret his tone. "Sorry," he mumbled.

"Why? You're right," Harlan said. "But you're not me, Drew. Grabbing every willing girl was never your style. So I want to know if you did this because, well, because her sister has a bit of a reputation, and God knows I do, and you thought we'd gotten married . . ."

Drew shook his head, brow furrowed in confusion. "What are you getting at, Dad?"

"I'm asking if you thought Lauren was an easy score, and maybe you wanted to get back at me by sleeping with Meg's sister."

Drew stared. "Hell, no!" He pushed off the refrigerator and paced a tight, frustrated circle, stopping to glare at his dad. "Yes, I thought the idea of you marrying Meg was ridiculous, but using that as an excuse to sleep with her sister would be . . ." He paused, searching for the right word. "I don't know what, but it'd be a whole lot worse. And Lauren is *not* easy. You have no right to—"

He broke off at his dad's upraised hands.

"Hey, whoa. I didn't imply that she was." The corner of his dad's lip quirked upward. "Looks like I hit a sensitive spot."

Breathing hard, Drew let his temper subside. "Yeah," he grumbled.

"Look, son, I asked because I have a lot of respect for Meg Sutherland, and after all we went through this past week it feels like Lauren practically *is* my sister-in-law."

The irony of it struck Drew as absurd, and he startled his dad with a bitter laugh. "Your sister-in-law? Hell, Dad, if I had my way she'd be your daughter-in-law. I'm just not sure I can talk her into it."

Harlan put the spoon down and turned his back on the chili. "Well, I'll be damned, Gerald was right."

Drew groaned. Was there anything that man didn't know?

"So why aren't you doing anything about it? She can't agree to marry you if you're standing in here with me."

Drew cocked his head toward the window. "As I recall, you just told me to leave them alone."

"Not if it's keeping me from my future grandchildren. Get movin', boy, I'm getting older by the minute."

"Huh," Drew gave an amused snort. "I wish Lauren were that easy to convince."

"How do you know she's not?"

"Because I was stupid enough to point out how regulated and dull her life was, and she bought it. She's decided to be more like her sister, and not tie herself to one man. Smart move on my part, eh?"

Harlan laughed. "Maybe smarter than you know. Meg's so sick with love for that Romanian boyfriend of hers I think she's about to get down on her knees and beg him to marry her."

A smidgen of hope sparked to life inside him. "Yeah?"

Drew took another thoughtful look out the window at Lauren and Meg. Both women sat in the strong spring sunshine, identical haircuts catching golden highlights. Anyone else might have said they looked alike, but Drew saw a big difference. Lauren had a sparkle, an aura around her that kept him entranced. It made her sister look ordinary in comparison.

"I think I'll go outside for awhile."

Lauren nibbled at the worn corner of her fingernail and considered Meg's comment. "I don't know, it sounds risky to come right out and say it."

Meg shrugged. "What have you got to lose?"

Everything. She could lose Drew.

He'd upset her entire life, rearranged her priorities, and now she didn't know how to go on without him.

But in one more day, she'd find out. She'd go home to Michigan. He'd go home to Colorado. She couldn't afford a long-distance relationship. They would have to say good-bye.

"Hi."

She hadn't heard Drew come up behind them. She flashed the goofy smile she always had when she was around Drew. It probably looked as dorky as it felt.

He held up a nylon jacket. "I thought you might be chilly out here."

"Thanks." She took it gratefully.

"Just one, huh?" Meg exchanged smiles with Drew. "Then I guess I'll be going inside."

" 'Bye." Drew waited until she left, but didn't claim her vacated chaise lounge. Instead, he straddled Lauren's, forcing her to pull her knees up to make room. With Drew's arms braced on either side of her, she was effectively trapped.

"I hope you weren't talking about me," he said.

"Why?"

"Because you're biting your nails again, which means you're nervous about something. You haven't been doing that lately."

"I haven't?"

"Not even when we were shot at in Florida. Which means this must be pretty bad."

"I guess only certain things worry me." Like saying good-bye to Drew. Like wondering if saying she loved him would make a difference.

"Like seeing Jeff again?"

She blinked, startled. "No. I hadn't even thought about him. But I doubt he'll want to see me again. I'm sure he's embarrassed about having to tell everyone we broke up."

"Probably annoyed, too. You've ruined his vacation plans. Probably can't even get a refund on his deposit."

Lauren gave him a puzzled smile, unsure why Drew had been giving this any thought. "I'm sure you're right."

"Ruined *your* vacation, too," he mused.

At least Drew appeared to be taking it well. "It doesn't matter."

"But now you have one more week off and no place to go."

She suddenly saw a possible direction to this conversation, and tried not to quiver with a hope that could be dashed at any second. "I hadn't thought about that."

Drew pretended to think. "You know, you could come visit me. I have to work with the camp kids part of each day, but we'd still have plenty of time together."

She couldn't prevent the tiny smile that crept to her lips. He wanted to continue their relationship. Even if these two weeks of vacation were all she could have with Drew, she'd take it.

But she couldn't appear too eager. "I don't know. What's it like at this place of yours?"

"My cottage is big, a house really. And there's just me, so we'd have lots of . . . privacy."

The lift in his eyebrow told her exactly what that meant, and she had to bite her cheek to keep from grinning.

"There's a large fireplace, and a big dining room table, and a comfortable couch, and of course, a king-size bed."

She felt a flush creep into her cheeks as she realized he was offering several unorthodox locations for making love. She cleared her throat. "That sounds nice."

Seeing he had her interest, he leaned closer with a sly smile. "There's a meadow out the back door that's very pretty in the moonlight. Also very private. And of course hundreds of acres of wilderness with no one around."

Making love with Drew outside, with the open sky above and acres of wilderness around them—just the idea made her warm all over. "I've never, um, done that."

"No?" His gaze held hers. "I could help you correct that oversight. The property also has a lake. Of course the water's freezing cold this time of year, so you might want to come back in the summer." He paused, watching her closely.

Her heart faltered. "Come back?"

"Or just stay. I close up for a couple weeks in the fall and let the entire staff have some time off. We'd have the whole lodge to ourselves then, just the two of us."

It felt like her lungs had constricted, each breath catching in her throat. "Stay? Until fall?" she whispered.

Drew's smile was gone, his gaze sharp as he leaned forward, caressing her arms. "Lauren, I know I shouldn't rush you. You've just bounced out of a relationship that stifled you, and you need some space."

He obviously thought she felt some sadness about ending her relationship with Jeff. Lauren opened her mouth to correct him, but he put a finger to her lips.

"No, hear me out. Right now you're probably afraid to hear words that imply commitment, and I understand that." He drew a deep breath. "But I have to be honest with you, Lauren. I'm in love with you, and I don't intend to let you go."

She knew she'd heard correctly because she saw the concerned look in his eyes, as if he were afraid of how she might react. Her mouth opened again, but all she could manage was, "Um . . ."

A deep crease appeared in his brow. The reason occurred to her in a flash of amazement—he was nervous.

"Honey, if you need time, I'll wait." His pained look made her want to kiss him senseless, but she was still paralyzed with disbelief. "But I have to warn you right now, I'm going to keep trying to change your mind."

He was waiting for a reply. She managed a shaky nod.

"And I won't be satisfied with a live-in relationship. I want marriage and children."

His jaw clenched with determination and he set his shoulders, apparently braced for the impact of rejection.

Lauren swallowed the lump in her throat. If her mouth weren't hanging open in shock she'd probably be grinning like an idiot. "That's quite a lot for me to think about," she told him, careful to keep her voice casual.

He nodded, looking as serious as she'd ever seen him. "I know what you're thinking," he said, wincing.

"You do?"

"You're thinking my place is remote and the town is too small for you to find the sort of responsible position you have now."

Actually, she hadn't given it a second's thought.

"But if you're willing to consider a slightly less

glamorous job, I'm planning to expand Camp Wind-haven's services in the future, and I could use a good financial planner."

"You mean, work for you?"

"Work *with* me," he corrected gently. "It would be your place, too. Your home."

Her heart had already decided, but Lauren weighed the decision one time to satisfy her conscience. She could return to her old job crunching numbers for an engineering firm and hope to find a man as wonderful as Drew, or live in a mountain paradise with the man she loved, the man she knew she would love for the rest of her life, building a home and family together, while giving troubled kids a second shot at life.

She bit her lip as she touched his chest and stroked down the hard muscles of his arms, the arms that would always be there to hold her.

She allowed a tiny smile as she met his eyes. She didn't want to appear too easy, which was going to be a challenge, because she was already visualizing those children he'd promised. "You said the house has a fireplace?"

He nodded cautiously. "Yes, a big one."

"I don't suppose there's a bear skin rug in front of it?"

Drew's eyes blinked with surprise. As he got her meaning, his mouth twitched upward. "I'll buy one. Tomorrow."

"Take your time." She leaned forward, pressing her lips to his in a lingering kiss. "We can start on the dining room table."

Turn the page
for a sneak preview
at the next sexy, romantic caper

from Starr Ambrose

Thieves Like Us

the sequel to *Lie to Me*

Coming soon from Pocket Books

Dumping the world's worst husband called for more than a celebration. It required a symbolic act—like hocking her engagement ring.

"You know what this is? It's poetic justice." Janet Aims admired the tasteful display of diamonds twinkling in Portman Jewelers' storefront window as if she were buying, not selling. "This is where Banner bought the stupid ring in the first place. I found the receipt."

"That doesn't mean they'll buy it back," Ellie pointed out, "I don't think jewelry stores do that, especially high-class places like Portman's." Ellie admired the diamonds, too, then glanced at her watch. She'd been doing that a lot today.

Janet pretended not to notice her friend's obsession with time. "They buy estate jewelry. This ring is now part of the Westfield estate, which ought to be enough to impress anyone in this town. I just have to suck it up and be a Westfield one last time."

She shifted to get a better view of her reflection and finger-combed the hairs that barely covered her ears. She wasn't used to the short haircut yet, but she liked it. It was all part of the new Janet—new haircut, new condo, and new marital status: single, with no dazzling diamond ring to remind her of the biggest mistake of her life.

"Do I look rich and influential enough to impress them?"

Ellie laughed. "You were born rich and influential. You can do rich and influential in jammies and bunny slippers."

"Not Westfield rich, I can't. That's a whole different class of wealth." She gave Ellie a significant eyebrow wiggle. "One you'd better get used to."

"Jack's a Payton, not a Westfield."

"Payton, Westfield, what's the difference? They all connect to Elizabeth Payton Westfield, and it doesn't get any richer than that, at least not in Bloomfield Hills, Michigan." She pulled a white ring box out of her purse. "Come on, I'll take advantage of my status one last time and show you how the rich folk throw their weight around. I can't wait to get rid of this thing."

"You demonstrate. I'll take notes." Ellie snickered and gave her watch another glance before reaching for the door.

That did it. "Okay, hold it." Janet stuck a hand in front of her friend.

"What? Why?"

"What's with the watch? That's about the fiftieth time you've looked at it today."

"It is?" Ellie looked embarrassed.

"Yes it is, and every time you do, you get all anxious and tense. Do you have an appointment somewhere? 'Cause we can leave, I don't have to do this now."

Ellie's lips quirked upward. "Well, it's not exactly an appointment."

Suspicion grew. "This isn't about my divorce being finalized, is it? Because if you planned a surprise party or something, I want to know about it right now. You know I hate surprise parties."

"No party, I promise. It's not about you. It's about me."

Ellie's smug little smile made Janet relax. She smiled back without knowing why. "Looks like something good. You gonna share?"

Ellie leaned closer so the few shoppers wandering by couldn't hear. "I have to be home by three o'clock so I can get pregnant."

Janet's mouth opened. "Huh?"

"My temperature chart says I'm ovulating, and Jack promised to leave the office early so we can"—she lifted her eyebrows—"make a baby. Maybe."

"Really? " She grinned at her best friend for several seconds. "It's about time!"

"Yeah, well, we didn't want to wait this long, but it's not happening as fast as we hoped."

Janet bounced on her toes, unable to contain her excitement. "It will, don't worry. This is a good day for both of us, I can feel it. I get rid of the last reminder of Banner, and you get started on a baby. This is exciting! Come on, let's get this over with so you can get home and get pregnant." Janet grabbed her hand and pulled her inside the store.

Ellie walked fast to keep up. "I'm glad you're so agreeable, since I have to ask you for a favor."

"Anything."

"It involves Rocky."

Damn! That was *not* what Janet wanted to hear. Ready to accuse Ellie of taking advantage of her good mood, a voice behind Janet said, "Mrs. Westfield! Welcome to Portman's. How may I help you?"

Janet hissed, "We'll talk about this later," then replaced her glare with a smile as she turned toward the man behind the counter. She didn't know him, so he must have recognized her from newspaper photos. The wife of the accused. One more reason to hate Banner.

"Hello, Mr.—"

"Portman. William Portman."

"Mr. Portman. I'm Miss Aims now."

He flushed. "Of course, I'm sorry."

Letting him feel a little embarrassed might work to her advantage. She reached into her purse and pulled out a small box. Opening the white silk lid, she set it on the glass countertop. "Do you remember this ring, Mr. Portman?"

He smiled as soon as he saw the large diamond flanked by two smaller stones. "Oh my, yes. A beautiful piece, we designed the setting exclusively for . . ." His smile slipped and he cleared his throat. "For Mr. Westfield."

"Yes, you did. So you can understand why, as beautiful as it is, I don't want it anymore."

"Uh, hmm, yes." He pursed his lips and frowned, apparently unsure of the protocol when acknowledging one's association with a notorious criminal.

"How much can you give me for it?"

Portman looked even more uncomfortable. "Miss Aims, Portman's doesn't accept returns on used jewelry."

"*Used*?" She arched an eyebrow. "Mr. Portman, this jewelry belongs to the Westfield estate. Do you, or do you not, deal in estate jewelry?"

Janet saw his gaze dart across the room to a tall display case labeled "Estate Jewelry," then look quickly away. "Yes, but those are heirloom pieces, crafted by well-known artists. They have historic value in addition to their intrinsic worth."

"I see." She smiled sweetly. "And my ring was crafted by—who did you say?"

"By, um, us."

"By Portman Jewelers. A name with a long-standing reputation for fine jewelry. One would hope it was well deserved." She nearly winced at her own arrogance and reminded herself it was for a good cause—getting rid of the last trace of Banner Westfield. "As for its intrinsic value, well, I am in possession of the original receipt for this ring. The price was quite impressive. I would hope that a diamond ring costing as much as my BMW would be worth what my husband paid." Whoops. The BMW had been Banner's idea, too; the car would have to go. Maybe she should make a list.

William Portman turned an interesting shade of dusky purple. "Portman Jewelers is competitively priced. The price on your ring was fair. Your diamond is of exceptional quality, Miss Aims."

"Of course it is. Heirloom quality, some might say. And it comes with a rather interesting history, don't you agree?" If you were interested in high-profile criminals who committed daring crimes like drug running and attempted murder, that is.

Janet lifted the ring box, admiring the brilliance of the stones. "I had many compliments on the ring. I'm sure you could sell it again. Or even reset the stones. The large one must be quite valuable on its own."

Portman took the ring from the box, allowing the diamond's facets to catch the bright overhead lights. Tiny arrows of color shot from its surface, as the smaller diamonds twinkled beside it. "I don't know." He spoke quietly, almost to himself. "It would be highly irregular, against store policy."

Janet felt a surge of excitement—if he was waffling, she had him.

"My father still owns the store, you know,"

Portman continued. "Going strong at seventy-six. He doesn't care to make exceptions to the rules."

The final hurdle; she knew just how to handle it. "Oh yes, Lewis Portman. I believe my mother-in-law, Elizabeth Westfield, knows him well." Janet inserted herself back into the Westfield family temporarily and hoped Elizabeth wouldn't mind. She seemed to like Janet better than her own son these days anyway. "She's purchased so many lovely pieces of jewelry from your store over the years." She paused deliberately. "The Westfields have always been good customers of Portman Jewelers."

"That's true."

She waited while he thought about the possibility of offending a long-term customer. A very *wealthy* long-term customer.

"Unfortunately, I couldn't give you anything near what Mr. Westfield paid for the ring."

Warm relief coursed through her, spreading heat to her cold limbs. "I understand completely, Mr. Portman, and I trust you'll offer a fair price. Oh, and I wonder if you could include this in the purchase. It was a gift from Mr. Westfield, and I would rather not keep it." Before he could object, she pulled a crinkled wad of tissue from her purse and set it on the counter.

Portman frowned at the tiny bundle as if she'd placed a toad on his immaculate display case. "I really don't think—"

Janet rushed to remove the tissue before he could reject the piece unseen. A double-strand pearl necklace slithered out, followed by a clunk from the attached pendant. Portman stopped talking.

Janet angled the pendant toward Portman. Inside an ornate, filigreed circle of gold, a large red stone glowed under the store's strong fluorescent lights. "If you don't want it, I'll take it elsewhere. I just want to get rid of it." No sense blowing the whole deal because he didn't want her ugly necklace.

Portman leaned closer. So did Ellie, showing her first glimmer of interest in the proceedings. "When did you get that?" Ellie asked. "It's kind of gaudy, isn't it?"

Janet nodded. "Banner bought it for my birthday. I didn't want to offend him by not wearing it, but it's awfully heavy and definitely not my style."

Portman touched the pearled chain, spreading it across the glass to get a better view of the pendant. Janet said nothing and watched his expression grow thoughtful. He was obviously intrigued as he lifted the necklace and let the pendant dangle. Areas of solid gold were decorated with curlicues and raised gold beads. In Janet's opinion, it skipped over being pretty and went straight to tacky.

"Where did your husband buy this?" he asked without looking away from the necklace.

She was tempted to correct her marital status, but decided not to distract Portman from his obvious fascination with the necklace. If she'd known it would get this sort of reaction, she would have shown it to him before the ring.

"I don't know where he bought it. I've never seen anything like it."

"I have," Portman murmured, lost in his examination. "Somewhere. The style is quite old; it might be a copy of a museum piece. Quality workmanship . . ." His voice faded out as he fumbled beneath his collar, pulling out a chain with a gold hexagon on the end. He opened it like a jackknife, revealing a jeweler's loupe. Portman held it to his eyes and peered closely at the stone. Seconds passed. He tilted the pendant at different angles, still saying nothing. Janet wondered if he'd forgotten about her.

Portman finally looked up, dropping the loupe and letting it hang over his tie. "Fifteen thousand."

Her mouth opened, but it took a couple more seconds for words to come out. "Sorry, what?"

"Five for the ring, and ten for the necklace. You understand, I'm taking a big chance on the ring. It's possible no one will want it, with its shady history." He didn't even look embarrassed when he said it.

Janet stared. The ring was worth ten times what he offered, but she hadn't expected more. It was the offer for the necklace that threw her. It had been an afterthought to bring it along, and she would have been thrilled if he'd offered a few hundred dollars for it.

"Ten thousand dollars for the necklace?"

"Again, a risk on my part."

He didn't strike her as the type to take risks with money. "Then the stone is real?"

"Real? Yes, it's a gemstone."

"A ruby?"

The corner of his mouth gave an arrogant twitch upward. "No. Quality rubies don't come that large. I'm sure it's a spinel."

His expression was unreadable. She had a feeling he wouldn't lie to her, but he also wouldn't offer information. "Is that good?"

"Depends. Historically, they were often mistaken for rubies and used in fine pieces of jewelry, most notably in England's Imperial State Crown. Today, they are less common but smaller ones are quite affordable."

She tried to sort out the pertinent facts. "Are you saying this could be one of those historically fine pieces?"

He shifted from one foot to the other, looking suddenly uncomfortable. "Possibly. It could also be a modern knockoff and relatively worthless." He pursed his lips as he took her measure, probably weighing how far he could push her. "My father is the expert on antique jewelry. If you'd like to wait a couple days for him to look at it—"

And risk having him reduce the price to two hundred dollars? "No need. I accept your offer."

Portman gave a brisk nod. "Is a check okay?"

"Of course."

He moved quickly to the back of the store. Ellie grabbed her arm. "Are you crazy? What's the hurry? You should let Rocky look at the necklace. No one knows more about precious gems than he does, and he wouldn't lie to you."

"I don't think Mr. Portman is lying."

"And he's not telling you the whole truth, either. That necklace could be worth a fortune. Rocky would know. Why don't you let me call him?"

Rocky again. Just the thought of him made her all jumpy and nervous inside.

Making an effort to keep her voice calm, she said, "No. I don't need his opinion, ex–jewel thief or not. You know I don't like him."

"So you keep saying."

"So why don't you believe me?"

"Because he's a great guy, and you can't give me any reason why you don't like him."

"He's an ex-con," Janet said.

She should have known Ellie wouldn't buy it. "Jack's an ex-con."

"That's different. Banner framed him, he was innocent." She still found it hard to believe that her former brother-in-law had been convicted of manslaughter and spent two years in jail. She hadn't known him then, though. To Janet, Jack was the guy who had helped her expose Banner's criminal activities and who had had the good sense to fall head over heels in love with her best friend. She could never think of Jack as an ex-con, and she knew Ellie couldn't either.

Unfortunately, it wasn't helping her argument against Rocky. "Rocky was framed, too," Ellie pointed out.

"Yes, but *Rocky* can't be trusted."

Ellie looked closely at Janet, no doubt wondering what in the heck happened at that New Year's Eve party last year. Janet had been snubbing Rocky ever since.

As they exchanged stubborn stares, Portman reappeared with Janet's check. She thanked him, tucked it into her purse, and gave Ellie a nod toward the door. The elegant interior of Portman Jewelers wasn't the best place to discuss a jewel thief, and for some reason, Ellie seemed determined to change her mind about Rocky. Today.

Once back in the June sunlight, she turned on her friend. "Okay, let's skip the setup. I can see you're determined to make me like Rocky. What does he have to do with this favor you want? Because I'm sure I can continue to dislike the man while doing whatever it is you want me to do."

Ellie sighed. "Probably. But you can't let it show, because you'll be in public. I need you to cover for me, helping Rocky with a demonstration we scheduled for tomorrow night."

"For Red Rose Security? I don't know anything about your business."

"You don't have to. You just have to act as Rocky's assistant. He'll show you everything you need to know."

"Uh-huh." She bet he would. "You know, you look so innocent with those big blue eyes and your hair in that cute little ponytail. Almost like you aren't trying to set me up."

"I'm not." At Janet's skeptical look, she threw up her hands. "Honest. Jack and I just want to *finally* take our delayed honeymoon. But I had the brilliant idea to have Rocky speak to some women's groups about home security, since he's so charming they fall all over themselves making appointments for personal consultations. We get a ton of business that way. You know I'm right, you've seen how they respond to him."

It was true, women ate up that big, lopsided grin combined with his former bad-boy life of crime, to which Rocky always admitted. His burglary skills were his credentials. Between his expertise at advising clients on the best security systems and Ellie's organizational skills, their fledgling security business was booming.

Janet motioned toward her car, parked a couple spaces away, to keep Ellie walking as they talked. "It's not hard, you just need to be an extra set of hands, then set up appointments for anyone who wants to make them. I'd ask Lisa, but she can't get a sitter at night, and anyway I told her the job never required evening hours. I cancelled everything else for the next two weeks, but I can't get out of this one. I know you're busy trying to reestablish Aims Air Freight, but—"

"Okay, okay, okay," she relented with a groan. "I'm not going to keep my best friend from her honeymoon."

Janet started the car, her heart pounding louder than the engine.

Five minutes later, Janet could still feel Ellie studying her as she drove. "You know, he doesn't feel the same way about you. He thinks you're great."

Oh, she knew. Better than she'd ever let on to Ellie. He hadn't made it a secret, and resisting such a devilishly cute, smooth-talking hunk of man went against some basic instinct that she had to stomp down every time she saw him.

"If you didn't already know him, I'd introduce you, because I think you two would be great together. Did you know he's nearly at the top of his class in law school? Smart guy. Plus he's cute, and funny, and he loves kids. Like you."

Another perfect man. She knew how those turned out. At least with this one she already knew he had criminal tendencies. They should all wear signs. If Banner had come with the warning "Willing to screw you over to get what I want," she could have saved herself a lot of trouble.

Ellie was watching her with a bemused expression.

"Stop matchmaking, El. You found the only perfect guy out there, and I'm willing to settle for watching from the sidelines."

"Jack *is* perfect," she agreed. "And no, you aren't."

Trust a best friend to point out when you're lying. "Stop being a pain in the butt and tell me about this honeymoon of yours. Where are you going to go?"

Ellie took the hint and quit lobbying for Rocky in favor of talking about her trip. It kept them occupied until they got to Ellie's house. Janet pulled into the driveway.

Jack stood beside his car, talking animatedly with a tall, broad man. Janet would know that body anywhere.

"Crap."

Ellie laughed.

Rocky.

* * *

Not saying hello would be rude. Janet was almost willing to tarnish her reputation for it, but Ellie took her sweet time getting out of the car, long enough for Rocky to stroll over to the driver's side. Not lowering the window would be beyond rude and probably make Ellie pretty mad. Crap again.

Janet hit the power switch and ordered herself to relax. Rocky waited for the glass to lower all the way, then folded his arms on the open window and leaned down. His dark eyes were level with hers, close enough for her to appreciate the thick lashes any woman would envy.

"Hey, Janet." His mouth curved into a lopsided smile and something tripped in her chest.

"Hi."

"Still avoiding me?"

Heat threatened to creep up her neck to her face. "Still deluding yourself that everything I do revolves around you?"

"Interesting fantasy." His gaze wandered over her for several long seconds while she tried not to squirm. "Nice haircut. It looks good on you."

"Thanks," she mumbled, unable to stop the automatic response good manners demanded. Damn her proper upbringing. "I thought you liked long hair." It was the only defiant thought that came to mind.

His smile grew. "Is that why you cut it?"

"No!" This time she felt the heat reach her cheeks, furious at her own reaction. The idea that cutting her hair had anything to do with him was absurd, but he always seemed to keep her off-balance. She needed to take control of their conversation somehow. "I just learned I'm filling in for Ellie at some demonstration you're doing tomorrow night. Can you tell me the time and place?"

"I'll pick you up at seven."

"I can meet you there," she started to protest. But when Rocky moved his hand and she felt his fingers brush her cheek, her words faltered.

"A mosquito," he explained when she narrowed her eyes. "If we use one car, we save gas. It's ecologically responsible."

He knew her well enough to use the one reason she wouldn't argue with. "Fine." She looked pointedly at his shirt. "Are you dressing like that?"

He feigned surprise. Glancing at the shirt, one of several that comprised what Ellie called his "surfer dude" look, he asked, "Is there something wrong with pineapples and palm fronds?"

She considered the loud yellow-and-green pattern. "I'm gonna go with *yes*."

He looked amused. "Don't worry, tomorrow night I will wear what proper Bloomfield Hills ladies expect me to wear."

She took that to mean something conservative and expensive. She had a wardrobe full of that. "Okay, I'll be ready."

"I can come early, if you'd like. We can practice."

She recognized the unspoken meaning, but was annoyed enough that she didn't flush at the thought. "No, thanks. I don't need practice."

He winked. "Good to know. See you tomorrow."

Arrogant jerk. He stepped back as she jammed the car into reverse. She barely remembered to wave at Ellie and Jack before speeding off.

* * *

Rocky strolled back up the driveway. Jack was watching his wife's rear end appreciatively as she walked to the house before turning his attention back to the matter at hand. Digging into his pocket, he handed a spare set of house keys to Rocky.

"Ellie said you only have to water the plants once."

Uh-huh. House-sitting while his friends were away was not at the forefront of his mind right now. "And what did she say about Janet?"

"That you shouldn't rush her." Jack's mouth quirked upward, obviously unperturbed at relaying his wife's message.

"Who's rushing? I've known her a year."

Jack leaned against the car and folded his arms. "Yeah, I know. I was there when you met. You decided you wanted her after knowing her a whole two hours. You don't call that rushing?"

"This from the man who got engaged after knowing a woman—what, two minutes?"

Jack's composure slipped into a slight frown. "That doesn't count. It wasn't real for at least a week." Seeing Rocky's smile, he apparently thought better of using the details of his impromptu engagement to Ellie as a shining example of restraint. "Come on, Rocky, Ellie has a point. I know you're set on putting your life back together. You've done a good job of it too, starting the business with Ellie and going to law school. But you don't have to have *everything* all at once. You can't just go out and get an instant wife and family."

"What family? Janet doesn't have kids. And I'm not looking to marry her. I just want to be with her. You know, in that very special way that requires taking off all your clothes," Rocky explained with a wink.

Jack snorted. "It doesn't all happen that fast, just

because you want it to. And you can't expect her to accommodate the accelerated schedule you've made for your life."

"Overlooking the fact that it happened exactly that fast for you, I have to repeat, I've known Janet for a year. Hell, I knew her six months before I even kissed her. That's beyond patient for me. I haven't even had a relationship that lasted that long."

Jack's brow lifted. "You kissed her?"

"You mean there wasn't a household news flash? She didn't tell Ellie?"

Jack waved it off. "I'm sure she told Ellie. Those two talk about everything. But no one told me. When did this happen?"

Rocky wasn't bothered his friend's intrusion on what he might normally consider private business. He'd met Jack in jail, where privacy was nearly impossible and personal issues were discussed openly. Jack Payton was closer to him than his own brother.

"It was here, at your New Year's Eve party."

Jack made a scoffing noise. "New Year's kisses don't count."

"It wasn't like that. And believe me, this one counted."

At least he gave it a moment's consideration. "Nah, I still gotta trust Ellie on this one. If you move too fast and she's not ready, you'll blow it."

It was a valid point. Janet had been uncertain and scared after her disastrous marriage to Banner. But her confidence was back now. She laughed a lot and had plans for her future. He needed her to know he wanted to be part of that future.

Rocky lifted an eyebrow with a knowing look. "She's ready. She doesn't know it yet, but she is."

Love
waits on
every page...

Pick up a bestselling
romance from Pocket Books!

JULIA LONDON
SUMMER OF TWO WISHES
When one wish came true, she suddenly needed a
second wish—and a second chance.

....

ROXANNE ST. CLAIRE
HUNT HER DOWN
A Bullet Catcher Novel
Some vendettas are hard to forget.
Some passions are hard to resist.

....

JOAN JOHNSTON
A Stranger's Game
A Bitter Creek Novel
Her game is vengeance . . . And she plays to win.

....

BARBARA FREETHY
Suddenly One Summer
She was looking for a place to hide.
She found love.

Available wherever
books are sold or at
www.simonandschuster.com

Experience the
excitement
of bestselling romances
from Pocket Books!

Eileen Carr
HOLD BACK THE DARK
When a clinical psychologist and a detective
investigate an unspeakable crime, they learn that
every passion has its dark side.....

Laura Griffin
WHISPER OF WARNING
Blamed for a murder she witnessed, Courtney
chooses to trust the sexy detective pursuing her.
Will he help prove her innocence...or
lead a killer to her door?

Susan Mallery
Sunset Bay
What if you got another chance at the life that got
away? Amid the turmoil of broken dreams lies the
promise of a future Megan never expected....

Available wherever books are sold or at
www.simonandschuster.com

20471

Get intimate

WITH A BESTSELLING ROMANCE

from Pocket Books!

❋

Janet Chapman
THE MAN MUST MARRY
She has the money. He has the desire.
Only love can bring them together.

Starr Ambrose
LIE TO ME
One flirtatious fib leads to the sexiest
adventure of her life....

Karen Hawkins
TALK OF THE TOWN
Do blondes have more fun? He'd love to know—
but it takes two to tango.

Hester Browne
THE LITTLE LADY AGENCY
IN THE BIG APPLE
She's a manners coach for men, and
she's working her magic on Manhattan!

Available wherever books are sold or at www.simonsayslove.com

19584